The Guys From Fargo

By

Delray K. Dvoracek

Saber Books
Published by Indigo Sea Press
Winston-Salem

Saber Books
Indigo Sea Press
302 Ricks Drive
Winston-Salem, NC 27103

First Saber Books edition published
June, 2016
Saber Books, Moon Sailor and all production design are trademarks of Indigo Sea Press, used under license.

For information regarding bulk purchases of this book, digital purchase and special discounts, please contact the publisher at indigoseapress@gmail.com

Cover design by Pan Morelli
Manufactured in the United States of America
ISBN 978-1-63066-244-8

Dedication

To my wife, Verlene, and my two sons, Kamron and Kent.

I must thank all the fellows with whom I enjoyed coffee breaks at the Powers Hotel in Fargo. You became the inspiration for *the guys* in my novel. And a special thanks to Peggy, the only girl in our group, whom I also considered as *one of the guys*.

A Word About Fargo

The story you are about to read took place in 1983 long before the movie, *Fargo,* splashed itself across the nation's theater screens. Strangely enough, not one frame of that movie was ever filmed in Fargo. Unlike the movie, the tale that unfolds here plays on the actual streets of this North Dakota city. Fargo lies on the eastern border of the state, and just across the Red River is Moorhead, Minnesota. People around here refer to Fargo-Moorhead as the twin cities, but don't confuse them with Minneapolis-St. Paul, the real twin cities. The big twins had a population of a couple million in the 1980's; the little twins were pushing 100,000.

So what's so unique about Fargo? This is the heart of the Red River Valley. The river itself is rather unusual, in that it is one of the few, which flows north in the United States. It eventually empties into Lake Winnipeg, Canada, and makes its way via the Hudson Bay to the Atlantic. Many claim the Vikings sailed this far in the 10th century, but like Noah's ark, no archaeological find, at least to date, has provided a semblance of proof, not that we need it.

This fertile valley lays claim to some of the richest, black dirt you'll find in America, and that's why it's sometimes referred to as *a farmer's paradise.* We're heavy on sugar beets, and when the wind is out of the northwest, which it is most of the time, we're heavy on residue from the beet plant on the north edge of Moorhead. Lucky for Fargo, the stink hangs mostly over their city and not ours.

Fargo has always boasted a fabulous park system. Kids are never without anything to do year around, because sports seem to dominate everything. This is the home of the *Bison,* NDSU's football, basketball and hockey teams. They're tough, and so are most of the people who live here, because winters can be relentlessly severe and unforgiving. Temperatures often drop to 20 or 30 below for weeks at a time. If you've never driven in snow before and for some reason end up here during the winter, you're a good candidate for a fender-bender.

The Bad Lands are one of the big attractions in the state. The town to visit near the western boundary is Medora, where Teddy Roosevelt used to hang out. The stretch between here and there covers about 300 miles of rolling prairie, and no matter where you stop along the way, you can usually see fifty miles in every direction.

For those of you, who have never visited the plains, let me give you a slight picture. Imagine New York City in the year 1500. Remove all the trees for a couple hundred miles around, then stand on the coast and look westward. You've got to take out all the rivers and canals, too, and then fill up what's left with grassland, and stock it with prairie wolves, coyotes, long-eared jackrabbits, fox, antelope, and deer. If you throw in a bunch of ducks, pheasants, grouse and prairie chickens, that gives you a fair idea what the plains are like. You have to understand, a lot of roads in North Dakota go nowhere, which doesn't seem to be much of a bother to those used to open country.

If you like the water, forty miles east is Detroit Lakes, or DL, where the lakes country begins. In Minnesota, you can't drive five miles without cruising by a lake. That's not totally true, but the Minnesotans like to think it is. That state is loaded with a lot of pine trees, heavy forests, and great summer fun and, of course, more people.

However, let's get back to Fargo. In many respects, it's a typical Midwestern town—the largest in the state. I mentioned NDSU, but we have two more colleges—Moorhead State and Concordia, both across the border. MS is a typical liberal arts college and Concordia is a goody-two-shoes school. If you don't understand that term, suffice it to say it is Lutheran driven, where none of the girls ever get pregnant and nobody swears.

West Acres is one of the largest shopping malls between Minneapolis and Seattle, but that's on 13th Avenue West, where most of the city is expanding. The downtown back in the 80's attempted to be progressive by modifying Broadway into a sort of mall-look. You know, angle the streets, remove most of the parking, and bottle up the only main thoroughfare through town—that sort of progressive stuff. However, that's all changed now.

Fargo is basically a Scandinavian town. It has its share of banks and loan companies and, in fact, is a rather substantial financial hub. Independent businessmen thrive here very well, and those that don't or can't stand the winters move out, which leaves only the hearty behind.

Something that is very cliquish to a Midwestern town is the corner restaurant, where the locals usually hang out. There's more than one in Fargo, but we're zeroing in on the Powers Coffee House on the corner of 4th and Broadway. The restaurant is on the main floor of the hotel by the same name. I never did understand why they called it the Coffee House, since it always served breakfast, lunch and dinner. Some call it the Powers Café or the Powers Restaurant or just the Powers. In any case, a coffee break is almost a ritual in Fargo, and especially at this place. At nine in the morning, Fargoans turn out in droves for coffee and a roll, or maybe wheat toast, and sometimes a full breakfast. The same people show up mid-afternoon for more coffee. It's an obsession. The city fathers estimate that over six million dollars in retail sales is lost annually due to coffee breaks.

The interior of the Powers Coffee House is very conventional. The Warner Realty group, next to the famous Fargo Theatre, thinks they own the one big, round table that occupies the center of the restaurant. If you should grab this table before their entourage arrives, you could quite easily be

3

glared into obscurity. The booths along the sides are for senior citizens and transients from the bus depot, which lies one block east. Most of the center tables that seat four are occupied by specialty groups—the employees from Schumacher Goodyear across the street, those from the clothing store down the street, other independent businessmen, and of course, a few of the filthy rich, who show up to take advantage of the low prices.

The Powers Coffee House has its share of weirdoes, too. They usually sit by themselves at the counter, stretching a 50-cent cup of coffee into a meal by pouring in tons of sugar and gallons of real cream.

Most of the clientele, who show up, it seems, are men, and if they talk about their business, it's that it is slightly up or down from last year, or it's the same, because nobody wants to confess that they're doing really well. Most of the time, however, the main stream of conversation is bullshit, which includes the weather, how the Bisons are doing, whether the Vikings have a chance, or how one managed to three putt a green.

They talk politics, too, but mostly during election years. Now and then, an occasional risqué joke slips into the conversation, and if anybody makes a sexual remark, it's spoken very quietly, because it seems everybody is listening to everybody else. Funny things happen, everyone laughs, everyone is having a great time, and it's the same old stuff day after day.

One of these small crowds is made up of a half-dozen guys who never miss the morning or afternoon sessions, and one of the guys at this table happens to be beautiful Pam Allison. They all love her, and when she sits down to join them, the guys clean up their act—not that Pam by any means is a prude. Every day it's the same; the weather, the Bisons, the Vikings, sometimes the same joke. The same old bullshit.

And then one summer day, that all changed.

PART I

One
The Powers Coffee House Crowd

Mr. Graybar locked his wheelchair into a firm position, his armrests stationed exactly four inches from the edge of the table. He was alert and recognized the footsteps of Millie as she scooted around the counter headed in his direction with two scrambled eggs, wheat toast and hash browns. His eggs were always scrambled lightly with just enough juice dribbling from around their yellowed edges so he could easily stuff them down. He had already tucked a napkin neatly over his narrow green tie that contrasted nicely with his tattered plaid shirt of red and blue. The thick-lenses pair of silver spectacles perched awkwardly on the end of his nose sharply reflected the neon lights from above against his pale and wrinkled face.

Henry Graybar was 82 years old. He always sat at the one table in the Powers that seated only two. However, Mr. Graybar's table had only one chair, obviously, because he always came down the elevator from his fourth floor apartment in a wheelchair, and he always wheeled himself to this particular table, which stood almost in the center of the lounge. The table rested against a long, mirrored pillar, which reached ten feet upwards to a relief-sculptured ceiling, once painted off-white, but now off-grease in color from years of cooking.

"Thank you, Millie," he said to the waitress in a raspy,

almost breathless voice. Then, in military fashion, Mr. Graybar sat stiffly upright and examined each utensil near his plate with the eye of a cock rooster spying a crawling insect. Spoon, fork, knife all in place, water glass four inches at an angle to his plate on the right side.

Millie shuffled around the counter again with a small orange juice, which she placed exactly four inches from his plate on the left side. Mr. Graybar's regimen dealt in measures of four. When he chewed his food, it was always in increments of four, usually twenty chews or twenty-four, rarely less, before he swallowed.

Even when he drank his orange juice, he took at least four short swallows at a time. His wheel chair had four wheels. Two large, two small. He had four pockets in his pants, two forward, two in the rear. He had four pockets in his shirt, two where they would normally appear on his chest, and two khaki brown ones sewed in below, obviously by his own hand. He had a pair of clip-on dark glasses, now flipped up, thus giving him four lenses. Usually Millie supplied him with an extra spoon or fork, so he would have four utensils, and his two slices of wheat toast were always cut in two, thus making four pieces.

But Mr. Graybar ordered only two eggs. "Too much cholesterol in four eggs," he was often overheard remarking to Millie.

Mr. Graybar's routine was so routine that none of the regulars in the coffee house paid much attention to him, none except for Carrigan Mulhouse, who had been observing Graybar's idiosyncrasies over a period of several months.

Carrigan was forty-two years younger than Henry Graybar and carried his age rather nicely. He was thinning slightly on the back of his head, receded heavily in front, and although his hair was streaked with gray, he had more of it than Graybar, and he wore glasses like Graybar, but his were styled in the mode of the day—light frames snugged nicely against a warm and friendly face. Carrigan Mulhouse was an educated man, and he usually wore a nice sport jacket and slacks to match. Only occasionally did he wear a tie, but he was always neat in appearance.

Carrigan usually sat at a round table in contrast to most other tables in the restaurant that were square. As usual, Carrigan was early, and while waiting for the other members of his coffee group to arrive, he was studying Mr. Graybar very closely. It was the way old man Graybar fidgeted before his meal arrived that originally caught Carrigan's attention. His head would nod a bit, and he would suddenly jerk upright. Carrigan was sure it was going to happen again, but his big wonder was who would come to the rescue today.

Carrigan eyed the two Indians sitting near Graybar. They were clad in Levis, both with knapsacks, both with long flowing hair, both mean in appearance. If they had been wearing war paint and Crazy Horse was still alive, these two might well have been members of his band. There was no doubt they were transients. They were either staying at the Salvation Army Center down the block or just passing through on the Greyhound Bus. The bus station was a block east, easily visible through the facade of windows that lined the street. During stopovers, transients were usually directed to the Powers Coffee House, the only eating-place within easy walking distance from the station. It was not at all unusual to see transients walking along the street long in advance of their entering the Powers. And they almost always carried knapsacks or bags or small suitcases. Some carried bedrolls, and once in a while, some arrived with nothing.

Transients came and went all day, mostly lower class people taking advantage of the cheaper bus travel fares. Sometimes families of two, three, four or more arrived, and whenever it was a group of four, Mr. Graybar was particularly attentive.

Booths lined three of the walls in the Powers, each with

enough room to comfortably seat four, or six pressed in. All the booths were occupied this morning. Four persons were in the booth near the door, transients Carrigan was sure, a young couple and two noisy kids. The next booth held two elderly ladies, newcomers to the Powers, since Carrigan didn't recognize them, and they were dressed quite nicely, each clinging on to a large leather purse.

Suddenly it happened. Graybar stiffened in his chair, totally catatonic. His eyes bulged fiercely as if they were about to pop out of his head, and then came the sounds—at first a long murmur droning out of him and then a slight cough and a sputter. His hands dropped limply from the table, and as he flopped back in his wheelchair, he whooped. A bellowing groan of rushing chair charged out of his mouth, and then he slumped forward, his face now smack dab in the center of his two uneaten eggs.

When the seizure took hold, his whole body bounced up and down like popcorn on an open grill. Just as Carrigan expected, it was the two Indians, who came to his rescue. If they appeared mean before, they had now become palefaces while they were deciding what to do. One of them grabbed Graybar and lifted his head while the other stood seemingly stunned, not sure how to help. People looked on in awe. The two old ladies gaped with their hands taught against their mouths, their faces flat and unbelieving.

The second Indian now reached to help the first, and when he did so, he hit the release lever on Graybar's chair. The Indian grabbed a handle to stop the backward motion of the chair, but it spun abruptly and Graybar began to slip forward out of the seat.

When they grabbed for him, he flopped backwards, tipping the wheelchair as he went. His feet caught the table sending Graybar's plate of eggs and juice and everything else splattering to the floor. Carrigan rolled in tears when the first Indian slid on the eggs. He went down dragging the chair with him, and now all three were on the floor. Graybar's feet flailed in the air as if he were the star acrobat of a flying circus. One of his shoes flew across the room, landing on the table where the two old ladies sat. A huge groan burst from Graybar's lungs as he rolled over and ended up face down on the floor.

By now, two other men from the counter came to the rescue of the two Indians making the rescue, and Graybar was mumbling, a sign that he was coming out of his seizure. One of the Indians writhed in pain, grabbing at his neck while his friend helped him up, and at the same time, the two old ladies in the second booth were scrambling out the door.

It was Millie who finally came to the rescue of the rescue of the rescue. She had been through this scenario a few times before. She dashed commands calming everybody down and had four men lift Graybar's frail body back into his chair. If Graybar had been totally coherent, he would have loved to know *four men* were helping him up.

In short order, Graybar was seated again, his lever locked, and the table was set upright and wiped clean. Millie brought him some fresh silverware, and someone from the back mopped up the floor. Five minutes later a fresh breakfast followed, and Mr. Graybar started his ritual all over again, as if nothing had happened.

When someone brought back Graybar's shoe, Carrigan chuckled. How many times had he seen Graybar go through this act? One? Two? Four?

The front door to the Powers swung open as one of the old ladies hurried over to the booth where she had left her purse. She snatched it up and left as quickly as she entered. Carrigan stirred his coffee and glanced at his watch. Five after nine. Paul Glitzberg would be arriving soon.

While he was waiting, he happened to glance out the window and focused on the dented Pinto standing on the street. Hardnuts Brodigan, the local beat cop, was on the

9

driver's side with his citation book out. While Hardnuts wrote out the ticket, the driver jerked his hands up and down, and now, on close inspection, Carrigan recognized him as an Iranian, who frequented the Powers Cafe.

Carrigan could imagine what the Iranian was now saying in his broken English. *I am for driving on corner, lady she is for walking crazy on the light for stop and not to hit for ticket, I am for helping her.* But Hardnuts would be persistent, Carrigan knew. He hadn't earned his nickname for patting Iranians on the head.

Carrigan could imagine the Iranian's next reply. *I am for Iranian. I come for to this country as citizen, you for are writing prejudice.*

Whatever the Iranian was blathering, Hardnuts wasn't listening. He handed the book inside the window, and when the Iranian finally signed it, Hardnuts tore out the ticket, handed it to him and started walking back to the curb.

From where Carrigan sat, the Iranian was quite a ways away, but Carrigan was sure he saw the student mouth the word *cocksucker* in Brodigan's direction. Though the Iranian's English was broken, he had evidently gained some prominence with English slang.

"So, the little Khomeini shit got a ticket, huh?" It was Paul Glitzberg, better known to the coffee group as Pavlov, Russian for Paul.

"Yeah," answered Carrigan. "I wonder what he did."

"Ran a red light." Pavlov dropped his big frame into a chair and grabbed a pot. "Little Iranian fucker. I insured his Pinto some time back. Inside of two months, he had three accidents. Had to drop him, but not before the little shit took us for about twelve hundred dollars. Shee-it! He never did have anything fixed."

Pavlov was good at labeling those whom he did not hold in high esteem. He liked short phrases like *little shit* or *little bastard.* When he was really mad, he used *little fucker.*

Everything was little this or little that but done in a big manner, because Pavlov Glitzberg was big. He was six foot two and had shoulders wide enough to fill the width of an open garage door. Carrigan envied his black and thick curly hair mopped around a rugged outdoorsman face. He was a few years younger than Carrigan—Mr. Joe College. He always wore a suit and tie, and his shoes were always spit shined. He had to look cool and successful, or so he said, because the insurance business demanded it.

Pavlov, strangely enough, was a graduate from Augustana College, a Lutheran goody-two-shoes school in Sioux Falls. He was a Nick. Nicks were the jocks and had a reputation for screwing anyone and everyone indiscriminately. Whether Pavlov Glitzberg ever lived up to those traits, Carrigan didn't know. What he did know was Pavlov Glitzberg was a good family man. He had married a girl from the same college, who was a member of the Delphic society. If you were anybody at Augie, you had to belong to a society. Pavlov and his wife, Emily, were good friends of the Mulhouses.

"The little prick," Pavlov went on referring to the Iranian. "He had the nerve to ask me for the name of another insurance company when we cancelled him. So I sent him over to Connecticut General. I gave him the name of a little cunt that was good at selling policies by flashing her body around. She can have him."

They both chuckled. Whenever Pavlov grinned, he displayed a perfect set of teeth, whiter than ivory piano keys. He was smooth, and although he expressed himself with little words at the coffee table, with clients he used big words like *necessity of protection* and *service beyond reputable quality.*

Carrigan had three policies with Pavlov—life, car and business liability insurance. Pavlov was in reality a good insurance salesman. He would run himself ragged for any and every client who showed the remotest sign of dissatisfaction, and he was prompt and dependable.

Carrigan himself thought he had lot of Pavlov qualities. After all, he was service minded. As the owner of an advertising agency, it was necessary to meet deadlines, keep clients happy and satisfied with promotions. Carrigan considered himself a good communicator. The advertising business dictated that, and he was a salesman, too, even though he sold mostly service. For all practical purposes, Carrigan carried his wares around with him at all times; a pencil, paper and ideas. Physically, however, he was the opposite of Pavlov. He was average height and a little stocky, not one who jumped out in a crowd. Whenever Pavlov entered a room, he could easily pass for a Viking tackle or the brother of the Hulk. Whenever Carrigan entered a room, he had to be careful so that the door didn't snap back and hit him in the ass.

"You missed old Graybar's fit again," said Carrigan.

"No shit?" Pavlov glanced at the table where Graybar was just finishing his eggs.

Carrigan pointed to the booth across the way. "Those two Indians came to the rescue this time. What a mess." Carrigan retold the scene, and when he reached the part where Graybar flipped out of his chair, Pavlov was howling.

At twenty after nine, Johann von Meer made his appearance. It was obvious he had spent a long night painting in his studio. He looked half-asleep as he limped his way over to the table. Johann had a clubfoot. When he was younger, he had had several operations, but the doctors had only managed to straighten the foot slightly, thus Johann wore a size nine shoe on his left foot and a size eight on the right. Whenever he went shopping, he always had to buy two pairs of shoes and throw one pair away. Actually, he always wore a half boot. The last time he had purchased a new pair was a month ago, and it appeared that he was finally feeling comfortable with these, since over the last week, his limp hadn't appeared so prevalent.

In spite of the handicap, Johann played football when he was in high school and unfortunately broke a leg in three places. Another series of operations left him with the same clubfoot leg a bit skinnier than the other.

Johann had a bad knee from the football accident, a bad foot at birth and by natural phenomenon had bad luck selling his paintings.

Carrigan was by no means a good judge of paintings, but Johann's paintings were unique. He strived to create oil colors that he himself likened to Rembrandt. The faces of his subjects were always rounded, and the noses had their own peculiarity. All had slight hooks to them, and the eyes were always filled with a guilty or death-ridden look. Always dark, always shadowed, always set closely together. When one spotted a *von Meer* painting and knew Johann's style, there was no doubt one was viewing a *von Meer*.

Johann studied and researched every painting he made, and there were hundreds. He wouldn't settle for simple two-foot by three-foot paintings; his paintings had to be colossal in size, so large that they would barely snug through a double set of doors. Johann thought big and painted bigger, yet he was a small, wiry fellow. His hair was soft and thin with a lock of it always hanging over his forehead, and his goatee beard, apropos to his profession, was always nicely trimmed. His attire never changed. Every day he wore blue Levis, a blue denim shirt, striped tie, black boots and a brown corduroy sport coat. Whenever he entered a room, the door really slammed him in the ass.

For the first several minutes at coffee, he seemed a bit ornery, although he really wasn't. He rarely showed any signs of life until he had downed two or three cups of coffee. He smoked incessantly, always with his jaw jutted outward, his cigarette stuck between his lips and pointed up, and since the smoke streamed upward, he squinted a lot.

He managed to let the ash grow to an ungodly length. Somehow, and quite often, he managed to remove the cigarette from his lip without dropping the ash, allowing him just enough time to gulp in a couple mouthfuls of coffee. Whenever the ash finally did fall, he managed, without even looking, to swipe it off the table.

"Graybar had another fit this morning," Pavlov told Johann.

"Uhhh," came his response.

"The old fucker fell out of his chair. Took four guys to get him back in place."

"Uhhh."

"See those two Indians over there?" Pavlov pointed to the warriors.

Johann managed to move his-head slightly. Smoke streamed upward from the end of his cigarette into his eyes forcing him to really squint, making him look like most of the faces of his paintings. "Uhhh," he commented.

"They came to the rescue," Pavlov went on. "The big guy slipped and fell on his ass."

"Uhhh, ya, ya, ya."

Johann was coming around now. He had managed four grunts in a row. The coffee was taking effect.

"Ya, ya... so...."

Carrigan and Pavlov smiled. Johann had spit out his first discernible word of the morning, and only a few minutes after he arrived.

"I'd like to paint that son-of-a-bitch before he dies," Johann said. "He's got good eyes. Mean, dark. Good nose, too, if he'd get rid of those stupid glasses."

Carrigan and Pavlov marveled. Two or three complete sentences, and all before he finished his first cup of coffee!

"So," said Carrigan, recognizing an opportunity. "How's the painting coming along?"

"Lousy."

"You're not happy with what you're doing?"

"I'm happy. Buyers aren't. I should go to San Francisco where there's a market. No market here."

God, thought Carrigan to himself. Five minutes after his

arrival, he was already talking business.

"So why don't you move to San Francisco?"

"Might," came the retort. "Too goddamn cold up here anyway."

Carrigan and Pavlov both laughed. It was the middle of the summer, but they knew what he meant. Johann couldn't take the winters. He hated snow, hated ice, hated wind-chill factors, and even hated Christmas, only because Christmas meant snow, which meant ice, which meant wind-chill factors. His studio was two blocks from the coffee shop in the old Burlington Northern warehouse, but even during that short jaunt during the miserable Fargo winters, he would show up with a pound of ice hanging from his beard and eyebrows.

Fargo winters were not Johann's climate. When the cold invaded the city, Johann considered it nature's way of perpetrating a personal attack upon himself. Therein lay a fundamental polarity with Johann's life; Johann loved nature, but nature hated Johann.

"Ya, ya, too goddamn cold up here. Person's got to be crazy to live here."

"We all live here," said Carrigan.

"Ya, and we're all crazy.'

"This is where my business is."

"It'd be easier in San Francisco."

"Too many people," answered Carrigan. "Too many cars, too crowded."

"But it's got aristocrats, and they've got money and they buy paintings. You betchum, Red Ryder."

"There must be some aristocrats in this town," Pavlov interjected.

"Yeah," Johann said. "And I already sold a painting to all three."

They all laughed as Pavlov filled his cup and passed the pot around.

"How about some toast here this morning?" It was Millie,

the waitress, the sweet mama type, so Norwegian, so efficient. She could carry thirty plates at one time, and never used a writing pad for orders.

"Carrigan? Wheat toast and peanut butter?"

"Yup."

"How about you, Paul?" She always called Pavlov by his real name.

"Hay-yal yes," he answered with a forced southern accent. "Ah needs sus-ta-nance. Ah'll have th' same."

Millie looked at Johann. "How about you?"

"Uhhh."

Mille gave him her usual nose wrinkle. "What does that mean?"

"Say," said Johann. "You've got good eyes. I'd like to paint them someday."

"What color? Red or green?" Millie quipped back. She snickered at her own joke when the table broke out in laughter. "You don't need anything," Millie told him. "Painters live on oil alone."

"How right she is," said Johann, after she scooted off. "Ya, ya. Should take her to San Francisco with me."

Sko Skofield maneuvered his way through the coffee house to the table. "Make way," he barked in a heavy voice as he pulled up a chair. "Let a man in here." Sko's first name was Everett, a name he dearly hated. He sold radio spots, so he picked up the nickname, Radio Sko, a name that he not only appreciated, but a name that reflected his business. Sko was big, like Pavlov Glitzberg, but when he was in college, he actually played football as a fullback. He was the senior citizen of the coffee crowd, now balding, with round eyeglasses, but suave in appearance. He always wore a suit and tie like Pavlov, and he was always full of shit like Pavlov

"Damn," said Radio Sko. "I need to sell some radio spots." His gaze naturally focused on Carrigan, because Carrigan was the only one at the table who dealt with advertising. "Got any clients who need some radio? Got a hell of a deal today."

"You've always got a hell of a deal, Sko."

His pitch came in one sentence. "Today only, ten percent off for every package of twenty spots, everybody needs Mayville radio, charge them the same four-fifty per spot less the ten percent discount, you get the normal fifteen percent commission plus ten percent more, you buy twenty spots, that's ninety dollars less twenty-five percent, that's sixty-seven-fifty, you make twenty-two-fifty profit."

"But I have to write the commercial for my client," said Carrigan. "Got to charge him for that."

"That's part of the deal," said fast talking Sko. "I'll write the spot, won't even charge you extra."

"I don't have a client who needs Mayville radio at the moment." Mayville was forty miles north of Fargo.

"Buy it anyway, I'll write the commercial and you can find a client later."

"How can you write a commercial if you don't know what the product is?"

"I'll make it general enough so it'll fit everybody." With that, Sko threw his head back and laughed heartily. In seconds, he lit up a cigarette and poured himself a cup.

"I'll tell you what," said Johann, as he eyed Sko with his dark, beady eyes. "I'll buy one radio spot."

"Can't sell just one. Twenty spots minimum."

Johann drew in a breath of smoke, the cigarette still sticking up in the air, the ash growing. "All right, I'll buy twenty spots if you can sell one painting per spot."

"Jesus," said Sko. "Only the rich can afford your paintings. I don't think there are twenty rich people in the county."

Johann grinned. "You're probably right, but that's my offer. Take it or leave it."

"You might sell one painting."

Johann's eyes lit up. "God, if I even sold one, I'd come out ahead."

Carrigan stirred. "Well, now, Johann. If you're serious about the radio buy, you'll need an agency to represent you, so I'11 make the buy."

"Hold it," said Sko. "This deal's between Johann and me. No agency in between."

Carrigan looked at Johann. "How about it? I'll be your agent. I'll keep the fifteen percent for myself and give you the ten percent discount. You get twenty spots for eighty-one bucks instead of ninety.

"Who'll write the copy?" asked Johann

"Sko will,' said Carrigan.

"Oh, no. Not on this deal. You're the agency, you write the copy."

"But you said you'd write it. That was part of the deal."

"Only with legitimate clients."

Johann von Meer sat upright in his chair, his hands clasped tightly to his lapels. "I'll have you know," he began in a stately voice, as his ash tumbled from his cigarette, "I am of Dutch peasantry, and though I may not be a wealthy painter or possess any blue blood, I certainly am not a bastard."

The whole table broke up with laughter, and for a moment, everyone else in the room became silent, all eyes focused on the loud, coffee group.

"Shee-it!" said Pavlov in his southern accent. "Ah'll write the fukkin' copy fer ten percent."

The sentence rang loud and clear in the room filled with customers, all eyes and ears still trained on the coffee group. Slowly, chuckles and laughter came from those who heard the comment. Pavlov turned a shade of red for a bit.

"Where's the Princess?" Sko asked. "Haven't seen her for a few days."

"Me neither," Pavlov commented. "Carrigan, she's in your building."

Carrigan nodded. Pam Allison, known as the *Princess* to the group, had an office down the hall from his. "I don't know.

I haven't seen her either. Usually she tells me when she's going out of town."

"Way'al hay'al," Pavlov remarked. "Ain't thet just like a woman to run off and not tell poor ol' Carrigan whar she done gone."

Everyone laughed, and then the table got down to some basic conversation.

"I hear the Vikings are lining up a new quarterback."

"We're not talking football," Carrigan charged. "I put up with that bullshit all last fall. No football conversation until August."

"Sales have been bad; I need a radio buy."

"Yeah, the bar in Ada burned down. Goddamn, I just insured it last month."

"San Francisco. That's where all the aristocrats are. They buy paintings. You betchum, Red Ryder."

"I don't know. The president has a democratic congress and house. How the hell is he going to pass anything?"

"Aristocrats. Need more aristocrats in this city."

"Ol' Hardnuts gave that little fucker a ticket this morning."

"I could come down to four and a quarter per spot. Yesterday I sold a fifty-spot package to Gate City."

"We're out of wheat toast. I brought white. Is that okay?"

"How about four dollars a spot?"

"That slimy little shit owns half the goddamn city."

"You pay for the coffee this time."

"I paid last time."

"Old man Graybar had another fit this morning."

"Somebody leave a tip."

Two
Rembrandt

Slim, young, good-looking Terri Brighton, the marketing director of American Bank and Trust, sat behind her desk looking over the proposal. "It's good, Carrigan. I like it." Carrigan watched the delicate, feminine hands as Terri again glanced over the layouts in front of her. "I especially like the newspaper. Nice graphics, nice use of space. I won't have any trouble running this past the marketing committee."

"Good," answered Carrigan. "I'll make the media buy. The campaign starts the first, runs through the twenty ninth." Carrigan was on his feet. "I'll leave the layouts and storyboards. Give me a call after you've met with the committee."

Carrigan caught the elevator to the main floor, and by the time he reached the front door, a heavy drizzle was coming down. Hurriedly, he made his way across the pavement to his car, and once inside he checked his watch. Nine-thirty. He was already late for coffee.

Five minutes later, he pulled up at the back of the Mark Building, dashed from his car past the *Carrigan Advertising* sign, and had his key in hand as he ran up the red brick steps.

Inside his office, he glanced at his recorder phone. No red light meant no phone calls. Just as he headed out the door, he heard the phone ding once. Someone was calling. He hesitated, checked his watch and thought, to hell with it. Before he left, he glanced down the hall to the doorway that led to Pam Allison's office. It was shut. He had checked earlier in the morning and it was shut then, too. When she was in, the door was always open.

And besides, her Volkswagen wasn't in the parking lot.

The Guys from Fargo

The drizzle had slowly evolved into a lazy rain, and as Carrigan hustled down the block, the gutters were slowly filling with water. With the collar of his coat pulled up around his neck, he quickened his pace. "Shit," he said. The sun had been shining brightly when he left home, but this was typical weather for Fargo; wait five minutes and you get something different. He recollected that rain had been predicted the night before on TV, but usually they were wrong. How come they were right today?

He made his way to the Powers Cafe double doors, and when he jerked the handle, his hand slipped away. It was then he saw the crude sign:

CLOSED TWO DAYS FOR REMODELING

"Shit." Carrigan gazed along the block toward the bus station, his body backed up against the door to protect himself from the falling rain. *Where the hell would the group go?* he thought to himself. *The Townhouse? No. Too new. Perkins? No.* That was the greasy-hole of Broadway. There was more grease there on the ceiling than here at the Powers.

Carrigan reread the sign, and then kicked his foot against the door. When he turned around, Hardnuts Brodigan was standing in front of him, rain dripping off his plastic covered cap. He was wearing a blue raincoat that stretched to his knees, and his pistol belt was strapped to the outside as if he might have to use the weapon.

"That's defacing private property," Hardnuts snarled in his usual demeaning tone. "I could write you up for that, but I'm going to overlook it this time." Hardnuts narrowed his eyes into a killing stare for a few seconds, and then casually strolled up the street.

Carrigan followed him with his eyes for a bit, feeling well protected knowing that Hardnuts was ever on the alert. He was probably searching for the stray dog that had been pissing on the fire hydrants a few days ago. God forbid he find him, thought Carrigan as he hurried back to his office.

The Princess' car still wasn't in the lot. He stopped short of the Mark Building and cast a quick glance diagonally across the block. On the third floor of the Burlington Northern building, he could see the lights burning in Johann's studio. Carrigan ran to his car, and by the time he reached the warehouse, the rain was torrential.

He made a mad dash for the back door and ran up the cold, open staircase to the third floor. He swung the wooden doors open and briskly walked through the junk-filled interior. It was dark in this portion, and from above, water dripped forming puddles here and there on the cement beneath his feet.

He entered the modern part of the building and hurried along the carpeted corridor and pushed through the fire doors at the opposite end into another old section of the building. Johann's studio was past the elevator, which never worked.

A huge set of double doors, wide enough to snug through Johann's gigantic paintings, was the initial amenity that drew Johann to this spot. This corner enclave was a great find for him at one-fifty a month. The warehouse dated back to the turn of the century, and at one time this particular room had been a bakery where maple syrup was mixed. Johann had removed the two large mixing bins, propped the overhanging vents with two by fours and built in a makeshift table underneath.

Hundreds of paned windows lined the two outer walls, half of them cracked, many filled with cardboard, but still, the incoming light was sufficient enough to illuminate the genius of Johann's artwork. Radiators ran all around the room. Some worked.

Johann's layout table was in the very center of the room, where he did his commercial artwork, something he detested, but which at least granted him a meager living. Carrigan had known Johann for a couple years and helped him along by utilizing his talents for some of his clients.

A partition ran half the length of the room. One side was devoted to the studio portion where Johann's giant easel stood, where all his oils were mixed, where all his colossal finished paintings stood, layer upon layer stacked against the two inside walls. Any open space on these walls portrayed Johann's sketches and charcoal pencil drawings—all faces with large noses and beady, black eyes, and dark, heavy eyebrows. All of his faces seemed sad, researched out of the past, or so Johann maintained, and clad in garb reminiscent of the Middle Ages.

Papers, books and oil pallets were strewn on other makeshift tables, giving the room a look of total disarray, but to Carrigan's keen eye, he knew different. This was orderly compared to its normal state.

With all the metal framework, pipes and electrical mazes of unending wire hanging from the ceiling, it was difficult for Carrigan to believe that at one time, someone had actually designed this room.

Carrigan could smell coffee brewing, and classical music came almost inaudible from a radio in the corner. Johann probably was in his darkroom, a conglomerate of two by fours hulking one corner of his studio covered with black tar paper. A purple curtain draped an entrance to it.

The cold and dampness of the room caused Carrigan to shudder. "Johann?" he called out.

"Uhhh."

He was alive.

Carrigan walked past the divider to discover Johann sitting in a wooden director's chair, staring at the huge painting he was working on.

"Have you had your coffee yet?"

"Uhhh.

Carrigan filled a couple cups and pulled up another director's chair. Johann sat, crippled knee folded over his leg, cigarette sticking out of his mouth upwards at a forty-five-degree angle, his ash almost an inch long. Smoke streamed upwards forcing Johann's eyes shut. Then he opened his eyes wider. He was only squinting this morning, a methodology he utilized when scrutinizing his work. Carrigan knew he should remain silent until Johann made his first observation.

It finally came. "It's a piece of shit."

Carrigan studied the figures on the canvas, focused on the large noses, the heavy eyebrows, the dark penetrating eyes. Johann had changed the color of the clothing completely since Carrigan had last viewed the painting.

"But it's a good piece of shit." Johann squinted again, and as he stretched his narrow face forward, the ash dropped from his cigarette. He relaxed back in his chair and turned to Carrigan. "Good morning."

"Powers was closed this morning," said Carrigan.

"I know. I was there. I rattled the doors until they practically shook off the hinges. Then Hardnuts came over and threatened me with a ticket."

Carrigan chuckled. Good old Hardnuts. By having him patrol the streets, the city was certainly safe from criminals beating on the Powers Coffee House door or from stray dogs pissing on hydrants.

Johann returned his gaze back to the painting.

"Have you seen Pam lately?" Carrigan asked.

"What?" Johann turned his head. "No, why?"

"Well, you sometimes do layout drawings for her clients."

"So?"

"Well, I haven't seen her for a few days."

"Carrigan," Johann said as he took a drag off is cigarette. "You asked about her yesterday at coffee. This is only twenty-four hours later."

"She hasn't been in her office for three days. It's not like her."

Johann was squinting at his painting again. "So, three days. Maybe she's sick or got a cold or something. Call her husband and find out."

"Call Jerry?" Carrigan smiled. "The last time I called Pam

and he answered the phone, he wanted to know the nature of my call. Talk about a jealous son-of-a-bitch."

"Well, she's a good looker. I'd be jealous, too." Johann said.

Carrigan was silent for a moment. "Why don't you call him?"

Johann snubbed out his cigarette. "Carrigan, what the hell is your problem?"

"I don't have any problem."

"Yes, you do. You're obsessed with Pam's whereabouts."

"I'm just concerned."

"It's more than that."

"Well, it isn't like her to just take off without telling me."

"Maybe she and her husband went somewhere together."

"No, I saw his car this morning in front of his office."

"Well, she's probably off to see a client somewhere. I wouldn't worry about her." Johann focused on the smear of oil before him as he lit up another cigarette. "What do you think of the painting?"

Carrigan was having a hard time concentrating on anything else beside the Princess. Finally, he made a comment. "I like it. I like the clothes. I like the rich colors."

"I like the elbow on the guy in gray. The right elbow," said Johann. Then methodically, and with the presence of a university professor, he stood up and explained in art terms how he had managed to blend the colors giving the illusion of a perfect shadow at the very tip of the elbow, yet lightening up the forearm along the sleeve. According to Johann, the elbow was Rembrandt-like, especially with its artistic use of dark and light colors, which, Johann explained, was a basic style change that Rembrandt utilized in his portraits from the year 1642 through 1669.

Carrigan was listening attentively to Johann's diatribe and studied the colors some more. There was something particularly striking about the forearm. It did appear three-dimensional. It was incredible. Johann had ten pounds of oil on the canvas, yet, the only portion of the painting that struck his fancy was the elbow of the figure on the right.

"When I finish, all of the painting should look like that elbow." Johann lit up another cigarette and sat down again. "Would you buy it?"

"No," Carrigan said candidly.

"Why not?"

"Couldn't get it in my house. Even if I could, I don't have a wall big enough for it."

Johann nodded, the ash growing on his cigarette. "It would sell in San Francisco."

"But this is Fargo. I doubt there are a dozen houses around big enough for this painting. Why don't you paint smaller stuff?"

Johann turned slowly to face Carrigan. "An artist paints what he has to paint."

Carrigan agreed. "Yes, but an artist who paints what he has to paint should paint what he paints where the painting will sell. There's not much demand for a painting six by ten feet here in the Midwest. You paint good stuff, and there's probably a market in San Francisco. Maybe you should make the move."

"Can t."

"Why not?"

"Don't have the money to move."

Carrigan was persistent. "You've got no family, Johann. No wife, no kids to worry about like the rest of us. You've got too much talent to waste it here in Fargo."

Johann's face turned to stone, his eyes seemingly staring right through Carrigan. He slowly turned to face his work of art, his eyes squinting again, his lower lip wrapped up under the butt of his cigarette, sticking it upwards into its traditional angle. When Johann nodded his head, Carrigan knew he was getting through to his friend. His reasoning was practical, his logic clear.

And then Johann spoke. "That elbow sure looks good."

Three
Death Ride

Damon Jamison, former Fargo resident, kept his foot to the gas pedal on his 38 Chevy pickup as he came down the highway. When he entered the outskirts of Moorhead, he slowed as he passed Bud's Roller Rink and angled off onto 1st Avenue. Within a few blocks he pulled up to a pump at the coop filling station.

Damon, known in familiar circles as Junkman Jamison, was a little man with big ideas. He had lived in Fargo for several years and at one time had amassed several pieces of property, but what took six short years to accumulate all went in a short six months. The stress was too much, and eventually he and his wife divorced. She got the two girls, but as a result of an amicable parting, he was able to see them quite often. He now lived in Detroit Lakes, forty miles east of Fargo, known as DL, the beginning of the lakes area in Minnesota.

"Want her filled?" asked the man in the tattered cap.

"Yep," replied Damon to the attendant. The two talked as the gas pump dinged with each gallon pouring in. It was an old pump, just like the man pumping gas. They discussed the weather, commented on the crops in the field and made their observations about the heavy flood that had inundated Fargo-Moorhead the spring before. During the short conversation the man running the pump couldn't help but notice the furniture in the box of the truck. "Antique collector?" he asked curiously.

Damon Jamison had never thought of his junk as antiques, but the term seemed attractive at the moment.

"Yes," he finally replied.

A white cat brushed against Damon Jamison's feet and

looked up at him with lazy eyes. When Damon petted the animal, the fur ball responded with heavy purring.

"Don't know where it came from," said the man at the pump. "I think someone filled up with gas and the critter got left. Been here for a couple days. That'll be eleven-fifty even."

Damon followed the man into the station, paid the bill and came back out. He had left the door open to his pickup, and when he crawled in, the white cat was curled up on the back of the seat enjoying the warm sunrays pouring through the window.

Damon stroked the fluff ball. "How would you like to live in DL? I've got a place where you can roam all over, and I've got mice by the hundreds."

The cat purred heavily, his lazy eyes almost shut in the warm sun.

Five minutes later, Damon parked across the street from the Powers Coffee House and left the windows open for the cat. As he crossed to the cafe, he was thinking about the term *antiques*. It was a much more eloquent word than *junk*.

When Damon first entered the Powers, he looked around realizing there was something different about the interior, but he couldn't quite put his finger on it. It had been awhile since he had visited the coffee shop.

The same old tables were still in place, still painted black with a dozen chips missing out of each one. At the far end of the restaurant, the long black counter where the singles sat seemed to be the same.

There were no new chairs, and the booths were still painted a dark blue, and the edges of the seats were still worn where people slid in and out.

Then it struck him. It was the wallpaper. It used to be a horrible combination of red, black and orange stripes running from the floor to the ceiling. Now it was papered with yellow and pink daisies set on a dark blue background. The former stripes were terrible, but this pattern was atrocious.

The Guys from Fargo

Carrigan Mulhouse saw Damon enter, and he could imagine Damon was having the same traumatic experience he had gone through only minutes before.

"Snuffy," Carrigan greeted. The nickname fit him perfectly. Damon was short, squatty, had light red hair and a scraggly beard speckled with gray. His favorite shirt was a blue and black plaid, which he wore almost daily. Over this, he usually wore a green, knit sweater, which he had donned today. The sweater had dozens of holes in it, as if it had been shot-gunned. Snuffy still had his eyes glued to the wallpaper when he sat down.

Carrigan saw the amazement. "Isn't it god-awful?"

"It's horse shit," commented Snuffy. "Their interior decorator must be blind."

Carrigan laughed. "And they washed the floor. Did you notice?"

Snuffy examined the skuzzy black and white tile. It definitely had been cleaned and waxed. "Will these wonders never cease?" Snuffy pushed his cup across the table and let Carrigan fill it.

"What tears you away from the lake country?"

Snuffy stirred in some sugar. "Oh, the usual earthly pleasures."

Carrigan wasn't sure what that meant. Since the divorce, Snuffy had dated a lady friend in Moorhead. Though he made regular trips back and forth from DL to see her, Carrigan hadn't seen him for a few weeks.

"How are the kids?" Carrigan asked.

"Fine. I get them every other weekend. They like it in DL. Lots to do." The two girls were both beautiful like their mother. "How's your family?" Snuffy asked.

"The boys are growing like weeds. They're either into football or soccer or baseball or something. This winter I suspect it will be hockey. Verna's still teaching in the school system."

"What would you like this morning?" Millie asked Damon. She always came around within a minute from the moment a new member sat down.

"Toast," said Snuffy.

"Wheat or white?"

"Wheat."

"Peanut butter?"

"Peanut butter." Millie was gone

"Where is everyone?" asked Snuffy.

Carrigan checked his watch. "Still early." He looked around. The Warner Realty crew of eight was packed around the big table, and all the booths were occupied. Graybar was at his place almost finished with his two eggs, and beyond him was Wandering Eddie.

Wandering Eddie was just one of many strange tenants of the Powers Hotel, which was filled with senior citizens or handicapped people. Wandering Eddie was one of the handicapped; he had his brain cleverly concealed in his right knee. He was sitting in one of the booths and had just received his breakfast from one of the other waitresses, but it wouldn't be long when he would be wandering off through the back doors to the men's toilet in the basement. Whenever he returned, he would occupy a different table and reorder his meal. Before that meal would be finished, he would be off to the can again, only to return to a third table and order another meal. If the waitress were alert, she would usually pick up his first meal and trail around after him.

Carrigan had no idea why Wandering Eddie spent so much time in the can. He either had a small bladder or else it was the attraction of the urinals. They were the old style, standing at chest height and extending all the way to the floor, so one didn't require much control. With eyes shut, one could stand back a couple feet from the urinal and still hit it quite easily. Wandering Eddie probably had just as much accuracy as a bombsite did on a Flying Fortress.

When he returned to the coffee shop, he always had his fly open. Today was no exception.

"So, how long have you been in the junk business now?"

"Three, four months," answered Snuffy. He hesitated, then, "I'm kind'a moving into antiques. I find a lot of furniture when I travel around. Seems a natural, junk and furniture."

"You like it?"

His eyes shined. "Nothing like it. I wake up in the morning and never know quite where I'm going. Never know when I'm coming home, never know what I'll find."

"Do you miss being a landlord?"

"Not a bit. Nothing but headaches." Snuffy whipped out his bull Durham sack of tobacco, tore off a paper and started rolling a cigarette. "I had fourteen employees, fifty-four apartments. Bookwork alone killed me."

"But you made money."

'Ha!" came the retort. "Until the crunch came. You don't know how fast a piece of property loses value when housing goes down. Everything mortgaged to the hilt, payments here, notes there, credit disappears, henchmen knocking on my doors in the middle of the night. I was lucky to get out alive. I'd never go back for all the money in the world."

"So now you're in antiques and furniture. Must be nice to find your niche in life so early."

Snuffy licked the cigarette paper and rolled it into a tube, slicked the ends and stuck it in his mouth. "Haven't you? Wasn't it you who told me some six, seven years ago, you were happier than shit to get out of the college setting?"

Carrigan shrugged his shoulders. "Yeah, I guess so."

"Do you miss teaching?"

No one had asked him that question in months, perhaps years. Carrigan had been a foreign language specialist, spoke German and Russian fluently. Like Snuffy, to a degree, he had come through a period of falling enrollments, just like the housing business fell off. He lost his job because he didn't have tenure. He had always enjoyed an excellent reputation as a college teacher, but in spite of that, he was forced to leave. The irony of it all was the fact that he could out teach anyone. He never got over losing the job.

"Oh, I guess I miss the contact with students. I always enjoyed being a part of the process responsible for molding the kids into something." When Carrigan dipped his head, Snuffy saw the empty look on his face and realized the topic must still be painful for him

Snuffy changed the subject. "How's the advertising business?"

"Okay. I'm working on a few new clients. But it's sort of the same thing over and over again. Write a TV commercial and produce it, buy some media. Do a layout for the paper, buy some media. Write a radio commercial, buy some media."

Snuffy dragged on his cigarette. "At least you've made your success already. I'm still working at it."

Carrigan found the remark amusing. *Did Snuffy really believe he had found his success already?* He wondered. He was antsy and wanted to move on to something different. He needed a change, a new challenge.

Carrigan reached for the pot and poured the remainder in his cup. He looked up, caught Millie's attention and motioned that the pot was empty. He looked over to where Wandering Eddie had been sitting, but he was gone. Then he spotted Eddie's crew-cut hair and beanpole frame at a different table, waiting to be served again.

As Carrigan sipped his coffee, a pair of warm, soft hands swept around his cheeks, then down over his chest. The unmistakable perfume of the *Princess* flowed into his nostrils.

"Hi, dah-ling," he heard her greet in a low Marlene Dietrich voice. Pam Allison gave Carrigan a quick peck on the cheek and slid around the table into a chair. "Hi. How are you this morning?" she asked in her normal voice.

Oh, sweet sweetness, thought Carrigan with a wide smile

and a blushing face. She had a habit of doing that—sneaking up behind him and giving him a big squeeze and a quick kiss. He loved it. Who could not love this beautiful, twenty-eight-year-old strawberry blond with immaculately clean skin and a body like Marilyn Monroe. Her gorgeous blue eyes lit up the coffee table like a pinball machine.

Oh, sweet sweetness! "You know Snuffy, don't you?" Carrigan asked her.

"Of course." Her warm smile floated across the table and swarmed like bees around Snuffy's grubby face. She tugged playfully at his beard with her long fingers. "How are you, Snuffy? I understand you're the number one junkman in DL nowadays."

"Yup, number one," he answered with a chuckle and still reverberating from the friendly little tug on his beard. "Got the best junk within a fifty-mile radius."

"What kind of junk do you collect?"

"Nothing but the finest. Bed pans, ball bearings and Ben Franklin burners."

She laughed. "I'll bet you had that phrase memorized."

Snuffy grinned. "Matter of fact, I did. Kind of cute, isn't it?"

Carrigan jumped back into the conversation, his words aimed at the Princess. "Where have you been the past week? I was worried about you. I even thought about calling Jerry."

The warm smile on her face suddenly disappeared. "What? Why would you call Jerry?"

"Well, I didn't call him, but I was worried about you."

The warm smile came back to her face. "I took my little VW for a trip out West. Hung drapes on all the houses in Williston."

"All the houses?" Snuffy inquired, not sure he had heard her correctly.

"Yes. Didn't you know, none of the houses in Williston has drapes? They're behind the times. The sod huts just got

windows a month ago, so now they need drapes." She laughed.
They all laughed.

"She's an interior decorator," Carrigan clarified.

"I knew that," Snuffy said, his eyes glued to her pretty face.

Pam turned serious. "In Williston I was redecorating the complete main floor of the most beautiful mansion you've ever seen." Her excitement rose. "I've got an order in for drapes, carpet, wallpaper and paint." She touched Carrigan on the arm. "You know what? The owner, Mr. Belmont, has a den on the main floor larger than my living room. And it has high ceilings and spacious walls. I told him I knew an artist here in Fargo that could decorate the den with the most fabulous sixteenth century art he'd ever seen. It would be perfect for Johann. He'd go wild!"

Carrigan was thinking about the conversation he had just had with Johann the day before. "Do you really think this Belmont fellow would consider Johann's paintings?"

"He'll be in town next month, and he said he'd look him up."

"I hope he does," said Carrigan. Johann needed a boost, and this Mr. Belmont sounded like a perfect client for him.

"So, you do wallpaper," Snuffy remarked coming back into the conversation. He made a wide sweep with his hand. "What do you think of the wallpaper in here?"

"Oh, good Lord!" she gasped as she looked around. "Isn't that the ghastliest pattern you've ever seen?"

Suddenly old man Graybar screamed out, "I came in with my glasses!" Everyone focused on him when he slammed a fist down on the table and rattled his plate. "I came in with my glasses! Someone stole my glasses!"

Millie was at his side trying to calm him down, but he was persistent accusing Millie or anyone nearby, that someone had taken his glasses. Carrigan couldn't remember if he was wearing them earlier.

"No!" Graybar hollered at Millie. "I'll wheel myself back! I'm perfectly capable. I'm not an invalid!"

Not an invalid? Carrigan mused. Graybar rolled his chair up to the table every morning at a speed of five feet per minute. Carrigan watched as the old man muttered and sputtered and wheeled his chair toward the rear double doors that lead to the lobby.

"You find my glasses or I won't pay for breakfast!" Graybar threatened Millie. Old Graybar had more strength than Carrigan realized. He had his chair moving at quite a clip when he rammed through the double doors, but once through, his chair spun awkwardly to the left out of control.

To the left was where the staircase led down to the men's bathroom. Too late! Graybar's whoop echoed like a thunderbolt from the stairway, and as he toppled down, the clatter of wheels and metal boomed like a cannonball flying through a K-mart store.

By the time Carrigan reached the top of the stairs, a crowd of people had already come to Graybar's rescue. He had ridden the stairs while upright in his chair, and at the bottom he had plowed through the door of the men's can. His chair, lying on its side had propped the door open, and there lay Graybar. He had scooted ten feet across the tiles and came to a rest with his head face down in the bottom of one of the urinals.

A couple men picked him up, dragged him back to his chair and flopped him into it. His face was sheet white, his eyes as big as ping-pong balls. "Okay, I'll pay!" he said half-coherent. "I'll pay!"

Carrigan shook his head in awe as he headed back to the table. Graybar had just taken a death ride and survived it! Absolutely amazing!

"Is he okay?" the Princess asked when Carrigan sat down.

"A little shaken, I suspect. I'm not sure he knows what happened."

As the crowd from the door slowly began to shuffle back into the restaurant, a low murmur hovered throughout like a church crowd waiting for the service to start. Wandering Eddie was one of the crowd, standing around, his hands in his pocket, his fly wide open. Millie guided him back to his seat.

"Wha-aat th' hay-al was that?" Pavlov Glitzberg plunked himself in a chair and stared at the people near the rear door.

"Graybar just took a ride down the staircase in his wheel chair. Ended up with his face lying in the urinal."

"Way-al, ah'l be damned! What a funny way t' take a pee!"

The Princess cracked up, spit out her coffee and dropped her cup. The hot coffee swirled over the edge of the table onto Pavlov's lap.

"Yow!" Pavlov bellowed as he flew up from his chair. Coffee stains covered his fly and were running down his leg.

"Way-al ah'll be damned!" he said as he pulled the cloth away from his legs. "Ah jus' peed mah pants!"

The table roared. The next table roared. Those in the booths against the wall roared.

"Where have you been the past several days?" Pavlov asked Pam as he sat back down.

"I was off to Dickinson. I've got a new client."

"Dickinson?" Carrigan asked. "I thought you said Williston?"

She pursed her lips. "I meant Williston."

"Shee-it," Pavlov remarked. "Ain't no dif-fence a'tween Dick'son an' Wills'ton. They's bof in da middle a' buff'lo country."

They were all laughing.

"What's going on here?" Radio Sko made his appearance and eyed Pavlov's wet pants, then glanced at the Princess. "What'd you do, get him a little excited?"

Everyone within earshot roared.

"Princess, haven't seen you for a few days," Sko said

36

"She been in da buff-lo country?" Pavlov answered.

"Dickinson or Williston?" Sko asked.

"Bof," Pavlov answered.

And then the coffee group got down to some serious conversation.

"Anyone need a radio buy today? Got a hell of a deal."

"This mansion was humungous. The potential is unending."

"Where's Johann today?"

"So, the Democrats are bitching about social security, but have they got a solution?"

"I think I'll build a separate garage for the antiques, and it's gonna have a lot of windows."

"You'll need drapes."

"Hi, Johann. How's the painting coming along?"

"Uhhh."

"So, you've got a little pussy in your Chevy, eh, Snuffy?" I hope she's over twenty-one."

"The way you guys talk!"

"You know you love it."

"How about a 250-time annual radio contract? That'll bring each spot down to less than four dollars, commissionable of course."

"Has anyone seen Reggie lately?"

"And Mr. Belmont wants to see some of your paintings. What do you think of that?"

"Uhhh."

"I was really worried about you."

"Ah think ah peed mah pants!"

Four
The Princess and Other Things

The manila envelope, on which was scribbled her name and address in pencil, had arrived the day before to her office. She pulled the envelope from a desk drawer and once again examined the two black and white photos within. The partially nude photographs were of her, depicting her in a compromising situation. If her husband, Jerry, ever saw these, he would fly into a rage. The only person she would remotely consider showing these to was Carrigan Mulhouse, the closest friend she had. Carrigan's office was in the same building just down the hall. She had spoken briefly with him this morning with the intention of seeking his advice on what to do concerning the arrival of the photos, but she could not yet bring herself around to discussing it. She required more time to rethink the situation, and when she finally decided to approach him, he had left his office.

She checked her watch, knowing she had a luncheon meeting in ten minutes with a client, so she put the envelope back in the drawer, grabbed a light jacket and walked the few blocks to PD's, the photos firmly on her mind every step of the way.

PD's was the restaurant portion of Elm Tree Square. The square itself was in downtown Fargo on Broadway, two blocks south of the Powers Coffee House, and basically held a group of boutiques, craft shops and fashion corners. The square derived its name from the huge elm tree with fake leaves and a trunk that extended from the basement floor clear to the ceiling. In the very center of the remodeled building, an iron rail ran around a square shaped balcony. A staircase at both ends led down a level to the eating area, and looking downward over the railing, one could view a large fountain that sprayed water in gurgling sounds, and, which was lit up by various colored lights. Around this fountain were dozens of tables fitted with chairs and an occasional picnic type table with benches. The lounge area was rather quaint, a sort of serve-yourself type restaurant, sort of hidden and sort of dark even during the daytime. In that sense, it was a sort of a nice hide-a-way spot to eat.

There were two ways into Elm Tree Square; one through the main door that fronted Broadway and another at the back that opened to the alley.

It was all innocent enough, at least in appearance. The Princess, Pam Allison, kept her appointment and was now munching on a sandwich sitting across from the suave, blond haired man. He couldn't keep his eyes off of her. He was so enraptured in her beauty that when he dipped his spoon in his soup and raised it to his lips, a few noodles dribbled onto his tie.

He was a natural klutz, and she knew it, and she always attempted to overlook his sloppy manners. He was hoping she had not seen his blunder as he tugged at his napkin ever so secretly, his gaze solidly on her sparkling eyes. His intentions were honest, but his coffee cup was on top of the napkin, and when he pulled the napkin away the cup came with it and fell from the table.

A crisp thump sounded when the plastic cup hit the tile, but pretending as if nothing had happened, the suave, young man began dabbing his tie with the napkin, unaware that it was smeared with catsup.

It was all the Princess could do to refrain from noticing the splotch on his tie, which was becoming larger and larger with each proverbial wipe. She continued nibbling at her sandwich, making small talk, forcing her eyes level with his.

He was so goggle-eyed with her beauty that she might well

have been asking an ethical question; *Is it true you always pick your nose when you eat a hamburger?* To which he might well have answered, *Yes, I do.*

Or she might have asked a philosophical question; *What ramifications does Franz Kafka attempt to clarify in his work, Metamorphosis?* To which he might well have answered, *Of course.*

Or she might have asked a simple question; *I understand your penis is three and one quarter inches long.* To which he might well have answered, *Exactly.*

So it was certainly innocent enough when this young, suave, blond haired man reached across and touched her delicate and warm hand. When he squeezed it, his eyeballs rolled as if they would pop out of his head.

His heart fluttered, and the spot on his tie became still larger as he excitedly wiped at it with his free hand. He was totally unaware of his actions, unaware how stupid he looked, unaware how terribly painful all this was going to be for him in a few seconds.

A few seconds was all it required for the man hidden behind the fountain to make his sudden appearance. So enraptured, and so excited was the young, blond haired man that he did not even see the ring attached to the fist approaching his nose at light-year speed. So painful came the blow, and with so much thrust that the young man rolled backwards, his feet sailing up in the air. And so immediate was the blood pouring from his nose that it was no longer necessary for him to continue wiping the catsup spot on his tie, nor could he for that matter.

Angrily, the man who delivered the stunning punch grabbed Pam Allison by the arm and jerked her to her feet. In seconds he marched her out of the restaurant, past the gurgling fountain, dragging her up the stairs.

"By God, I've been watching you!" her husband spat out between his teeth. "Three times you met this idiot in the same place. If you were going to have an affair, I would at least expect you to carry it out in some remote spot and not here in the center of town where everybody and his goddamn brother can see you!"

She was as calm and collected as she always was. "I would say," she began with a soft voice, "that I just lost another client. That was Mr. John Raphardt, the architect on the new medical building going up by West Acres. I was about to close a deal in which I could have easily made six thousand dollars profit in six weeks time."

Big Jerry Allison's mouth dropped down near his beltline. He slowly released his grip on her arm as he glanced over the railing where a small group of people had gathered around the blond haired man. Jerry turned back to his wife.

"Oh." He took another glance at the man with the blood on his face. The young man had a towel shoved up against his nose, and now, with his head tipped back, someone began leading him away.

"Oh," said Jerry Allison again. He hung his head down and stuck his hands into his overcoat. "Well, in that case, I, ah..."

"I think you owe Mr. Raphardt an apology."

"Yes, well, ah, yes, I ah. . ." Jerry Allison quickly headed down the staircase, but as soon as Mr. Raphardt saw him coming, he tore away from the person guiding him to the restroom.

"Come back!" Pam heard her husband shout as he chased after the fleeing Mr. Raphardt.

Mr. Raphardt scaled the opposite staircase as if a grizzly was charging after him. His feet clattered against the tile as he banged his way out the back door to the alley with Jerry in hot pursuit.

This was not the first time Jerry Allison had made such an error. A month earlier, he had broken the middle finger of a gentleman who was giving the finger to another gentleman. Jerry just happened to be in the wrong line of sight for the man with the nasty digit. That scene also ended in another hot pursuit.

And there were other occasions similar to this incident, in which Jerry Allison had accosted an innocent bystander. He was very good at tailing the Princess and her clients, and he was very good at delivering an unsuspecting blow to unsuspecting noses.

Of course, his rage and jealousy helped reduce his wife's income by several thousand dollars a year. Indeed, this six-foot-four, two-hundred-thirty-pound giant was the total ruination of any success the Princess might have potentially acquired in her decorating business.

As the Princess headed for the doorway, she sighed a frightful breath. She could not help but wonder how her husband would react if she was having a *real* affair with someone. Of course, he would kill the *someone*, and he would not at all be gentle while he beat her to a pulp. She knew that she would suffer the same fate if he should ever discover the nude photos, which secretly occupied her desk drawer.

She left the building and walked back to her office.

Reginald Richthoffen, instructor in the geography department at Moorhead State, was one of Carrigan's few close friends remaining there. He was nicknamed Reggie the Baron after Baron von Richthoffen, the World War I German Ace. However, their last name was the only thing they had in common, since Reggie couldn't fly a plane. If one considered the Baron as top gun in his squadron, then one might consider Reggie as top gun in the geography department, because he was chairman. But not everyone knew he was the *only teacher* in the department.

Reggie was known as a *fornagainst* college teacher. He was for the Union at the college when the benefits fell his way, and he was against it when certain benefits became a detriment. He was for the new course curriculum being developed over the past six months, but against it when he discovered none of his ideas was being adapted. He wanted the old library torn down, but didn't want a new one built in its place.

Being pro and con everything, Reggie could attend any meeting on campus regardless of the goal. He was also very adept at acquiring scuttlebutt on anyone and anything at the college. If there were no latest scuttle to report, he would invent something, spread it around and later deny such scuttlebutt existed.

There was only one thing on campus Reggie was not for or against, and that was the geography department. He was totally for it, and he had the backing of his students, especially if they wanted to get through his courses.

Reggie loved college life. As chairman of the geography department, he usually taught three courses a week, all arranged on Tuesday, Wednesday and Thursday. That provided him with a four-day weekend every week. Now, he was teaching summer school, which gave him much more time off, since he only taught two courses on Wednesday and Thursday, which now offered a five-day weekend. In the course of the normal school year, he devoted some time to administrative duties, and as chairman, he had direct contact with Dean Wimpleton, whom he thoroughly detested.

It had been rumored that the prior chairman, who had been gone for the past three years, ruled with an iron fist, which was not really true. But there was no doubt in anyone's mind that Reggie ruled with a wooden club. He was a table-pounder, a shouter, and a great naysayer. He was loud and boisterous, and if he had ever possessed any tact, it was probably before he reached puberty, and whenever he engaged in an argument he always won whether he was right or wrong.

Dean Willard Wimpleton hated Reggie Richthoffen as much as Reggie hated him.

Reggie was now sitting in the Dean's office, where he had

been summoned earlier in the morning for an urgent conference.

Dean Wimpleton, referred to as *the Wimp* by Reggie, had a stack of papers on his desk. For the past fifteen minutes, he had been going through them while Reggie Richthoffen sat waiting, slumped in his chair, mouth turned down, his Brezhnev eyebrows dipped in a scowl to match the rest of his face. Reggie was just about to froth at the mouth when the Dean finally spoke.

"I see here that you have recommended a rather major revamp of the geography-geology department."

"That's right," said Reggie.

The mousy mustached, bald-headed Dean studied the papers some more. "I'm accustomed to seeing curriculum change come across my desk, but I'm not going to waste time on your so called need to relocate the department."

"Dean Wimpleton," Reggie protested. "Our office is jammed into 400 square feet, the staff equipment is stored in the annex at the library a block away, and our labs are in the science building. We're spread out all over the campus."

"That's the way it's always been."

Reggie's black eyebrows dipped lower as the scowl on his face broadened. He felt an immediate urge to bang his fist on the Dean's glass-top desk, but he held his temper.

Dean Wimpleton challenged him. "And what is this *our* and *we* and *the staff,* when you're the only person in the department?"

Reggie thought a moment. "I have a secretary."

Dean Wimpleton sighed a breath of resentment and turned the page to the next topic. "I see you want to resign from the grievance committee."

"Yes."

"I think that's an excellent idea. Have you also considered resigning from the curriculum committee and the union affairs committee?" The Dean turned the page and went on to another topic. "Now, about this draft protest group you're associating with. You realize we don't allow such participation from the faculty. We're here to educate the students, not to encourage riot."

"They need a voice," Reggie barked.

"Let's leave that rowdiness to North Dakota State. We don't need that sort of thing here in Minnesota." The Dean turned over the sheet to another topic. "Your request for the visual equipment has been denied."

"Why? The equipment at the library annex is outdated. It's World War II vintage."

"There was nothing wrong with fighting World War II. I was in it myself, and proud of it."

"I didn't say..."

"Of course you imply it with your analogy. No, I'm afraid this will be out of the question."

Reggie was near boiling when the dean went on to the next topic. "As to the heavy workload your department is supposedly undergoing, or rather *your* workload. No one else on campus has complained about having too heavy a workload. What specifically did you want me to do with this request?"

Reggie quietly rose from his chair, reached across and gathered up the request sheet and rolled it into a tube. He took a rubber band from the desktop, twisted it around the roll and held the tubular paper upright. With a broad smile, he said, "Dean Wimpleton, whenever I come up here you always give me so much shit, so why don't you give this request the attention it deserves by sticking it up your ass?"

When Reggie slammed the door to his office, a picture fell from the wall. Dean Wimpleton calmly reached into his drawer and produced a competency report and began filling it out on Reginald Richthoffen, his fourth one on him in as many months.

Delray K. Dvoracek

It was early afternoon when Carrigan Mulhouse walked down the corridor to the familiar sign sticking out above the doorway to the Geography Department. Someone had crossed out the *Geo* at the beginning and added a *T* at the end. The sign read;

graphyT

Carrigan smiled as he walked through the doorway. He only glanced at the gray-haired secretary with the beak nose and passed her by directly to Reginald's office.

Nothing had changed. Four hundred books jammed into a bookcase that held two hundred. The top of Reggie's desk was not visible, cluttered with papers, pencils and an assortment of maps and books. On the corner of his desk sat the same fifteen-pound meteorite that took up a square foot. He used it as a paperweight, but there was nothing underneath it. A pair of lamps sat on each side of his desk, both which he had brought from his home, and, which definitely belonged in a living room setting. Neither of them was plugged in.

All of that was the usual. The unusual was the back wheel of a bicycle on his desktop, complete with the sprocket and brake band assembly. Reggie was in the process of removing the sprocket. He was wearing a nice sport coat and pants, but his hands were covered with grease.

He put down his wrench when Carrigan entered. "Well," he boomed in a heavy voice. "What the hell brings you this side of the border?"

"I like to be reminded once in a while how the elite make a living."

"Haw, haw, haw!" Reggie boomed. Two test papers flew off the desk with the verbal blast.

Carrigan marveled at Reggie. He was a big man, built more out than up. Whenever he laughed, the vibrations could easily shake the toupee off of the president in the next building. With his coal black hair and bushy eyebrows, he very much resembled Brezhnev, except Reggie wore black, horn-rimmed glasses.

"Sit down," Reggie invited.

Carrigan looked around. There was not an extra chair in the room.

"Oh," said Reggie. "Grab one from the outer office. Don't have extra chairs in here. Gets the students in and out faster. No one likes to stand around, you know."

Carrigan secured a chair from the outer office, swung the door shut and sat down.

"Same old utopia over here, I imagine?" Carrigan questioned. "All the professors still putting in a twenty-hour week?"

"Naw," said Reggie as he pulled a handkerchief from his pocket and began wiping his hands. "Some put in as much as twenty-two or twenty-three. Teachers are dropping dead in the halls daily from the pressure. We had one professor put in thirty hours last week. Didn't have a heart attack, but the tension got him. He's on the fourth floor over at the hospital."

Carrigan chuckled. The psycho ward was on the fourth floor.

"So," said Carrigan. "I haven't seen you at the Powers for awhile. Thought I'd check up on you. Where were you all last week?"

"Test week. Finals. Big exam, lot of tests to grade."

"It takes a whole week to correct papers?"

"It did this time. I was teaching a geology course. I had twenty rocks lined up in the lab that students were supposed to identify as part of the test. The night after I set them up, someone came in and switched my rocks around. One goddamn mess. I had everybody failing until I found out. Had to retest."

"Probably the same person who changed your outside geography sign."

"Yeah. I think I know who the culprit is. I can't prove it

though, so I'll just fail him." Reggie had a solution to everything.

"Got time for coffee?" asked Carrigan.

"It's afternoon."

"I know. But I need a break."

"Don't you ever work, Carrigan?"

"Sure I work."

"You're always at coffee."

"Guy's gotta have sustenance,"

"You should be out digging up new clients."

"Don't need any more. I make more money now than I ever did when I was teaching."

"Everybody makes more money than a teacher."

"How about the deans of the college? They make a lot of money."

Reggie let out a defiant guffaw. "Deans aren't teachers, they're administrators. They're up there with the Prez and Vee-Pee. Teachers are the working class, the brown shit collar workers. Deans are the top echelon shit workers."

Carrigan smiled. "Sounds like you had another run-in with ol' Wimpy."

Reggie laughed. "How'd you guess? You know what I'd like to do with him? I'd like to stick this bicycle wheel up his ass and spend the afternoon rolling him around campus."

"Oooh, must have been a bad meeting."

"Not one of my best performances, but I believe I drove my point home."

Carrigan sat for a few seconds more. 'Well, then I'm off."

"Where to?"

"See Pavlov. I have to check on some insurance."

"When are we going fishing?"

"How about this weekend?"

"Can't. Taking the family to Wisconsin."

"Next weekend?"

"I'll check with the war department."

He meant his wife.

"Sorry I can't make coffee. Got this wheel to fix for my kid."

Carrigan stood up. "Come on down when you get a chance."

"I will. Pretty Pam still has coffee with you guys?"

"Yep."

Reggie just smiled.

Pavlov Glitzberg walked swiftly out of his office past the divider behind which the office girls had their desks. "Good afternoon Marian," he said to the blond receptionist. "Nice to see you back."

"Thank you, Paul," came the reply from the buxom blond. What Pavlov Glitzberg really wanted to say was, *Nice to see your big tits back in the office.* Pavlov liked girls with big breasts, perhaps because he had married one with small ones. Marian had been sick for three days claiming she had a mild case of influenza, but Pavlov knew she was having her period.

Pavlov made a Shakespearean sweep across to the copier and ran off a couple pages, then dashed past the blond back to his office. "I believe you'll find these in order, Mr. Fryerman," he said to the client waiting in a chair. Pavlov displayed his large teeth as if he were Burt Lancaster.

"I appreciate your promptness," Mr. Fryerman said as he stood up and offered a hand.

"No problem," replied Pavlov shoving his teeth out even further. "It's our policy to run these claims through with minimal repercussion."

Fryerman left the office and the building.

"Dumb shit," Pavlov said under his breath after Fryerman was gone. What he really wanted to say to Mr. Fryerman was, *Why the hell don't you take your business somewhere else?* Fryerman was always having something stolen from his house or garage or his million-dollar summer home on Pelican Lake.

His phone rang. "Good afternoon, Paul Glitzberg." His

49

teeth were flashing again, his mood forced into a jovial pose. "Yes, Mrs. Bannerfield, the necessity of protection dictates your decision in this manner." He hesitated, then, "Yes, ma'am. The assets should definitely be covered. You can rest assured I'll give you service beyond reputable quality. I'll have the policy drawn up and mailed forthwith."

He waited for her response, gave a salutation and hung up.

"I'll take care of you, old woman," he said between gritted teeth. He scribbled out a few notes on a piece of paper, and when he finished, he glanced into a mirror. He drew a comb out of his pocket and ran it through his hair a couple times, then turned his head first this way then that to make sure everything was in order. He snugged up his tie, rose out of his seat and smoothed the tails of his coat, then sat again.

Marian was in the doorway again. "Paul, I've finished the reports for Kansas City."

"Thank you," said Pavlov as he took them from her. "Have you had a chance to review the Grandlund account yet? Those papers should be mailed forthwith."

"No, I haven't."

"That's nice." He didn't mean to that, but he was staring at the buxom chest on the girl, and the words came from nowhere. "Well, ah, review them... forthwith, and mail them, if you will, please."

"Very well."

Pavlov turned to his dictionary, opened it and randomly focused on a word. "Indubitable." He read the definition. "Too evident to be doubted."

The blond was back in the doorway. "Paul, about the Kansas City papers. They're due there by the end of the week. Should I send them registered mail to make sure they arrive on time?"

Pavlov showed his beautiful Burt Lancaster teeth. "That would be an indubitable decision." She wasn't sure what he said. "Fine," Pavlov clarified. "Send them registered mail."

She was gone.

The phone rang. "Hello, Paul Glitzberg." There was a pause "Ahhh, Mr. Cosborn." He stretched his lips, let his teeth hang out, then after a few seconds the wide smile slowly disappeared, "You have my complete condolence... Indubitably... Ah, yes, I'm sure it was God's will. May she repose in eternal solitude... Yes, sir, Mr. Cosborn... Oh, I understand completely, Mr. Cosborn... I'll have a check sent just as soon as the death certificate arrives... Yes, Mr. Cosborn... Again my condolatory sympathy."

He hung up. "Shit. Another one kicked the bucket."

"What are you shittin' about?" Carrigan Mulhouse entered his cubicle and sat down.

Pavlov's face reeked from disgust. "Four weeks ago I insured this guy's wife. She had a history of heart problems, but they were long ago. I ran through paperwork like you wouldn't believe to make her insurable, and now she does the crappie-flop. I talked him into a fifty thousand dollar policy instead of a ten. Shit."

"You have my condolatory sympathy."

Pavlov smiled. "How long have you been listening?"

"Long enough. How about coffee?"

He checked his watch. "Kind of early, isn't it?"

"I know, but I need a challenge."

"Drinking coffee is no challenge. Any dumb ass can do that."

They both laughed

"I got a better idea," said Pavlov. "How about the two of us drive up to Ada and get drunk?"

Carrigan wasn't comprehending.

Pavlov went on. "I have to check out this guy's bar that burned down a couple days ago. Got to deliver some papers."

"I don't know," answered Carrigan.

"Might even pick up some Indian ginch near the reservation."

Carrigan chuckled.

"What do you say? We deliver the papers, pick up some snatch and get laid."

Carrigan knew Pavlov wasn't serious, but he played along with his little game. "What if we don't find any Indians?"

"Then we'll catch a Boeing 707, fly to England and screw the queen."

Carrigan rolled his eyes and looked back to see if the blond bombshell had heard him, but she was near the copy machine.

"Come on, Carrigan." Pavlov grabbed Carrigan by the sleeve and pulled him out of his office. He dropped off an envelope at the receptionist's desk and told her, "Mail these off if you will, please, forthwith."

"Yes, sir."

"If anybody calls tell them I have urgent business in England."

The receptionist had no idea what he meant. She watched as the two went out the door, crossed the street to Pavlov's car and drove off.

Five
The Need for a Challenge

It was the Fargo-Burnout Carrigan had his eye on this morning. Carrigan arrived early at the Powers Coffee House, had even beat old man Graybar by ten minutes. But now Graybar was already half way into his eggs and toast, his wheel chair parked exactly four inches from the edge of the table, his toast sliced into four pieces, four utensils at his setting. He had two spoons this morning with his fork and knife and was swallowing his orange juice four short gulps at a time. Carrigan was counting.

Carrigan switched his attention back to the Fargo-Burnout. None of the coffee group knew his real name. They only knew that the tall, gaunt replica of a human being had supposedly burned himself out on drugs. He was young, maybe twenty-five years old, Carrigan guessed. He always wore a white pair of Levis, which probably had never been washed, since their color quite closely matched the color of the ceiling in the Powers. He wore a knee-length, black coat, oversized for his frame, and had the cuffs rolled up a turn exposing his boney hands.

Carrigan watched as the narrow-faced fellow poured his cup with half water, then added coffee, then sluggishly poured two small paper caps of cream and followed with a couple heaping spoonfuls of sugar. He stirred the mixture, downed the brew in a few seconds and then repeated the maneuver.

The Fargo-Burnout drank as many as eight or ten cups of coffee that way. Carrigan had never seen him order breakfast and guessed he probably was short on money.

The fellow set his cup down and tugged at his long coat. It was more like a slicker like the Jesse James Gang had worn when they pulled the famous Northfield Bank raid. Carrigan had just seen the TV movie. All of the gang had worn long, light colored coats, so they could recognize each other during the bank holdup. But the Fargo-Burnout's was black. Perhaps it had been cream colored like his pants at one time. Carrigan thought it strange to see him wearing a coat when it was so warm out.

The Burnout's feet were wrapped around the pedestal of the seat, so Carrigan could easily see the holes in each of his soles. To state that his hair was unkempt was too kind of a description for the messy, greasy mop on his head. Probably had lice, Carrigan thought.

"M-m-more coffee," he managed to stammer to the girl behind the counter.

Carrigan shrugged and let his gaze move about to others in the crowd. The two Indians, whom he had seen a few days before, were back at the same booth. Perhaps they weren't transients and had made the Salvation Army their permanent home.

Carrigan looked around some more. Old man Ruckles, whose first name was Roman, was sitting quietly at the next table. He owned Ruckles Chemical Supply and was usually quiet, because he had a hearing problem. The receptacle to his hearing aid was clipped to the lapel of his coat, but often it fell down and hung below the table, so when someone was talking to him, he never heard them. Carrigan wondered why the man didn't have the hearing aide placed in his glasses. Or better yet, in his nose. His nostrils were huge, and the ugly hairs sticking out from them would certainly camouflage a receptacle. Except for the wire, of course.

Roman Ruckles had iddy-biddy blue eyes, so small that Carrigan guessed he probably couldn't see more than fifty feet, if size of eyes had anything to do with how far one could see. Ruckles was a tall, pear-shaped individual. Thick gray hair hung over his ears, but he was bald on top with a white wisp of hair sticking up above his forehead.

"Do you have the time," Ruckles said suddenly. He was only a few feet away, and although Carrigan had been staring at him, he hadn't expected the question and he didn't understand what the man had asked.

"I beg your pardon?" Carrigan asked politely,

"Half past what?" Ruckles asked, as he fumbled with his hearing aide.

"Half what?" asked Carrigan not comprehending old man Ruckles.

Ruckles pointed to the top of his hand. Carrigan's eyes fixed on a lump a few inches back from his knuckles.

"Arthritis," said Carrigan.

"What's that?"

"Arthritis!" Carrigan now shouted.

Ruckles fumbled with his hearing aide again, and then he leaned forward, his hand cupped around his ear. A lot of good that did, thought Carrigan. The receiver for his hearing aid was on the front of his shirt.

Carrigan moved leaned over into his shirtfront and said quite clearly into the receiver, "Arthritis, I suspect."

"Arthritis?" questioned Ruckles. "Harrumph!" he guffawed with his lower lip sticking out. "I ask for the time, and all I get is arthritis." He pushed himself away from the table, propped a homburg over his bare head and headed toward the door.

Just as Ruckles was leaving, the Iranian was entering, the same fellow to whom Hardnuts Brodigan had given the ticket a few mornings back. The dark glasses he was wearing were just a shade darker than his Iranian skin. He was wearing a dark pullover sweater, expensive looking, and a dark pair of trousers with pleats rippling from his beltline to his fly. Black shoes. Black hair. The only thing on him that wasn't black was the blond hanging onto his arm; Harriet the whore, queen of the streets. Harriet had a flat fee for her services, which included a night of adult-rated sex, a foot massage and breakfast. At least, that's what Carrigan had heard. He guessed the breakfast was continental; a bun and juice, something like what she had probably supplied him with last night.

Carrigan checked his watch again. Quarter past nine and none of the coffee group had showed up yet. As he poured himself another cup, he began to wonder where everybody was. It was strange. The Princess was usually at work by eight in the morning, but she hadn't shown up at work yet, and in the last few days, she had not been her usual self. She normally carried a smile on her face and was so upbeat all the time. But lately, she seemed to be holed up in her office, and though he had stopped in to see her during the day, she seemed preoccupied with something.

Maybe she was going through a midlife crisis like Carrigan, though she seemed a bit young for it. Carrigan's mind wandered some more. *You already made your success,* Snuffy had told him a few days ago. Success? What sort of success had he achieved? Advertising was easy for him. He had been at it for six years, the same amount of years he had taught at the college.

Carrigan needed a challenge, something new, something different.

"Why so glum?" It was Radio Sko, former football hero.

Pavlov trailed in after him. "I see that little Iranian fucker has the nerve to occupy the premises."

"Uhhh." Johann was with them.

They were all seated now, cups rustled in place, the fine aroma of caffeine steaming upwards out of the pot.

"Why so glum?" Sko asked again. "Need a radio buy, I bet. Got a hell of a deal this week."

"I need a challenge," said Carrigan.

"This is a challenge," said Sko. "I'm lowering my radio rates. I know the boss is going to raise hell with me when I take an order back, but I'll suffer the consequences. Five

56

hundred spots with an annual contract, rock bottom price three-twenty-five commissionable. If you don't use all five hundred in a year, I won't even short rate you. What do you say to that?"

"I need a challenge.

"Hay—al, ah'l give you a fukkin' challenge," Pavlov said in a hushed voice. "How am ah goin' ta rebuild an $80,000.00 burned out building with $40,000.00 worth'a insurance?"

Carrigan knew he was referring to the bar in Ada.

"Prefab," suggested Sko.

"Uhhh," said Johann. His cigarette was already an inch long, and his eyes weren't fully open yet.

Carrigan was feeling a bit more refreshed. The coffee group always had that affect on him.

Reggie the Baron pulled up a chair after having sneaked in through the back door. "Got her fixed," he said to Carrigan. His hands were still covered with grease from the wheel he had been working on the day before. "And I flunked the kid who messed up my Geography sign. He said he'd confess to messing up my rocks if I'd give him a D.

"Did you?"

Nope. Gave him the big F. Haw, haw, haw!" A napkin blew off the table.

"Ah'l tell you who got th' big F," said Pavlov as he pointed to the booth across the room. "That little Iranian fukkah ovah thay-ah with ol' Hay-et. Las' night he got the big F."

Everybody at the table was laughing.

"Hey, you guys got room for Junkman Jamison?" Snuffy stood by the table, grubby-faced in his green sweater while the guys gave him a cheer.

"Hey guys, listen to this," he said as he hooked his thumbs under his armpits and began reciting

"I'm called Junkman Jamison and I come from DL

I told the big city to go plumb to hell

I'm now a junk collector at the corner of Turners.

I got bed pans and ball bearings and Ben Franklin burners."

"What th' hay-al is all that shit?" asked Pavlov.

"Kind'a cute, huh? Made it up myself." Snuffy pushed a chair in between two of the guys. "It all rhymes too. I've been working on it since I last saw you guys."

"What's this Turners stuff?" asked Radio Sko.

"I live on Turner drive. Turners rhymes with burners. Get it? Turners, burners."

Carrigan offered his critique. "Turner is singular form. You used it in plural. How many Turner streets do you live on?"

"I can do what I want," responded Snuffy as he began rolling a cigarette. "I'm a free American. This is democracy at its finest. Ain't that right, Johann?"

"Uhhh."

"Should make Ben Franklin Burners singular. Turner, burner," said Carrigan. "Ain't that right, Johann?"

"Paint it," said Johann.

Ooohs and ahhhs belched from the coffee group. Johann had spoken!

"Ya, ya, ya. Paint the goddamn stove purple and green, sell it as a Rembrandt to some dumb aristocrat. You betchum, Red Ryder."

And then the coffee group got down to some serious talk.

"Found fourteen of them in a junk pile. They'll bring ten dollars apiece easy."

"Yeah. He switched my rocks around. But I gave him the big F!"

"That little Iranian shit got the big F."

"I need a challenge. Something different."

"Paint that purple and green, too. You betchum."

"You're damn right I was mad. I told Wimpleton where he could stick it."

"Wimpleton? I think I know him. He gambles at cards, doesn't he?"

"I know old man Crawford burned the bar down."

"It's a nuclear standoff. Democrats know it. Republicans know it."

"How about three dollars a spot?"

"Where's the Princess this morning?"

"There's more grease on your hands than on the ceiling of this place."

"Here's your wheat toast. What would you other guys like?"

"Graybar's got a wobbly wheel this morning."

"That's funny. I haven't seen her for a couple days either."

"I have a rocker without a cushion. I could let that go for about forty dollars."

Who? The Fargo-Burnout? Naw he's harmless."

"I need a challenge, something different."

PART II

Six
The Challenge

Carrigan sat behind his desk, his feet propped up and his hands folded across his stomach. He had filled the past few days with as much excitement as he could. He had talked to his plumbing account and had a set of newspaper ads underway. The food store was extremely happy with the results of the most recent TV commercials he had produced.

The bank promotional campaign started a week ago, and the travel agency happened to be on a hiatus at the moment.

Carrigan's mind wandered. Why was it that all of his friends at the Powers had found their niche in life? Pavlov, the successful insurance man. Snuffy, happy as hell collecting junk. Reggie, secure with tenure at the college and doing what he dearly loved. Radio Sko, twenty-five years selling radio spots, a job he wouldn't give up for anything.

And the Princess? She was successful in her interior decorating business in spite of her husband.

Johann didn't have it as good. Carrigan could certainly identify with him. His commercial artwork was super, but he didn't enjoy it. He was a fine artist, and although his work hadn't been recognized yet, it would someday, Carrigan was sure.

But what about himself? Former teacher, former parts and warranty manager at Silverline Boats for a year, and then advertising owner for the past six. He liked teaching best of all, but he couldn't in good conscience go back to the incompetence of the college system, and the desk job at Silverline had been nothing more a daily battle with everyone else's boat problems. Whoever was in that job now was a glutton for punishment. He was successful in the advertising business, but somehow he found himself with a lot of free time. Perhaps this is what constituted *midlife crisis*.

The morning and afternoon sessions at the Powers had become his only entertainment during the day, but only an hour out of each day. What would that lead to? He had too much free time to *think of all the things one might* possibly accomplish in a lifetime. If he wasn't careful, he might think away his entire life.

He glanced at a list on his desk. Three new prospects, but he didn't have the drive to pick up the phone and make a contact. Suppose he did manage to pick up a few new clients? Then what? He'd be too busy. No more free time to have coffee with the group.

"Carrigan Mulhouse," he told himself out loud. "You've got to get your life together. You need a challenge."

"Do you always talk to yourself?"

When Carrigan turned his head, the Princess was standing in the doorway that led to the inner corridor of the Mark Building. Her decorating office was just fifty feet away down the hall

Oh, sweet, sweetness! Carrigan suddenly felt rejuvenated, refreshed. The Princess dropped into a chair in front of him and crossed one of her slim, beautiful legs over the other. She was wearing black patent leather shoes with dainty straps running across her ankles. Her tight-fitting white blouse today was so very striking against the speckled gray tweed skirt, and the sunrays pouring through the window from behind made the fringes of her strawberry hair glisten like a blooming flower.

"Hi," she greeted.

61

"Where have you been hiding the past few days?" Carrigan inquired as he gently let his feet slip to the floor. "I checked your office every time I went to the can."

"You only miss me when you're on your way to perform a bodily function?"

Carrigan felt embarrassed. "No. I missed you at coffee, too."

"That's nice. I like being missed. I was in Williston working on Mr. Belmont's house. I told you I picked up a decorating job there."

"I thought you had ordered everything."

"He made some last minute changes. I mentioned Johann's paintings for his walls again, and he's still interested."

"Is it a big job?"

"For me or for Johann?"

"Both."

"Pretty good for me, but it could be a super undertaking for Johann. Belmont's a big spender. He could keep Johann busy for a year if he likes his work."

"I'm happy for you, and for Johann, too. He needs a break. Sometimes I worry about him."

"Oh, I wouldn't worry about Johann. He can take care of himself." She raised a leg a bit and delicately picked a piece of lint off her skirt with her long, pointed fingernails

"What's that in your hand?" Carrigan asked. He had just noticed the small packet, and when she handed it over, the radiance in her face slowly faded.

Carrigan opened the package and drew out two photographs, both of the Princess. He felt his heart jump as he leaned over his desk, unable to take his eyes from the nude photos. He rose up surprised and a bit embarrassed, and then his eyes were back on the photos. She looked much younger, and her face was painted quite heavily with makeup. In one photo she was poised without a bra, only a G-string. In the other, a large plume covered part of her body, one foot raised up high behind her, yet it was clear that she was totally naked in this photo. He glanced up and quickly noted the tight fitting blouse she was wearing. There was no doubt in his mind that what was underneath the material was the genuine thing.

"This is you, isn't it?" Carrigan asked sheepishly.

"Yes."

He scanned the photos again, sneaked a quick glance at her breasts protruding from underneath her blouse, and sneaked a look at her beautiful, slim legs.

"I was twenty when those photos were taken. Eight years ago at the Gay Nineties bar in Minneapolis."

Carrigan could hardly believe what he was hearing. "You were a stripper?"

"Yes. But that's all," she quickly added. "It was a foolish thing now, I know, but at the time, it was just a… a fantasy, I guess."

Carrigan placed the photos on his desk and sat back, his eyes falling on her troubled face. He was about to ask how she came by the photos when she volunteered the answer.

"They came in the mail a few days ago."

Carrigan checked the postmark on the envelope. It had been posted here in Fargo. "And you have no idea who sent them?"

"Carrigan, I didn't even know these photos existed. Someone in the audience must have taken them. They don't look like professional photos, do they?"

Photography to a degree was Carrigan's business. He utilized them periodically when he designed brochures or newspaper ads, but taking photographs was not his expertise. He studied the black and white photos, both five by sevens, both grainy in appearance as if they had been enlarged. "They're nicely cropped," he finally said, "but I don't think they are necessarily professional photos. Amateur, I'd guess."

She still carried a somber look on her face.

"No letter attached?" he asked.

"No. Nothing."

"Perhaps someone sent them as a joke."

The Princess had her fingers clasped together so tightly that her knuckles were white. "This isn't much of a joke, Carrigan. Do you realize what would happen if those photos fell into the wrong hands?"

Carrigan's thoughts quickly jumped to her husband, Jerry.

She was reading his mind. "If Jerry saw these, he'd kill me."

"Oh, I don't think…"

"You know John Raphardt, the architect?" she interrupted.

"Yes."

"A few days ago, Jerry punched him out in Elm Tree Square right in front of everybody. Three months ago he punched Scott Harrison from the newspaper. And you remember the man with the finger? I told you about that."

"Pam," Carrigan began.

"Jerry is so jealous. He'll kill me first and ask questions later." She gave a frightful, nervous laugh. "It'll be hard for him to ask questions after I'm dead."

Carrigan rose to his feet and stepped stiffly around the desk, his hands stuck in his pockets. He didn't think Jerry would kill her, but the man had an uncontrollable temper. He just might beat the hell out of her.

He shuddered with the thought. There was no doubt that if Jerry ever caught the culprit who sent the photos, he would be dead for sure, and Pam…?

"You know how jealous Jerry is," she repeated.

Carrigan had met him on a few occasions. He had sat in with the coffee crowd once or twice, but that was well over a year ago. He had a fuse shorter than a one-inch wick on a stick of dynamite.

Carrigan cleared his throat. "Pam, I wouldn't get overly excited about this yet. Maybe there's some explanation, some mix-up, some..."

"There's no mix-up, Carrigan. That's me in the photos. I'm not proud of it, but I'm not denying it either."

"But they're not bad photos," Carrigan said trying to console her. "I mean, they're not pornographic. There's no other person involved here. Surely Jerry would understand..." Carrigan stopped mid-sentence. No, he told himself. Jerry would not understand. He would beat her to a pulp, just like the Princess said, and ask questions later.

"What about my work?" she asked. "If these photos ever got out, it would ruin my business. And what about my parents? They don't even know I worked as a stripper." She was just short of tears, and her lip was quivering.

"At least they're living in Florida now," said Carrigan. He happened to be looking out the window at Ivers Funeral Home across the street. Pallbearers were just loading a casket into the rear of a hearse, and cars were lined up behind it in an unending line around the block. Carrigan wasn't superstitious, but the scene did seem to indicate a bad omen.

Carrigan turned to face the Princess. He was staring at her blouse, but he was mentally visualizing a big plume in front of her. Mentally, he removed the plume and imagined those beautiful breasts, then shook his head, forcing the fantasy away.

"What shall I do?" she asked abruptly.

He knew the question was coming. When he sat, he tapped a finger nervously on the desktop, unable to tear his eyes from the photos. "Nothing we can do. Just wait There's no letter, no threat of..."

"Blackmail?" she finished.

That was the exact term floating around in his brain, but he didn't want to say it. The normal warmth and glow on her face was nothing more than a statue, a frozen mask. There was no doubt she was scared, frightened. Right now she was terribly in need of some reassuring words, anything that would console her.

Carrigan wracked his brain. "We'll simply consider this a joke for now. We have nothing more to go on. It could be a prankster, perhaps an old boyfriend."

It hurt him to see her torn face, and he now realized he wasn't playing his role as counselor very well. "Let's just wait and see," he said firmly. "If nothing else turns up, we forget about it."

"But if something does turn up?"

"We'll go from there." He knew that wasn't much help.

A phone rang from somewhere down the hall. When it rang a second time, the Princess jumped to her feet. "I think it's mine."

She dashed out the door, and as the sound of her footsteps faded away, Carrigan relaxed. He needed a moment to think. When she came back, he wanted to have something more concrete to tell her, something more reassuring.

Carrigan jumped when he heard something thump in the hallway. A roll of wallpaper bounced into his office. He got to his feet and stuck his head around the door to see Pam Allison beckoning him from her doorway. He hurried down the corridor and saw the panic in her face as she ducked back into her office.

She was just lowering the receiver when he walked in. "Who was it?" he asked.

"A man. Whispering. He asked if I received the photos."

Carrigan's mind whirled. "Is that all?"

"No." she hesitated. "He said that he saw me at the Powers last week."

"Did he demand anything?"

"No, nothing. That's all he said."

"It was definitely a man?"

"I think so." She thought a moment. "The voice was whispered. I think it was a man." She looked up, her face pleading. "Carrigan, what should I do?"

He saw the tears come on, and when he crossed to her, she

threw her arms around him and pressed her face against his, now sobbing. He had always had a desire to hug her, but not under these circumstances.

Oh, God, he thought. Ten minutes ago he was looking for a challenge, and now he suddenly had one.

But he wasn't ready for this.

Seven
Hidden Messages

It was not at all unusual for Carrigan Mulhouse to spend an evening in the attic on the third floor of his home. He often spent hours working on budgets for his clients, writing scripts or simply meditating.

The area was cramped, every wall peaked to conform to the roofline. He had make-shifted a tabletop by setting a door on top of two file cabinets. A small desk filled a corner with a lamp and typewriter on top, and two metal bookshelves were stuffed with paperback novels, mostly adventure and espionage. Though this space could hardly be labeled as a den, at least it was comfortable.

The only other set of instruments in the attic were exactly that—instruments. His eldest son's drum set occupied another corner. For the past thirty minutes, Carrigan had listened to his incessant banging—music, his son labeled it. But he was gone now.

Throughout the practice session, Carrigan had somehow managed to remain deep in thought, an unfathomable feat if he had been concentrating on one of his clients. Tonight, his thoughts were decidedly pointed in a far different direction, a totally bizarre direction.

He opened a folder and pulled two sheets from it. On the first sheet he had carefully noted the exact words of the conversation that the Princess had heard that afternoon with the stranger on the phone, at least what she could recall. He had conveniently numbered each line and now read over the conversation.

1· Allo, Princess?

P· Yes·

2· *Welcome back·*

P· *Who is this?*

3· *I see you got my photos·*

P· *(Princess doesn't remember what she said here, or if she said anything)*

4· *I seen you at the Powers·*

That was the extent of the telephone conversation as near as the Princess could recollect it. From this text, Carrigan had already gleaned a great deal of information.

From line one: *Allo* instead of *Hello*. If she heard him correctly, that could possibly indicate a foreigner. The caller had used the name *Princess*. Only members of the coffee house group called her that, so whoever the caller was obviously must have overheard her nickname at one time or another.

Line 2: *Welcome back.* The Princes had been on a trip to Williston. Did the caller know that she had been away? Or did he know where she had been?

Line 3: Particularly interesting. The caller knew she had already received the photos, and secondly, the caller used the word *got* instead of *received*, a lower form of stylistic usage. Of course, even educated people utilized the word *got*, so perhaps it wasn't all that important, but as a former linguist, it was something Carrigan could not overlook.

Line 4: *I seen you at the Powers.* Two interesting clues here. First, the caller either frequented the Powers Coffee House or had, at least within the past week. Of course, he obviously knew her. Second, if the greeting in the first line was not *Allo*, rather *Hello*, then it was quite possible the Princess may have well misunderstood the fourth line. The caller may well have not said *I seen you,* but rather, *I've seen you at the Powers*, which, of course, would be proper grammar.

To Carrigan that was significant. If the phrases were *Allo* and *I seen*, then the caller might well be a foreigner or someone unschooled in grammar, someone with a lower level of education.

And then again, not necessarily, since Carrigan knew many prominent businessmen in the community who used extremely poor grammar, and some of them were college educated.

"How's the advertising executive?"

It was Verna. She had sneaked up the stairs with a cup of coffee without him even aware of it.

"Okay," Carrigan answered as he casually slipped the folder shut.

"What have you been doing?"

"Thinking," said Carrigan. "A great deal of thinking always precludes the masterpiece."

She laughed, and as silently as she appeared, she turned and descended the staircase.

Carrigan sipped at the coffee, and as soon as her footsteps were no longer audible, he pulled the two photos out of the folder, laid them side-by-side and produced a magnifying glass from a desk drawer

He ran the glass over the photos looking for anything peculiar. Her nude body was perched against a dark backdrop, a black curtain, he guessed. In both photos the floor was visible, oak boards toe nailed closely together, a common flooring for a stage.

As he moved the glass across her face, the view magnified her long fake eyelashes. The splotch on her cheeks was more than likely rouge, and her lips were dark colored. She had tiny specs on her earlobes, pierced earrings, he surmised.

He moved the glass downward across the nipples of her breasts and felt a little tingle rip throughout his body. He lowered the glass some more to her pubic area and was strangely amused. The Princess wasn't a strawberry blond after all.

He set the magnifying glass on the desk and leaned back in his chair. Who would blackmail the Princess?

Someone who knew her nickname was *Princess.*

Someone who had obviously seen her perform in the Gay Nineties Bar in Minneapolis.

Someone who had seen her at the Powers last week, and more than likely at the coffee table with the rest of the guys.

As for motive, there was none, yet. Money was a good possibility, jealousy another. Someone might have been secretly in love with her but knew he could never have her.

After some thought, that reasoning didn't seem too logical. *I need something a little more concrete than that,* he was thinking.

Maybe it was a joke after all, a prankster. Someone who had accidentally seen the Princess in the Powers and just happened to recognize her.

"And just happened to have a couple photos of her, too. Shit," he said, disgruntled with his logic. He once again turned to the page where he had written the text.

The man on the phone had whispered, the Princess said. To disguise his voice? Carrigan reread the text, whispering each line to himself. When he finished, he sat back in his chair rather envious. He discovered one more revelation; when one whispered, it was difficult to discern whether the voice was male or female. The culprit could well be a woman!

Carrigan sipped at his coffee, very pleased with his amateur investigative work. This was indeed becoming a challenge. He let his mind float from one aspect of the investigation to another and then dialed the phone.

"Hello?" the male voice responded on the other end.

Carrigan's mind twisted. He shouldn't have called! "Hi, Jerry," he said collecting himself. "This is Carrigan. Is your wife home?"

"Jes' a minute."

Jes' a minute, Carrigan repeated to himself. That was

71

sloppy speech. A revelation struck Carrigan. Had Jerry said *Hello* or *Allo*?

"Hello?" It was the Pam.

"Hi, Princess. It's just me. Can you meet me at the Powers at eight tomorrow morning?"

"Yes."

"Before the regular coffee group arrives. If Jerry asks why I called, tell him I have a potential client for you. Okay?"

"Fine, I'll be there."

When Carrigan hung up, his heartbeat had increased. He could have blown that one, knowing Jerry was so jealous. He'd have to be more careful from now on.

It seemed ironic to remotely consider Jerry as a suspect just because he answered the phone with sloppy speech, but Carrigan was glad he made the phone call. That put a new perspective on things. No matter who he talked to from now, he was sure he would be scrutinizing each individual as the potential blackmailer.

Or was he just jumping to conclusions? Maybe in a day or two, all this would blow over. "Yeah," Carrigan said sarcastically to himself after a few seconds. "Blow over just like a winter in Fargo without snow."

Carrigan was calm and casually looked around the coffee crowd, naturally suspicious of everybody he was looking at. Graybar was in his place at the center table near the pillar. He must have ordered already, since he had water and a place setting in front of him. He was early this morning, sitting perfectly still, upright, as if he were dead. But then Carrigan saw his eyes blink.

The Fargo-Burnout was at the counter, his usual place. He normally came in only once or twice a week, but this was two days in a row.

Mumbling Mike was in the far corner today. The group had nicknamed him the *Music Man* for a few months because whenever he passed by the group's table on the way to find a seat, they all thought he had a pocket radio in his jacket. It turned out that he was always talking to himself. So they dropped the nickname and attached the moniker, *Mumbling Mike*. He was nice enough. It was just that he walked around the coffee shop always having a conversation with himself, usually whispering. *Whispering?* Carrigan questioned. Good lord! Mumbling Mike did whisper all the time!

"Hi, Carrigan," the Princess greeted. When she flipped over a cup, Carrigan filled it up.

"Pam," he said in a low voice. "I want you to act natural, as if you never received a phone call yesterday. It's quite possible the person who called is here today. That's what I want to find out, so act natural."

"Should we both act natural?" she whispered back.

"Of course."

"Then why are we whispering?"

Carrigan carried a stupid look on his face for a moment and then came back to his normal voice. "I think we should keep all this quiet from the coffee crowd. Agree?"

"Of course. I don't want my photos splattered all over the place."

"Good. I've got a hunch that the person who called frequents this place, and he's probably looking at us right now."

The Princess glanced over the coffee crowd.

"Don't look around," said Carrigan. "Act natural."

"Wheat toast and peanut butter this morning?" Millie plopped a fresh pot on the table.

"Please, answered Carrigan."

Pam ordered a blueberry muffin.

"So what if this person is looking at us now?" she asked. "How are we going to know who it is?"

"We aren't, but if he calls you later on, it could be that he might have been here today. I want to find out."

"Then what?"

"I've got a plan."

"Maybe you could let me in on it since I'm the one that's being blackmailed."

"We don't know that for sure."

"Did you learn anything from the photos?"

"Only one conclusive fact."

"What's that?"

"You're not a strawberry blond."

"Carrigan!" she scolded. "Don't embarrass me. That's not funny."

Carrigan had a straight face. "No, I guess not. But it was revealing."

She playfully slapped him on the arm just as the front door slammed shut. Hardnuts Brodigan came in carrying his two-way radio, his big gun dangling low near his groin. He scanned the room, and when he saw Carrigan, his glare hung on him for a few seconds. He only glanced at Pam and then strutted off. Carrigan watched as Hardnuts moved through the crowd toward the counter. His uniform was shabby looking, and he was carrying the usual scowl on his face. He had been twenty years on the beat, but Carrigan heard he hadn't been able to save a dime.

Unable to save a dime? Carrigan's thoughts jumped to the blackmailer. Money obviously was a very good motive. Hardnuts stopped at a table and was speaking to a few men. "I seen a stray dog around here a couple days ago. A black German shepherd. Anybody here seen him?"

Seen! Twice he used the word grammatically wrong, just like the person on the phone!

The Princess noticed his crazed look. "What's the matter, Carrigan?"

Carrigan felt a sense of paranoia overcome him.

"Wheat toast and a blueberry muffin," said Millie. She plunked the two plates on the table, dropped off some peanut butter and jelly and shuffled off to another table.

Radio Sko and Pavlov Glitzberg tromped through the

door, jabbering and laughing as they made their way to the table. "Well, hello Princess," Sko greeted as he sat and gave her a snuggle. "How would you like to run off with me to Alaska today? It's going to be a hot one. We'll be able to cool off and it'll solve all your problems."

"What problems?" the Princess asked curiously.

"Hell, we all got problems don't we? This is your chance to toss it all."

Sko was blathering, but for a moment, the princess thought he was referring to the photos, and then she perked up. "You go on ahead, Sko. I'll come just as soon as I sell my car, get rid of the business and my husband."

"Now you're talking," Sko chuckled.

Pavlov started his silly antics early. He grabbed a piece of Carrigan's toast and stuck the entire piece in his mouth, then dunked a finger in Carrigan's coffee cup and licked it off. "Too hot," he said in between chews.

"I thought you liked it hot?" said Sko.

"Yeah," said Pavlov still chewing, "but ah don' wannit so hot that it set mah pyoo-bik hairs on fahr."

"Insure them," quipped Sko. "Write yourself a policy."

"Hay-al, even mah comp'ny don' got a policy with a high nuff premium. Matta fak, ain't no comp'ny in town what kn' insure pyoobik hairs what surround a million dollah peenus."

The Princess sank her head into her hands. "Oh, good Lord."

Carrigan chastised Pavlov, but not too convincingly. "Your manners and vocabulary are atrocious." It was hard to believe this was the same man who used business phrases like *beyond reputable quality* or *standards of commensurate responsibility*.

Luckily Johann showed up and the table turned to a more serious note.

"How's the painting coming along, Johann?"

"Uhhh."

"I have to spend the afternoon picking out wallpaper."

"No, I think I'll have eggs this morning."

"I heard you might be doing some paintings for a guy in Williston?"

"Uhhh, ya, ya."

"Pavlov's going to have his pubic hairs insured."

"Show me a Communist who has got freedom and I'll show you a Communist who lives in the United States."

"By golly, it's Reggie the Baron. Looks like Hardnuts is giving him a ticket."

"Of course, I'm going to insure my penis. What else could I do with it?"

"Paint it. Paint it purple and green. It'll sell. You betchum, Red Ryder."

"Hi, Reggie."

"No, I'm using commercial carpet."

"Have I tried to sell you some radio spots today?"

"He's giving me this ticket, see, and next thing I know he's asking me about a stray dog pissing on fire hydrants."

"It's too cold in Alaska."

"I'm called Junkman Jamison and I come from DL."

"No. Foreign language requires study daily."

"I picked up a wood statue today. Should be worth a fortune."

"Naw. Graybar already had his breakfast."

"Who's that guy always staring at our table?"

"That's the Fargo-Burnout. He's harmless."

To his own ecstatic surprise, Carrigan's hunch paid off. Later in the afternoon, the Princess received a phone call from the same stranger. *I seen you at the Powers* was all the caller had said. The Princess had immediately informed Carrigan. The voice was whispered like before, and the Princess emphatically maintained the caller had said, *I seen you.*

That definitely put some direction in Carrigan's line of investigation, and he now knew exactly what he wanted to do.

Eight
Leroy R

Leroy Ridgebutte lived near the college campus in Moorhead, and although his last name was pronounced *Ridge-byoot*, almost everyone referred to him as *Ridge-butt* when he was a student. Ridge-butt became Plateau-butt among his college peers, which became Flat-butt, which became Flat-ass, which remained with him. It was not easy living with a name like Leroy Flat-ass, so he assumed the pseudonym of *Leroy R.*

Leroy R had taken a few of Carrigan's Russian classes years back and was an excellent D student. He was not much of a linguist, but he worked hard at the language, so for his effort, Carrigan had always granted him a Gratis C. After three courses of the Russian language, he suddenly disappeared from the face of the earth only to turn up in Moorhead a few years later. He was presently living in a huge broken-down two-story home on South 9th Street. He considered himself a landlord, but really, all he did was run errands for the 97-year-old lady who owned the place. He kept her checkbook straight, picked up groceries and medicine, and haphazardly acted as landlord for the one other tenant occupying the upper floor.

Leroy R was heavy into Marxism, but he was honest. And he had a particular talent that Carrigan was interested in, and that's why Carrigan went to see him

He parked in front of the familiar weather-beaten structure and ambled up the sidewalk. After pressing the doorbell three times, he realized it wasn't working. There was no doorknocker, so Carrigan thumped against the oak barrier with his fist.

When Leroy R answered the door, Carrigan stared at him a moment. He never remembered Leroy wearing anything more than the shabbiest of clothing, but now he was growing the most god-awful replica of a beard Carrigan had ever seen. He couldn't have had more than a couple dozen long and gnarly hairs sticking down from his chin, and he was working on a dozen more on his upper lip. If he thought they would help cover up his pimples, he was wrong, and if he would have squinted when he answered the door, Carrigan could have easily mistaken him for a member of the Tongs.

Leroy R adjusted his glasses and whipped out a wide smile. "Well, Gospodin M. To what do I owe this pleasurable and unexpected visit?" Leroy R always addressed Carrigan Mulhouse as Gospodin M, which meant *Mister M* in English. It was secretive, and besides, M also stood for *Marxism*. Carrigan was momentarily having second thoughts about stopping in and considered saying he just happened by and decided to pay a visit, but that didn't make any sense.

He reconciled himself to the moment. "I'd like to talk to you about a project, Leroy. If you have a minute, that is."

Leroy R's curiosity was at a peak. No one had ever paid him a visit to talk about a project, and he highly respected Carrigan Mulhouse.

"Pozhaulista, maya komnata vasha komnata." Leroy R said in Russian. *Please, my room is your room.* What he meant to say in English was the Spanish equivalent of *Mi casa es su casa,* or in Russian, *Moj dom vash dom.* Carrigan overlooked the error like he used to when he taught Russian.

Leroy R made a sweeping motion with his hand. "Step into my reception room if you will, and allow me to reiterate my distinct pleasure with your unexpected presence. Might I be so bold as to ask you to partake of a brandy?"

Leroy R's language was eloquently out of place. If he had been dressed in a black suit with tails, white-frocked shirt and tie and was thirty years older and bald, he might have passed for a butler, but he would have to get rid of that god-awful growth on his face. That was what Carrigan was thinking as he stepped in. "I don't mind if I do," he said referring to the brandy.

The reception room was nothing more than a sun porch off to one side of the house. The entrance to it was built with French doors, but one was missing. Light poured through one-third of the bay windows; the other two-thirds were blotted out by massive bookshelves filled with a throng of paperbacks. The wood was simple unstained pine. In the middle of the room stood a huge oak desk, and although cluttered with anything and everything, what stood out were the three leather volumes of Karl Marx's *Das Kapital.* A gooseneck lamp sat nearby, its neck turned to focus on the three important books.

Leroy R produced a decanter out of a desk drawer, then grabbed two crystal glasses from a windowsill and blew the dust out of the bottom of them. He filled them and handed one over. "Na zdorove, Gospodin M." *To your health, Mr. M.*

Carrigan sipped at the vintage brandy. It was definitely smooth.

"Sadites pozhauilsta," *Please sit down,* Leroy R said to his former teacher as he motioned to a chair.

Carrigan was to a slight degree impressed with Leroy's Russian. Those were simple words, and an early phrase he learned in class, but at least he was utilizing his talent, as restricted as it might be.

Leroy R hadn't changed much in terms of his attire. He still dressed the same—grubby shirt, worn leather vest, Levis, combat boots. He was also wearing the same peasant cap he had worn to his classes, but the bill was greasy from fingering it all these years. Carrigan couldn't remember if he had ever seen him *not* wearing it. From underneath it, a mop of hair stuck out in every direction.

Carrigan's eyes focused on the gooseneck lamp above the three volumes of Marx's works. "I'm surprised you don't have the light on," he commented.

"Bulb burned out," said Leroy R

"Why don't you replace it?"

"It's an excellent reminder of Marxist philosophy."

Carrigan raised an eyebrow.

Leroy R explained. "It represents an example of the proletariats who manufactured the bulb in the factories. I refuse to purchase a new bulb because the profit earned properly belongs to the working class and not to the owners of the factory. It's a constant reminder of the struggle between the workers and the bourgeoisie."

It seemed like an unusual reminder to Carrigan, but then, Leroy R himself was an unusual individual.

"Well, Leroy," said Carrigan. "What have you been up to these days?"

"I rarely go by the name of Leroy, Gospodin M. I have long shed myself of the embarrassment my parents inadvertently placed upon me when I so unexpectedly entered this world."

Carrigan again raised an eyebrow.

"I now use the nom de plume of Ivan Gladkijzad."

Carrigan smiled. Ivan was the name he had been assigned when he was a student in Russian class. For his last choice of family name, Leroy obviously had done a remarkable bit of research. *Gladkij* meant flat or smooth in Russian. *Zad* meant the ass end, but of an animal rather than the buttock of a person. *John Smoothass* was his English counterpart.

"I see my new name amuses you, Gospodin M. Rest assured, it is not at all amusing to my close friends. Of course, if they were learned in various cultures, as I am, they would find the name quite titillating. They call me Leroy R simply because they can't remember the Russian equivalent. Unfortunately, I cannot control the destinies of those who choose to remain illiterate."

Leroy R tipped his brandy glass and savored the flavor with red-purplish lips. "Ahhh," he sighed once he had swallowed the smooth brandy. "Otlichno!" *Excellent!*

The Guys from Fargo

Carrigan was totally amused. "I don't think Marx would appreciate the fact that you're enjoying your brandy so much." "Undoubtedly," Leroy R remarked. "However, I did not purchase this quality brandy. That's the difference. I didn't have to pay any profit, thereby stealing from the working class who produced it. As you can see, I have been heavily researching the three aspects of Marxism—antitheses, thesis, and eventually the synthesis of the two. Perhaps you'd care to share in an exchange of ideas?"

"No, Leroy. I'm here to ask if you are still dabbling in photography."

"Dabbling," repeated Leroy R, as he pondered the term. "I'm not sure that is antithesis or synthesis. Dabbling demands clarification before I am able to respond accurately."

"Leroy, I haven't got time to clarify definitions of terminology. Marx spent a lifetime doing that, and I only have about ten more minutes before I'm due to meet a client. Are you still dabbling in photography or not?"

"Yes," he answered simply.

"Do you still have that miniature camera you used to bring to Russian class? The one you sneaked pictures with?"

He pulled open a drawer and flopped the cigarette lighter sized camera on the desk. "I do."

"Do you want to make some money?"

"How much?"

"Fifty dollars."

"What do I have to do?"

"Spend about one hour a morning doing some special work for me for the next four mornings. I'll pay for the film and developing expenses above the fifty dollars, and I'll throw in a breakfast each morning."

Leroy R sank back into the leather-backed chair pondering the request. "Gospodin M," he said finally. "An assignment of this nature would require a temporary cease and desist in my research. On such short notice, I. . ."

81

Carrigan stood up. "Do you want the job or don't you?"

"I'll take it."

Carrigan sat back down and drew a piece of paper from inside his coat. He unfolded the pencil sketch of the Powers Coffee House interior, spread it out on the desk and pointed to a corner booth. "At exactly nine a.m. for the next four mornings I want you seated in this booth and none other. I want you taking pictures and I want you seated alone. Do you think you can handle that?"

"I presume the people in the Powers are of the working class?"

"Yes. Some even lower."

"I can handle that."

Carrigan produced a second piece of paper with complete instructions and a photograph of Pam Allison. "Follow these instructions and memorize this girl's face. When you get to the Powers, I want you as inconspicuous as you can be. You are never to talk to me, although I will be there every morning. You never even acknowledge my presence in any shape or form. Is that clear?"

"Right."

Carrigan thumped the sheet with the details on it. "Memorize everything. I don't want you with any paper, I don't want to see the camera, and I don't even want anyone to know you're there."

"Right. Anything else?"

Carrigan cringed when he looked over Leroy R's atrocious attire. "Shave your face, get rid of that hat, comb your hair and put on some decent clothes."

Leroy R's face sagged, and his eyes saddened like a puppy that just peed on a rug. "All for fifty dollars?" The question seemed to squeak out of him.

"And free breakfast," Carrigan reminded him. "If you do a good job, I'll give you a bonus."

Leroy R slowly stood up. "Well, ah, I…"

"Do you want the job?"

"Yes, but you see, at the moment, I seem to be a little strapped. I wonder if..."

Carrigan pulled out his wallet and handed over twenty dollars, "That'll cover the film and breakfast. You'll get the rest at the end of the week."

Leroy R's eyes bulged. "Very good." Carrigan made his way to the door and was already down the steps when Leroy R cried out, "Do svidaniya, Gospodin M."

Goodbye in Russian. He had remembered a third phrase.

The next morning Leroy R, alias Ivan Gladkijzad, felt naked. He had spent six months growing the brush on his face, and in a single sentence from Mr. M, he had been forced to shave it off. He was now wearing a pair of street shoes, something he hadn't donned in years, and he missed his Russian peasant cap, a reminder that he was a Marxist, although he had no idea if Karl Marx ever wore one.

He had combed his hair and washed it, but it was so unruly that he decided to get a haircut from a real barber. That had cost him five dollars, but he was confident that he might be able to recoup the amount as part of his expense account.

He was now wearing a white shirt with a pullover wool vest and cords. Clean ones. *My God*, he thought to himself. He was sacrificing his lifestyle for a mere fifty dollars. It was like becoming a whore, but he never forgot the C's Gospodin M had given him, so he considered this payback time.

It was strange. Though he was making a major sacrifice in his appearance for a mere fifty dollars, he still didn't know precisely what his mission was. He had the specifics down, but to what end he was secretly photographing the Powers Coffee House crowd, he had not the faintest idea.

At ten to nine, he was sitting in the exact booth Carrigan had recommended, and his waitress had just plopped the food down in front of him. Two scrambled eggs, toast, bacon, a muffin with raspberry jam, a bowl of oatmeal and a large orange juice. This was a feast compared to the cookie and Pepsi he habitually had for breakfast, and without a doubt, it was the first balanced meal he had eaten in a long time. To a rather enjoyable degree, he was secretly gaining a renewed perspective on how normal people lived and ate. Four mornings of huge breakfasts, an hour's work each day and still fifty dollars at the end of the week. Maybe this change in his appearance was worth it, especially when he considered that all he made was fifty dollars a month for keeping his landlady's checkbook straight. He dug into his breakfast and savored every bite. *I never thought I'd ever get a taste of how the rich lived!*

Everything was working like clockwork so far. He had a couple books propped up just like when he was in Russian class. The mini camera was cleverly concealed between the hardback covers, the device secured in place with Velcro. A fine thread extended backwards between the two books. All he had to do was shift the books in the desired direction and trigger the thread. He had collected hundreds of clandestine photos utilizing this method before.

He ate away at his food and noted that at precisely 8:55 Gospodin M made his appearance. Out of the corner of his eye, Leroy R watched as his benefactor found his way to a table.

By the time he finished his breakfast, the good-looking strawberry blond, the girl he had memorized from the photo, had arrived. She, too, seated herself at the same round table with. Mr. M. Leroy R noted the time on his watch and began his first photographic endeavor. After each tug on the string, he shifted the books slightly, covering all of the faces in the coffee house crowd. He took four shots and was to wait ten minutes before he shot another series and was to continue the routine until the strawberry blond left the Powers.

Still not knowing exactly why he was doing what he was

doing, he was feeling quite comfortable. By now, five people were sitting at Mr. M's table. One was a big guy, older than the rest, dressed in a nice suit and tie. The other big guy was black haired, but younger, and he seemed to be doing silly antics, talking loud, breaking up the guys at the table at every instant.

The third fellow was a strange little man, bearded, who rarely spoke, and his eyes seemed to be half closed most of the time. By his attire, Leroy R thought he might easily identify with him. Just as a sixth person joined Carrigan's table, he clicked off another set of photographs. This fellow was large, too, a robust fellow, and on close inspection, Leroy R was sure he knew him. He scrutinized the black bushy hair, the bushy eyebrows, and whenever he spoke, he seemed to drive his point home by banging a fist on the table.

Then it came to him like a bolt out of the blue. Mr. Richthoffen from the college! He had failed him in a geography course, primarily because he had cut almost all the classes. The man was too demanding, not near as forgiving as Carrigan had been as a teacher. Leroy R figured out early there was no way to earn a D from Mr. Richthoffen, so he just quit attending.

When the entire group at the table broke into hysterics, Leroy R wondered what could possibly be so funny. Not long afterward, the strawberry blond got up from the table, mentioned something to the group and left the Powers. Leroy R's work for the day was over. He summoned Millie, paid his bill and went home.

The second day began pretty much like the first. Leroy R arrived at 8:30 and had already purchased his breakfast and eaten it by the time the strawberry blond arrived. Today, she remained with the group at Carrigan's table for a little over twenty minutes and then left. Leroy R had taken three sets of photographs, paid his bill and walked out. Another easy day.

The third day began with a slight conflict when he entered

the Powers. A younger couple was already seated in the booth from which he needed to take the photos. He waited patiently at a table across from them, and when nine o'clock neared and the couple was still in the booth, Leroy R approached them and offered to pay for their breakfast if they would take their food and switch places with him. They considered the request rather unusual, but they agreed. Breakfast that morning cost him over ten dollars, but he managed to photograph the coffee crowd over a thirty-minute time span from the moment the strawberry blond girl had entered until she left.

The fourth and final day started off with total havoc for Leroy R. He caught the bus near his home across the river, but en route the bus developed motor trouble and stalled a mile short of the Powers. Already behind time, Leroy R panicked. He hailed a taxi and arrived at the Powers just short of nine o'clock. The fare was a flat two dollars, and when Leroy R checked his pocket, he had only a dollar and nine cents. Paying for the couple's breakfast the day before had cut him short for the week. He offered the amount, but the cabby snapped back, "Who the hell do you think you are, a senior citizen? And what about a tip?"

Leroy R panicked for the second time that morning. The cab was facing north, so Leroy ran south across the street, down the block and into the alley. He peered around the building, and when he saw the cabby coming his way, he ran down the alley past the barbershop and ducked into the back entrance of Prat's Coats, a luxury store for women. When Leroy appeared from the back room, a lady clerk, suddenly startled, inquired if she could help him.

Leroy R answered quite calmly. "Has my wife been in this morning yet?"

The lady clerk asked him to describe her.

"Five foot one, 270 pounds."

The clerk's mouth dropped. "No."

"Are you sure?"

She stared back.

Leroy R excused himself and left through the door onto the street. Checking both ways, he couldn't see the taxi. He ran across to the Powers and was ten minutes late when he entered.

He panicked for the third time. A blond bombshell was sitting in the booth, her face painted with enough rouge and makeup to put the tail feathers of the NBC peacock to shame.

Leroy stood looking at her, his mouth gaping.

"Hi, sweetheart," she said. "My name's Harriet. Would you like to sit down?"

Leroy nervously glanced at the table where Carrigan was sitting with two of his friends. Luckily, the strawberry blond had not arrived yet.

"I'm in luck!" he blurted out.

"You certainly are," said the queen of the streets, thinking he was addressing her.

He stared at her. "How would you like to make a dollar and nine cents?"

She wrinkled her face like a walrus, insulted with the offer. "Well," she spat out. "I know my rates are economical, but I don't give anything out for that price."

Leroy R was panicking again. "I think you may have misunderstood me."

"Oh," she said as her wrinkles smoothed out. "In that case, why don't you sit down and let's talk it over."

Leroy R had no choice. Outside on the sidewalk, he saw the strawberry blond coming.

"Right," he said, as he slid in across from Harriet.

Millie scooted into place. "The usual?" she asked Leroy R after having served him the same breakfast three days in a row.

"Right," said Leroy R as Pam Allison strolled past him. He was fumbling with his books trying to line up the camera lens to take the first series of photographs.

"I'll have the same," Harriet said, even though she didn't have the faintest idea what Leroy R had ordered.

"Right," said Leroy R, his concentration on setting up his books.

"You don't really have only a dollar and nine cents on you, do you big boy?" Harriet asked.

Leroy clicked off the first photo and moved his books slightly, not in the least paying attention to her. "Right," he said as he clicked off his second picture.

Harriet flashed her fake eyebrows. "How about after breakfast the two of us mosey up to my apartment for a little dessert?"

"Right," said Leroy, as he snapped the third photograph.

Harriet was fully engrossed in him now. "We could start with the usual."

"Yeah, the usual," Leroy said excitedly as he triggered the last photo in this series.

"And work up to a blowjob."

Leroy R's eyes bugged out when he realized what she had just said.

"I see you brought a couple books with you," she snickered. "Planning on studying while we play house?"

Leroy R was finally paying attention, but he wasn't following her.

"Are you a college boy?" Harriet asked.

"How'd you guess?"

"I'm very perceptive," she said, and then she blathered on for the next ten minutes, pouring out her life story and the woes of having been a neglected child for years. Leroy R pretended to be listening, but he was ever alert, snapping the photos regularly.

Finally their breakfasts came. Scrambled eggs, toast, bacon, a blueberry muffin, oatmeal and a large orange juice for two. Millie scribbled out the ticket, dropped it on the table and raced off to the kitchen.

Leroy stared at the bill. "Oh, Jesus! I have only a dollar nine cents!"

The Guys from Fargo

A smug look broke on Harriet's face. "For a dollar nine cents I wouldn't even squeeze your cock, and try not to take the Lord's name in vain."

Nausea suddenly swept up the back of Leroy R's throat as he looked across at Harriet. She was gobbling down the food like this was the day before a nuclear holocaust. Leroy R checked his watch, and while the minutes flew by, Harriet kept stuffing in her breakfast. Leroy R nervously fumbled with his two books to start off another series of photographs. He had no sooner finished when the strawberry blond sitting at Mr. M's table got up and left. At least he was finished with his photo session for the week. Harriet, slurping down her juice, brought his attention back to her. "You better eat, big boy, cause when I get you up in my apartment, I'm going to screw all the strength right out of you."

Leroy R's face went numb, his legs rubbery. *What the hell am I getting into? I've got to get out of this!*

"This the guy?" Hardnuts Brodigan perched himself in front of Leroy R's table, his feet spread apart, his nightstick thumping into an open palm.

"Yeah, that's him." It was the fat cabby. Before Leroy R had a chance to respond, the cabby yanked Leroy R up from his seat and stuck his nose in his face. "Two bucks, buddy, and don't forget the tip."

"I'll handle this," said Hardnuts as he stepped between the two.

Leroy R's frantic level jumped a notch. "This is all a misunderstanding! I can explain! I only had a dollar and nine cents but I had to be here by nine o'clock for a meeting."

"Yeah," the cabby snarled as he eyed Harriet. "I can see you had a meeting." He had hauled Harriet home many times. "Anybody who meets with Harriet sure as hell has twenty bucks in his wallet."

"No!" Leroy protested as the cabby grabbed for his shirtfront again.

"I believe I can clear this up." Carrigan Mulhouse quietly shoved a ten-dollar bill into the cabby's hand. "Will that take care of the matter?"

The cabby snatched the ten and stuck it in his pocket, then turned to Hardnuts. "It's like the kid said, a misunderstanding." The cabby abruptly turned and walked out of the Powers.

Hardnuts continued to slap the nightstick across his palm, first eyeing Harriet, then eyeing Leroy R. He finally jammed the stick in Leroy R's chest. "I see your face in here again and you'll be spending your nights in the slammer. Understand?"

Leroy R managed to shake his head up and down. "Right."

And then Hardnuts turned to Harriet, tipped his hat and gave her a warm smile. "Ma'am," he said. He turned and walked out the door.

"Come on," Carrigan said to Leroy R as he flopped another ten dollar bill on the table. "Let's get out of here."

"Hey!" Harriet hollered as the two headed for the door. "What about me?"

Carrigan was fuming when they reached his car, but by the time he drove Leroy R back to his house, his normal color had come back into his face.

"Really, Mr. M, I'm sorry how this turned out."

"It wasn't your fault, Leroy. Did you get the photographs?"

"Yes, sir.

"You have a darkroom in your house?"

"Yes, sir."

"Can I get the photographs tonight?"

"Yes, sir."

"Good." Carrigan took a fifty-dollar bill out of his billfold. "If the pictures are good, I'll throw in another ten."

Leroy R's eyes widened. "Spasibo, Gospodin M."

Leroy R was half way up the walkway toward his house

when Carrigan shouted after him, "Leroy, you should dress like that more often. You don't look half bad."

Leroy R waved and disappeared inside the home.

Carrigan spent the remainder of the morning at the WDAY TV studio finalizing production on two more commercials for the Food Store. That afternoon, he dropped off the final newspaper layouts at the bank, called on his plumbing account and spent an hour at the dentist.

At 3:30 p.m. he had a meeting with one of the account executives at The Fargo Forum, the local newspaper known in wide circles as *The Fargo Fool-em.* When the Watergate scandal broke and Nixon resigned from the presidency, Carrigan thought sure the paper would at least offer its readers an apology for supporting Tricky Dicky all those years, but it never did.

In fact, even though a decade had passed since the Watergate incident, Carrigan would read an occasional editorial that sought to have Nixon run again. Carrigan was a staunch Democrat, so the meeting at the Forum didn't last long.

At four o'clock, Carrigan returned to his office, relieved to discover no messages had been left on his phone but disgruntled that no checks were in the mail.

He removed his sport coat, plopped into a chair and propped his feet up. For the longest time, he simply reflected. The Princess had not heard from the caller since Tuesday morning, the first day Leroy R had begun taking pictures. His plan was simple. If the caller phoned the Princess again, she was instructed to play along and find out if the caller had seen her in the Powers, and if so, on which days. And she was to immediately write down an accurate account of the conversation with the caller.

Carrigan would look over the photographs on the particular day the caller said he had seen her, *if he had seen her,* to determine if any of the coffee house patrons were depicted looking in the direction of the Princess.

It was a long shot, but it was the only logical direction Carrigan had at the moment. After all, the caller had not yet threatened with blackmail. That seemed the only motive, yet in four days' time, the Princess had not once heard from the would-be blackmailer.

He abruptly got up and walked down the corridor to the Princess' office. She was standing at a window opposite him gazing out onto the street, and when she turned around, he saw the distraught look on her f ace. They met in the middle of the room where she wrapped her arms about him and hung on for several seconds. There were no tears, but Carrigan suspected she had been contacted again.

She returned to her desk and produced another envelope from a drawer. More photos. Five this time. The Princess was in a variety of poses, some exposing her breasts, some with the same plume covering her nude body, and one with the plume raised high in the air. This particular photo was a frontal shot with both arms and legs spread apart. If there had been any doubt before, there was none now; the Princess was definitely not a strawberry blonde.

Carrigan replaced the photos in the envelope. "No message?"

"No," she replied. Her body was limp, her face as unhappy as he had ever seen it. "But he called again."

Carrigan stirred.

She produced a piece of paper on which she had scribbled out as much of the conversation as she could recall. He read over her notes.

Caller: You got my photos?
Yes.
Caller: I seen you again.

Where?

Caller: At the Powers.

When?

Caller: Couple days ago. Tuesday. I remember the pink blouse. Very sexy.

I wore my pink blouse on Wednesday.

Caller: No. White.

What do you want from me?

Caller: I am watching you.

That was the end of the text. "This is incredible!" Carrigan exclaimed.

"There nothing incredible about this. I'm scared, Carrigan."

Carrigan could hardly contain his excitement. "You did marvelous. Don't you see? We know he was there on Tuesday and Wednesday."

So?"

"Why do you suppose I wanted you at the Powers every morning at nine o'clock?"

She stared back, not at all understanding

"Because each day, I hired a photographer to take pictures of the entire coffee house crowd. The blackmailer has got to be on some of those photos! Don't you see?" Carrigan headed for the door.

"Carrigan, wait! What do you mean, you hired a photographer?"

Carrigan's face flashed from excitement. "Princess, I'm going to spend the weekend doing some analysis. If you hear from the caller again, get hold of me. If I don't see you this weekend, I'll see you at coffee first thing Monday morning."

"Carrigan!" she called after him. "Why didn't you tell me?"

Carrigan couldn't contain his excitement. He grabbed his coat, locked up and ran for his car. With a little bit of luck, maybe Leroy R already finished developing the photos.

Carrigan was sitting at the dinner table with his family picking over his food with a fork.

"Hey, dad," his fourteen-year-old son, Kelly, inquired. "Can I play football next year?"

"Sure, I think it's a good idea."

"See, mom," Kelly said. "Dad said I can."

Carrigan gave him an evil eye. "You asked your mother first and she said no?"

"Yes," he responded.

"It's too dangerous," Verna said to Carrigan. "He might hurt himself. It's such a rough sport."

Carrigan chewed on a piece of beef. "Can't be any more dangerous than wood carving. Remember last summer when I sliced my hand and bled like a stuck hog."

Verna smirked. "We're eating."

Carrigan went on. "Wasn't it last year about this time he broke his arm when he fell off his bicycle? Does that mean he shouldn't ride one anymore?"

"Does that mean I can play?" Kelly asked.

"No. That means your mother and I have to discuss it some more "

"But I wanna play. Everybody in my grade is trying out."

"Our family isn't run like everybody else's family in your grade," said Carrigan.

"Aw, cripes."

"Did you make any money today, dad?" his ten-year-old, Kurt, inquired.

"Yes," said Carrigan.

"How much?"

"Thousands."

"How many thousands?"

"Two, three," said Carrigan.

"Dad, some families in Africa don't even make a thousand dollars a year."

"That's right," said Carrigan. "How did you know that?"

"I read it in the National Geographic."

Carrigan smiled, pleased the National Geographic was being read by someone in the family.

"We must be rich," said Kurt. "I'm going to tell all my friends you make thousands of dollars each day."

"Do that."

Verna locked her eyes on Carrigan. If they had been lasers, she would have melted his face. The two boys were up from the table and ran for the TV room.

"Is everything all right at work, Carrigan?" Verna asked.

Carrigan felt uneasy. "Of course. Why do you ask?"

She shrugged. "You've kind of been on edge lately."

"No I haven't," Carrigan denied.

"Then why have you buttered three pieces of bread and not eaten any of them?"

Carrigan looked at his plate. He had buttered three pieces.

"Paul and Elaine asked us over tonight."

"For what?"

"It's Friday."

"They invite us over because it's Friday?"

"No," she said as she began clearing the table. "I think a night of relaxation would be good for you."

"What do you mean, relaxation?" Carrigan protested. "I feel great."

"You're on edge."

"I'm not on edge."

"The last three nights you've been rolling and turning in bed. And what's this *plume* you're muttering about in your sleep?"

Carrigan's jaw dropped. While Verna innocently gathered up some dishes and walked into the kitchen, his mind was working. "What plume?" he finally asked.

Verna came back into the dining room after more dishes. "I don't know. You kept saying in your sleep, "Throw away the plume, throw away the plume.""

Carrigan played dumb. "What do you suppose that means? There must be some explanation for it."

"How would I know? It's your dream." She gathered up another handful of dishes and went back to the kitchen.

Carrigan's mind kept working. He did not want to mention the problem with the Princess to the coffee house crowd, simply to protect her reputation, but he had no idea that he had been talking in his sleep, and he certainly didn't want to involve Verna. "I think I know what that plume is," he explained feebly. "I'm making some commercials for the Food Store. A couple days ago, I filmed one in the meat department. I distinctly remember telling Dean, wouldn't it be funny if they sold chickens with feathers on." Carrigan gave a sick laugh. "Feathers, plumes. Get it? I must have been talking to Dean in my sleep. Sure, that's it. I was talking to Dean."

She stuck her head around the door of the kitchen.

"Dean's bald, isn't he?"

"Why do you ask?"

"Because in your dream, you kept telling him he wasn't a strawberry blond after all." Her eyes zeroed in on Carrigan again. "I think you need to consult Freud on that one."

"Maybe so," Carrigan agreed.

"I think you need a night out on the town."

"But I planned on doing some research for a client," Carrigan protested. He could hardly wait to get to the photos Leroy R had developed.

"We're going out on the town."

Carrigan was running out of excuses. "I have a headache,"

"That's my line," Verna shot back. "We're going out with Paul and Elaine."

"Okay. My research can wait until tomorrow."

"Not tomorrow. We're going to Grand Forks."

That was eighty miles away. "What for?"

Verna looked around the doorway again. "Carrigan, where has your head been this week? I told you Tuesday we were invited to the Davies. They're your relatives. I distinctly remember asking you if you had anything planned for the weekend and you said no. And I distinctly remember you saying, yes, we could go."

"Oh, yeah, right." Carrigan vaguely remember something about Grand Forks. "Then I'll research Sunday."

"Can't," said Verna.

Carrigan slumped in his chair, his hands dangling loosely while Verna went through another commitment he had agreed to. A day at the lake. The kids were heavily planning on it.

"Then I'll research Monday!" Carrigan said defiantly.

"That'll be fine," said Verna, as she ran a dishrag across the table. "In your office where you should be doing your work anyway."

Carrigan's mind whirled with frustration, thinking about the photographs Leroy R had developed. The quality was excellent, and he was sure the suspect was on one of those shots.

"...a nice challenge for you," Verna was saying.

"What?" Carrigan questioned. Verna was sitting on his lap, her hands draped around his neck. "I said a full weekend would be a nice challenge for you. A change of pace. A couple days of relaxation."

"Right, right," said Carrigan. "A good challenge. Change of pace. Right."

When Verna left the room, Carrigan dipped his head. He was starting to sound like Leroy.

Nine
The Suspects

Carrigan sat at his layout table in the adjoining room to his office where he did all his design work, where he typed TV and radio scripts, where he wrote copy for brochures.

Unable to sleep and anxious to examine the photographs, he left home at seven o'clock that morning, unusually early for him, but Verna hadn't suspected anything.

For over an hour, Carrigan sat staring at the photos lined up on the table, sorting them, studying them. These photos had been taken on Tuesday and Wednesday, the two days the suspect claimed he had seen the Princess in the Powers.

On Tuesday, Leroy had taken four sets of pictures, ten minutes apart. Carrigan had the four sets lined up at the top of his table from left to right in four neat rows. On Wednesday, Leroy had snapped three sets of photographs, because the Princess had remained in the coffee house for only thirty minutes that day.

The Wednesday photos were lined up under the Tuesday photos. So then, Carrigan was now thinking to himself. Seven sets of photos. On these two days the potential blackmailer had definitely been in the Powers and had seen the Princess, or so he claimed. He might well have been in the cafe on Thursday and Friday, too. If he had, Thursday's sequence of photos was also excellent, very sharp, very clear. However, Friday's photos were anything but what Carrigan had expected. Half of them were out of focus. Two were clear shots but only depicted the corner of the booth. Another was an extremely clear shot of Harriet the whore stuffing her face with eggs.

Other shots displayed extreme close ups of Hardnuts Brodigan's gun and holster and belt buckle. Clearly engraved on the buckle was the word, *Mother.* Another photo depicted a hairy knuckle with a ring on a finger, slightly out of focus, probably the cabby. On three other photos, nothing was discernible.

Of course, that had been a particularly tough day for Leroy. Carrigan once again focused his attention on the Tuesday and Wednesday photos.

Suspect number one: Graybar. On all seven sets, seven different photos depicted old man Graybar at his table, all seven times his gaze focused in the direction of the Powers Coffee House group, where the Princess had been sitting.

Suspect number two: Wandering Eddie showed up on five out of seven sets of photos. Four of the times he was definitely looking in the direction of the Princess. That was particularly interesting to Carrigan, and what was not interesting was the fact that on all four photos, he had his fly open.

Suspect number three: Old man Ruckles from the Chemical Company. He had also been photographed five times, all five within a table length of the guys. In fact Carrigan's table was on every one of these photos, and all five times, Roman Ruckles without a doubt was looking directly at the table. On three of the photos he had his hand up to his chest as if turning up his hearing aide. That was suspicious.

Suspect number four: Hardnuts Brodigan. Interesting. Photographed three times, all near the rear door of the Powers. One showed him standing in the doorway looking in the direction of the group. On the other two, he was leaning on the counter. Carrigan did not remember seeing Hardnuts on Tuesday and Wednesday, only on Friday. In fact, Hardnuts had visited all four days.

Suspect number five: Mumbling Mike. Once sitting in a booth by himself, once sitting with Wandering Eddie, once sitting at the counter next to the Fargo-Burnout. All three times he without a doubt was looking in the direction of Carrigan's table.

Suspect number six: The little Iranian fucker, as Pavlov would call him. Once photographed with Harriet, twice with two other individuals that Carrigan did not recognize, both dark skinned, both probably Iranians.

Of course others had been caught looking at the table, but one time was not enough to bring them under suspicion. The bad part was all six of his suspects turned out to be weirdoes.

For one whole week Carrigan had tossed and turned in his sleep, and his wife, although not suspicious of anything specific, was certainly aware something was going on. Worse yet, he had shelled out over a hundred dollars of his own money on this *challenge*.

And for what? "For six fucking weirdo suspects!"

Several nude photos of the Princess, three whispered phone calls and not even a hint of blackmail—yet! What a strange way to go about blackmailing somebody.

The revelation suddenly boomed in Carrigan's brain like an elephant fart in a ballroom. All of the suspects are weirdoes! And the way the suspect is carrying out the blackmail, he has definitely got to be a weirdo himself!

Carrigan was sure he was on to something.

He heard a slight rap on the door, and when he turned, the Princess was standing in the corridor.

"Hi," she greeted as she walked in.

"Did you get any more phone calls?" Carrigan inquired.

"No."

"Any more photos?"

"No."

"A letter?"

"No.

"That's it!" Carrigan exclaimed.

"That's what?"

"It's one of these weirdoes!"

A puzzled look streamed across her face. "I don't have the faintest idea what you're talking about."

The Guys from Fargo

"Come on," said Carrigan. "We'll discuss it at coffee."

"So you see," Carrigan was saying in a whisper. "Those are the six suspects. And Graybar is on the top of the list, photographed all seven times. He's always looking at you." Carrigan glanced in the direction of Graybar. "As a matter of fact, he's looking over here now." The Princess stared unbelieving. "But he's a cripple." "I'm not so sure. I've been watching him. He's been flipped out of that chair, rode it all the way downstairs to the men's can and survived. I'm beginning to think maybe his seizures aren't even real. I think he's misleading us."

The Princess made another glance at old man Graybar, and then turned to Carrigan. "You've gone to a lot of trouble for me," she said as she patted the top of his hand. "I sincerely appreciate this, but maybe we should go to the police."

"What!?" exclaimed Carrigan. "With the police involved you know this will all come out in the open sooner or later. Is that what you want? Your photos splattered all over the Fargo Fool-em? You know the editor would do that. That's the price you pay for being a Democrat in this town. And besides, Jerry would beat the hell out of you."

"I suppose you're right, but isn't this costing you something? I don't want you spending your money on me. I'll be happy to reimburse you."

Carrigan knew she wasn't reaping grand profits from her decorating business. "It's only a few bucks. We'll worry about that later."

"I really appreciate this, Carrigan," she said softly as she patted his hand again.

Carrigan smiled and glanced at old man Graybar. He was looking at Carrigan and then abruptly turned his head away. "Yeah," said Carrigan confidently. "Graybar is our number one suspect."

"I got bed pans, ball bearings and Ben Franklin burners."

Snuffy pulled up a chair and slouched into it. "Why so serious over here?"

"Hi, Snuffy," the Princess greeted. "How's the junk business coming along?"

"Glad you asked," he said as he began rolling a cigarette. "I got canisters, cotton and cardigan sweaters, benches and back rests and a sack of potaters."

"Oh, that's cute," said the Princess.

"Thought you'd kind'a like it. Rhymes, too." Snuffy's eyes flashed at her as he licked his cigarette and popped it in his mouth. "How about you, Carrigan. Pick up any new accounts?"

"Nope. Don't want to work any harder than I have to."

"Move over and let a man in here." Radio Sko pulled up a chair and reached for the coffee pot. "Hi, Princess. Still want to go to Alaska with me?"

"Sure, when are we leaving?"

"Just as soon as I make a sale." He turned to Carrigan. "How about sixty-second radio spots? I'll give em' to you for the same price as thirties. Four-seventy-five."

"You were down to three-twenty-five a couple days ago."

"We'll start at four-seventy-five and work down during coffee."

They were all laughing when Pavlov came through the door. Reggie the Baron was right behind him. Chairs shuffled as the two sat down.

"Wheat toast this morning?" Millie squeezed between two of the members with another pot of coffee.

Carrigan nodded, Sko nodded, Snuffy nodded, Reggie nodded. "Muffin," said the Princess.

"How about you, Mr. insurance man?" Millie asked Pavlov.

"Way-al, ah'll tell ya. Ah wants two aigs this morn'n scram-belled, hay-ish browns, a big joose and wheat toast."

"A Graybar special," said Millie. Pavlov looked at her. She

102

clarified. "That's what Mr. Graybar orders every morning."

"Every morning?' asked Pavlov.

"Without fail. He's a man of habit."

"Way-al, if it's good nuff fo Mistah Graybah, it's good nuff fo me."

Millie scooted away.

"Yessah," Pavlov went on. "What evah Mistah Graybah likes, ah likes."

Mr. Graybar likes the Princess, Carrigan was thinking.

"What evah Mistah Graybah does, ah does".

Mr. Graybar is blackmailing the Princess, Carrigan was thinking.

Johann pulled up a chair from a neighboring table. "Uhhh."

"Well, Jesus," said Sko surprised. "We're all here and it's only ten after nine."

"We're all here except for Johann," Reggie quipped. "Well, he's sort'a here, but he ain't all here. Haw, haw, haw!"

"Uhhh.," Johann commented as he snugged his chair in closer. He was already working on his first inch of cigarette ash. Reggie poured him a cup and Johann started coming around, "Uhhh, ya, ya, ya."

Everyone marveled. Johann was already muttering multiple syllables and hadn't even drunk any coffee yet.

It was then that Carrigan noticed the way old man Graybar was fidgeting.

"Hey, guys!" Carrigan said getting the coffee group's attention. "This is it!"

"This is what?" asked Pavlov.

"Old man Graybar is about to have one of his seizures. See the way his hands are jerking, the way he's sitting upright in his chair. Look at his eyes!"

Everyone in the coffee group was now focusing on the old gent. "I wonder who's going to come to his aid this morning." Carrigan questioned.

"Probably that little Iranian shit," said Pavlov. "Or maybe Eddie."

Carrigan glanced at the booth in which the Iranian was sitting. He was curiously watching Graybar, his dark eyes wider than wide, his dark skin now turning gray.

Wandering Eddie was in the next booth with Mumbling Mike. All the booths were occupied, and everybody was now focusing on Graybar.

Carrigan scanned the rest of the room. Hardnuts Brodigan was at the counter next to the Fargo-Burnout. Ruckles was across at another table, a hand fumbling with his hearing aide, his eyes glued to Graybar.

Then came the traditional *whoop* as Graybar slumped back in his wheel chair and kicked his legs up. *What the hell?* Carrigan thought. *Can a cripple kick his feet that high in the air? By God, Graybar's my number one suspect. I'll bet the old son-of-a-bitch can walk!*

Another *whoop* belched from Graybar and now his face was turning gray. The man was having a hell of a fit this time, and the entire coffee group was witness to the comical, but habitual occurrence.

Then came the finale as Graybar stiffened and his eyeballs rolled back in his head. His face was really gray now, his mouth rounded, forming deep wrinkles on his lips. Then he slumped forward and banged his face flat on the table in front of him.

It was the Iranian and a buddy who came to the rescue. They each grabbed an arm and pulled him, but this morning, the fit was lasting longer than usual. And when the Iranian hollered for help, Hardnuts Brodigan jumped into the scene and Millie tore around the corner.

In seconds, Hardnuts jerked old man Graybar from the chair and laid him flat on the floor. By now, several people had gathered around.

"Call an ambulance!" someone shouted.

Hardnuts was now bent over the old man blowing into his

mouth, pumping his chest up and down.

Five minutes passed before the ambulance pulled up outside, and seconds later, two paramedics rushed through the door with an oxygen tank, its hoses and nozzles whipping like wild vines in the wind.

"Give us room!" one of them shouted

Everybody moved back as the two started working on him. Graybar was now completely the color of his name as they strapped an oxygen mask to his face.

Graybar was not moving.

Hands jostled the old man and flopped him onto a stretcher.

Graybar did not have a fit this morning .

Graybar was dead

It happened so fast. The paramedics hauled him out the front door, and in no time the ambulance was gone, its siren fading away.

Hushed voices and whispered conversations hovered around the tables like a mushroom cloud hangs in the air. This was the first time in at least two years that Carrigan could recollect the people in the coffee house being so quiet.

"He was 82 years old," said Carrigan.

Radio Sko whisked a hand over his bald head, his face blank. "That's only twelve years older than me."

Reggie stared into his cup. "My father-in-law went the same way."

Johann held loosely onto his coffee and snuffed out his cigarette.

When Millie slipped the plate of food in front of Pavlov, he stared at the two eggs, hash browns, wheat toast and orange juice. This was the same breakfast Graybar had ordered. It was not a good feeling.

Carrigan and the Princess exchanged glances, their thoughts identical. They had just lost their number one suspect.

And then the table got down to some serious conversation.

"Too bad about Graybar."

"He had good eyes. Wish I could have painted them before he kicked off."

"How's your breakfast, Pavlov?"

"Ah think ah feel a fit comin' on."

"Haw, haw, haw!"

"Wandering Eddie and Mumbling Mike have been hanging around together lately."

"More coffee here?"

"No, I learned to roll cigarettes when I was in the service."

"Maybe it was food poisoning."

"He kicked his legs before he died. Do you suppose he wasn't a cripple?"

"Want to make a radio buy?"

"Hey, Princess. What are you and Carrigan always whispering about?"

"Ya, ya, ya. He had good eyes. I should have painted em'. You betchum, Red Ryder."

"What photos? What the hell are you two talking about?"

"Pavlov, you don't look so good."

"Maybe Ruckles is a bit kinky, but you will be too when you reach his age."

"Who's that guy always staring at our table?"

"That's the Fargo-Burnout. He might be crazy, but he's harmless."

PART III

Ten

T.B. Harvey

Tarragon Bromeliad Harvey was his given name, but most of his friends called him T.B. or Harvey, but rarely both. Those who didn't know him invariably inquired what the initials T.B. stood for, to which Harvey would simply answer *Tarragon Bromeliad*, to which the inquirer would usually answer, "Oh," or "I see," or "That's different."

That's different was an understatement, for there was scientific methodology behind his name. T.B.'s father held a professor's rank at the university level and taught a variety of sophisticated courses in Botany. After having done sixteen years of research, all in an effort to leave a mark in the field of Botany, he died a rather obscure man. The only mark he left behind was T.B. Harvey.

In the few months prior to T.B.'s birth, T. B's father had been writing a dissertation for his Ph. D. on the subject of Tarragon, a bitter, aromatic perennial herb from the family *Compositae.* Tarragon was an ally to wormwood and sagebrush, a native plant of Europe and Asia. The leaves of this plant, which grew to a normal height of two feet, were dried and used commercially to flavor vinegar. T.B. Harvey was five foot two inches tall.

T.B. Harvey's middle name came from the family of the *Bromeliad Order,* two words which on several occasions occurred in the footnotes of his father's dissertation. The Bromeliad Order, or *Bromeliales,* stemmed from a group of tropical plants that grew on branches or trunks of other species and were often referred to as parasites, but, which, in fact, they were not. Examples of Bromeliads were Spanish moss, aechmea and pineapple.

T.B. Harvey was bald through the center of his head, yet, he appeared to be wearing a two-part toupee—one part glued to each side. Though his hair was not green, it did resemble Spanish moss, so very fuzzy, that people often thought he was shedding.

Thus, Tarragon Bromeliad was a fairly accurate description of the little man. T.B. was quite young when his father died and he had not yet obtained his five-foot-two height, so his father never really appreciated the extent of naming him *Tarragon*. At that point in his life, T.B. had a full head of hair, but it had not yet fully matured, nor did it resemble Spanish moss. So, on both accounts T.B.'s father expired without knowing the profound significance of his botany-labeled son.

Besides being short and carrying around a mop of Spanish moss hair, T.B. possessed other striking features. On initial inspection one would swear his mother had copulated with an elephant. T.B. had enormous ears, even larger than Abraham Lincoln's, and besides being huge, they stuck out like a curved lean-to. T.B. often commented about himself in jest, that he had to fight off birds, which had mistaken his big ears for open-ended eave spouts, a perfect place to build a nest.

He also had the misfortune of possessing a tiny bulbous nose that stuck out from underneath a pair of round wire-rimmed glasses.

Some of his greatest heroes were Peter Falk, Paul Williams, Dick Cavett, Mickey Rooney, Napoleon, and parts of Abraham Lincoln. He also liked the seven dwarves.

T.B. Harvey's office was on the third floor of Strauss Clothing located on the corner of 1st Avenue and Broadway in downtown Fargo. Actually, his office was at the extreme rear of the building, which was a three story affair. The elevator only went to the second floor, so T.B. had to walk the staircase to the third. He called it his private staircase, since no one else was located on the third floor. The door to his office was easy to find, since it was the only door in the corridor with a window in it, thereby allowing light to shine through. On the window, black, elaborate letters spelled out his business.

T.B. Harvey—Private Investigator

T.B. had been a private eye for almost six months. Prior to that he had been a salesman for Richtman's Printing, a sales rep for KFGO radio, and an account executive for the Fargo Paper Company. Unfortunately, he had never lasted even a few weeks in either position before he was politely let loose. He had spent three months as the president of Command Enterprises, a mail order house he started up on his own, but which never got off the ground. He finally found his niche working at Silverline Boats as a truck dispatcher. He managed somehow to remain there for almost three years before he was fired for incompetence. He sued the company, complaining that he lost his job because he was so short, but the judge threw him and the case out of court

All of this experience, according to T.B., was preparatory work for becoming a P.I. The only background he had for this kind of work came from the forty-plus detective novels he had read. His favorite detective was Shell Scott, primarily, because he could find these age-old detective mysteries at a premium price at Ernie's book store. He liked Mickey Spillane, too, and had read a few of Ian Fleming's 007 novels, but Shell Scott was his hero. He was a suave, handsome fellow with thick, white hair. It was the hair that mostly attracted T.B., something he would have wished upon himself, even if it was white, and Shell Scott was also a hulking six-footer, a height that T.B. could admire.

T.B. sat behind his desk, the only piece of furniture in his office besides a steel file cabinet, a chair, a piano stool and a wall map of Fargo-Moorhead. The single window in the room had one of the panes missing, and in its place, T.B. had stuffed a piece of cardboard.

He was now cleaning his gun, a cheap Saturday night special, the only firearm he could afford. A new, highly polished leather holster hung over his shoulder and would easily conceal the pistol when he had his jacket on.

He attached a piece of his handkerchief, with a dab of oil on it, to the end of wire and ran it through the barrel of the gun a few times. He held up the gun, cylinder extended to the side, and peered down the barrel.

"Clean," he said.

He loaded the bullets back into the cylinder, flipped it shut and pointed the muzzle into his waste basket. The bottom was laden with two-by-four blocks of wood and covered with a large pillow to muffle the sound. He jammed the muzzle into the pillow, squeezed his eyes shut and pulled the trigger.

The hammer snapped, but the weapon did not fire.

"Damn," he said.

He jammed the muzzle in place again, squeezed his eyes shut, grimaced and pulled the trigger for the second time.

Nothing.

Damn," he said again.

He flipped the cylinder out and inspected the firing pin, then worked it loose with a paper clip and dropped a spot of oil on it.

He flipped the cylinder back in place and pulled the hammer back. The shot exploded before he even got his eyes shut, sending a bullet into the plate glass on top of his desk. T.B. Harvey jumped excitedly, and although he dropped the gun, the distinct aroma of gun powder was music to his nose as he inhaled.

Suddenly, his elephant-sized ears heard footsteps coming down the corridor. T.B. nervously jammed the gun into his holster, then quietly slipped himself into his closet, leaving a crack wide enough to view the door. A shadow swung across the glass, and a moment later, Carrigan Mulhouse stepped into the room and looked around. He raised his nose, obviously smelling the gun powder residue hanging in the air.

"Ah Carrigan," T.B. Harvey said as he opened the closet door and made his appearance. "Thought it was the landlord." He stuck out a stubby hand. "How are you? Haven't seen you in months."

"Good," said Carrigan. He was still sniffing the air. "Did I hear a shot?" Carrigan's gaze focused on the hole in the plate glass on his desk.

T.B. chuckled and patted his shoulder holster. "Once in a while it gets away from me. Got to have her looked at. Have a chair."

Carrigan sat on the round piano stool in front of T.B.'s desk. "How's the P.I. business?"

"Great, just great" said T.B. as he sat down. "Been busy as hell. Can't keep up."

Carrigan looked around the room. He was recollecting the yellow pages of the phone book in his office where he had spent over twelve dollars on phone calls inquiring about private detectives in Minneapolis. He still wasn't convinced he had made the right decision in coming to T.B.'s office, but he had good reason.

"I heard you opened a detective agency," Carrigan finally said.

"That's right," T.B. snapped with authority. "I did a little research. Not another detective agency between here and Minneapolis. Fargo needs an agency. There's a big demand for private investigative work."

"Silverline Boats, evidently wasn't your bag, huh.?"

"No, I guess not. Wasn't your bag either, was it?"

Carrigan smiled. T.B. Harvey, as strange as he was, was the one friend Carrigan had made during his year with the boat company. The two of them had something in common from their earlier relationship; both were highly frustrated with their jobs, both highly underpaid. T.B. had been a fairly good truck dispatcher, although on one occasion he sent a truckload of boats to the West Coast instead of the East Coast. He got out of that dilemma by making a few phone calls and establishing a new dealer in Sacramento, but there were other little screw-ups that followed. T.B. never was very good with paperwork.

"Are you in need of a good detective?" inquired T.B. He had one ear cocked, waiting enthusiastically for a response.

"Could be. Are you on a case right now?"

"No, I'm free at the moment. Lucky for you."

"What sort of work do you do?"

"Oh, the usual detective work. Tracking down runaways, investigating extra marital activities, drug traffic, murder. You know, the usual stuff."

"What have you done recently?"

T.B. sat back in his chair, his mouth hanging open, but nothing came out.

"I see," said Carrigan.

"I've only been in business six months," said T.B. "Guy's got to build up a clientele." He was quiet for the moment, his eyes saddened like a munchkin out of the Wizard of Oz. "Carrigan," he said almost pleading. "I need a case. I need a case badly."

"Things haven't been that good?"

"No. Whatever services you need you can count on me. I'll even become a hired killer if you need one."

Carrigan smiled. "I not sure killing is sanctioned by the National Detectives Association."

"It's not, but I'm desperate. Sometimes a guy has to bend the rules a bit. You need somebody killed?"

Carrigan was laughing inside. This five-foot-two man in front of him was lucky if he weighed 110 pounds. Ready to kill? Carrigan knew he was not serious—at least he hoped he wasn't.

Desperation was imprinted on his face like a Coca-Cola logo on a t-shirt. The man needed work, and after all, he was his friend. "What are your fees?"

"What's the case?"

"I think blackmail."

"Ooooh," T.B. said with a grimace. "Those are kind of sticky. Never know how a blackmailer is going to react. Could be gunplay."

"Harvey," I don't want anyone shot. How much for a blackmail case?"

"Have you got a suspect?"

"Several."

"Hmm. A hundred a day?"

"A hundred!?" It was more a revelation than a question. In Minneapolis, detectives were going for three hundred a day.

"All right, seventy-five since we're friends."

Carrigan raised an eyebrow.

"Plus expenses," T.B. quickly added.

Carrigan raised his other eyebrow. He had already shelled out $110.00 for photography expenses. "Okay. Seventy-five a day plus expenses." Carrigan hesitated. "What expenses?"

T.B. reeled back in his chair. "The usual. Disguises. Meals. A new gun."

"A new gun? I said I didn't want any gunplay. Besides, you have a gun."

"It isn't reliable," said T.B.

"No new gun," said Carrigan.

"I'll need a retainer."

"How much?"

"Couple hundred."

"Two hundred dollars?"

"A hundred since we're friends."

Carrigan took out his billfold, counted out five twenties and mentally added that to the already spent near one hundred on Leroy. He then produced the envelope from his jacket and spread the photos of the Princess on the desk so T. B. could examine them. T.B. licked his lips and adjusted his glasses so he could see more clearly with his bifocals.

"Nice looking. How tall is she?"

"Five-four."

"Not bad."

"Her husband is six-two."

"That's bad."

"Her name is Pam Allison." In sketch form, Carrigan gave her background, her former but brief occupation as a stripper, her association with the Powers Coffee House group, and then he dwelled at length on the size of her gigantic and jealous husband and emphasized the importance of keeping the investigation in strict confidence.

"Strict confidence," said T.B. "I won't say shit. And don't worry about the husband. I'll leave him alone."

Carrigan wanted to laugh out loud. T.B. said the last sentence as if he were capable of beating big Jerry Allison black and blue. Carrigan produced photos of all the Powers Coffee House suspects and strung them out in front of T.B.

"Six suspects," said T.B. as he studied the photos.

"Some of them reside in the Powers Hotel, some outside. You can forget about Graybar. He just checked out."

"Went to another hotel?"

"No, he died."

"Ah. Could still be a suspect though. Lot of the dead ones tend to fool you."

"Forget about him."

"Right."

Carrigan produced a sheet of paper on which he had written a sketchy background on all of the suspects. T.B. scanned the sheet quickly. "Looks like a bunch of weirdoes."

"My exact sentiments. I think we're after a weirdo. The guy has called Pam Allison a few times, but he hasn't demanded any money yet. Just keeps sending her photos."

"That's weird," said T.B., as if he had just thought up the word himself. "This shouldn't be tough. I think I can clear this up for you in short time."

"How short?"

"A week. I'll need to do some investigative work first. You say this gal was a stripper in Minneapolis?"

Carrigan was multiplying seventy-five dollars times five. "Ah, yes, in the Gay Nineties Bar. Seven years ago."

"Good place to start."

"Where?"

"In Minneapolis."

"On seventy-five bucks a day? I'm not paying you to fly to Minneapolis and check into a hotel. You do your investigative work from here. Use the telephone."

T.B. looked at his phone. It had been disconnected a month ago. "Right."

"And no gunplay."

"Right." T.B. scanned the photographs again. "Who did the photography?"

"A former student named Leroy Ridgebutte. He lives in Moorhead."

"Good stuff. In a clandestine manner, I presume?"

"Yes. Clandestine."

"Good. Don't want any more faces floating around this case. Got to keep everything clandestine."

That was the exact reason Carrigan Mulhouse came to T.B. Harvey. He had initiated the investigation by hiring Leroy, but there was no way he could continue it himself. Now that he studied T.B. again, he wasn't sure he had done the right thing in coming to see him.

"T.B.," Carrigan said as he stood up. I'm counting on you. I want results. I came to you because…" Carrigan stopped mid sentence. He wanted to say because he couldn't afford to hire any detectives from Minneapolis.

"Because you wanted results," T.B. repeated. "You could

count on me at Silverline and you can count on me now."

T.B. spoke as if the two occupations were synonymous with each other. He was a spirited little man, if nothing else.

"Good," said Carrigan

They shook on the deal and Carrigan exited the office. He was about to descend the staircase at the end of the corridor when he heard a pistol shot. Carrigan jumped, turned and stared down the hallway. The bullet had gone through the window of T.B.'s office door.

Seconds later, the door opened and T.B. peeked around the doorway. "Got away from me." He waved and ducked back inside, and when he slammed the door, the rest of the window dropped from its frame and crashed to the floor.

Carrigan questioned his own sanity as he made his way down the staircase to the elevator.

Eleven
The Investigations

Carrigan Mulhouse had been sitting at the Powers Coffee House table for fifteen minutes chatting with the Princess and Pavlov when Sko Skofield came in.

"Make room for a man," he said when he reached the table. Immediately, he was engaged in a conversation with the Princess, planning their so-called trip to Alaska. Pavlov, too, was engaged in the conversation, making his bid for the escapade.

While the other three bantered back and forth, Carrigan was watching the door as he had been all morning, scrutinizing each coffee house patron that entered. Graybar, obviously, was not sitting at his table, since he was dead. Three of the four booths against the wall were filled already, and other patrons were slowly occupying the tables here and there.

Carrigan's eye caught the front door again as a squat, plump lady came in, fatter than fat, rouge smeared from one ear to the other. She was carrying a huge rag satchel stuffed with something or other. Carrigan eyed her curiously as she waddled to the end booth and shoved herself in, her feet dangling several inches off the floor. Her head was covered with gray, stringy hair, which had the definite quality of a mop head. A transient, Carrigan was convinced, from the bus depot.

Wandering Eddie made his appearance from the back door of the hotel lobby. He stood nervously, looking about, his bean frame swaying as if he were about to fall over. Finally he sat at a free table, his knees wide apart, his fly fully open.

Beyond Wandering Eddie, the fat lady in the end booth was looking in Carrigan's direction, but he thought nothing of it as he turned his attention to the guys at his table.

The fat lady wasn't staring at Carrigan Mulhouse at all. She had her eyes fixed on Wandering Eddie. Quite innocently, she took a note pad from her satchel, checked her wristwatch and noted the exact time Wandering Eddie sat down at the table.

T.B. Harvey felt excited, nervous. This was his first case, and so far he had managed to make his way to a booth in the Powers unnoticed, or so he thought. It was a perfect disguise. The old, gray striped dress had been hanging in his closet for the past several months. He had a choice of four different wigs, and had selected the gray one, the best of the lot. His feet hurt, since he was wearing sandals a size too small for his already small feet. They pinched even now as he wiggled his feet to relieve the pain.

Wandering Eddie ordered breakfast. T.B. noted the time.

Coffee came to Eddie's table. T.B. noted the time.

Wandering Eddie started to fidget in his seat. T.B. noted the time.

Five minutes later, Millie came by with Eddie's breakfast, and after a few bites of food, Wandering Eddie got out of his chair and left his food steaming.

When Eddie disappeared through the back doors to the lobby, T.B. left his satchel behind and crawled out of his seat. On the way past the counter toward the back doors, the distinct odor of burning toast poured out of the kitchen.

The hotel lobby, with its high gold painted arches and the grubby black and white tiled floor, was practically barren. The only person visible was a man standing near an open elevator. T.B. could see up the empty staircase that led to the second floor.

He calculated that Wandering Eddie must have gone downstairs. He made his way down the dank staircase and was about to enter the door to the men's room when he realized that he was dressed as a lady. When he heard talking at the top of the stairs, he quickly moved out of view into a short hallway. There was no ladies room down here, only a door at the end of the hall. Footsteps echoed in the staircase, more men for the men's room, T.B. was sure. He jerked at the handle of the lone door, and once inside, the door automatically swung shut. He pressed his ear against the door, listening to the voices of two men carrying on a conversation as they entered the men's room.

A minute or so later, he heard the audible squeak of the door open. Wandering Eddie's peculiar short steps sounded against the tile floor, and when Eddie began ascending the staircase, T.B. groped for the closet door handle. His hand pressed against a protruding piece of metal, and when he heard a clank outside the door, he realized there was no handle on the inside. He had just pushed the door knob out of its slot, and now, he had a small peek hole through which he could view the corridor.

The other two men from the toilette finished their business and went up the staircase before T.B. even thought about hollering at them to let him out. Fifteen minutes slipped by with no one else coming downstairs, and then he thought he heard the door to the men's room squeak open. By the time he looked through the peek hole, whoever it was had already entered the men's can. A minute later, Wandering Eddie came out and T.B. hollered at him.

"Eddie! Over here!" He could see Eddie staring down the hallway in his direction, but he wasn't moving.

"Here, Eddie, the closet door!"

"Who's there?" Eddie responded.

T.B. shook his head. "Your fairy godmother, for god's sake! Let me out of here!"

Eddie came down the hallway and saw the door handle lying on the floor, picked it up and inserted it in the hole.

When the door opened, T.B. came out and simply said, "Next."

Eddie had the most bewildered look on his face. Just as

119

T.B. reached the staircase, he heard the door slip shut behind him. When he turned, Eddie was locked inside the closet.

"Godmother?" he heard Eddie call out.

By the time T.B. reached the restaurant, his satchel and note pad were gone and someone else was sitting in his booth.

That afternoon, T.B. was back in the Powers lobby sitting at a corner table. He sat as inconspicuously as he could, wearing a black hat with a brim pulled low over his head. He wore an extra long gray coat and had donned dark glasses. A white cane hung over the back of his chair.

T.B. was in luck. Wandering Eddie wandered through the lounge directly past him and exited the front doors to the street. T.B. was in quick pursuit as he tapped his way out the doors and hurried after him. It was easy going, since Eddie was not a fast walker.

Down Broadway Eddie went, T.B. not far behind, tapping his cane as he went.

Eddie crossed to the east side of the street and entered a building. It used to be the old Roxy Theatre, but some months back, someone had turned it into a porn shop. From outside the shop, T.B. dropped his glasses and nonchalantly peered through the window, but Eddie was nowhere in sight. He tapped his way inside, but still, Eddie was nowhere to be seen. He made his way to the counter where a husky, mean looking proprietor curiously eyed him.

"Want somethin' buddy?"

T.B. was stuck for a quick response. "Ah, your heavy porn section, please."

The man behind the counter stared incredulously at the little man and the white cane, but he came around the counter. "This way."

"Just lead the way and keep talking," said T.B. as he banged his cane on a bookrack, struck a table leg, slapped another rack.

"Right this way," the big husky man grunted. "Right over here, that's right, keep coming."

T.B. tapped his way into a cubicle area where the covers of the pornographic books jumped out at him from every shelf. The proprietor made his way back to the counter but kept his eyes on T.B.

Realizing he was supposed to be blind, and, knowing the proprietor was still watching him, T.B. began feeling the pictures on the pages as if they were in Braille. He purposely groaned a couple times, breathed as heavily as he could simply for effect.

Then, beyond the cubicle, he spotted Eddie in a back room. He was carrying an envelope similar to the kind in which Pam Allison's nude photos had arrived.

Aha! he thought. Was it possible this was the pick-up point?

The proprietor was still watching T.B., so he faked another heavy sigh, ran his fingers rapidly over the pages, and then, when he actually viewed the page, he gasped! A three hundred pound woman was straddling a skinny man. He quickly thumbed through a few more pages, totally engrossed and amazed at the number of positions the two had tangled themselves into. *How on earth could this skinny little man take on all that flesh?* he was thinking. "My God!" he said out loud as he grabbed at the bulge in his pants. He took a second book from the shelf and started flipping through the pages. By now, he forgot about running his fingers across the pages, and his groans were genuine, the bulge in his pants so huge that he thought he would punch right through his zipper.

He was perusing his third magazine when his thoughts abruptly came back to Eddie. He looked over the cubicle toward the back room, but Eddie was gone!

He glanced around the shop and then quickly tapped his way over to the big man behind the counter. "That skinny fellow in the backroom with the crew cut. Did he leave already?"

"Five minutes ago," said the man. "How did you know he was in the backroom if you can't see? And how did you know he had a crew cut?"

"It's all in the ears," T.B. said as he pointed to one of the floppy digits. He was about to leave and then added. "By the way, I represent the National Academy for the Blind. None of your pictures are in brail. Next time I come through you had better have representative stock on your shelves, otherwise I may be forced to make out a report on you. Could flat close you down."

T.B. started away. "Equal opportunity," he said as he tapped his way out the door onto the street.

Once outside, he strained through the dark glasses in both directions. Wandering Eddie was nowhere to be seen. He cursed his luck, but at least he was on to something. Wandering Eddie had picked up an envelope and was probably on his way to the post office to mail another set of nude photos.

T.B. spent the next hour in the lobby of the post office, but Wandering Eddie never showed up.

At 5:30 that afternoon, T.B. was again in the Powers Hotel Coffee House, sitting in the same corner he had occupied earlier in the day. This time he had donned a flat cap with a bill. Underneath, he wore a wig with scraggly strands of hair draping over his shoulders. Several necklaces and chains dangled around his neck and draped down over a long leather vest with frills on the edges. The pant legs of his green cords were so long that the cuffs lapped over a pair of black brogans.

It wasn't long before crew-cut Eddie came through the lobby doors into the coffee house and took a seat in a booth. He ordered a meal, but before it came, he walked back through the lobby doors. T.B. was sure he was headed down to the men's room, so he patiently waited.

When he returned, he sat at a different table and the

waitress had to chase him down with his plate. Before his meal was over, Eddie repeated the habitual excursion to the men's can and back two more times. By now, T.B. pretty well had the man's strange habits down. Wandering Eddie was as predictable as a growing cucumber.

An hour passed before Wandering Eddie finally left the coffee house. He was wearing a light jacket, and interestingly enough, the same manila envelope that T.B. had seen earlier was protruding from a pocket.

T B. was immediately on his tail. Eddie headed north on Broadway and disappeared around the corner of the Empire Bar. By the time T.B. reached the corner, Eddie had crossed the Burlington Northern tracks. It appeared he was headed toward Hardees, but then he swung left along the tracks and disappeared inside the door of an old, white-washed, concrete block storehouse. The only visible light came from a window on the second floor.

T.B. cautiously approached the building, stopped short of the doorway and reached inside his vest for the Saturday night special. When he tried the door handle, he was surprised to discover it was open, so he stepped in. The bottom floor of the building appeared to have been abandoned long ago. It was completely gutted except for a few long counters and a lone wall extending from floor to ceiling. A staircase led upwards, and obviously, that was where Eddie had gone.

T.B. had no idea anyone lived in the building. Cautiously, with gun in hand, he sneaked upwards to the top of the wooden staircase. At the far end of a long hallway, a faint light shone through a window. No more than twenty feet away, a yellow light peeked out under a door.

T B. made his way along the corridor, his squat body pressed against the wall. Short of the entrance, he heard voices coming from within. Eddie was not alone. His high squeaky voice was easily recognizable, but T.B. could not make out the other voice, a sort of mumbling, rattling sound.

It was then T.B. heard Eddie's voice again. Faintly but clearly, he said, "What do you think of the photos?"

It was a conspiracy, T.B. was convinced. At least two people were in on the blackmail. Under normal circumstances, Shell Scott would have blasted off the door handle with his pistol before bursting into the room, but T.B. couldn't trust his revolver for a first shot. In the back of his mind, he tried *not* to recollect that Carrigan had explicitly said *no gunplay*.

He would have to kick the door in, rush in with his gun pointed and catch the men in the act. However, on close inspection, T.B. noticed the door was not closed completely. He could just push it in!

He pressed an ear to the door, straining a final time for any audible words. Someone mumbled and Eddie was talking again. T.B. shoved the door open and jumped into the room with his revolver pointed at the two men.

"Freeze!" he hollered.

When they froze, T.B. gulped, could hardly believe what he was witnessing. Skinny Wandering Eddie was clad only in his underwear and had struck a pose like a muscle builder. His knees were slightly bent and if he had any muscles on his body anywhere, it was difficult to perceive them. T.B. recognized the other man with him as Mumbling Mike. His pants were down over his ankles and shoes, and he was still wearing his shirt, but he, too, was posed similarly to Eddie.

T.B.'s heart fluttered, but he held the handgun steady. "All right, all right!" he barked. "Don't anybody move!"

Not sure what else he should say, T.B. made a quick survey of the room. Two old stuffed chairs with hardly any stuffing left in them were off to his left. To his right stood a dilapidated iron-rung bed with a heavily stained mattress on it. That was where the god-awful stench was coming from. The two, still as stiff as mannequins were standing at a table covered with magazine after magazine. In front of them was the envelope Eddie had been carrying, and spread out on the table top were some photos.

"The photos," T.B. commanded. "I want the photos!"

Eddie gave a helpless stare, as if he were about to cry, but he gathered the photos and handed them to T.B. "I p-paid for them," he managed to squeak out.

T.B. turned red as he gazed at the photos. There were five in all, all muscle builders, and not one of them in the least pornographic. They were simply men in various poses, muscles bulging, veins popping out all over, all wearing tights.

Good God, T.B. was thinking, his mind running a mile a minute. Was this what Eddie had picked up at the porn shop? It seemed inconsequential at the moment, but he had to ask.

"Have either of you ever been in Minneapolis?"

Eddie shrugged as he sought an answer from his friend, Mumbling Mike. "I don't know. Have I?"

Mumbling Mike shrugged and mumbled something that T.B. could not remotely decipher.

"Do either of you know where Minneapolis is?" T.B. questioned.

Eddie looked at Mumbling Mike again, his face as blank as a sheet of paper. "I don't know. Do I?"

Mike mumbled something again.

Holy shit, thought T.B. Here he was confronting two of the suspects. One couldn't utter a coherent sentence, and neither one had the remotest idea where Minneapolis was. The only thing T.B. was sure of was that they were definitely weirdoes.

"All right," said T.B. trying to think of something clever to say. "As long as neither of you know where Minneapolis is, you can go back to doing whatever you were doing."

As an afterthought, he verbally blasted them. "And by God, I never want to see either of you in Minneapolis!"

"No, no," the two said together. This time even Mumbling Mike's words were discernible.

T.B. drove a final point home. "If I ever catch either of you in Minneapolis, you're dead meat! Is that clear?"

Death was riding their faces as T.B. eased himself out of his squat position and handed the photos back to Eddie. Confident and completely in control of himself, T.B. jammed the pistol back in his shoulder holster, spun smartly on his heels and exited the room.

Reaching the outside, he hurried back to the Powers where he left his car. This incident with Eddie and Mumbling Mike was not something he could report to Carrigan, yet at seventy-five dollars a day, he would have to report something.

"Shit," said T.B., as he started the motor. "Shit, shit, shit!"

Twelve
What Price Blackmail?

Carrigan Mulhouse was sitting in T.B.'s office reading the report. "Uh-huh. Both of them incarcerated in the Jamestown Institution." Carrigan examined the dates of the stay. "There's no way either of them could have been in Minneapolis at the time Pam Allison was stripping?"

"No way," T.B. said.

"I see you have the doctor's signature on this report. How did you manage that?"

"I started with the Vets Hospital on a hunch and made a couple phone calls from there. Off and on for the past two years, Eddie and Mike were institutionalized at the Vets. Eddie's living at the Powers, Mike has his own apartment downtown. Looks like they're doing all right." T.B. rolled his eyes. "That's the rehabilitation procedure. Allow them to mix in with society."

"Good," said Carrigan as he folded the report shut. "Next on your list?"

"Roman Ruckles from Ruckles Chemical."

"Does he strike you as a likely suspect?"

"I heard he's hurting financially. He runs his plant like a modern day Scrooge. No bonuses, one day off a year on Christmas, minimum wage, no benefits. He's one tight son-of-a-bitch. If he's going to stay in business, he's going to need money."

Carrigan nodded.

T.B. went on. "Could be he blackmails people daily like Eddie takes a leak."

It was a strange analogy, but Carrigan was pleased. T.B. had evidently learned what Wandering Eddie's favorite pastime was. "Well, you've certainly earned your money. You've eliminated two suspects in one day."

T.B. grinned. Carrigan had got his money's worth but perhaps not in the way he thought.

"Keep up the good work. Give me a call when you get a rundown on Ruckles." Carrigan left the office and walked down the corridor wondering whether he would hear a gunshot or not.

He didn't. He walked down a flight of stairs, caught the elevator to the lobby and returned to his office.

Ruckles Chemical occupied the southwest corner two blocks east of the Powers, where T.B. made his appearance the next morning. The company was primarily a wholesaler of chemical products, but Ruckles had a small retail store on the main floor where he sold supplies in small quantities to the public.

T.B. pushed his way through the heavy oak door, and immediately, a heavy waft of soap swept up his nose. An office girl was sitting behind a huge desk, her head buried in a set of books. T.B. guessed she might be an accountant besides being a clerk. She was a good-looking brunette, but big and hefty with large gold earrings dangling from her ears. She approached him wearing a huge smile, and when she pressed against the counter, both of her breasts, the size of huge cantaloupes, rested easily on top. She reminded him of the 300 pounds of flesh he had seen in the pornography shop.

"Good morning, Father," she greeted.

T.B.'s eyes remained on the humongous breasts as he tugged at the white clerical collar about his neck. A certain excitement charged within him. He straightened his black frock coat that matched his black pants, which matched the oversized black homburg he was wearing.

"Can I help you, Father?" she offered again

T.B. dropped an envelope on the counter, an identical one

in which Pam Allison had received her photos. "I wonder if you carry these kinds of envelopes?" he inquired.

She studied the envelope for a moment. "You must be mistaken, Father. We don't sell envelopes. We sell chemicals."

T.B. played dumb. "Really? You don't sell envelopes?" He looked at the shelves behind the counter as if he didn't believe her. "I was told this was Northern School Supply."

"Oh, no, sir. That's a couple blocks over and south on Roberts. This is Ruckles Chemical Supply."

T.B. had his line ready as he checked his watch. "Ah, I'm just traveling through and my bus leaves in a few minutes." He gestured to the depot across the street. "Do you happen to have an envelope like this one, which I could perhaps purchase?"

She glanced at the envelope. "A number one bubble mailer. You, know I believe we do." When she bent over to search underneath the counter, T.B. stretched up and glanced at her. *Big ass, too.* She raised up and produced an envelope identical to the one T.B. had showed her, but his eyes were fully focused on her breasts where one button had popped open.

"Would you like to purchase one?" she inquired.

"Oh, wow!"

"I beg your pardon?"

He lifted his eyes to meet hers. "Ah, yes, two please."

"I don't know exactly how much they're worth, but would twenty-five cents each be appropriate?"

"They're certainly worth that," he said as he fished a dollar out of his wallet. He watched her wiggle her way to the cash register and ring up the sale.

"Thank you, Father," she said as she handed him his change.

When he turned to leave, the big breasts hung in front of his eyes like a mirage, reminding him of a vacation he had once made to the Tetons. Just as T.B. was headed out of the building, Ruckles was coming in.

"Good morning, Father," Ruckles greeted.

T.B. nervously tipped his hat. At the oak door, he hesitated, fidgeted with his envelopes long enough to take one last glance at the girl with the big breasts. When the phone rang, Ruckles lifted the receiver and adjusted his hearing aide.

"No, dear," Ruckles was saying into the phone as he sneaked a glance at his big-titted secretary. "I'm flying to Minneapolis tonight... A new client, dear." He sneaked another glance at his secretary and made a wild, devilish grin.

"Oh, that's right. You have bridge tonight. Well, have a nice time. I'll call when I return tomorrow." He hung up the phone, glanced at the brunette and headed for her desk, but when he noticed T.B. was still standing in the doorway, he made an abrupt turn and seated himself at the desk next to hers.

"Aha," thought T.B. as he quietly let himself out onto the street. Ruckles was headed for Minneapolis tonight, and he stocked the exact envelopes in which the nude photos were sent.

"Aha," he said to a passing lady as he tipped his hat.

"Aha," he said to himself as he got into his beat up Chevy.

From a pay phone, T.B. called the airport identifying himself as Roman Ruckles and said he hadn't received his reservation yet for the flight to Minneapolis.

"I'm sorry, sir," came the retort. "We don't have a reservation for you listed as a passenger on Northwest, but we have availability on this afternoon's flight and one later this evening. Would you care to book one of those?"

T.B. hung up. Ruckles was flying to Minneapolis, but he hadn't made a reservation. From the way Ruckles had been ogling his secretary, it would not surprise him if Ruckles would not do the same in Minneapolis. Of course, bars would offer the best opportunity for such affairs. The Gay Nineties, for example.

T.B. pondered his thoughts. If Ruckles did not have a reservation for Minneapolis, then what was he going to do tonight? He dropped another dime into the phone and called Carrigan's office only to reach his recorder. "Carrigan, this is Harvey. Tell Pam Allison she might be expecting a call sometime today or perhaps tonight. If the blackmailer calls, I want to know the exact time. I think I'm on to something."

Shaking with excitement and cackling, T.B. hung up and clasped his pudgy hands together in a gesture of defiance.

Late that afternoon, T.B. sat in his beat up Chevy, parked strategically across from Ruckles Chemical and Supply where he could easily view the front and side exits. He was conveniently disguised in his old-man outfit, quite appropriate, he thought, since his suspect now was an old man. T.B. adjusted the heavy, gray hat and moved the full beard around on his chin to relieve an itch. He had crawled into a horribly wrinkled gray coat and threw on a brown pair of pleated slacks with cuffs. It had not occurred once to T.B. that anyone in town who knew him would also know his car. It was rust colored, primarily because most of it was rusted. He drove a 1967 Chevy, a V-8, but he called it a V-6, since most of the time in only ran on six cylinders.

For three hours, he had been sitting behind the wheel, his head barely above the steering column. With field glasses, he could see quite clearly through the office window of the first floor where Mr. Roman Ruckles had spent most of the afternoon. The old boy also had a private office on the second floor, and during the few hours T.B. had been making his observations, he had seen Ruckles make a couple trips to that office. Ruckles was, of course, out of sight during the time required to ascend the staircase, but the window in the second floor office was large, easy for T.B. to view him again.

For T.B., looking through the field glasses was an exciting experience. Every free moment Ruckles had, he was sitting on the edge of his secretary's desk, the girl with the huge lungs. On two occasions, T.B. saw Ruckles pinch her on the boob, and from the snickering face she gave, she apparently loved it.

At 4:30, the working crowd exited the side doors, but Ruckles was not among them. At 5:15, two more employees exited the front door. At 6:03, the secretary left by herself.

At 6:04 Ruckles turned off the lights in his upstairs office and came to the downstairs office, busy behind his desk, working off hours like he normally did.

After another hour of spying, the binoculars seemed incurably heavy, and T.B. could no longer hold them up to his face. His eyes had become blurry and strained from the constant surveillance, but now, more than ever, he needed to be ever watchful. No one else was in the building, and if Ruckles ever dialed the phone, T.B. needed to note the time.

At eight o'clock, Ruckles was still at his desk, and he still hadn't dialed. The gas lights along the curb had already come on creating a yellow-gold haze over the street. At least the night was comfortable, not too hot, not too cool. He became bored and aggravated. He thought for certain Ruckles would have made a phone call to Pam Allison by now, but the old fart was still bent over his desk, probably devising a way to embezzle money out of his own business.

A figure appeared coming up the street, a lady he could tell by the walk, and as she neared the front door of the building, T.B. recognized her as Ruckles' secretary. Even though she was wearing a light coat, the huge chest was unmistakable.

The girl, after a glance left and right, ducked inside the building. *What the hell's this all about?* T.B. was thinking as he excitedly shoved the binoculars to his eyes. Ruckles got out of his chair, and immediately the lights went out in his downstairs office.

T.B. dropped the glasses and looked at the front door, expecting the two to exit any moment, but the door didn't open. Suddenly, the lights in his second floor office went on. T.B. jammed the binoculars to his face and held his breath, his heart pumping. There, magnified six times right before his eyes, he witnessed Ruckles give the secretary a huge embrace. Even now, T.B. could feel her big tits jutting into his own chest, could feel the heavy thighs pressing up against his groin. And now, Ruckles had his decrepit hands firmly tearing into her buttocks.

"Oh, Lord!" said T.B. to himself.

Ruckles abruptly tore away from her, and like a film breaking in the middle of a movie, the drapes to the window slapped shut.

"Not now! Not now!" T.B. yelled out as he pressed his eyes into the binoculars. A portion of the curtain was open, but from T.B.'s low angle, he could not get a clear view.

He was alert, excited, and felt the bulge in his pants. He glanced across the street at the outside fire escape of the Colonial Hotel.

In seconds, he was out of his car and on a dead run for the fire escape. Puffing and nearly out of breath, he clambered up the iron steps not at all aware of the racket he was making with his feet. "Wait! Wait!" he hollered. "Not yet!"

On the second landing, he once again focused the binoculars on the window across from him. "Oh Lord!" he said as he saw her blouse practically ripped from her body, and then her brassiere snapped off.

He grabbed his groin and groaned when he caught sight of the huge, fleshy breasts. "My God!! Just like the three-hundred pounder in the magazine!"

"Oh, Lord!" he said as he felt the rush of warm semen stream into his shorts. What ecstasy! What pleasure! Stars seemed to burst in front of his eyes, lights were flashing!

Lights flashing?

133

"Hey! What the hell's going on up there?"

T.B. jumped. The lights were real, and the flashing he saw was coming from a flashlight down below.

Hardnuts Brodigan! T.B. was still holding tight to the wet spot in his groin. "Holy shit!" His mind raced, and now stars really flashed in his head. Brodigan was climbing the stairs!

T.B. panicked and nervously fought his way to the third landing where the fire escape ended at a door. He tried the handle, but it wouldn't open. To the right was a window. He pulled at the frame, but the effort was useless. Chapter four from an obscure detective novel raced through his mind. He balled himself up like the hero in the novel and thrust himself through the window. As he rolled onto the floor, the entire frame broke away with him. He was in the dark and had no idea where he was or if anyone even lived here. He raced across the room when he heard Hardnuts still coming up the stairs. He threw open the door that led to a hallway but remained inside behind the door. His heart pounded when he heard Brodigan grunt his way through the broken window, heard the size eleven shoes bang across the wooden floor out the door and down the hallway.

Holy shit! It worked just like in Shell Scott's novel! He climbed out the window and made his way back down the fire escape, his binoculars dangling, his feet scrambling as fast as they could go.

Half way down the last flight of stairs T.B. tripped, and like a circus star, he made a somersault, and at the bottom, he miraculously came to his feet and ended up on a dead run covering the fifty some yards to his Chevy in a little over five seconds.

Once in his car and with the motor engaged, he reasoned the shortest distance to his office was a straight line, and that's the direction he went. Over the curb, through the depot parking lot. A thunderous *karummp* ripped through his ears as the car top scraped under a billboard. Beyond, his bumper caught a wire fence, and as he tore down the street, sparks flew like a boiler spitting fire at a steel mill. Once around the corner, he slowed the vehicle as if nothing had happened. He had no idea the roof had been squared off and now resembled a huge, flat card table, nor was he aware that he was dragging seventy-five feet of wire fence.

Feeling somewhat safe, he did not drive back to his office. What would his hero, Shell Scott do? He certainly wouldn't stop now when he was on such a roll.

T.B. recollected the phone call Ruckles had made to his wife. She was playing bridge tonight and Ruckles was back in his office screwing the big-titted brunette. That meant no one was at Ruckles house tonight! He hoped, at least, that Ruckles wife was playing bridge somewhere else.

"Aha!" he declared. This was the night. Yes, sir! Hardnuts Brodigan didn't scare him, and neither Ruckles nor his wife were a threat tonight.

On the way north, T.B. realized he was dragging a fence behind him. He stopped near the El Zagel golf course and spent a few minutes detaching the wire, then drove on to the Ruckles' home, a nice neighborhood west of the Veterans Hospital. He parked a block away and sat in his car with the lights off for a few minutes, studying the house. The Ruckles' residence was dark, which meant Mrs. Ruckles was still at her bridge game. That was good.

He scurried down the block and up the driveway around to the back of the house. In the shadow of the garage, he stood for several seconds listening for any sounds. Nothing.

Now that his eyes had easily adjusted to the dark, he worked his way to the back of the house, defiantly swung open the screen door and rummaged in his pocket for his picklock. Though he had practiced using one on his office door, his best time was ten minutes and fifteen seconds, an embarrassing time for Houdini, but not too shabby for him.

He examined the opening to the lock, selected two pointed picks, locked them together and jammed them into the lock. For a complete minute he worked the lock, but he could not hear the faint click that indicated he had opened it.

Another minute passed. Five more minutes passed. Sweat was dripping his forehead, his chin itching terribly from the false beard.

Frustration tore at him, and angered, he stood up and just by chance turned the handle. The door was unlocked all this time!

"For crissake," he swore silently as he put the pick away and stepped inside. He listened some more, not in the least thinking that Ruckles might own a dog. Light from an outside lamp lit up the inside allowing him to move through the kitchen into the living room.

The big question was where would Ruckles keep the photos?

He pulled at drawers wherever he could find them, flipped open the doors to a china cabinet and examined the contents with a lit match. He searched through a secretary desk in the hallway, but nothing.

Into the den, more drawers, more matches. Nothing.

He moved into a bedroom and was going through a chest of drawers when his elephant ears picked up a buzzing sound as if an alarm had gone off on a stove. It seemed strange that Ruckles' wife would put something in the oven and leave with the timer on, especially when she wasn't home. He had smelled nothing cooking when he came through the kitchen. The buzzing stopped, and he felt relieved. Then the buzzing started again, and seconds later, a door slammed and voices pierced the night. No lights came on in the house, but someone had entered through the door from the garage. The buzzing was the garage door going up and down!

Oh, Jesus!

He could easily hear the hushed and giggling voices

nearing. Seconds later, someone was coming down the hallway! T.B. panicked and bound into a huge closet and slid a sliding door shut, leaving a narrow crack.

Two figures came into the room, both whispering, still giggling. It was Ruckles and his wife! Was she finished with bridge already? And what was Ruckles doing at home? He was supposed to be with the brunette!

T.B. could see the big man, his bald head silhouetted against the faint light coming from the window. It was Ruckles all right! More giggling, more excited voices. T.B. could just make out the tall, skinny frame of Ruckles' wife. Ruckles' pawing hands were ripping off her clothes, just like with the big titted brunette. An hour ago, he was banging his secretary, and now he was jumping in bed with his wife. For an old coot, the man possessed an insatiable sexual appetite.

They ripped the covers aside, and now their groaning voices penetrated the night. T.B. cracked the door open a bit more. *Oh, Lord*, he thought. *Not again?*

Their whispering continued, the bed bounced as Ruckles' ass pounded up and down. *My God, the guy's gonna have a heart attack if he keeps this up!*

The steady rhythm of the squeaking bed tore at T.B.'s ears, and now the bulge in his pants was growing. On and on Ruckles pumped away until he let out huge groans of pleasure.

A few seconds later, T.B. creamed his pants for the second time that night, and uncontrollably, he let out his own little groan.

"What was that!?" Ruckles' wife had heard T.B.'s faint verbal discharge.

T.B. froze, his groin sticky wet, his feet cramped. He stared through the crack in the door and decided it was time to act. He whipped the door open and sprang from the closet into a squat position with his Saturday night special held firmly in both hands. Though the light was dim in the room, enough of the moon shining in set off a glint on the barrel of his gun, and they saw it.

Delray K. Dvoracek

"He's got a gun!" Ruckles' wife screamed out.

Her hellish scream shook T.B. He was sure he was just as scared as the two naked people, but in the moment of excitement, he hollered out, "What price blackmail! Photos! Where are the photos?!"

She screamed back, "He's got photos! It's blackmail! I'll pay!" she yelled, as she scrambled to pull the covers over her skinny body. Ruckles had bunched himself up under the covers in a fetal position.

"The photos!" T.B. demanded again, his voice as mean as he could make it.

"I'll pay!" she yelled back frantically. "My husband has money! I'll pay! I'll pay!"

What the hell was she talking about? T.B. kept the gun steady, letting his brain sort out her words. *She was willing to pay for photos? What photos?*

"Harold! Do something!"

Harold? Who the hell is Harold? Then it struck him like a bowling pin being shoved up his rear end. He groped along the wall for a light switch.

Mrs. Ruckles screamed when the lights went on and shoved her head under the covers. It was her all right, but *he wasn't Ruckles*! He was as old as Ruckles and as bald as Ruckles, and obviously just as hot as Ruckles, although he had cooled off for the moment.

Holy Jesus!

"W-what do you w-want?" the man named Harold stuttered, his eyes popping over the top of the covers.

"Excuse me," T.B. said quite diplomatically. "I think I may have the wrong house." He switched off the light and said, "Carry on." Then as fast as his feet would carry him, he scrambled out of the room and dashed out the front door. His car was a hundred yards away, but he reached it in nine seconds flat. He started up the Chevy in a cloud of smoke, and after a quick u-turn, he raced all the way back to town.

Once in the safety of his office, he put away his disguise and sat behind his desk exhausted but relieved that the night was over. "Oh, shit," he said to himself. "What do I tell Carrigan?"

The next morning, Carrigan was sitting in front of T.B.'s desk reading over the report. "Uh-huh. So, Ruckles has a girlfriend."

"Yes," said T.B. That was a fact.

"And you think he spent the night with his secretary?"

"Yes. I was parked outside her apartment. Ruckles never left." The fact that he said he was parked outside her apartment was a lie, of course, but Ruckles may have well done exactly that, which wouldn't be a lie, sort of, if it was true.

"According to this," said Carrigan, as he snapped a finger across the report, "Ruckles has millions."

"I have friends at his bank. I checked his records. He has money all over the place. Here in Fargo in three banks, in Dilworth, in D.L., in Northwood. He's got money and he's got a lover. That doesn't sound like a blackmailer to me." Most of that was lies.

"No, it doesn't," agreed Carrigan. He nodded, a satisfied look on his face and very pleased with the research and progress T.B. was making. "By the way, the blackmailer called again last night."

T.B. cocked his head to the side. "What time?"

"At exactly 9:28."

T.B. knew he had been on the fire escape glaring through the binoculars at Ruckles laying his secretary across the desk, and in fact, he had creamed his pants for the first time about 9:30. Like Pearl Harbor, that was a time and date that would go down in infamy.

"That definitely puts Ruckles out of the picture," said T.B. "He was in his office at that time, but he wasn't on the phone." T.B. was amused with his little joke. Ruckles was on something, but he definitely was not on the phone.

"Shit," said T.B. "If I had known the blackmailer called at 9:28, I wouldn't have had to go through last night."

"That couldn't have been so bad, could it? Sitting in your car watching the brunette's apartment. That's what I'm paying you for."

T.B. just realized what he had said. "You're right. Not so bad after all."

"So, who's next on the list?" Carrigan asked. "Brodigan?"

"It couldn't be Brodigan," said T.B. "He was on the fire escape at the same time the blackmailer called."

Carrigan twisted his face. "What fire escape?"

"Ahh..." T.B. stammered. "Th-that is, he was walking by across the street, by, ah, the fire escape at the Colonial Inn. Hardnuts was making his patrol at the same time the blackmailer called."

"Interesting," said Carrigan with another satisfied mile. "You've eliminated four of the suspects in two days. I'm impressed."

"And on only seventy-five a day," T.B. quickly added.

"So, that leaves the Iranian," Carrigan mused.

"Right, the Iranian," said T.B. "I'll check him out tomorrow."

Carrigan started to get up.

"By the way, Carrigan, where was Pam Allison when the blackmailer called?"

"At her office."

"That means she was working late." said T B.

"Once in a while she works late. So do I."

"Interesting," said T.B. "She's always been at her office when the blackmailer calls. Doesn't that strike you rather odd?"

Carrigan raised an eyebrow at what he thought was the obvious. "You wouldn't expect the blackmailer to call her at home, would you? If her husband ever found out, there'd be no way to blackmail her."

"Right, right. Still it's as if the blackmailer knows her

schedule. He knows when and where to call her at all times. Whoever he is, he's sly like a fox." T.B. leaned back in his chair, amused with his choice of words. He was reminded of General Rommel in Africa.

"The Iranian Fox," said T.B. out loud.

"What's that?" asked Carrigan.

T.B. smiled defiantly. "Nothing. Just thinking out loud."

Carrigan could tell his little friend was off in another world, gloating on the word *fox*. Carrigan's mind was unraveling a few things, too. Just a few days ago, they had six suspects, but now they were down to one.

The Iranian was a strong suspect, Carrigan conceded privately. Whoever had called the Princess had an accent. Yes. It was quite possible that the Iranian was the blackmailer. Carrigan got up to leave.

"Ah, Carrigan," said T, B. as he rose to his feet. "I wonder if, ah, that is, the retainer fee…"

"Oh, sure," said Carrigan. He had sixty dollars in his wallet. He counted out fifty. So far, the investigation had cost him a hundred fifty to T.B. and a hundred ten to Leroy. He had already cashed two private checks without telling his wife and hoped the investigation would not go on much longer. She would have a hard time understanding his motive in this situation, but it was simple; the Princess needed help.

"Keep me posted," said Carrigan, as he left the room.

T.B. leaned over the fifty dollars on his desk. With the first hundred, he got his phone back and paid off a portion of his rent. With this fifty and his Saturday night special as a trade in, he was prepared to make a down payment on a new .357 magnum handgun, just like the one Clint Eastwood used as Dirty Harry.

That gun would make noise. Tomorrow he would carry a *big gun* on the job. Too bad Shell Scott didn't carry one. That was about the only thing he did not admire about Shell. A detective should always carry a gun.

Delray K. Dvoracek

Thirteen
After the Fox

At eight-thirty the next morning, T.B. Harvey returned to his office with excitement driving every cell in his body. He sat at his desk and nervously opened the box he had brought with him.

Gloating like a child with a new toy, he very carefully removed the .357 magnum handgun from the box and admired the gunmetal color, the crosshair oak handle, the gold trigger. With fifty dollars and his Saturday night special as a trade in, he was now the proud and security-minded owner of one of the most powerful handguns devised by man.

"Aha!" he said. He knew that a bullet from this weapon would penetrate the block of a car engine as if the metal were made out of balsa! "Aha!"

At exactly eight-thirty that same morning, Carrigan Mulhouse arrived at the Powers Coffee House and waited patiently at his table until Millie brought him coffee. He ordered wheat toast and peanut butter and was feeling very confident. He had been skeptical initially when he hired T.B. as a private detective, but it appeared the little fellow had more on the ball than he had imagined.

Across the room, the Iranian, the one remaining suspect, was sitting in a booth with Harriet, the lady of the night, queen of the streets. Carrigan scanned the coffee crowd thinking perhaps T.B. might be here, but he wasn't

By eight-thirty-five, T.B. had oiled the newly acquired .357 magnum, although it already was sufficiently oiled. There was a certain thrill behind oiling a gun, something only

142

he and Shell Scott would understand. He and *Clint Eastwood,* he corrected himself. The new weapon was sensual in his hands, and heavy. It possessed far too large of a grip for T.B.'s tiny hand, but he didn't care. This was a policeman's gun, a detective's gun, a killer, his means of protection. He no longer felt so naked as when he carried the Saturday night special. And he had no doubt that this weapon would fire every time.

This magnum was indeed a formidable weapon, and it had, in only a few short minutes become an important adjunct to T.B.'s life.

T.B. Harvey. Private Eye. Protectorate of Fargo. And Moorhead.

He carefully loaded the bullets into the cylinder and marveled at the metallic click when it snapped shut. With the hammer thumbed back just a fraction, he spun the cylinder and listened attentively to the ball-bearing hum the mechanism emitted. Then, as a test, he pointed the muzzle of the newly oiled magnum into his wastebasket and shoved the barrel into the pillow above the pile of two-by-fours. Noting the clock on the wall, he fired the weapon into the bottom of the basket. It was exactly 8:42 when the gun exploded, deafening T.B.'s sensitive hearing.

At exactly 8:42, Millie swung past Carrigan's table, wiggled the pot and moved on. Carrigan returned to his surveillance of the coffee house patrons. Hardnuts was near the back doors by the counter and Ruckles was sitting at a table with a couple of his cronies.

Wandering Eddie was visibly not visible this morning, in fact he hadn't been in for a couple days, which was unusual, since Eddie lived in the Powers Hotel.

The Princess came through the front door and scurried over to Carrigan. When she sat down, she fumbled in her purse, and he knew she was troubled.

"More photos?" Carrigan asked in a hushed voice.

143

"No," she answered almost on the verge of tears. Something else." She produced an envelope identical in color and shape to the ones she had received previously. Carrigan slowly, curiously, began to open it.

The recoil of the .357 magnum jolted T.B. so hard that he was sure his elbow had jammed into a locked position. It felt like he had been stung by a wasp with a six-inch stinger. The gun almost tore out of his hand when it fired, and the wastebasket jumped a foot in the air. Now, as T.B. moved the basket to the side, he could see why. The bullet had penetrated the wood blocks, went through the bottom of the basket and left a fine hole in the floor. At least this time the hole was not in his desk top.

"Jesus," said T.B. as he shook his arm. "Powerful little sucker." He set the magnum on his desk while he rummaged through his closet for a new disguise. Today would be devoted to the last suspect, *the Fox*, as he now labeled the Iranian.

"Aha," he said as he pulled the brown wig and bib overalls from the closet. He reached behind the remaining garments and withdrew the wooden configurations from out of their hiding place. No one in the world would recognize him when he put on his disguise today.

Carrigan read the note again.

```
$50,000 for foto negatives.
No police. I am always watching. Maybe now.
```

Carrigan had expected the words to be cut out of a magazine or newspaper and pasted on a sheet of paper. But this note was typewritten on a plain white sheet of bond typewriting paper.

"Fifty thousand dollars!" she whispered excitedly.

Carrigan shook his head as he read the last line. "No police. I am always watching. Maybe now."

The Guys from Fargo

Carrigan looked up, glimpsed the Iranian in the booth. The dark skinned man was looking back at Carrigan, then abruptly changed his gaze back to Harriet. Both were eating eggs and toast. Carrigan reread the note again, studied carefully every word. Then he caught the glaring error. Funny he had not noticed it before. The word photo was spelled *foto*, an uncommon spelling in the United States, but quite common in foreign countries all over Europe. Even in the Arabic countries, like Egypt, Syria, Iraq, and also in…

"Iran!" Carrigan blurted out. He hunched his shoulders realizing he had said the word overly loud.

"What?" the Princess asked.

"Look at the word foto," he pointed out. He went on to clarify the significance of the word, the abnormal spelling. He also told her the Iranian was sitting behind her and cautioned her not to look in his direction.

Out of the corner of his eye, Carrigan could see that the Iranian's gaze was set on his table again. Carrigan scanned the room searching for T.B. Harvey. He should have been here by now.

Suddenly, a blaring siren rang from outside as a fire truck zoomed by on the street. Those on the sidewalk were all peering south on Broadway. Hardnuts Brodigan rammed his way out of the Powers and ran off in the direction of the fire truck. Among the crowd, Carrigan spotted Pavlov's head of curly black hair towering over most of the people. Moments later, he came in the coffee shop.

"Where's the fire?" asked Carrigan.

"Don't know," said Pavlov. "The truck stopped a couple blocks down in front of Strauss Clothing. I couldn't see any smoke."

Harvey's office was in the back of the store on the upper floor. Carrigan hoped nothing had happened to him.

T.B. already had the wig in place and darkened his eyebrows. He had donned a tweed cap, a heavy woolen shirt and pulled on bib overalls. The overalls were normally far too long for T.B.'s short legs, but not today. He had strapped on short, wooden stilts with fake feet and shoes attached, and now when he stood, he was five-foot ten, eight inches taller than his normal height.

T.B. left his office and carefully thumped his way along the corridor on the long, stiff legs, so abnormally long compared to the length of his short arms. He had stuffed the .357 magnum into the Saturday night special shoulder holster, but only the barrel snugged in leaving the cylinder and handle protruding, bulging under his coat. In order to keep the bulky weapon from slipping from side to side as he walked, he forced an arm tightly against it. With each step, he gave the appearance as if his arm was malformed, and of course, with the stiff-legged walk, one would easily believe he was a cripple.

However T.B. did not at all think about the ramifications of his disguise. As far as he was concerned, he was now five-foot ten inches tall.

In this way, T.B. made his way extra carefully down the staircase to the second floor elevator, and once he reached the lobby, he was surprised at the activity. At the corner on Broadway, a throng of people had gathered on the street, all looking through the show window. Firemen were coming in, fighting the customers, and near the entrance to the clothing store, the manager was pumping his arms up and down, aiming his comments at the fire chief. Patrolman Brodigan was standing next to the two as more firemen charged past. It was strange, T.B. was thinking, that he could not smell any smoke.

"I don't know," the little wiry manager of the store standing in his water soaked suit was explaining to the fire chief and Brodigan. "I heard this muffled explosion, and when I looked up, the sprinkler in my office had gone off. Before I knew it, all of the sprinklers in the store went off! Look at this mess! I'm ruined!"

T.B. gaped through the glass windows to the interior of the men's clothing store. Every sprinkler was on spraying every square inch of the floor space.

"When did this happen?" the fire chief asked.

"At exactly eight-forty. I checked my watch."

T.B. hurriedly walked off in gigantic steps, knowing the manager's time was wrong, but unwilling to correct him. The sprinkler had gone off at exactly eight-forty-two, the moment T.B. had fired his magnum for the first time.

"Oh, Lord," said T.B. as he turned the corner and headed his crippled looking body up Broadway toward the Powers. "Oh, Lord."

Chairs shuffled as Radio Sko sat down and elbowed his way in. "Move over and let a man in here. "Coffee," he said to Pavlov. "I need some brew."

"Ya look nervous," Pavlov chided him. "What didja do, set a fahr or somethin'?"

"Ain't no fire," said Sko. "But there sure is a hell of a lot of water. The boys at Strauss are probably having a hemorrhage about now."

"No fahr?" asked Pavlov. "Shee-it. Gotta be a fahr. Ah seed a coup'la trucks."

"I don't know," said Sko. "But there ain't no fire." He looked at Pam. "How are you doing, Princess?"

Pam was wearing a flat face, but Carrigan's eyes suddenly bugged out when he noticed the person fighting his way through the doorway. He recognized the short arms, saw the abnormally long legs and knew T.B. had made his appearance. *Good God, his disguise is atrocious!*

Pavlov noticed him, too. "Hey, who's the guy with the fudsicle stuck up his ass?"

Incredible! thought Carrigan as he watched T.B. try to sit on a stool at the counter. The distance from the bottom of his shoes to his knees was so long that his legs would not fit underneath. He had mounted the stool and leaned his elbows on the counter, but his feet stuck out backwards behind the stool, and the soles of his shoes were now facing Carrigan. Carrigan shook his head in awe and put on a dumb face. The little detective was reminiscent of something out of a Madd Magazine.

And then the table got down to some serious conversation.

"Look at the long legs on that little shit at the counter."

"I tell you what, if you won't talk radio, I won't talk politics."

"How come so glum, Princess?"

"Make room. Here comes the Baron."

"Anybody want breakfast this morning?"

"No fahr. Jes' waddah."

"Hi, Johann."

"Uhhh."

"You still painting those pictures for that guy in Williston?"

"Watch your ash, Johann."

"Watch whose ass?"

"Haw, haw, haw!"

"We're all here except Snuffy."

"He's got such short arms, but look at his legs. Poor guy."

"Paint it. Paint it purple. You betchum, Red Ryder."

"So, how's the decorating business?"

"I'll bet you don't even know where Somalia is."

"How about a small package of radio spots?"

"Who, Andropov? He's been dead for some time. Chernenko's running things now."

"That funny guy with the long legs is headed for the door."

"Oh, jeez, he fell!"

"Looks like his foot is caught in the door."

"Damn! I think his foot tore off!"

"What do you mean, tore off?"

"Check that out Pavlov."

"Must be a transient."

"Well, he might run again. Who else have the Republicans got?"

"Dean Wimpleton? Is he bald? I think I know him."

"That little sucker was wearing stilts."

"Ain't that weird?"

"No, Harriet left shortly before that guy with the stilts."

"I wonder what Snuffy is up to this morning."

PART IV

Fourteen
Christians and Gentlemen

From head on, the 38 Chevy pickup coming down the dirt road resembled a huge bug. The headlights on the fenders were like two big eyes, and the spring-steel bumper beneath them gave the appearance of a wide smile. The Chevy moved at a nice pace, its engine quiet, humming like the wings of a bumblebee in flight.

And if anyone were within a mile, they would hear Snuffy singing:

I'm called Junkman Jamison and I come from DL.
I told the big city to go plumb to hell.
I'm now a junk collector at the corner of Turners.
I got bed pans and ball bearings and Ben Franklin burners...
Oh yeah...
I'm now a junk collector at the corner of Turners.
I got canisters, cotton and cardigan sweaters
Oh yeah...
Benches and backrests and sacks of potaters...
Oh, yeah...

"Pretty cute, even if I say so myself." Snuffy smiled, happy with his made-up words and melody as he maintained a steady speed over the rolling Minnesota hills. "Yes sir, I love this country."

The countryside reflected the beauty of the day—

everything green. Every hump and rise in the road brought a spectacular view of rich, fertile fields. Even rocks would grow on this western edge of the state, he mused. All a farmer required was just a little bit of rain at the right time. The farmhouses and buildings were nicely painted. Holsteins dotted the open pastures. Wheat, oats and sunflower reached skyward mile after mile.

Everywhere, groves of birch and aspen shimmered in the breeze. Occasionally a grove of pines came into view, but the big pine tree forests began a little more to the east.

Today was a typical day for Snuffy Jamison. The gravel road he started on turned into a dirt road, which he pursued, knowing it would lead somewhere where he'd never been before. A different road meant different soil, different groves of trees, different ravines and different junk piles.

It was almost instinct now. He suddenly caught a glint of the sun bouncing off of a tin can or old glass bottle. He slowed the truck, shifted down and turned onto a cow path along a fencerow. A hundred yards in, he pulled the truck to a stop and swung a door open. As he walked toward the pile of trash and discarded debris, he started rolling a cigarette. Trash piles were good. Some items had been chucked away years ago, some not so long ago.

The best place to start was on the edges of the pile farthest from the present dumping spot. His methodology was simple; dig down a layer or so and let a keen eye search the stuff underneath. This pile of junk on which he now stood, was very typical. He selected a spot, dug down, examined a few bottles and tossed them aside. He found a piece of metal angle iron and started probing with it, working downward. Then he pried the bar to the side revealing more stuff.

For ten minutes he threw cans and bottles aside, discarded bent up containers, sheet metal and wire. "Well, hello," he mused, as he picked up an oilcan and read the inscription on the side. "Buko Oiler." He looked at the bottom of the soft

151

metal container and read the date—1921. It was complete with handle and squirter, and though the drum was dented, it could be straightened. This was a very good find, a fifty to seventy-five dollar find, and he had hardly begun.

He probed for several minutes more, selected a few items but rejected most. Then came the nicer find. He knew at once it was a treasure as he held it for up for inspection.

It was a coin safe about half the size of a cigar box. On top stood a momma eagle, with two smaller eaglets to the side. Snuffy knew how it worked. When one placed a coin in either of the beaks of the small eaglets, the momma eagle bent over, grabbed the coin and deposited it to an interior chamber, which later could be opened from the back with a key. It dated back probably to the early 1800's. This one was not too severely corroded, and it appeared all the parts were present. Once cleaned up, and if the inside mechanism functioned, it would easily bring four or five hundred dollars to the right buyer.

The sun was warm and beating down enough to cause him to sweat as he sat on the rubble and rolled another cigarette. Not bad, he thought, as he lit up. After several puffs and an investigative glance about him, he went back to probing for more stuff.

And softly, almost silently he sang:

I'm called Junkman Jamison and I come from DL
I told the big city to go plumb to hell...

After Sko Skofield left the Powers, he drove directly to the Appliance Center on NP Avenue and entered the store without his radio rate schedule or any related radio information. Nobody was in the store as he walked down a cluttered aisle. Like normal, he was wearing his tan suit, tailored nicely to fit his big frame, and his shoes were shined beyond Army standards. He entered the back room where Frank Newsom, owner and proprietor of the store, had his office. Frank was on the phone and motioned for Sko to take a chair. After a patient minute of waiting, Sko lit up a cigarette and waited some more, during which time Frank's main comment was several "Uh-huhs," until he finally hung up.

"Hi, Sko," the cigar-smoking-blubber-lipped figure behind the desk greeted. Frank rarely smiled. His cigar was already half smoked, and the end of it clamped in his teeth was wet and slimy from spit.

"I've got it," said Sko as he pulled four hundreds and a fifty from his wallet.

"Well, that's what I like." Frank's fat fingers scooped up the bills and stuffed them into his shirt pocket. "Yes, sir, I like a man who pays his debts."

"I told you I was good for it."

"Yeah," Frank spit out. "Course, you were supposed to pay a week ago."

"Times are tough," answered Sko. He should have never joined the night game with Frank and his gambling buddies. If Sko's wife ever learned of this, she would tear him apart, and it would do no good to tell her he had been cheated, and he knew he had been.

He had spent the better part of an evening winning and was ahead by almost fifteen hundred dollars when it dropped on him. First Frank took a giant pot, then Lenny Buckmeier, Frank's buddy, then the University man, an unfamiliar face known as Arnie Wimpleton won big. The cards were marked, Sko firmly believed, but he had not had a chance to examine them.

In his younger years, he had wasted many hours at cards, and when he married Emily, he promised to give up the habit. For the most part, he had. But now and then, the urge to gamble ran through his veins. Most of the time he came out all right, but he regretted the day that he sat at a table with Frank, Bucky and the University professor. It was a set up and he had no one to blame but himself.

When Sko got up, Frank Newsom labored his grossly obese figure out of his chair. "Thanks, Sko. It's always nice to play a gentleman's game. We'll let you know when we have another if you're interested."

"I might be," said Sko as he left the office. He walked back through the messy showroom of appliances. *A gentleman's game, eh?* he thought to himself as he left the store. *He* was the only gentleman in the last game.

Back in his car, Sko checked the address of Lenny Buckmeier, or Bucky, the next man he owed money to. Not as much, but enough to hurt.

As he drove off, he repeated again, "A gentleman's game. Someday I'll get even with you gentlemen son-of-a-bitches."

It was late afternoon when Snuffy Jamison finished unloading his pickup. It had been a good day. He placed the Buko Oiler, eaglet coin box and several other items in his garage and locked it. Tomorrow he would sort it out and check his catalogues for values.

He entered the back door of his small cottage on the corner of Turner Street, less than a block from the Holiday Inn. Tucked in among towering oaks, his cottage bordered the lake edge of Big DL, the name the locals gave Big Detroit Lake. Narrow blacktopped pathways, barely wide enough to cover the spread of a car's wheels, angled around his cottage and up a hill to other cabins.

Snuffy's was one of the few two-story homes. He was a good carpenter and had added the top half by himself during one summer. The cottage was brown, trimmed with white and resembled a Chalet of sorts commonly found in the Bavarian Alps. It was, however, far from authentic. But at a glance, the cottage was more than quaint, and, for Snuffy Jamison, quite comfortable. The lower level contained a bedroom, a kitchen and a living room filled with too much furniture. A small wood burning stove was the only source of heat. A fan, hanging by a piece of twine in a doorway, had its blades pointed into a hallway that lead to the other rooms, a means of moving the heat around in the winter.

The second floor was reached by means of a steep staircase that led to the two bedrooms and a bath on the second floor. All of the walls in his bedrooms were painted dark blue, his kitchen dark green. Every piece of trim in the house was beige as were the cupboards, the bookshelf in his bedroom, the bookshelves in the living room and all built-in cabinets.

This was more than a home for Snuffy. It was a palace. What he lacked at the cottage, he made up for with a membership at the Holiday Inn. That gave him privileges to the outdoor pool, a sauna, a Jacuzzi bath and the billiard room. The membership also gave him access to an occasional cache of single ladies—summertime vacationers.

But Snuffy was not exactly a ladies' man, and was, in fact, more of a hermit by self-proclamation, but he was not very good at being a hermit, since the Holiday Inn was stuffed to capacity at least six months out of the year. Cars, pickups and campers jammed the lot near the outdoor pool, and hundreds of vacationers strolled the park, which lay just beyond the hotel. The only saving grace from this throng of people was the fact that his cottage was situated a half block off the beach. The only traffic that passed directly by his cottage was by those people who owned cabins further up.

The coffee pot was on and emitting a fine aroma now. Snuffy utilized a Mr. Coffee Maker and surmised if it was good enough for Joe DiMaggio, it was good enough for him.

He had just poured himself a cup when a car pulled up outside. He recognized the Lincoln Continental as that of Mr. Coddington, a man, who only a month ago had accidentally stumbled across Snuffy Jamison's hideaway, and, who ever since had made it a habit to drop in weekly.

Snuffy came through the back door just as Mr.

Coddington, dressed smartly in a black suit and tie, emerged from the flashy automobile. It seemed Mr. Coddington always arrived late every Thursday. Today was no exception.

"Just thought I'd see if you've picked up anything recently," Mr. Coddington inquired. He was about fifty, Snuffy guessed. A kind fellow, short, with a full head of gray hair and a thin gray mustache. He seemed to be every bit a gentleman as he extended a warm and friendly handshake.

Like before on at least four occasions, Snuffy led Mr. Coddington to his collection of furniture in the garage and waited patiently while the antique collector examined the most recent pieces Snuffy had acquired.

"Someday I'll clean up the place, Mr. Coddington," Snuffy said apologetically.

"No need to just for me," he answered politely.

His eyes expertly scanned the room. "That's an interesting piece," he said pointing to a table in the corner. "That wasn't here last week."

"No," said Snuffy. "Just picked it up a few days ago."

Mr. Coddington carefully made his way through a narrow passageway, set a floor lamp aside and knelt down to examine the table.

"It looks Victorian," Mr. Coddington commented, "but obviously a copy." He studied the underside, ran his fingers across the trim, and with a fingernail, he scratched away some paint.

"It seems solid," he said as he stood up. "Have you priced it?"

Snuffy had picked it up in a barn with a lot of other furniture pieces. The entire lot had cost him eighty dollars, but he had no idea what the value of the table was. "Yes," he finally said, punting. "A hundred fifty."

Mr. Coddington nodded his head, then pulled a small leather-bound book from his inside pocket. The pages were not visible to Snuffy, but after a moment Mr. Coddington nodded again. "I could offer a hundred, but I'm afraid that's all."

"Fine," said Snuffy. "You've been a good customer."

Mr. Coddington moved to the side and let Snuffy clear other items away to free the table from the cluttered corner. As Snuffy pulled the table out, he accidentally struck it against another piece of furniture and laid a small gash in the leg. Snuffy saw the cringe on Coddington's face, a most painful look of despair.

Snuffy felt badly, and then, very carefully, he carried the table to the door and set it on the floor. Mr. Coddington produced his wallet and took out two fifties.

"I'll write up a slip for you, Mr. Coddington," Snuffy said as he headed for his desk.

"That won't be necessary," he answered with a warm smile. In the past Mr. Coddington had always paid in cash, and not once had he demanded a receipt.

Mr. Coddington opened the back door to his Lincoln and eyed Snuffy closely as he set the table on the back seat.

"Thank you, Mr. Jamison," he said with a polite nod. He was abruptly behind the wheel, turned the Lincoln around and headed out the driveway.

Snuffy returned to the antique shop, sat behind his desk and fingered the cash he had just received from Mr. Coddington. It was almost all profit for him. A good purchase, a good sale. Mr. Coddington was turning out to be a very good customer, a very likable man, so kind, so polite, so Christian-like.

Fifteen
To Outfox the Fox

T.B. Harvey swore as he walked stiff-legged on one stilt through the glass doors into his building. Although firemen were still walking in and out of the entrance, the sprinklers were off, and the manager was pacing like a nervous ex-millionaire, while another man, an insurance investigator, T.B. guessed, was questioning him. The elevator was still working, so he rode to the second floor, his mind on Harriet the whore and the Iranian Fox. They had given him the slip somewhere near Elm Tree Square. He was sure he could have kept up if he hadn't lost one of his stilts in the doorway at the Powers.

He cursed and kicked the remaining wooden stilt into the elevator door just as it opened. He stepped out and stomped up the staircase to the next floor. By the time he reached his office, he was totally dejected. Shell Scott never would have lost two people in plain daylight.

He changed out of his bib overalls and unstrapped the one stilt and stashed everything in the closet. Still angry with himself and bemoaning his bad tailing job, he stood at the one window in his office and stared across the street. T.B. cringed when one of the fire trucks passed by on the street below. He hoped no one would find out that he probably caused the sprinklers to go off when he fired his weapon through the floor.

Of course, he shouldn't be blamed; he had no idea the weapon would be that powerful. As his eyes followed the fire truck along the street, he stared in disbelief. Almost directly below him, the Iranian Fox had just come out of the building across the alley! T.B. knew there were apartments in the adjoining structure. "Aha!" Without a doubt, Harriet the whore was domiciled in one of the apartments.

His excitement soared as he watched the Iranian cross the street. His curiosity soared again when he saw Hardnuts Brodigan strut up to the same doorway from which the Iranian had just left. The policeman appeared to make a security check in both directions and then entered the building.

T.B. eyeballed the Iranian again as the guy hurried up 1st Avenue past the sport shop.

With no time to don a disguise, T.B. threw on his jacket, slammed the office door and ran down the corridor as fast as his feet would carry him, his arm jammed against his chest to prevent the giant magnum from falling out of the holster. He skipped the elevator and ran down the stairs past two firemen. He pushed his way out the set of double doors onto the street, but the Iranian Fox had outfoxed him.

"Shit," he said to himself. "Shit," he said to a fireman standing by his truck. "Shit," he said to an old lady passing by.

And then luck rolled with him for the second time this morning. There at the corner waiting for the red light to change was the Iranian Fox sitting in his banged up Pinto.

"Aha!" said T.B. as he ran for his Chevy. He set the vehicle in motion and barely made the yellow light, but he was now only a half block behind the Pinto.

"Aha," he barked. He was feeling like Shell Scott again.

The pursuit took T.B. to Owens Hall, the administrative building of Moorhead State College, where he managed to follow the Fox to the second floor without detection.

T.B. found a spot behind a pillar but within view of the Fox, who sat in an office only a few feet away. T.B. had his note pad out and noted the time the Fox arrived, jotted down a few more notes concerning his present location. It was strange. Why was the Iranian sitting in the office of student loans?

"Aha!" It suddenly made good sense. The Fox was the one

remaining suspect, and if money were the motive, then this foreigner was now a *prime suspect* since he was obviously seeking a loan to support his education. T.B.'s logic was working. The Fox needed money, so naturally he would turn to blackmail. *That's what foreigners do.*

He was still leaning up against the support pillar when the Fox exited the student loan office and descended the staircase to the main floor. T.B. saw him get into a line of five people in front of the administrative affairs window. He would be there for several minutes. On with the investigation!

T.B. strode confidently into the Student Affairs office, the same place the Fox had entered. The same lady that had attended him was working on some reports. When he closed the door behind him, the lady, surprised, looked up over a set of Pince-nez glasses. She was skinny with wrinkles on her face that would put a prune to shame.

"Yes?" she chirped as she dropped the frames from her face. They hung on a chain and were obviously bifocals since they were only half-lenses.

T.B. hadn't given the remote thought to what he was going to say. "Ah, that Iranian student who was just in here."

"Yes?" she chirped again. Her eyelids drooped like a snob, and now a scowl on her pruney lips slowly slipped into place

"I'm here to… verify his name."

"Verify his name?" she asked, not comprehending.

"That is, I'm the official verifier from American State Bank. I noticed he was applying for a student loan, and we bank verifiers occasionally need to check up on those, ah, foreign students who have checking accounts with us, and well, in this case…"

"American State Bank, you say?"

"Yes," said T.B. enthusiastically. He felt the magnum slipping out from its holster and shoved an arm against it. The secretary opened a folder on her desk as she suspiciously eyed T.B.

"Well, you see," T.B. went on, "this individual has applied for a bank loan and we're following up on his credit."

"I've never known Hahmeed to have any credit," she said snobbily.

"Hahmeed?"

"Yes, Hahmeed Bagdiagalliy."

"Oh, yes. Bag..."

"Bag-dee-a-gal-liy," she pronounced ever so clearly in a monotone.

T.B. pulled out a brochure from his pocket that had been there for months and studied it as if it were some important piece of documentation. "Ah, yes, Bag-a-lilly, he said, mispronouncing the name. The gesture seemed to appease her.

"Well," she said, still using her artistic and snobbish tone. "Hahmeed stated he has no more than $350.00 in his checking account, if that's what you're interested in."

"Exactly," said T B. glancing at the brochure again. When she pulled out a bank statement and placed it in front of her, he leaned over to look at it, and when he did so, the magnum fell from the holster and thudded on her desk.

Her eyes bugged out at the gun, its barrel pointed directly at her. T.B. nervously picked up the gun and shoved it back in place. "You're from the bank?!" she questioned as a mild fear swept over her wrinkled face.

"Ah, no, not exactly." T.B.'s mind raced. "I'm actually with the CIA. He retrieved his billfold and flashed his Private Eye license hardly long enough for the prune lady to catch a glimpse.

"You see," T.B. continued, "we have reason to believe this Hahmeed Bag-a-lilly may be connected with SAVAK, and..."

"SAVAK?" she retorted as if she knew the organization for the Iranian equivalent of the CIA.

"Yes, I'm here on an assignment from Washington, direct orders, from the President."

"You know President Reagan?"

"Shhh," cautioned T.B. as he thrust a finger to his nose. "No one at the college knows I'm here, but I've been assured you would assist in this matter and not breathe a word. It's in your file that you would cooperate."

"Washington has a file on me?"

T.B. felt his contrived conversation getting away from him.

"Right. Well, thank you Miss Pruneface," he said as turned to leave. When he reached for the door handle, the magnum again fell from its place and dropped to the floor.

As T.B. walked out of the office, he had the gun in his hand and was in the process of jamming it back in place. Two students and the Vice President of Academic Affairs were passing by, none of whom he knew, and all stared on as he fumbled with the weapon.

When he reached the staircase, he knew the three were still watching him. He whirled quickly and flashed his Private Eye license. "CIA," he said.

He walked directly down the staircase to the main floor and did not even glance at the academic affairs window where Hahmeed Bagdiagalliy was now second in line. T.B. hurried out of the administrative building and headed for his car.

Five minutes later he found a phone booth and called Carrigan, and a few minutes after that, he parked in the lot outside of Lommen Hall on the other side of the campus. Confidently, he strode into the building and made his way down the wide corridor filled with students going to class.

At the end of the hall, he discovered the big man with the black hair and a big stomach standing on a chair placing a new geography sign back in place.

"Reginald Richthoffen, I presume?" T.B. said looking up at the man. From his perspective, Reggie looked like Goliath.

"T.B. Harvey, I presume," answered Reggie.

"At your service."

Reggie came down from the chair and pulled it into his

office next to his cluttered desk. "Have a chair."

When T.B. sat, his feet dangled a couple inches off the floor. He produced a business card along with his Private Eye license and then moved his coat aside to show Reggie his gun, as if that were proof he was a detective. Reggie smiled. Carrigan had described the little man before him perfectly

T.B. initiated the conversation. "I presume Mr. Mulhouse, my client, called you on my behalf?"

"Hardly ten minutes ago," said Reggie.

T.B. produced a photo of the Iranian Fox. "Do you know this man?"

"Hahmeed?" Everybody on campus knows him."

"Have you ever had the pleasure of his presence in your class?"

"Only once," said Reggie. "Before I threw him out. Haw, haw, haw!" A couple sheets of paper on his desk wavered with the belly laugh.

T.B. was amused. "I require some information on this Hahmeed Bag-a-lilly, and my client, Mr. Mulhouse, stated you might be able to help me."

"What's this all about? Is Carrigan in trouble?"

"No, nothing like that. A personal favor, you might say. I was instructed not to divulge any of the particulars in this case."

Reggie leaned back in his chair and twisted his lip. "What can I do for you?"

"I require this piece of information." T.B. handed over a sheet of paper with some notes on it.

Reggie read the peculiar informational request.

"Can you get it?" T.B. asked.

Reggie reached for the phone and dialed a couple digits. "This is Mr. Richthoffen in Geography. Can you tell me what room Hahmeed Bagdiagalliy is located in?" He spelled the last name and waited patiently. "And who's his roommate?" He waited another few patient seconds and then said, "Thank you," and hung up.

"You're in luck. His roommate is Carter Houseman."

"And what does this Carter Houseman have to do with luck?"

"Carter is taking a class from me right now, and he's doing an excellent job of failing, so he might be willing to earn a D this quarter."

"That sounds like blackmail," T.B. commented.

"Sounds like a good way to get your information, too, eh? Haw, haw, haw!" This time, the two sheets on his desk flipped to the floor.

"How soon may I expect the information?"

"Before the day is out."

"Very good," said T.B. "Mr. Mulhouse said you would be most accommodating."

"No problem, but I am curious what this is all about."

"That," said T.B. as the magnum slid out from under his coat and dropped to the floor, "you'll have to take up with Mr. Mulhouse." T.B. replaced the magnum, thanked Reggie and walked out of the office.

Sixteen
Tally-ho the Fox

For two hours, T.B. Harvey had been sitting in the bar across the street from Harriet the whore's apartment building. He stationed himself at a window from where he could observe the street both ways, and since he was out of fresh disguises, he was once again dressed as an old-woman.

He was also on his sixth tap beer, his eyes already becoming bleary. A huge pillow stuffed underneath the striped dress gave him his fat stature, but he was terribly hot. Sweat had already worked its way from under an itching wig and was dripping down over his rouged face and painted lips.

"Buy ya' a drink, shweetheart?" T.B. took his eyes away from the street and looked into the face of a drunk trying his utmost to remain upright. A foul stench of liquor and barf loomed off of him like hot cow piss steaming up from a frozen Dakota meadow.

The heavy consummation of beer was feeding T.B.'s courage. "Shove off, Mac," he told the drunk as he returned his gaze back to the street. Any time now he expected Hahmeed Bagdiagalliy and Harriet to come stomping down the sidewalk, and he wanted to be ready for them.

"Frisky little broad, ain'tcha," said the red-eyed drunk as he slid into a chair and edged an elbow against T.B. He tried to wink but couldn't get his eyelid closed.

"You got balls, Mac?" T.B. challenged.

"Damn right I got balls," the man snapped, loud enough to turn a few heads in the bar.

"So do I, so push off," T.B. snarled.

The barf smelling man seemed taken aback for a moment as he looked over T.B.'s pot belly and huge breasts. "Well, goddamn," he said. "A lady with balls? Holy shit! Ain't that somethin'."

T.B. shoved his purse to the center of the table. "I got balls and I carry a big gun, too."

"Shit, you ain't got no gun, lady," the drunk responded as he maneuvered to throw an arm around him. T.B. slapped the man's arm aside and opened his purse enough to expose the magnum.

"B'Jesus!" the drunk exclaimed. "You do gots a big gun!"

"I sure do," said T.B. bravely. "And if you don't shove off, I'm going to stick this big gun up your big ass and splatter your big gut all over that big mirror behind the bar."

The man seemed to suddenly sober up. "No offense, ma'am," he said, as he rose from the table. "I ain't never minded a lady with big balls, but I do mind a lady what got a big gun." He staggered his way back to the bar where he stuck a foot up on a rail and ordered a drink.

T.B. cast his gaze back to the street again. Hahmeed and Harriet were nowhere in sight. He reflected on the pair. Harriet, as well as Hahmeed, had appeared in several of the photos that Carrigan had showed him. Were the two in this together? The more T.B. thought about it, the more it seemed plausible. A conspiracy. Harriet wasn't a ravishing beauty, so she probably didn't make a very good living at her profession, and Hahmeed was applying for a student loan, so he needed bucks.

T.B. Harvey checked his watch. It was already late afternoon.

What if the two didn't show up? T.B. was now thinking. After six beers, his mind was flowing freely, and he was feeling brave and mean and tough. He had handled the puke-faced drunk at the bar just like Shell Scott would have done, and that made him feel good.

T.B. dropped a quarter tip on the table and raised his half-drunk frame up. Shell Scott wouldn't spend an entire afternoon sitting in a bar waiting for the culprits. Shell would get the jump on them.

T.B., now on his feet, wheezed a couple large breaths trying to steady himself, then grabbed his purse and went out the door. He ambled across the street and stepped into the entryway of Harriet's apartment building, but after a quick examination of the names on the mailboxes, he did not find one labeled *Harriet*, but he did find one box labeled as *H. Ambrose*, Room 207.

He pushed his way into a dark hallway, adjusted the purse strap over his shoulder and quietly labored his way up the stairs. Several doors lined the corridor, dimly lit by a lone bulb at the end of the hallway. Room 207 was the third door down. A sign was stapled next to the door that said *No Soliciting*. T.B. found that amusing, since soliciting was Harriet's business.

The hallway stunk, but T.B. couldn't exactly place the foul smell. The aroma was something between a chicken coop on a hundred-degree day and a four-pound dump of fresh bear shit.

His head was still spinning from the six beers he drank. Two was his limit, but the excessive amount was what bolstered his courage. He pressed an ear against the door to room 207 and listened for a moment. Obviously no one was inside, nor could he hear any other noise coming from anywhere in the building.

He scratched around in his purse and found the picks, selected two points after examining the lock, jammed the picks in and worked the handle.

To his utter surprise, the door popped open. This was a legitimate break-in, not at all like at Ruckles' house. He slipped inside to a one-room apartment with a bathroom off to the right and an open closet door to the left. A mussed up bed, a dresser, a small night table and a bathroom. This would be an easy search.

He started with the dresser, ran through all the drawers looking for photos of Pam Allison. He checked the nightstand. Nothing. Rummaging under the mattress left a pungent smell in his nose. The closet contained Harriet's clothes, hats, several pairs of shoes and a box with a variety of personal items including a dildo, a leather strap and a chain. "Tools for the trade," he whispered to himself as he closed the closet door.

The only place left to search was the bathroom. He no sooner entered when he heard voices from outside the room. "Oh, Lord!" he said to himself. "Not again!" He closed the bathroom door to a crack's width so he could view the interior of the bedroom.

The door to the outer corridor opened and shut and there stood Hahmeed and Harriet, giggling and chatting. T.B. wasn't even listening to the conversation. Sweat was pouring down his face, and he was experiencing the bitter taste of rouge on his lips. Whatever courage he had managed to muster a little earlier seemed to have folded up into a huge ball pressing somewhere near his bladder.

"...and make yourself at home," Harriet was saying to Hahmeed as he sat on the bed and began unbuttoning his shirt.

Oh, shit! Now what?

"I'll just slip into something comfortable," Harriet said as she undid a strap and let her dress slip to the floor. "I'm comfortable," she said to Hahmeed with a snicker. The Iranian Fox was now unzipping his pants.

When Harriet made a few steps toward the bathroom door, T.B. panicked. The only thing he could think of was to sit on the toilet. He jerked up his dress and plopped himself down.

When she entered, mascara was streaming down his face. She let out a yell that even Tarzan would have appreciated. Hahmeed came off the bed clad only in his tee shirt and shorts, and when he charged into the bathroom, T.B. peed right through his pants.

168

"What you are here doing?" Hahmeed barked in his Iranian accent.

"Ah, taking a leak," T.B. squeaked out, making every effort to mimic a woman's voice.

"Throw her out!" Harriet shouted. "Nobody takes a leak in my toilet without paying. Get her out of here!"

Before T.B. knew what was happening, Hahmeed grabbed him by the arm and jerked him off the stool. When T.B.'s feet hit the floor, he stumbled and went down. Off flew the wig leaving the top of his head shining brilliantly.

"What is the hell this?" Hahmeed cried out in broken English. "She is man!" Then the shouting and screaming began. T.B. didn't know who was hollering or who was swinging a fist, but he had just become a punching bag. The blows came one after another, to his head, to his gut, to his back. His feet flopped out from underneath him, and now Hahmeed was kicking the hell out of him, and he still had his shoes on! *Oh, my face, my back, the pain! Oh my God!*

"Stop, Stop!" T.B. hollered, frantically trying to think what Shell Scott would do under the circumstances.

"Damn person!" he heard Hahmeed yell. A foot caught T.B. in the butt and stars shot through him when his head bounced off of the radiator. Another blow caught him in the side of the face. *Oh, hurt! Oh, pain!* T.B. scrambled for his purse to get at his gun. If he didn't react somehow, Hahmeed was going to beat him to death.

"Decadent!" shouted Hahmeed using a high-level English vocabulary word. "Fiend, scumbag, shit-person!" With each common noun came a hellish blow to the body or head.

T.B. got to his feet with a burst of energy and swung the purse at Hahmeed, but the Iranian ducked and the purse thumped against the wall. He swung the purse again, and this time the mirror above the sink cracked from the weight of the magnum inside.

Hahmeed wrestled the purse away and swung it around

169

like a bolo. The purse caught T.B. in the back of the head and knocked him into the tub. Again the purse came at him and drilled him in the head sending stars everywhere. Somehow the faucet turned on and now water was pouring down over his face, the only refreshing test of the battle.

"Time out! Time out!' T.B. hollered. The phrase held Hahmeed off just long enough for T.B. to grab the Iranian Fox and jerk him off balance. He stumbled over the side of the tub and cracked his head against the faucet, stunning him long enough to give T.B. a slight reprieve.

He had just enough time to scramble out of the tub, dragging the purse behind him, and as he barreled through the bathroom door, Harriet swung a chain at him, *one of her tools of the trade.* The links wrapped around T.B.'s throat like a python squeezing the guts out of a wild pig.

He gagged and choked his way to the corridor, all the while lambasted by Harriet's verbal abuses. Eventually, he fought his way down the staircase, through the door onto the street, gasping for breath and pulling at the chain wound around his neck.

As he hobbled along the street toward his office, blood was running down his forehead and passersby stared on. Hardnuts Brodigan was coming from the opposite direction and looked on incredulously at his rouge running face, his disheveled and beaten up body.

"What happened?" he asked?"

An answer came to T.B. like a dart from heaven. "In Room 207! There's a man raping a woman!"

"What?" Hardnuts knew right away it was Harriet's room. He was off like a shot, but T.B., unable to refuse the pleasure he would gain if he followed the policeman, ran back to the apartment building. He reached the bottom of the staircase just as Hardnuts reached the second floor. In spite of the pain in his back, his swollen eye and battered head, T.B. gloated when he heard the merciless screams coming from Hahmeed

Bagdiagalliy. From a floor away, T.B. heard the nightstick crunch against Hahmeed's head, heard the blows from Hardnuts' huge fists. Furniture overturned, glass was breaking. Room 207 was being completely remodeled, and Hahmeed was getting a free facelift.

The ruckus was still going on when T.B., with his purse draped over his shoulder and his face covered with blood, strutted up the street. "Yes, sir," he gloated. "There's more than one way to outfox the Fox."

By the time he reached his office and removed his disguise, his feet hurt, one eye was swollen beyond swollen, and he felt like his head had been turned inside out from the blows he had taken from his own purse. He practically fell into his chair and hung his head down. "I think Shell Scott would have handled this differently."

The phone rang, and after listening to the voice at the other end, he simply said, "Thank you," and hung up.

It was Reginald Richthoffen from the college. He had called Hahmeed's roommate, Carter Houseman, who checked out Hahmeed's desk. The Iranian Fox had two additional bank accounts; one in Duluth, one in Chicago. Between the two separate accounts, his statements showed over a forty-thousand-dollar balance. That did not at all sound like a man who needed to blackmail Pam Allison. It did not sound like a man who was applying for a student loan either, but for certain, the Iranian bastard was not in need of money.

The goddamn Fox is loaded! If only he had waited for Reginald's phone call before he went to Harriet's apartment, he would not be suffering a head full of lumps and a body laden with welts and bruises.

He reflected. Carrigan Mulhouse had told him earlier to conduct his investigations using the yellow pages. Why didn't Shell Scott use the yellow pages? Why did his goddamn hero always have to go looking for trouble?

With every bone in his body feeling broken, he heaved

himself out of his chair and hobbled down the corridor to the bathroom. "I should learn something from this," he said to himself softly as he splashed cold water in his face. "I should learn something."

Punctually at eight the next morning, Carrigan Mulhouse showed up at T.B.'s office. He sat on the piano stool across from T.B., his eyes glued incredulously to Harvey's face. One eye was deep red and as big as an egg. A band aid ran over the bridge of his nose, another on the top of his head, and his earlobe was puffed up horribly. It was amazing, thought Carrigan, that the only thing on Harvey's face that wasn't broken, was his glasses.

T.B. Harvey spoke first. "Sorry, Carrigan, but I had to get a little rough with Hahmeed." He delicately patted a cherry ball on his cheek. "Sometimes we detectives just have to be persuasive."

"Jesus Christ," said Carrigan feeling sorry for his little friend. "I told you no rough stuff."

"You said no gunplay," T.B. corrected him.

Carrigan glanced at the magnum in the shoulder holster draped over the back of T.B.'s chair. It struck him funny to see such a big gun in such a little holster. Obviously Harvey had purchased a new gun, and although Carrigan had an urge to inquire about it, now did not seem be the appropriate time.

"Yeah," said T.B., as he handed over his report. "In this business one has to get tough to get a confession."

Carrigan had a hard time taking his gaze off of Harvey, but finally he read over the report. It was all there, how T.B. had confronted Hahmeed Bagdiagalliy in Harriet's apartment, had forced the man to his knees, forced the man to plea for his life, forced the truth out of him with his naked fists as Harriet Ambrose, petrified in her bed, stared on. T.B. had also noted a brief account of how he had slipped at the top of the staircase and toppled to the bottom, the cause of his battered face. What was most impressive, however, was the fact that Hahmeed Bagdiagalliy possessed two additional bank accounts, and that the man was not hurting for money.

"This guy has a lot of dough." Carrigan said.

"Yeah. Enough to buy a couple dozen two-humped camels."

Carrigan almost wanted to laugh. "That was a good idea to check out his financial status," he commented as he laid the report on the desk,

T.B. smiled painfully. That was the most brilliant thing he had done concerning Hahmeed. In the past ten days, T.B. was indeed learning something about being a detective.

Carrigan came back to Harvey's grotesque looking face. "You don't look good."

"I called the hospital this morning," T.B. said casually.

"What for?"

"To check up on Hahmeed. Not a good report, I'm afraid. Broken arm, broken nose, two broken ribs and multiple lacerations about the face."

"You did that?!"

"These did that," Harvey said as he lifted up his tiny fists, then quickly dropped them below the desktop, since none of his knuckles was even scratched.

"Do you realize Hahmeed could sue you? He could sue us both!"

"He didn't tell the doctor shit, and he won't. If he does, he knows he'll have to deal with me again. Don't worry, Carrigan. I protect my clients."

Carrigan was uneasy as he glanced over the report again. "We don't have any more suspects."

"I know.

"And Pam Allison heard from the blackmailer again. He wants fifty thousand dollars by next week. I thought we'd catch the bastard before then."

T.B. sighed. "Fifty thousand? How are you going to raise

that kind of money?"

"I was hoping I wouldn't have to, but I've been thinking about it just in case none of our suspects turned out to be the blackmailer."

T.B. winced like he had a bad tooth. "That *is* a problem. What are you going to do?"

"I'll have to talk to the guys in the coffee group. I didn't want to, but I haven't got anyplace else to go."

"You could go to the police."

"The Princess suggested that, but her husband would kill her, and it would ruin her business."

"Well," said T.B. after a moment. "If he kills her, she won't have to worry about the business. Say, speaking of her husband, have you ever considered he may be the blackmailer?"

"Jerry? Are you kidding? He's not smart enough to blackmail anybody, especially his wife. He'd rather beat her to death than blackmail her."

"Still," said T.B. "I could go over and talk to the guy. Might have to rough him up a bit, but I think I could get a confession out of him. Just like with Hahmeed."

Carrigan wanted to laugh. T.B. Harvey rough up big six-foot-two Jerry Allison? Big 230-pound Jerry Allison? Jerry's fist was bigger than Harvey's head. Still, Carrigan conceded that somehow Harvey had managed to break Hahmeed's nose and an arm and break a couple ribs. He wondered how little T.B. could have possibly done all that. The Iranian wasn't that big, but he certainly outweighed the little fellow by sixty or seventy pounds

"No,' said Carrigan emphatically. "Keep away from Jerry Allison. You've encountered enough trouble already." He stood up. "I'll keep in touch."

"About the bill," T.B. said before Carrigan reached the door. Carrigan eyed the report again, saw the outstanding dollar figure.

"I'll have to pay you later."

"No problem. I know you're good for it."

Carrigan Mulhouse again eyed T.B.'s beat up face feeling extremely sorry for him. The fall down the staircase had done a real job on him.

As soon as T.B. heard Carrigan's footsteps disappear down the hall, he picked up the phone and dialed his bank and waited patiently until the man on the other end answered.

"T.B. here," he said into the receiver. "Orville, I need a favor. Can you check out a guy named Jerry Allison for me? He banks with you people. All I need to know is if the guy has got any money." He paused. "Orville, do you think I'm stupid or something? Of course I know you're not supposed divulge that information." Another pause. "Good. I really appreciate this."

T.B. hung up and immediately pulled out the pictures of Pam Allison that Carrigan had left with him. He strung out the nude photos on the desktop, then held up a magnifying glass over one of them.

Uh-huh," T.B. muttered to himself. He examined a second photo with the glass. "Uh-huh," he said again. He examined a third and fourth photo and then produced some of the photos that Leroy Ridgebutte had taken in the Powers Cafe.

He began examining Leroy's photos with the magnifying glass and uh-huh'ed his way through several of them and then began comparing these with the nude photos.

"Aha," he concluded as he set the magnifying glass aside. He searched through the telephone directory looking for Leroy Ridgebutte's number, but nothing was listed under Ridgebutte. He pulled a sheet from his drawer.

"Alias Ivan Gladkijzad." he searched the directory again. "Aha," he said when he found the number. "Aha," he said again even before Leroy R had a chance to answer.

Seventeen
Stratagems

It was stupid, Carrigan Mulhouse kept telling himself all the way back to his office. Harvey had investigated and discredited all of the suspects except for Graybar, however, he had died before they had a chance to investigate him. The Princess had heard from the blackmailer several times since the death of Graybar, so the old boy was out, unless his spirit was paying a visit.

Hardnuts Brodigan and Ruckles had been accounted for, and Mumbling Mike and Wandering Eddie turned out to be couple of fairies. The chance of Harriet being involved at all in the blackmail was negligible. She had her own agenda, and unfortunately, the Iranian, Hahmeed, had more money than Carrigan was worth.

"Damned Iranians," Carrigan cursed as he slipped a key into his office door. "They always have money." He went directly to his recorder phone and listened to the messages.

"We've got a change in price," Dean from the Food Store reminded Carrigan politely. "Hope you didn't produce the commercials yet." He had.

"Did you forget to place the ads for the bank campaign?" Teri Brighton from the bank wanted to know.

"This is Butler," the next message said. "On the front of our brochure the Vice President's name is misspelled. I believe we discussed that change." Carrigan had just printed 5000 of them in two colors.

"Shit."

Carrigan put down the recorder phone when the messages ran out and turned to his checkbook. He had a little over four thousand dollars in his account. He owed twenty-eight hundred of that to various media, which left him with less than a thousand after he paid the rent.

"Shit," he said again.

He swiveled his chair around and headed for the Princess' office, but all he found was a sign on her door that said she was out of town and would return tomorrow.

Carrigan returned to his office, quickly dialed the Princess' business phone. Her recorder said she was in Williston and would return the next day. Leave a message if he would.

Carrigan hung up. The account in Williston must be a good one, which was healthy for her under the circumstances. She seemed to keep her mind off the blackmailer when she was busy, but now the blackmailer was playing cat and mouse with her. Fifty thousand dollars within a week would be hard to come by. The culprit would contact her later, he was sure, to tell her when and where to deliver the money.

"Shit," repeated Carrigan as he examined his checkbook again. He had purposely held off paying some of the media bills in order to gain a little cash, but even with more money coming in, he could not remotely acquire fifty thousand dollars. Maybe six or seven thousand at the most.

He reached into a drawer where he had a few of the nude photos of the Princess. He tucked them inside his coat pocket, put his phone on record and left the office.

Pavlov, Sko and Reggie were already at the Powers. "Damn" Pavlov said when Carrigan pulled up a chair. "You just missed it."

"Missed what?"

"Hardnuts," said Pavlov. "He just dragged Harriet the whore out of here kicking and screaming and cussing a blue streak. "You should have seen 'em."

"What was that all about?"

"Don't know. They were just sitting there, had a few loud words, then suddenly ol' Hardnuts grabs her and out they go."

"Their food's still on the table," said Reggie

"That little shittin' cop is jealous," said Pavlov. "He's always had the hots for her. I'll bet he caught somebody else screwin' her last night."

"That's her occupation, ain't it?" said Sko. "Can't blame her for working."

A slight revelation struck Carrigan. Hardnuts had confronted Leroy and Harriet a week or so ago. He had chewed out Leroy, but when he tipped his hat to Harriet, a coy smile had edged over his face. If Hardnuts had a little heartthrob for the lady of the night and discovered someone else was screwing her, he wouldn't let something like that pass by easily—in spite of the fact that she was a whore.

Another revelation struck Carrigan. He was now imagining Hahmeed Bagdiagalliy lying in the hospital with a smashed in face, a broken arm and two broken ribs. Harvey claimed to have done that, but now, Carrigan had his doubts. "Well, I'll be damned," he mused.

"Uhhh," said Johann as he set his skinny body into a chair. An ash dropped off his cigarette when he reached for the coffee pot.

"Anybody else want wheat toast here?" Millie asked.

"Uhhh," answered Johann.

"What does that mean?"

"That means he ain't awake yet," said Pavlov.

"How about you?" she asked Carrigan.

"Please."

Millie left a fresh pot and whisked herself away.

"So," said Carrigan. "Hardnuts has the hots for Harriet."

"Yas-sah," said Pavlov. "Ol' Hawd-nuts got the hots fo Hay-ets box."

The table roared.

It was shortly after nine when T.B. pulled up in front of the old house. He checked the slip of paper to make sure the address was correct, and then walked up the sidewalk. After trying the doorbell a couple times, he resorted to pounding against the massive door with his tiny fists.

When Leroy Ridgebutte opened the door, T.B. looked up into the week-old bearded face, examined the tattered sweater, the grubby vest, Levis and combat boots. "Ivan Gladkijzad I presume?"

Leroy was not only surprised to hear his Russian name but also very amused to see this little man's face replete with a few bandages and a swollen eye. "Yes, comrade, come in please." He had no idea who T.B. was, but anyone who knew him by his alias had to be important. "Might I offer you a morsel of liquid sustenance at this pre-noon hour?"

T.B. stared uncomprehending into the cap-covered thin face. "Care for a cognac this morning?" Leroy R asked.

"Why not," T.B. agreed

"Please," motioned Leroy R. "My study."

"Gentlemen, the name's Junkman Jamison." Snuffy jerked a chair in place and sat down.

"Hi, Snuffy," Pavlov greeted. How's the antique business these days?"

"You really want to know?" Snuffy asked as he poured himself some coffee.

"Shee-it. Ah wood'n ass if ah did'n wanna know."

"Well," said Snuffy, as he began to roll a cigarette. "I sold a Victorian table worth $3000.00 yesterday. That's the good news."

"What's the bad?" asked Sko.

"I sold it for a hundred dollars." The guys all groaned as Snuffy slicked the cigarette and lit up "Yes, sir. I sold a royal Victorian $3000.00 table for a hundred dollars.

"Sounds like you got a royal screwing," said Pavlov.

"But there's some good news," Snuffy went on. "The guy I sold it to was a Christian."

"Oh, that's good," the guys agreed.

"But this Christian was also a son-of-a-bitch."

"Oh, that's bad," said the guys in unison.

"But he bought some other things from me."

"Oh, that's good."

"And screwed me on those, too."

"Oh, that's bad."

They all laughed, even Snuffy.

"The little Christian fucker," Pavlov smirked. "Someone ought to get a knife and remove his little Christian balls."

More laughter.

"More coffee here?" asked Millie.

"Breakfast," said Snuffy. "The whole nine yards."

"Yeah," added Sko. "Something fit for a king. You're looking at royalty here."

"Haw, haw, haw," Reggie laughed as he blew a napkin off the table.

As soon as Millie left, Carrigan asked seriously, "How do you know this table was worth three grand?"

Snuffy's face sagged. "I found one identical to the one I sold in an antique catalogue."

"You're sure?"

"I'm so sure, it hurts. And this Christian Mr. Coddington took me on a couple old railroad lanterns last week and beat me out of a couple hundred dollars."

"You're sure?" asked Carrigan

Snuffy's face reeked from total dejection. "This antique stuff is new to me. I should have been more careful."

"Well, you didn't know," Carrigan consoled him.

"I will next time."

"Where's the Princes this morning?" Pavlov asked.

"In Williston."

"Is she still decorating that fancy place?"

"Yeah. Johann, you got those paintings done for that guy, yet?"

"Uhhh, yup. You betchum."

"Make any money?"

"Uhhh, little."

"How much?" Carrigan asked curiously.

"A little," Johann said.

"Fifty thousand?" asked Carrigan.

"Johann lit up another cigarette and smiled at the comment. "I'm good, but I ain't that good."

"Haw, haw, haw."

"So," said Leroy R, alias Ivan Gladkijzad, "you require my expertise as a photographer?"

"Well, not exactly," T.B. said as he eyed his empty glass.

"Well, in a way," he said changing his mind.

"Was it Mr. M who recommended me?"

Mr. M? T.B. reflected. *Mulhouse?* "Well, indirectly." He eyed his empty glass again.

"I see," said Leroy R, not seeing anything. "Care for some more cognac?"

T.B.'s eyes lit up. "Indeed I do," he said, as Leroy R filled his glass halfway this time. He was beginning to like Leroy.

"You're shittin' us!" said Pavlov, more serious than he had ever been.

"No," said Carrigan. "Fifty thousand dollars by next week." Carrigan looked at the faces around the table. Pavlov leaned on his elbows, his fingers clasped together, his chin resting on top. Sko was stone still as smoke streamed up past his blank face. Reggie sipped cautiously at his coffee and Snuffy had stopped rolling his cigarette.

"Fifty thousand?" Johann asked. "Dollars?"

"Yes. She needs fifty thousand dollars."

"And I'm not to mention this to Mr. M?" Leroy R, alias Ivan Gladkijzad, asked.

"No" said T.B. "Mr. M said you could be trusted. He said you would keep everything confidential."

Leroy R examined the few photos of the stripper that T.B. had brought along. He looked up into T.B.'s badly beat-up face, scrutinized the bandages, the fat ear. "If I might be so forward to ask," he inquired. "Are you in any kind of trouble with Mr. M?"

"No, not at all. It's a favor, you might say."

"I see," said Leroy R. He studied the nude photos again, looked back at the little round face in front of him. "You understand. I'd never do anything to harm Mr. M. He's sort of a benefactor for me, a mentor, you might say."

"Completely understood." T.B. was not sure he had gained the shaggy faced man's confidence. "You might also say, we'd be helping out Mr. M. He's a dear friend of mine. We go clear back to Silverline Boats."

Leroy R had no idea that Carrigan Mulhouse had once worked at Silverline, thus the statement meant absolutely nothing to him. "Well," he said after he gave the matter some thought. "If you two to back that far, then I suppose we could have a go at it."

"Fine," said T.B. as he started to get up.

"But of course," Leroy R went on. "Some synthesis in this matter will be required."

Little T.B. Harvey slowly sat back down.

"Your request for service," went on Leroy R, "demands action. This is thesis and antithesis in motion. The result is synthesis."

"Synthesis?" T.B. didn't having the faintest idea what he was talking about.

"Are you a Marxist by any chance?"

T.B. paused, his eyes looking skyward as if someone higher up might give him an answer. "I don't know."

"Do you have an office?

"Yes."

'Do you own it or rent it?"

"Rent it."

"Ah, good. That means you are not a member of the bourgeoisie."

T.B. had voted Democratic in the last election. "No, I don't think I am."

"Then I could accept some remuneration for my services."

"You mean money?"

"I prefer to call it a contribution."

"I suppose," said T.B. "How much?"

Leroy R paused, looked over the photos again and then figured a firm amount in his mind. He let a few more seconds pass as if he were making a careful calculation. "There will be some material expenses, and this will take a few days."

"I understand."

"Shall we say in round figures two hundred fifty dollars?"

"How about seventy-five?"

"Seventy-five?"

"Well," T.B. clarified, "according to Marx, a person who gives all he has for a cause is more worthy than he who holds back a dollar for himself. And seventy-five dollars is all I have." T.B. had no idea if Marx had ever said that, and, in fact, he didn't have the slightest idea who Marx was.

Leroy R was pondering the statement. He couldn't recollect ever reading those words by Karl Marx, but they were words Marx might have said. He figured T.B. Harvey must have read them somewhere, and rather than show his ignorance, he went along with the figure. "Seventy-five will be fine."

T.B. counted out the money.

"So, you've studied Karl Marx?" asked Leroy R.

"Ah, well, I, ah..."

"Perhaps you'd like to discuss some of his philosophy? Over another cognac, of course."

The cognac was very good. T.B. had never tasted better,

and the longer he sat with this fellow, the more he liked him. He was different, like himself, but he wondered, as he glanced at the shabby surroundings around him, how Leroy R could afford such good cognac.

Leroy R filled his glass this time, and as they clinked glasses, T.B. said, "To Marxist philosophy!" He took a sip and savored the taste as it rolled down his throat. "You start."

Their mouths hung a foot from their faces as each of guys in the coffee passed the photos of the Princess from hand to hand.

"She's not a blond, is she?" commented Pavlov. Carrigan knew which photo he was examining.

"No, she's not."

"I can't believe it," said Snuffy.

"Believe it," Carrigan confirmed.

"Fifty thousand dollars?" Johann inquired. He wasn't even smoking.

"Fifty thousand."

"What are we going to do about it?" asked Reggie.

Silence.

"Where are we going to get fifty thousand dollars?" asked Sko.

Silence.

Then the table got down to some very serious conversation.

"Don't you think the police should handle this?"

"No. If Jerry found out, he'd kill her."

"That's for sure. He's one jealous S.O.B."

"Does she suspect anyone?"

"No. Frankly, she doesn't have a clue."

"So, where are we going to get fifty thousand dollars?" It was the second time Sko asked the question.

"I could scratch up fifteen hundred," said Snuffy.

"Four hundred for me," said Sko. "Maybe five."

"There goes my painting money. Twelve hundred."

"Maybe five," said Reggie.

"Me too," said Pavlov.

"I could scratch maybe two grand," said Carrigan. "But I'll have to hide it in my business. Any one total that up?"

"You'd give two thousand dollars?" asked Snuffy.

Carrigan paused. "If I had to. Anyone total that up?" he repeated.

"Little over six thousand," said Reggie "If my wife knew I was planning on handing over five hundred dollars to help another woman, she'd skin me alive."

"Mine would divorce me," said Sko.

"You don't have to worry, guys," said Pavlov. "We're not even close."

They were all talking in hushed voices now.

"Can we borrow it?"

"I can't."

"That kind of money without our wives finding out?"

"Who in the hell would understand us giving her money anyway?

"My wife would believe that as much as she believes I've got a nine-inch cock."

No one was laughing.

"Is it all agreed," Carrigan asked, "that we want to help out the Princess?"

"Yeah."

"If we can."

"Sure."

"But where do we get the money?"

"Steal it."

"Rob a bank."

"Beat some rich little mother-fucker over the head and take his money."

"Set up a fake business."

"Chain letter?"

185

"How about a lottery?"

"Send somebody to Vegas."

"For what?"

"To gamble. Anybody good at cards here?"

"I am."

Everyone turned to Sko Skofield. His eyes flashed from left to right, as if he were not sure he should have responded to the question, or as if he wished he hadn't. "Well, I used to be good," he said.

"Used to be?" Reggie asked.

"I was usually a winner." Sko's voice was very hushed now, as he scanned the thinning crowd in the lounge. "I once lost eight grand in a card game. I quit for a long time after that. Had to. My wife about killed me. Since then I've been playing a few small games here and there in town. I was on a hell of winning streak until a couple weeks back. I lost a few hundred again. But I know I was cheated. Ever since I lost that eight grand that one time, I've stayed sober. That's the trick. I play excellent cards when I'm sober."

"You said you were cheated last week?" asked Carrigan.

"Damn right I was."

"For sure?"

"For sure. I know cards. There was no way those three could have beat me. They were all in on it."

Carrigan's mind was working.

Everyone at the table was silent, their eyes fixed on Sko. They knew he wouldn't lie. If he said he lost eight thousand at a poker game, he did. And if he said he was now an excellent card player, he was.

"I'd do anything to get back at those sons-a-bitches."

"Anything?" asked Carrigan curiously.

Sko's mind was working.

"That sets up some interesting possibilities," said Snuffy. He reached for the pot and began to fill everybody's cup. "You know," he said with a sly smile, "There is one Christian son-of-a-bitch I'd like to get even with."

Pavlov smiled, exposing his fine set of teeth. "Didn't I say we should find some rich little mother-fucker and take his money. Course, it would help if this rich little mother-fucker was a crook."

"They are," said Sko.

"He is," said Snuffy, his eyes glowing. His mind was back in Detroit Lakes back at his antique shop where Christian Mr. Coddington had ripped him off.

"Are you thinking what I'm thinking?" said Johann.

Everyone was catching on.

"You mean a scam?" asked Reggie. "We're talking about a couple scams, aren't we?"

"It sho' nuff do look that way."

Snuffy's mind was working a mile a minute, his blue eyes gazing as if he were in a trance. A rolled unlit cigarette hung on his lip. "Damn," he said. "It's coming to me like a vision from Heaven."

Carrigan smiled.

"I'll need some game money," Sko said quietly.

"Yeah," said Snuffy. "Let me work on this for a day or two. I may get that Christian S.O.B. yet."

Reggie looked around the table and adjusted his horn-rimmed glasses. "We're talking about a couple of scams, right?"

"You betchum, Red Ryder."

"I'll need some game money," Sko repeated. "And a couple guys to help."

"Yes, sir, it's coming to me like a vision from heaven." Snuffy looked around the table and finally pointed at Johann. "I need you and the Princess. Ah, yes. It's all falling into place."

"Me?" asked Johann.

"Yes, you. And the Princess."

"Why the Princess?" asked Johann. "Don't you think we

should keep her out of this?"

"No. It won't work without her." He was on his feet. "I think I've got it," he said excitedly. "Yes, sir, I think I've got it!"

"I want a plan," said Carrigan.

"You'll get it!" Snuffy said as he gulped down his coffee and headed for the door. "You'll get it!" He was gone.

"I'll need ten thousand dollars to start with," said Sko. He looked at the empty faces around the table. "If you wanna make money, I need ten grand as a stake."

Silence.

"Can you really do it, Sko?" asked Carrigan.

"I'll need ten thousand smackers."

"We'll get it somehow."

"Jesus," said Reggie. He hadn't cracked a smile in five minutes. "Are we talking about a couple scams? I mean, are we..."

"You're damn right we are," said Johann.

"I mean *scam* scams." Reggie looked around the coffee house and then leaned in and spoke more softly than he had ever spoken before. "I mean, we're talking about taking money from some people, aren't we?"

"Exactly," said Pavlov. "But remember, when you take money from a crook, you aren't stealing."

Reggie didn't look convinced. He turned to Carrigan. "Do you know for sure what's going on here?"

"I think so."

"We'll need details," said Reggie.

"I'll get 'em," said Sko. "Don't worry. I'll lay it all out."

Carrigan searched the faces at the table. "We're all in this together, aren't we?"

"Damn right," said Pavlov.

"You betchum, Red Ryder."

"Boy," Reggie fidgeted. "This is nothing like being a college teacher."

"Are you in?" asked Carrigan

Reggie looked at the envelope that contained Pam Allison's nude photos. He wasn't smiling, but he finally said, "I'm in."

Pavlov slapped Reggie on the back. "Shee—it! Ah knowed all along you was an ol' scammer from way back."

They all laughed, but it was a nervous laugh, and one of short duration.

Millie came to the table. "More coffee anyone?"

"Thiz' zom good shid," said T.B. as he downed another cognac. One eye was bleary on the little man, and the other would have been if it hadn't been almost swollen shut. "Yezzir, zom good shid."

"Hav' 'nother," offered Leroy R as he poured some more.

"Yep. Garl Margs god zom good ideas on clazzless soziety."

"Right, clazzless," T.B. agreed.

"Rev'lushun's what we need," said Leroy R.

"Right, rel-o-vushun."

"Garl Marg's zed we godda liberade th' proletariat," Leroy burped out. "Whadya zay boud that?"

T.B. forced his one working eye as open as he could get it, but it slowly slipped shut again. He opened his mouth as if to answer, and instead, he vomited all over the front of his shirt.

"Damn," remarked Leroy R. "Garl Margs ain't that bad, izz he?"

Eighteen
Homework

It was mid-morning the next day when T.B. stopped his car at the red light on the corner of fourth and Broadway. The Powers Hotel was off to his left, and when he glanced in that direction, he recognized Pam Allison standing on the corner. She was talking with a man T.B. did not know personally, but a man who was a member of the coffee group. He was the small, wiry fellow with the nicely trimmed goatee.

As the two headed for the door of the Powers Coffee House, T.B. noted that the man had a slight limp. When the horn honked behind T.B., he pressed on the gas and drove through the intersection.

T.B. was not feeling well this morning. It was as if someone had squeezed his head in a vice, as if he were wearing a huge clothespin clamped over each ear. His head pounded, and his stomach, as empty as it was, churned horribly. But he had made a commitment at the First National Bank this morning to see Orville, an appointment he did not want to miss.

He parked the car in front of the bank and groaned as he leaned his head on the steering wheel, groaned some more as he reflected on the number of cognacs he had drunk the day before with Leroy Ridgebutte, alias Ivan Gladkiyzad. He felt light on his feet as he exited the Chevy and even lighter as he slowly walked along the sidewalk to the front door of the bank. After he entered, he turned and pressed his forehead against the glass window facing the outside. He was still groaning when he saw a car pull up behind his. A tall, well-built man emerged from the car and quickly crossed to the other side of the street and walked into the Appliance Center. The man, dressed in a tan suit, looked vaguely familiar, but for the moment T.B. could not place him, nor would his pounding brain allow him to think much beyond his arrival at the bank.

Sko Skofield adjusted his tie and smoothed down his suit coat as he walked down the aisle to the back room where Frank Newsom had his office. Frank rarely showed up before ten in the morning, and Sko was counting on that.

"Frank in?" he asked the girl in the back of the store.

"No, not yet."

"Care if I leave a message on his desk?"

She knew Sko Skofield was Frank's radio rep and had seen him often enough in the store. "No," she replied.

Radio Sko pushed his way through the double swinging doors into Frank's office. He sat in Frank's chair and spun around to a credenza and removed a key from the top drawer. He turned back to the desk and unlocked the front drawer, which released all the other drawers to the desk. In the bottom of the lower right drawer were six decks of cards. Sko picked up one of them and slipped it into his coat pocket just as he heard the squeak of the swinging doors. He had a pen in hand and was scratching out a note on a pad when the girl casually glanced into the office, obviously checking on him, or so he thought. She disappeared toward the back of the store as Sko finished writing a message. He had the drawers shut and locked and the key back in place when the girl passed by again. Sko was out of the seat and headed for the front door! "Thank you," he said courteously to the girl before he left the center.

Sko couldn't help but notice the Chevy parked in front of him. He wasn't sure it was there when he first pulled up to the curb, but he found it amusing to see the top of the car squared off completely and could not help but wonder how that could have happened.

He started up his car and headed for the Powers Coffee House.

T.B., wearing a blue tie and a green face, sat across from gaunt Orville.

Orville twisted his face and fidgeted in his seat. "I can't do that," Orville whispered to T.B.

T.B. focused his best blood shot eye on the paper in front of him. It was a simple accounting of Jerry Allison's deposits and withdrawals within the past six months. Jerry Allison had only $287.00 in his checking account and did not possess a savings account, at least not at the First National Bank.

"It's not asking much," T.B. pleaded. "It's all on microfiche. I just want you to take a picture of his checks for the last six months."

"I can't do that!" Orville exclaimed under his breath. With huge owl eyes, a hook nose and a thin face sunk half way into his collar, he could easily pass for Ichabod Crane. His eyes moved wearily from side to side eyeing anyone in the outer office that might be looking at him. His voice was still hushed. "It's against the law! I can't open up a customer's files to just anyone. That's confidential information."

"Orville, I'm not just anyone, and you owe me. Have you forgotten about the boat?" Orville had wrecked his fifteen-foot Hilo due to his own stupidity, and insurance wouldn't cover him. T.B. had managed to run the repairs through warranty at Silverline Boats. That little favor had saved gaunt Orville over nine hundred dollars, and although the accident had occurred several years ago, T.B. wasn't going to let Orville forget it.

"You owe me," he reminded Orville again.

"All right, all right, give me a couple days."

"Tomorrow."

"All right, tomorrow!"

T.B. felt his stomach lurch as if a ten-day-old onion lay dormant inside and was now beginning to make a move. As he slowly raised up from the chair, he swore he would never again drink six cognacs in a row. He steadied himself at

Orville's desk, his head caving in as if an imaginary vice were still clamped to it. "Tomorrow," he said as he very slowly, one step after another, made his way to the front of the bank.

He managed to leave the bank lobby and was standing between it and the outer set of doors when the attack hit him. At first he gagged, and then a convulsive peristaltic movement tore at his insides as if he were going to wretch his esophagus inside out.

He steadied himself against the glass, felt the sweat drain down his forehead as he heaved dry puffs of air again and again. Nothing came up from the empty stomach.

The attack lasted only a few seconds, and when the dry heaves passed, he found himself looking into the face of an elderly woman, her eyes bulging behind thick-lenses glasses, her mouth hanging down to her waist.

In spite of the sickness and throbbing head, T.B. managed a faint smile. "Just a hairball, ma'am," he apologized. He pushed his way out the door and staggered across the street to his flat-topped Chevy. He checked his watch; almost nine thirty. He had to meet Leroy at the Powers Café, for what, he did not exactly know. Leroy had called him early in the morning and said it was urgent.

Sko pulled up a chair and joined the guys at the coffee table. Pavlov was sitting quietly, Johann was smoking and had a cigarette ash an inch long already, and Pam Allison sat complacently, both hands cupped around her coffee.

"Hi, Sko," Carrigan offered.

Sko just nodded and produced the deck of cards he had acquired from Frank Newson's desk. All eyes focused on the cards as Sko carefully peeled away the cellophane wrapper. He drew out the cards, and with remarkable speed and dexterity, he fanned them out on the table top. After a few seconds of searching the backs of the red spotted cards, he told Carrigan, "Pick one."

As Carrigan selected one, Sko looked over the coffee house crowd realizing how conspicuous he might be passing out cards, but there was no other way to prove his point.

"Ten of clubs," Sko said. Carrigan turned over the ten of clubs.

Pavlov pulled a card. "Jack of diamonds," Sko said.

The Princess selected a card.

"Six of spades."

"Jesus," Johann said.

Sko collected the cards and put the deck back in his pocket. "I knew they were cheating me," he said to the group. "It was an old trick. They used regular decks for the first part of the evening, and since I was winning, they switched to a deck like the one I just showed you. I'd been drinking and didn't think to check for spots on the cards. It wasn't until the next morning that I put two and two together."

"By God, they were marked, weren't they?" said Pavlov.

"You're damn right they were. You can see why I'd like to get even with those sons-a-bitches."

"Wheat toast anyone?" It was Millie.

"Wheat toast," said Sko.

When the rest of the group passed, she left a fresh pot and scurried away.

"I need ten thousand dollars," said Sko.

Pavlov slumped into his seat and Johann just shrugged.

"I haven't got that much money, Sko," the Princess told him.

"Don't worry," said Carrigan. "I'll take care of it."

The Princess stared at him. She knew he didn't have that kind of money either.

Carrigan went on. "I've been letting the kitty build in the business. I haven't paid my media bills yet, so in a week I should have the money."

The Princess grabbed Carrigan's arm and leaned in on him. "I can't let you do that. What if Sko loses?"

Sko threw his shoulders back, insulted with the remark. "Hey, honey. I ain't going to lose. I'm going to win, and I'm going to win big."

They all stared at him.

"Of course he's going to win big," Carrigan said, hoping to console the skeptical faces around the table. He eyed Sko, a worried look on his own face. "You can win, can't you, Sko?"

"I can do it," he said with conviction.

"Then that's that."

"I can't let you put up the money, Carrigan," the Princess protested. "Maybe we should go to the police."

"Goddammit!" Carrigan scolded. "He's going to win!"

When the Princess pulled a handkerchief from her purse and pressed it to her eyes, Pavlov wrapped an arm around her. "Ain't that like a fuckin' woman to cry."

The Princess smiled in between the tears, then slipped an arm about Carrigan's neck and planted a sweet, innocent kiss on his cheek causing him to turn the shade of a turnip.

Ooohs and aaahs came from the rest of the group just as Reggie slipped into a chair. "What's going on here," he asked. "Ooohs and ahhhs and the Princess is crying? Crying for happy or sad?"

"For both," she said.

"By God, Reggie," said Pavlov, "You just missed Radio Sko's sleight of hand."

Reggie made a face. "Where'd he stick it? Up his ass?"

They were all laughing so hard that almost everyone in the café trained their eyes on the table. Then, Carrigan's smile slowly faded when he noticed the two sitting across the room, and he wondered why they were here today.

"They always seem to be having a good time, don't they," said Leroy R. He and T.B. had been sitting in a corner booth near the back door of the Powers lounge and were watching the group at Carrigan's table.

"Yes, they do." T.B. raised the coffee cup to his lips and let the warm flavor slip down his throat. It tasted so good, so refreshing, the first sustenance he had had since the night before at Leroy R's home,

"Any of you boys want breakfast?" Millie asked.

"You know, said T.B., "1 believe I could eat some dry toast.

"Dry toast. And you?" she asked looking at Leroy.

"I'll have the breakfast special."

"Dry toast and a special." She shot off toward the kitchen.

Another roar of laughter from the table across the way caused Leroy and T.B. to glance in that direction. The big man with the curly black hair was explaining something, his hands waving up and down, and then the crowd roared again. Almost all of the people at the counter had turned to look at the group having so much fun. When the laughter subsided, those at the counter turned back to their food and drink, except for one. He was a tall man, grubby faced, dressed in a long black coat and white pants that were no longer white, and his tattered tennis shoes were beyond labeling as shoes. One lace was badly knotted on one shoe, the other was tied with a white piece of string. He had eyes like a weasel, small, penetrating and staring. He finally turned back to the counter and emptied two milk creamers into his coffee. As soon as he drank the cup down, he refilled it, loaded it again with cream and sugar and sat almost motionless as he stirred it.

"Who's he?" asked T.B.

Leroy R glanced at the fellow. "Don't know his name. 'Bout a year ago, he used to work on the NP docks unloading freight. So did I. Met him once. He's kind of spaced out. I heard he was a heavy drug user, and then one day he just went bloohy."

"He was on a couple of the photos you took, wasn't he?"

"Yeah. Hard not to remember that."

"What's he do for a living?"

"Don't know now. He's got an old brown Ford, I think. I haven't seen him driving it lately. Don't know where he lives."

"Is that all he does, drink coffee?"

"No. He gets a meal at the Salvation Army once In a while."

The dry toast and breakfast special came. T.B. felt his appetite grow with the first bite. He drank some more coffee and looked up when Carrigan's table again broke into hysterics.

Leroy forked up some eggs. "They sure are having a good time."

"Yep. You'd never know one of them was being blackmailed, would you?"

"What?" Leroy asked with a surprised look. "Is that what this is all about?"

T.B. realized he had blundered.

"Is Mr. M in trouble?" Leroy R asked.

"No, it's the girl."

Leroy R chewed on a piece of toast and shoveled in some more scrambled eggs. "I should have known. I was taking photos only when she was here."

"Speaking of photos," said T.B. "why'd you want to see me, and why down here at the Powers?"

"Well, this is a good place to eat, and I've been analyzing the pictures of the girl."

"And?"

"I've been studying the grain of the photos." T.B. raised an eyebrow. "The grain affects tonal shadows. I'm not so sure the photos were taken at a distance and then blown up, or else taken at close range by a photographer who had his lens partially out of focus. The quality of the paper is good, but the clarity isn't."

"They looked good to me."

"They'd look good to most, but not to me, so I thought I'd

take a couple long shot photos of the girl and then make some comparisons after I blow them up on the same quality paper that the… blackmailer used."

"When are you going to take the pictures?"

"I already have." He produced the miniature camera from his pocket, showed it to T.B. and then tucked it back in his pocket. "I took them ten minutes ago when we first sat down."

T.B. hadn't even noticed the camera, but he had been in no condition to be seeing much of anything when he first arrived at the Powers. Now, he was feeling much better. His stomach was clawing at the food, his taste buds demanding more coffee.

Once again the laughter at Carrigan's table rose to a roar. Faces at the counter turned to view the happy group, and when the laughter subsided, the faces turned back again, all but the face on the tall thin man with the overcoat

"You know," Leroy R said, after he had finished his last bit of food. "Whoever took the pictures of the girl might well have been a professional. All the photos were cropped nicely, spaced perfectly as if someone had carefully centered the girl in the photo. They were also shot to depict her best features.

T. B. screwed up his face. "A couple minutes ago you told me they weren't good photos."

"That could be, too," Leroy explained. "There's a light blur in the background on some of the photos. If they were shot from a distance, it's possible the photographer purposely set his depth of field out of focus just to sort of class it up a bit."

T.B. did not at all understand what Leroy was getting at or what he was saying. "What exactly are you telling me?" he finally asked.

Leroy pondered the question. "I'm not sure." He looked at the girl. "She is beautiful, isn't she? She has a model figure, a striking face, slim. Very photogenic. She'd look good no matter who was taking the pictures, don't you think?"

"Yes, I'd agree to that."

"And I think," continued Leroy R, "that my first impressions are... that the photographs might be professional."

T.B. was totally confused. First Leroy says the photographer wasn't any good, then he is, then he isn't, then he is.

"Well, Goddammit, what is he? A professional or amateur?"

"I'll know after I develop my own photographs. But for now, I'd say, yes. He's a professional photographer." Leroy drank some coffee. "But then again, you never know."

T.B. rolled his eyes as he looked around the coffee crowd again. Was one of these people here, now, a professional photographer? He wondered if there was a professional photographer near the Powers. Of course, he wouldn't have to be nearby. He could be anywhere in Fargo, or for that matter, anywhere in Minneapolis where the photos had been taken.

T.B. was using all his logic. He might not be looking for a professional photographer now. The guy could have changed occupations, however, he had been in the Powers. That's where he had seen the girl. The blackmail note confirmed that. The phone calls confirmed that. Then again, blackmailer may not have even been in the Powers. He could have said that just to throw an investigator off his tracks.

"Aha!" T.B. exclaimed.

Leroy R turned, wondering what the *aha* was about.

Deep in thought now, T.B. was rapidly beginning to feel the role of a true detective. His role wasn't as glorious as that of Shell Scott, who was always fighting his way to the culprit, coming across pretty ladies, beating the truth out of some individual in order to get to others.

No. His investigative work was closer to what Carrigan Mulhouse had said in the very beginning; *do your research by telephone.*

Search, seek, find clues, collect evidence, present a portfolio, analyze, detect, and draw conclusions. "You know, Leroy R," T.B. said after his thoughtful moments. "I've enjoyed our meeting, and I'm thinking it might not be a bad idea to make a few phone calls to some Minneapolis bars. We could start with the one in which Pam Allison did the stripping."

"What bar was that?"

"The Gay Nineties."

"Good idea," Leroy R agreed. "That might help me determine the distance from which the photos were shot."

"And I might find somebody who remembers her," T.B. added.

"And then you might not," said Leroy. "Bartenders change like the customers. Here today, gone tomorrow."

"You're right. The bar might not even be there anymore."

"Right," Leroy R agreed.

"So where does that put us?" asked T.B.

"In the Powers Coffee House."

"Right."

Nineteen
Scam plans

"I'm called Junkman Jamison," Snuffy was singing almost silently. The words switched to a hum as he thumbed through the catalogue of antiques searching for a particular item. "...and I come from DL," he sang on. He turned another page and focused on the pictures. "Uh-huh," he said quietly as he spread the catalogue on his desk and flopped a paperweight on each corner. The page before him depicted several pictures of the eaglet coin box, the treasure he had discovered in the junk pile less than a week ago. Snuffy had already cleaned up the treasure, removed the rust, straightened a few key iron bars, oiled the gears inside and polished the outside. The coin box was in perfect working condition.

In spite of a small dent on one side and a few scratches, it was rated, according to the catalogue as good condition. The only thing it was not, was an original. In appearance, that could not be determined. Only the serial number on the inside casing verified that. The casing had to be removed in order to read the serial number, and removing the casing was a five-minute endeavor, which Snuffy had already done. Obviously, no serial number existed inside this coin box; it was a reproduction of the original, but a good reproduction with a value near $350. Not a bad find for a morning in a junk pile.

He smiled to himself and quietly sang on.

"...and I come from D.L.

I know a Christian gentleman

who can go plumb to hell...."

"Ah, yes," said Snuffy out loud as he pulled another magazine from his desk and started paging through.

"I know a Christian gentleman
Who appears to be rich
He may be a Christian,
But he's a son-of-a..."

Snuffy suddenly stopped singing when he saw the dollar amount. "Whoa!" he said. He rolled a sheet of paper into his typewriter and very carefully began thinking out his words, accounting for every detail. By tomorrow morning, he would have the plan in Carrigan Mulhouse's hands.

Yes, he would require the services of the Princess and Johann. And, of course, the Christian gentleman, Mr. Coddington. It was all falling neatly into place.

This was indeed a vision from heaven for Snuffy, who, like the rest of the guys at the Powers, very much liked the Princess.

Big, blubber-lipped-cigar-chomping Frank Newsom screamed into the phone, "Goddammit, I said no, and don't call me again!"

He slammed the phone down and turned to face Sko Skofield. "I got your message. What's up?"

Radio Sko was cool, calm. "I want another game."

"That right?" Frank appeared to be eating his cigar rather than smoking it. "Last time it took you a little time to pay up. I don't know if the boys will go for it again."

"I just came into some money, Frank. You just get the group together."

Frank sank back in his chair, chewing his cigar. "I don't know."

"You guys owe me a game. You took me for several hundred last time."

"We didn't take anything from you, Sko," Frank scowled. "We won it."

Sko realized he hadn't said exactly what he should have, but he was still calm. "Well, then it's time I won some of it back."

"That was a small-time game, Sko. I think the boys want to go for bigger money. That puts you out of our league."

Sko was ready for the smart remark. He took his wallet from his pocket and opened it to show the hundred dollar bills bundled inside. Frank Newsom's eyes popped open like ping balls "How much you got there, Sko?"

"Enough.," said Sko as he patted his breast pocket. "Got a few here too."

"Damn, you did come into some dough." Frank Newsom grinned, and when he did so, his ugly, yellow teeth held tight to the cigar. "Well, now, the boys might go for that."

"Damn right they will. And none of this dollar-five-dollar shit. Tens, twenties, fifties. I feel lucky."

Frank was still grinning. "By God, I do believe you are serious."

"Never more serious in my life." Sko was confident as he thought about the five remaining marked decks in Frank Newsom's drawer.

"When?" Frank asked so very politely. It was the first time Frank had ever been polite that Sko could remember.

"Thursday night."

"Where?"

"Bucky's, at Dakota."

"All right. I'll line her up."

Sko stood up. "And Frank," he said still keeping his composure. "Cash. No IOU's."

"Cash?"

"You better bring plenty. And one more thing. I'll be bringing a friend along."

"To play?"

"No. To keep an eye on me and my money."

"Don't you trust me, Sko?"

"I don't trust myself when I walk around with ten grand in my pocket."

When Frank Newsom's mouth hung open, his cigar

dropped to the desktop.

"See you Thursday," said Sko as he left the office.

Frank picked up his cigar and thrust it in his mouth. The grin came over his greasy face again as he grabbed the phone and dialed. "Bucky, Frank here. Get hold of Wimpleton. We're playing cards Thursday night... Right. Our sucker's back... No, this time he's got money. I seen it... Ha! You're goddamn right. We're going to take him to the fucking cleaners."

Sko Skofield sat across from Carrigan in his office. He had handed over his game plan and waited patiently while Carrigan scanned the information.

"Jesus Christ, Sko," Carrigan said when he finished looking it over. "I was hoping for something foolproof, but you're taking a risk here. Pavlov's taking a risk. Reggie's taking a risk."

"Nothing ventured, nothing gained. Can't scale a mountain without some risk."

Carrigan sat back in his chair. "This is a big mountain. Pavlov will probably go along with it, but I don't know about Reggie. He might be loud at the table, but I think he'll probably back down when it comes to this."

"Don't worry about Reggie. He'll go along with it."

"How can you be so sure?"

Sko smiled. "You'll see."

Carrigan wondered what he meant, but he let the comment ride.

"The princess is worth it, ain't she?" Sko asked.

"We all like her, and we all want to help her out, but this is really risky."

Sko stood up and faced the window to the outside. "In all the years I've played cards, I never cheated anyone. Getting back at these cheats is as big a vendetta for me as it is getting the money for the Princess. I want to get these bastards so bad

I can taste it." He whirled around and pointed to his plan. "And that's the way to do it."

"The stuff you need. That's somewhat sophisticated."

"There must be someplace we can get it. It's a must."

"Oh, I know where we can get it."

"You do? I thought that was our biggest problem."

Carrigan grunted. Getting the items for him was the least of the problem. It was the rest of the plan that bothered him. "Someone could get hurt."

"Not if we do everything according to my instructions. You get the equipment, I'll get Pavlov and Reggie to go along."

"And me?"

Sko laughed. "Hell, you've got the easy part."

"All right." Carrigan checked his watch. It was almost nine. "Let's go have coffee and run this by the guys."

At eight o'clock that morning, T.B. Harvey had been sitting in his car parked across the street from the computer firm. He had observed Jerry Allison drive up and saw him disappear inside the building to his office. At quarter to nine, he followed Jerry to Elm Tree Square, where Jerry met his wife.

It was now nine, and T.B. was standing upstairs near the railing that overlooked the pit where P.D.'s restaurant was located. The two had ordered coffee and rolls, which. T.B. noted in his notebook. At nine fifteen, Pam Allison left the table, walked upstairs and exited the front door onto the street. She was headed north in the direction of the Powers.

T.B. made a note in his pad, which was rapidly filling up. Taking notes had now become a solid tool for his research. It was much better than being cornered by Hardnuts Brodigan at the top of a fire escape, more productive than being caught in the closet while Harold, or whoever he was, was banging Old man Ruckles' wife in his own bedroom. And a notepad was certainly much easier than getting his head bashed in with his own purse!

It was a fact that Shell Scott never took notes, but without a doubt, taking notes was much more comfortable. For T.B. Harvey, Jerry Allison had now become his number one suspect. Even though Carrigan told him to keep away from him, T.B. felt sure he was on to something, but exactly what, he did not know.

T.B. looked over the railing again into the restaurant. A man had joined Jerry Allison at the table. T. B. noted the event in his pad and scribbled a short description of the man. Almost immediately the two left the table and were coming up the staircase. T.B. slipped behind the trunk of the fake elm tree and observed the two as they exited the building to the back alley. Fifteen seconds later, T.B. stepped into the alley and caught a glimpse of the two as they disappeared behind the Graver Inn on the corner.

T.B. ran across the parking lot to catch up. When he peered around the building, the two were on the corner talking. Moments later, Jerry crossed the street and headed west past the post office, and the other man turned south on Roberts.

T.B. knew Jerry was headed for his office, so he tailed the other man maintaining a good distance behind. The man disappeared around the corner of the fire station and went east on NP Street. By the time T.B. reached the corner, the man was just entering a store front. T.B. casually headed in that direction and gasped with an "Aha!" The man had entered Epko Photography, and even now, T.B. could see the man through the window standing behind the counter. Whoever he was, he worked here!

"Isn't that a revelation?" he mused as he headed back for his car. Leroy had told him the blackmailer might be a professional photographer. It was impossible not to think that Jerry and this man might be in cahoots, which meant it was very possible Jerry Allison was blackmailing his own wife!

"Aha!" T.B. said to himself as he neared his car.

"Aha!" he said to the German Shepherd pissing on a fire hydrant.

"Aha!" he said a final time as he started up the Chevy and headed for the bank.

"Cripes!" said Reggie to the rest of the group. The Princess, Carrigan, Sko and Pavlov had their heads buried in the plans Sko had prepared.

"Cripes!" Reggie repeated under his breath. "I have to wear a cop's uniform?"

"That's right," said Sko.

Pavlov had his own misgivings. "Dark glasses? A pullover sweater? Cotton balls in my mouth? Why cotton balls?"

"Make you look bigger and meaner," said Sko, "Change your face a little. We don't want anyone recognizing you."

"I can't let you guys do this for me," said the Princess. "It's too dangerous."

"I agree," said Reggie as he lay down the set of papers. "I can't play cop."

"You mean you won't do it?" asked Sko.

"This is nothing like teaching geography."

"I can't let you guys do this," said the Princess.

Sko scowled.

"A gun?" Pavlov exclaimed, as he read some more.

"With blanks of course," Sko soothed him. "We don't want anyone getting hurt."

"Reggie needs a gun, too."

"I do?" He looked over the plan again. "Cripes!"

"I can't let you guys to this for me."

Sko looked at Pavlov. "Are you in?"

"Hay-al yes. Anything for the Princess."

"I can't let you do this. You guys are crazy!"

Sko eyed Reggie. "Are you in?"

"I don't know. I've never done anything like this before."

"None of us has."

"It's dangerous."

"Of course, but it's a chance to get back at Dean Wimpleton."

"What?" asked Reggie.

"Wimpleton. He's one of the guys in the card game, one of the bastards that cheated me. You must know him."

"Wimpy? That bald-headed, dumb shit, incompetent Wimpy?"

"Yeah., Wimpy, with the round eyeglasses. Looks like a guard from a Nazi prison camp."

Reggie looked like a snake just bit him. "That's him! Wimpy Wimpleton gambles?"

"And cheats." Sko leaned in close to Reggie and put an arm around him. "You know what I'm going to do to that smart-mouthed cheater? He's going to go home so broke, his wife will pound hell out of him."

"Haw, haw, haw! I'm in! Anything to get that prick!" He looked at the Princess and wiped the grin off his face. "And of course, to help you out."

"I can't let you guys…"

"Shut up!"

"Well, that's settled."

"Here comes Johann."

Pavlov fired up his accent. "Johann, ah gits ta' carry a big gun."

"Uhh, ya, ya. So does Red Ryder."

"And ah gits ta' stuff cotton balls in ma' mouth!"

"We'll never find cotton balls big enough."

They were all laughing except Reggie, who was looking over the scam plans again. He, too, had to carry a gun, at least according to the instructions. He wondered if he hadn't acted a little hastily. The plan was dangerous. He looked around the coffee table. "I was wondering…"

"I was wondering, too," Sko interrupted. "Where the hell

is Millie with the fresh pot?"

"Ah, yeah, coffee," Reggie mumbled. 'Ain't thet som'th'n. Ah gits ta' carry a big gun."

"Uhh, ya. So what's goin' on here?"

T.B. Harvey reached across the desk and took the large envelope from gaunt Orville, who, bent over in his chair, resembled the Hunchback of Notre Dame.

"Thanks, Orville. You sure it's all here?"

"It's all there," he whispered back. "Six months of checks from Jerry Allison's account. Now leave, and don't forget I don't owe you anymore."

"Right," said T.B. as he got up. "You don't owe me anymore." He left Orville's office and pushed himself through the first set of double doors.

"Did you recover from your hairball?' an old woman asked him. T.B. stopped. She was the same old lady whom he had met yesterday when he left the bank.

"Oh, yes," he answered. "Coughed up four of them. Big ones. Pound each." T.B. confidently pushed his way to the outside, strode over to his Chevy and drove back to his office.

Snuffy Jamison was late, but they were all there. He had copies made of his plan and passed a sheet around to each of the guys.

"Wheat toast anyone?" Millie slipped a fresh pot of coffee in place and stood patiently waiting.

"Yeah," said Snuffy. Lot of peanut butter this time."

"How about you," she asked Johann.

"Uhhh."

"I take it that means no?"

"Uhhh, yuh, yuh, yuh."

"I take it that means yes?"

"Uhhh, wheat toast'"

Everyone marveled. Johann von Meer had just ordered

wheat toast. No one could ever remember him ordering a breakfast before.

"Yuh, yuh, you betchum. Wheat toast."

Everyone marveled some more. Johann was functioning after only a few minutes in his chair, and long before he finished his first cup of coffee or cigarette.

Johann focused on the paper Snuffy had given him, his eyes stuck to it like glue. Unaware, he ground out his cigarette a couple inches to the right of the ashtray.

"Thursday?" Johann said after reading some more.

"Thursday late afternoon," Snuffy clarified. "That's when our Christian friend Mr. Coddington shows up."

"Every Thursday?"

"Late Thursday afternoon for the past six weeks. Without fail."

"What if he doesn't show up?" asked the Princess.

"He'll show. He's a greedy Christian. Don't worry, he'll show."

"It looks simple enough," said Carrigan.

Snuffy finished rolling a cigarette. "It's so simple, it's foolproof."

"A limousine?" asked Johann, reading some more.

"Damn right. A fancy, black Cadillac."

"Lavonya LaRue?" inquired the Princess.

"Lavonya LaRue."

"What's an eaglet coin box?" she asked.

"Just happen to have it in my truck. I'll show it to you after coffee at Carrigan's office. Fellas, this is a master plan dreamed up by a genius." He smiled confidently with his words and hooked his thumbs under the armpits of his tattered green sweater. "Only Junkman Jamison could think up something like this." His blue eyes sparkled at the Princess.

If Carrigan didn't know better, he would have sworn Snuffy was in love with her. He might be, for all the trouble he was going to.

"At least no one's got to carry a gun," Pavlov mused. "It isn't as risky as Sko's plan."

Carrigan shrugged. "No, but you're taking a lot for granted. First of all, Coddington has to show up, and then he's got to bite."

"He'll show and he'll bite." Snuffy said.

"Lavonya LaRue?" the Princess asked again.

Snuffy produced a magazine page from inside his sweater and spread it out on the table. Everyone stared at the woman on the page.

"You can't be serious," she said to Snuffy.

"I've never been so serious in my life." He lit the end of his rolled cigarette. With too much paper at the end, it flared up and startled him. When he jumped back, his knee hit the table and two coffee cups spilled, one of them directly into Pavlov's lap.

Pavlov was up in a flash and pulling his pants away from his crotch. It was Sko to mimicked Pavlov's southern accent. "Wal, looky' thar. Ah think Pavlov jus' peed his pants agin."

Everyone in the restaurant was looking at the table when the group roared. It took a minute for the table to get back to normal, and afterwards, all patrons in the lounge were back at their breakfasts, all except the Fargo-Burnout. He remained looking at the coffee group for an unusually long time.

But nobody noticed him.

PART V

Twenty
Big time in the cities

T.B. Harvey had placed an X across the faces of several of the checks with a red marker, those that, at least to his methodical and calculating mind, showed some interest. Jerry's tastes, for the most part were typical. Several checks were written to the Fargo Country Club, which was not unusual, since Jerry was an avid golfer. Several checks were also made out to Gold's Health Spa. Jerry was obviously the athletic type who participated in racquet ball, saunas and the whole health bit.

Other checks indicated that Jerry belonged to the American Legion, the Eagles and the Rotary Club. Jerry had run up a lot of money for liquid refreshment purposes, as indicated by the numerous checks made out to various bars and liquor stores in Fargo and Moorhead.

Payments were made out for typical bills such as life insurance, house, car, etc.

Pam Allison's tastes were somewhat extravagant. She also spent a lot of money on jewelry, and she loved clothing. Black's, one of the most expensive women's stores in all of Fargo, was the recipient of numerous checks.

Pam was good at labeling what she had purchased on the bottom of each check. She was heavy into brooches, beads, necklaces and earrings. One of the most expensive purchases was for a set of pearl imbedded earrings at a cost of almost two hundred dollars.

The Guys from Fargo

She got around. Checks were made out to Metro Drug, to Penney's and Sears and boutique shops in Block Six, the downtown craft building. Grocery checks were written to Hornbacher's Foods mainly, a few to Sun Mart, and two were made out to Carrigan's Advertising Agency. T.B. knew Carrigan had done some advertising for her.

One page listed an accounting of deposits and the days on which they were made. Jerry and Pam possessed a joint savings account with a little over twelve hundred dollars in it. Whether the two had stocks or other securities, T.B. did not know. Without a doubt, the two lived quite well. They owned a nicely kept up two story Tudor home on South 8th Street, the old but ritzy part of town.

Whoever the blackmailer was, he must have assumed the Princess had money, but in fact, the Allisons did not appear to have a substantially high amount of money or capital. It seemed to T.B. that the blackmailer didn't know Pam's financial status, which was strange. Why try to blackmail someone who didn't have the finances to cover it?

And it would have been most difficult for the Princess to accumulate any money at all without her husband knowing about it. Everything in the bank was in both of their names, and if the Princess ever withdrew any savings, which was not much to begin with, Jerry would be sure to find out.

No. The blackmailer wasn't very smart on this accord, yet, he was asking fifty thousand in ransom for the photos.

The checks that T.B. found most interesting were four written to Epko Photography, a total of almost eleven hundred dollars. That was quite a sum of money. T.B. was used to using a Polaroid that cost fifty bucks. He had no idea how much a 35 millimeter camera cost. Two hundred? Five hundred?

Unfortunately Jerry Allison rarely noted on his checks what he purchased, and none of the payments to Epko stated the purpose.

"Shit," T.B. said. He was sure he had some sort of

213

evidence before him, but he didn't know exactly what. Was it in the photography checks? Was Jerry Allison paying the camera store for photographic services?

Was it at all possible that Jerry Allison knew about his wife's escapade as a stripper in Minneapolis? And why would he blackmail his own wife? Obviously, the money she would have to accumulate would he out of his savings as well as hers.

Unless Jerry Allison counted on someone else helping her out, like the Powers Coffee House group. It all made very good sense now. Yes! That was a very strong possibility. But could the guys cough up that much money for the Princess?

She must be quite some lady if they could or would, and it did appear Carrigan was up to something. For T.B., this was just a strong gut feeling, like eating a Hardee's quarter-pounder smothered in horse radish

The more T.B. thought about it, the more he was convinced that Jerry Allison was involved in this whole blackmail mess.

"Aha!" he said. The phrase seemed to make him feel as if he were on to something

"Aha!" he said again, but nothing was registering in his brain.

"Shit," he finally said as he methodically began stacking the checks into a neat pile, just like he had received them from gaunt Orville that morning. He stuffed them into the same envelope Orville had provided and set it on the corner of his desk.

At that moment he heard the footsteps coming down the corridor, and obviously they were headed for his office, since he had the only business on the third floor. Business, he was thinking. His name was getting around.

T.B. quickly donned his sport coat, inched his tie tight to his throat and shoved his shoulder holster and pistol around the corner of the chair so it would be more visible to the on-comer. First impressions were important.

214

The Guys from Fargo

When the door opened, T.B. had a magnifying glass positioned over a photo to give the impression he was busy.

"Hi, Harvey." It was Carrigan.

T.B. dropped the magnifying glass on the desk, mildly surprised to see his friend. "Hi," he offered. He stood up and stuck out a hand as if he had not seen Carrigan in months. "In need of more services, I presume?"

"Indirectly."

"More suspects?" T.B. asked, as he motioned Carrigan to the piano stool. "Need someone roughed up? How about a bagman to deliver the ransom?"

Carrigan noticed the scab on the top of his little friend's head. The size of his left ear was almost back to normal, and the shiner on his eye had practically disappeared. T.B. was almost back to his own dwarf-like self.

"You're looking better," Carrigan complemented him.

"Well, the past few weeks have been lucrative for me, thanks to you. I hope you were pleased with my services."

"Very much so. As a matter of fact, I could use a few more services, or at least some advice."

"Shoot."

Carrigan produced a piece of paper from the inside of his coat pocket. "Can you procure these items for me?"

T.B. scrutinized the list. "The cop clothes I can get. Let's see, a .38 police special and another gun with blanks? Yeah, I think so." He read the last item. "Hmmm. That device might be a little difficult to come by. I'd need to contact a security firm. Minneapolis is probably the closest."

"How much would it cost?"

"Oh, probably two, three hundred dollars."

"That much?"

"That's an educated guess. When do you need this stuff?"

"By Wednesday."

T.B.'s eyebrows flipped up. "That's two days away. I'd have to go to Minneapolis for the electronics."

"How much for everything?"

"Five hundred." Carrigan's mouth didn't drop, but T.B. knew he was debating the amount. "Gotta fly to the cities. That'll cost at least a hundred round trip. Two, three hundred on the rental for electronics, taxi, food. A guy's gotta make a profit somewhere along the way."

When Carrigan opened his wallet, the hundreds bulging within did not escape T.B.'s keen eyes. "Six would be better," he added.

Carrigan hedged, then produced six one-hundred-dollar bills. "Wednesday night, no later."

"Right. How are you doing on the ransom money?"

"We're working on it."

"The coffee group?"

Carrigan nodded.

"Got a bagman for the money? You'll need a bagman. I've had experience."

Carrigan wondered what experience T.B. was talking about. "We don't have the details yet. We should know later on in the week."

"You planning on paying the money?"

Carrigan spun slowly on the piano stool while he was thinking. "We hoped somehow to catch the blackmailer, but just in case, we also thought we should have the money."

T.B. nodded. "You must be very fond of her to go to all this trouble."

"We all are. She's just a victim. And one of the guys. I'd hate to have her husband find out. We all know what he'd do to her."

"I've been thinking about Jerry Allison lately."

"You haven't been following him, have you? I told you to keep away from him."

"Oh, no, no. Hell no. You tell me to stay away, I stay away. I'm your friend. Shit. I wouldn't do anything you wouldn't want me to do."

Somehow, Carrigan perceived some untruth behind T.B.'s squeaky voice. "You're sure you're not tailing him?"

T.B. crossed himself. "Honest Injun. Christ. What do you take me for? I'm a professional, and besides, you pulled me off the case."

Carrigan was satisfied with the answer. "I don't know how we're going to handle the ransom money. We'll have to work that out Saturday."

"Saturday's the delivery day?"

"Delivery night, I imagine. Isn't all ransom delivered at night?"

T.B. thought back on some of his novels, but he couldn't remember reading a novel about ransom money. "Right," he finally said as if he were the authority on the subject. "Usually at night."

Carrigan got to his feet and pointed to the list in front of T.B. "Wednesday night. We have to have everything by then."

"No problem."

"Good." Carrigan was gone.

T.B. shuffled the hundred dollar bills between his little hands and grinned. Immediately, he was on the phone and dialed the FM Community Playhouse. "Marty? This is Harvey. Are you going to be in for a while?... Good. I'll be right over. I need a few things."

He hung up and quickly dialed again. "Leroy? How would you like to go to Minneapolis?" There was a pause. "That's right, the big cities, Minneapolis-St. Paul." Another pause. "Nope, it won't cost you a dime. Get your stuff together. I'll be over in a half hour."

He hung up and counted the six one-hundred-dollar bills again. He and Leroy could drive to Minneapolis and back for less than fifty. His tires were bald and the engine was knocking, but the Chevy had never failed him before.

He was out the door. "Aha!" he said as he vaulted down the staircase two steps at a time. "Aha!" he said to the lady standing near the elevator.

On the main floor, he tore out of the building and ran for his car where he discovered a ticket on his windshield. "Aha!" he said, as he ripped it to pieces and let it flutter to the pavement.

He started his car and headed for the FM Community Playhouse.

"Wheat toast and peanut butter?"

"Please," said Carrigan.

"And you?"

"The same," said Reggie.

"Anybody else?"

"I'll have tea this morning," said the Princess.

"Uhhhh."

"Mr. Rembrandt wants nothing. How about you, Mr. Radio?"

"Just coffee."

"Junkman special for me."

"What does that mean?"

"Just a special. Scrambled this morning."

Millie hiked off toward the kitchen.

"So, it's all settled," Carrigan said to the group. "We four guys meet at my office after coffee. We play cards until noon, then back at two o'clock."

"Maybe we should just play right on through."

Carrigan shook his head. "No. I've got a TV commercial to produce, and the bank needs final proof on a brochure."

"Is it necessary we play cards at all?" asked Reggie.

"We're playing," said Sko emphatically. "I want the practice. I'm gonna beat those bastards bad."

"What's your schedule, Princess?"

"I just have to order some carpet for Williston. I'm in the rest of the day."

"I'll need you tomorrow," Snuffy reminded her. "And you

too, Johann. We've got to make a trial run at my place."
And then the table once again settled on some very serious conversation.
"What if we don't raise the fifty thousand?"
"We'll raise it."
"No problem."
"Uhhh, yuh."
"Any more notes or calls from the blackmailer?"
"No."
"Who's going to deliver the money?"
"We'll find out Saturday."
"What if we deliver the fifty thousand and don't get the negatives?"
"I don't know."
"If my husband finds out, he'll kill me."
"I know."
"You guys are going to a lot of trouble."
"Shee-it. We'll take care a' thet litt'l blackmailin' bastard."
"Damn right."
"Uhhh, ya, ya. You betchum, Red Ryder."

T.B. Harvey and Leroy R had a lot in common. T.B. no longer tolerated Tarragon Bromeliad, his real name, and Leroy Ridgebutte preferred Ivan Gladkijzad, but that was a mouthful for T.B., so Leroy remained Leroy R. T.B. claimed to be a private detective, and if it weren't for the case that Carrigan Mulhouse had granted him, he would still be unemployed. Leroy R really didn't have an occupation, other than overseeing the home of his landlady and occasionally moving freight around on the docks, so in that sense, both were living on a shoestring.
They both had unusual physical appearances.
T.B. tried to dress neatly; Leroy R rarely did.
Both of them highly respected Carrigan Mulhouse, and

both, to a large degree, felt indebted to him; Leroy R for his gratis C's in college and his first photographic assignment, and T.B. for his first detective assignment.

Both, technically, were not supposed to be involved in the blackmail case anymore, but the two had other ideas.

Both were single. Both had no particular goals in life. Both were misfits in society. And both had spent four hours in Fergus Falls waiting for a mechanic to put a new universal joint in T.B.'s Chevy.

At the moment, they were sitting in a restaurant just outside of St. Cloud drinking coffee. Across the street at the auto repair facility, another mechanic was busy putting a new fuel pump in the Chevy.

Both checked their watches, growing impatient with the loss of time. They still had another seventy-five miles to Minneapolis.

Both ordered another cup of coffee.

It was almost four in the afternoon. "Deal," said Sko.

Carrigan, Reggie, Pavlov and Sko sat around the layout table in Carrigan's office. Carrigan had turned out the lights in the front, locked the door and put the telephone on record.

They all had poker chips in front of them, but Sko's stack was six times that of anyone else's.

"Open for ten," said Sko. They all flipped in a chip.

Reggie asked for cards. Sko took two, Pavlov and Carrigan took three each and Reggie took one.

Pavlov threw in his cards.

"Couldn't even pair up, huh?" Sko asked.

"Shit, this ain't even fun. You win all the time."

"That's the way it's supposed to be.

"Bet," said Reggie.

"Twenty," said Sko.

Carrigan and Reggie both folded.

Even with the gas pedal pressed to the floor, the Chevy was barely doing fifty miles an hour. They had just slipped off of Interstate 94 onto 494 heading south, confident and ecstatic now that the skyscrapers of Minneapolis were finally in view.

A used universal joint in Fergus Falls had cost sixty dollars, the fuel pump in St. Cloud about the same.

"She's humming right along, isn't she?" T.B. remarked to Leroy R concerning the sound of his automobile.

"For a moment there I thought we weren't going to make it."

"No sweat," said T.B. as he slowed at the Wayzata exit. The Chevy coasted to a stop at the red light on the corner where, without a single cough or sputter, it simply died.

"Shit," said T.B.

"Double shit," said Leroy R.

It was almost six-thirty. "Whose deal?'

"I'm tired."

"Gotta play some more."

"My wife will wonder where I'm at."

"Call her. Deal."

"You've already cleaned us out three times over."

"And I'll keep cleaning you out. Deal."

"For Christ sake, how much practice do you need?"

"All I can get. I gotta stay sharp, I gotta keep a poker face and I gotta keep winning."

"What happens if they switch decks on you again?"

"What do you mean if? They will eventually. I just want to be far enough ahead at that point."

"But what if they start using the marked cards early?"

"I can read 'em, too."

Reggie snickered. "I want you to nail that wimp Wimpleton. I hope you get that sucker bad."

Sko smiled confidently. "Reggie, when I get through with him, he'll be on food stamps."

Delray K. Dvoracek

"Haw, haw, haw!"

Snuffy Jamison swept the dust into a pan and dumped it into a waste basket. He looked around the garage, examined the chairs, tables, lamps, clocks, glassware and eyed the trinkets under the glassed-in show case.

"Very nice," he said as he put the broom away and settled behind his desk. He selected a magazine and thumbed to a particular page.

"Lavonya LaRue," he said out loud, as he studied the picture of the beautiful girl with the coal black hair. She was a petite woman, striking in appearance, clad in a black fur coat and long black dress that reached below the knees. He couldn't make out exactly what she was wearing around her neck in the photo, but whatever it was, it was sparkling, and it looked expensive.

He read the caption underneath the photo and nodded in agreement to himself. He knew precisely what he had to do Thursday evening when Mr. Coddington showed up.

He put down the magazine and glanced across the antique-filled room to where the eaglet coin box sat on a shelf against the wall. The eagles all appeared suspended in air, as if they were about to swoop down for some morsel of prey.

The box was in very good shape now. Snuffy had brought back the initial luster of brass with a good cleaner. It wasn't in mint condition, but it didn't need to be. Without a doubt it would easily bring $350.00.

It would, of course, have been worth upwards of thirty thousand dollars if it had contained a serial number inside the casing. That minute detail would not escape Mr. Coddington, unless of course, he was presented with some incentive to purchase it for such a price without being able to make a close inspection.

A sense of euphoria overtook Snuffy when he returned to the magazine and again scanned the article concerning Miss

Lavonya LaRue. "I think everything is working beautifully."

It was late when T.B. and Leroy R got off the bus in downtown Minneapolis. The night sounds of cars whizzing by on Hennepin Street was music to their ears. They stood in awe. This was it, the big city, big time. From this corner, they could see four major strip joints. In the next block, the crawling sign of the Gay Ninety's bar loomed out at them. The air was brisk as they crossed with the light, their faces mesmerized at the sight of all the flashing neon signs.

The distinct smell of rancid cooking oil swept out of an open doorway where several men lined the counter of a hot dog stand. The streets were jammed with pedestrians scurrying in every direction. A police car zoomed past the corner with lights flashing but no siren. It turned at the next corner and went out of sight.

Every so many steps, they passed a man leaning against a building or hanging in the shadow of a dark doorway. A cigarette butt flew past T.B.'s feet. He didn't bother to look at the person that flipped it, since he was beginning to feel uncomfortable. If he wasn't doing his best to keep up with Leroy R's long strides, he would have been walking even faster.

"Goddamn car," said T.B.

"They said they could fix it."

"Yeah, for over a hundred dollars. I've already blown half my wad and we haven't even bought any of the electronic gear yet."

"Don't worry about the money, T.B.," Leroy R comforted. "I think the mechanic working on the car is a Marxist, a pure member of the proletariat. Did you see the cap he was wearing? Just like mine. I doubt the bill will be over a hundred. Someday we'll all be liberated from the bourgeoisie."

T.B. had no idea what Leroy was alluding to, yet he liked the guy. Leroy had a good outlook on himself and life in general. He was never in a hurry to reach any place in particular, and he never appeared disappointed if he never got there. He had a strange philosophy about life, which revolved around this Marx character. The only Marx T.B. had heard of was Groucho, but somehow he didn't think they were related.

Leroy just might turn out to be a good friend, he was thinking as they stopped in front of the Gay Nineties bar and looked up at the red and white lights flashing in the night.

"I was here once sometime back," Leroy R commented. "They used to have a billboard outside with the pictures of the strippers. I wonder if Pam Allison ever had her face pictured here."

"Probably," said T.B. He tugged at the handle of the gigantic red door. Inside, a foul smell of cigarette smoke and liquor met them as well as a big bruiser sitting on a bar stool checking ID's. T.B. was sure the hunk of man, bigger than a 300-pound wrestler, had never learned to smile. He looked the two over, grunted and motioned for them to pass through.

Plush, red carpet was comfortable under their shoes as they stood for several seconds allowing their eyes to adjust to the dim interior. Tables were all over with couples sitting at most of them. Cocktail waitresses bustled about with drinks balanced delicately on round trays. A long bar lined the right side of the interior, and directly across from them was the stage and wall-to-wall black curtains behind it.

T.B. felt a renewed confidence. "Well, this is where the action is." As the two meandered toward the bar, T.B. cast a glance in the corner where several guys were playing electronic games. Buzzing and dinging, laser shots, screeches and other weird sounds flowed out of the game room.

T.B. turned his attention to the center of the lounge. From somewhere, speakers spit out some jazzy music that drowned out the voices of the noisy crowd.

"What'll it be, boys?" the bartender asked.

"Schlitz," said T.B.

"Two," said Leroy R.

The beer came and T.B. paid for them. While they sipped at the cold brew, they turned their backs to the bar and observed the crowd at the tables.

"Look at that," Leroy R pointed with his bottle.

T.B. saw the two guys sitting next to each other with their hands clasped together underneath the table. They were making eyes at each other, as if they were madly in love.

"I think we've got a couple funny ones, here," T.B. commented. When he turned back to the bar, the bartender gave him a sour look and began rinsing some glasses.

T.B. whispered to Leroy R, "Not too damn friendly around here, are they?" He motioned to the bartender. "When's the floorshow start?"

"Ain't no floorshow," he answered.

"How come?"

The bartender just smiled coyly and moved down to another customer.

"Damn," said T.B. "Must be somebody friendly around here. Let's move around a bit."

The two walked toward the end of the bar where the stage was located. Leroy R had his miniature camera out, clicking away every so many feet as they neared the stage. It was a strange setup, T.B. was thinking. No band, no floorshow and no dance floor where guys and gals could rub against each other.

The tall curtains on the stage were jet black, just like the ones in the photos of Pam Allison, and the wood floor appeared to be oak, exactly like in the photos.

The two found an empty table in the center of the room where Leroy R could easily look over the stage from left to right. "If I'm right, the pictures of the girl had to be taken from a distance anywhere from here to door. Forty to fifty feet, wouldn't you say?"

T.B. made a wild guess. "I guess so."

Leroy R got up and took his beer with him. "I'm going to get a few more photos from further back."

Leroy R was no sooner gone when a set of long slender arms swooped around the back of T.B.'s neck. Her hands reached under his coat and squeezed the little rolls of fat around his midriff. T.B. loved the smell of her perfume, savored the moment when the beads from her necklace flopped over his face and clicked against his glasses.

"Hi, sweetheart," she whispered with a husky and inviting voice.

She slid into the chair next to him, portraying a Cinderella elegance about her. Long swirling red hair drooped over her shoulders onto the front of a brilliant red dress. Both of her wrists jingled from brass bracelets. Her skin was smooth and tan, and now he noticed the circular earrings that matched her bracelets. She had beautiful thin eyebrows and dark blue eye shadowing that brought out her long eyelashes. A strong nose, painted red lips and heavy rouge on her cheeks tormented him.

She offered a warm smile. "Buy me a drink, big boy?"

T.B. was breathing heavy. Things like this always happened to Shell Scott, and now it was happening to him. Being a detective had its perks. He snapped his fingers for a waitress and didn't even hear what she ordered. He was fazed, enraptured with this beauty before him.

"You're new here, aren't you, big boy?"

She has a real way with words! he was thinking. He loved the husky voice, loved her tanned skin, and loved everything about her. He had never discovered anything like this in Fargo.

"Y-y-yes," he finally managed get out. "J-just got into town."

"Looking for a little excitement tonight?"

"C-Could be." He felt a warmth building up inside him and reached up to loosen his tie.

"Here, let me do that," she offered. Her slender hands tugged at the button on his collar, gently tugged at his tie and blew a little air across his face as she did so. When she patted his hand, his penis came up hard as a rock.

"Do you come here often?" he asked.

"All the time."

T.B.'s mind clicked. "Have you been coming here for the last seven years?" That was how long ago Pam Allison had worked here as a stripper.

She seemed amused with the question. "Seven years?" She thought a moment, then, "Yes. I suppose. Yes, since before that. This has always been one of my favorite places."

T.B. probed further. "Do you remember when this place used to have strippers?"

"Oh, my, yes. That was a long time ago. They've been gone for at least four years. Maybe more."

T.B. had a picture of Pam Allison in his coat pocket. It was a long shot, but he showed it to her. "Have you ever seen this girl?"

She examined it closely. "No, I don't believe so, but then there were so many. And really, I wasn't particularly interested in strippers." She smiled at T.B. and flashed her big eyelashes.

"I can understand," T.B. said. And he could. Why would a beautiful girl like this remember another beautiful girl like Pam Allison? He should be asking men about Pam Allison. They would remember.

Her drink came, something red in color with a twist of lemon and a cherry. She sipped at the drink through her straw and batted her eyelashes at him again and smiled invitingly. She eased her chair closer to T.B. and innocently rested one of her hands on his thigh. She was saying sweet things to him now, but T.B. couldn't concentrate. All he could feel was her hand moving a centimeter at a time toward the inside of his groin, until finally her long slender fingers edged against his bulge. He felt the excitement and jerked back when her hand grabbed his bulge expertly and squeezed.

"My," she said as she draped her free hand around his neck, "You're pretty big for a little fellow."

T.B. gulped. In fragmented flashes he visualized Ruckles laying the big titted brunette over his desk, visualized the man called Harold driving his ass up and down on top of Ruckles' wife.

"Oh, Shell, Shell!" he puffed as she squeezed him again.

"What's that?" she asked. "Shall we what?"

Oh, Lord! She had firmly established a steady rhythm against the outside of his pants.

Leroy R suddenly pulled up a chair at the table and sat down. "Hi," he said.

T.B. groaned when she took her hand away.

"Aren't you going to introduce us?" the redhead asked in her sexy and husky voice."

"L-L-Leroy, this is, ah, ah…"

"Bert," she finished with a huge smile."

Leroy R reached across to shake hands. She hesitated and then daintily shook his hand. "Well, we might make it a threesome," she suggested.

Leroy R looked curiously at her and then at T.B., totally clueless to what she meant.

"Bert," repeated T.B., his face aglow. "Short for Bernadine or Bertha, I presume."

"No, just Bert."

"What do you do, Bert?" Leroy R asked innocently as he sipped at his beer.

"Drive truck," she said.

"Drive truck?" T.B. blurted. He curiously examined her face, then grabbed one hand and flipped it palm up. Calluses lined the underside of the slender fingers.

T.B. stared behind the beads at her chest. She had no breasts! The jumble of beads around her neck hung straight down.

T.B. shot out of his chair. "She doesn't have any tits!"

The Guys from Fargo

"My God!" Leroy R said to T.B. "Don't insult the lady!"
T.B. sheepishly looked over the crowd. How come he hadn't noticed it before? There were no women in the bar except for the waitresses! Only guys! Couples everywhere, but men couples!

The Gay Nineties Bar! "Jesus Christ!" T.B. screamed. "She's a man!" He reached inside his coat and jerked the magnum from its holster.

"No!" Leroy R shouted as he grabbed his arm. "Don't kill her!"

"Him!" T.B. hollered back. "No goddamn man is going to squeeze my cock and get away with it!"

Bert drew back and screamed out, "Help! Help! A maniac!"

"For Christ sake!" Leroy shouted as he tried to wrest the gun away. The explosion from the magnum brought the entire crowd noise to a halt. Another shot barked in the silence of the bar. Two huge globes from the chandelier above popped and drained shards of glass down to the floor. In a flurry, men were heading for the door like a runaway herd of sheep with Bert in the lead. Every waitress that held a tray, dropped it and ran.

"He's got a gun!" somebody shouted. T.B. fired the gun a third time as Leroy R struggled to calm him down.

"Police!" someone shouted. "Call the police!"

"Jesus!" Leroy R hollered in T.B.'s face. "Let's get the hell out of here!"

T.B. came to his senses, and in seconds, the two of them were running down the middle of the bar, stumbling past chairs and tables, scrambling for the door like everyone else. Waitresses screamed, guys screamed, T.B. screamed as he and Leroy R plunged into the escaping crowd.

On the street, men and women were scattering in all directions. T.B. and Leroy R were on a dead run, even passing some the fastest runners. From somewhere, a police siren screamed in the night, and when the flashing red lights of the police car reached the corner, the two ducked into an alley and kept running. T.B.'s lungs were about to burst, but he was keeping up with Leroy R's long strides, just seconds behind the sound of his combat boots clomping against the cement.

At the end of the alley, they slowed to a normal gait as if nothing had happened and lazily walked along the sidewalk, puffing and wheezing. T.B. still had the magnum in his hand and quickly tucked it away.

A fire truck turned the corner two blocks down and headed their way, zipped by them and turned at the corner in the direction of the Gay Nineties Bar. Finally all sirens were quiet, and as the two puffed their way across the street, people were scurrying curiously in the direction of the bar.

"Oh, Lord," T.B. said to himself. "Oh, Lord."

Twenty-One
Nervous Wednesday

"Cards right after coffee," Radio Sko said as he tipped his cup.

"Goddamn," said Pavlov. "You cleaned us out yesterday."

"And I'll clean you guys out today."

"I want a different seat," said Reggie.

"Take any seat you want."

Carrigan looked at Johann and the Princess. "How are you two doing?"

"We're going to DL after coffee. Snuffy is expecting us."

"Good."

Reggie fidgeted. "Have you got the clothes and electronic stuff yet?"

"No. We should have it by tonight." Carrigan wondered how T.B. was doing. He left for Minneapolis the day before. His flight should have returned last night, but a phone call to T.B.'s home and office drew no response. Carrigan had called him this morning, too, but nothing.

"How's the coffee this morning?" Millie wiggled the pot then replaced it with one she was carrying. "Anything else here?"

"No, we're fine." Millie darted off to another table.

"We need the clothes and equipment," Radio Sko demanded.

"I know, I know," said Carrigan. "Don't worry." But he was worrying. He would call T.B. again when he got back to his office.

"There's that guy looking at our table again," said Reggie.

"Who?" When Carrigan checked the counter, the Fargo-Burnout was looking back.

231

"I don't like him," said Sko. "Burnout or no burnout, he gives me the willies."

Carrigan shrugged but agreed. "We're all getting jumpy."

The Fargo-Burnout got up from the counter and slowly made his way to the cashier where he paid his bill. Carrigan watched him all the while, watched the man walk through the coffee house and exit to the street.

It was strange, mused Carrigan. The Fargo-Burnout did seem to spend a lot of time watching their table. He wondered if it was just a coincidence.

"This is exactly what I need," T.B. told the salesman behind the counter. He again thumbed the switch on the transmitter that lit up the bulb on a separate black box. Leroy R stood to the side, simply observing.

"Simple device," explained the clerk. "Quite a few radio stations request them. They're used in production booths. The light blinks on when they have a phone call, and that way the ring doesn't disturb them if they're recording or they're on the air."

"I see," said T.B. The device did not seem to be such a secret instrument after all. He wondered if he might have been able to purchase such a device in Fargo. Probably.

"How much is it?"

"We have this unit which transmits up to 350 feet, and we have other units which reach as much as a couple miles. That and bugging devices."

"Bugging devices?" The man instilled a sudden curiosity in T.B.

"Sure," said the clerk. "We sell a lot of security devices. Transmitters, receivers, microphones..."

"Microphones?" T.B. remembered Shell Scott often used such devices.

The clerk raised an eyebrow and smiled, feeling a nice sale coming on. "Would you care to see some?"

"Absolutely."

As the clerk retired to the back room, Leroy R eyed T.B. "Why do you need bugs?"

"Just curious," T.B. said with a sly smile. "Just curious."

The phone rang in Carrigan Mulhouse's office, and when he picked it up, he hoped it was T.B. calling.

"Cards," Pavlov said to the remaining two.

"One," said Sko.

"I'm pat," said Reggie. He grinned like he might have a good hand.

Pavlov took two.

Sko looked at Reggie's cards. "You think that little straight will beat the full house I'm drawing to?"

"Reggie looked bewildered. "How did you know I had a straight?"

"I can read the spots on your cards."

Reggie and Pavlov both turned over their cards and examined them. "This is the deck?" asked Reggie.

"Yep. Pavlov just drew a four of hearts and a ten of clubs. He's got nothing."

"Shee-it," exclaimed Pavlov. "That's cheating."

"That's right," said Sko. "Now you guys know what it was like when those guys cleaned me out."

"So," Reggie asked Sko. "Did you draw the straight?"

"Nope. And I wouldn't have made a bet. Not betting a bad hand is just as good as betting a good one."

Carrigan sat down at the table again.

"Was that T.B. on the phone?"

"No. I want three cards."

"Watch it. They're marked."

The Princess turned the Volkswagen onto Turner Street and slowed her speed as she entered the back lot of the Holiday Inn. She passed the outdoor swimming pool and drove onto the stretch leading to the cottages behind the hotel.

"It's the first one," Johann directed her as he took the cigarette from his mouth and ground it out in the ashtray. The Princess pulled the Volks to a stop in front of the cottage and shut off the engine.

Snuffy Jamison banged a screen door open and came out carrying a white cat. "Coffee's on," he beckoned as the two got out of the car. "I see you found the place."

"It wasn't hard at all," said the Princess.

"Hi, Johann," Snuffy greeted.

"H'lo." Johann whipped out another cigarette as he and the Princess followed Snuffy into the cottage.

The salesman behind the counter totaled up the amount. "The whole package will run about twelve hundred dollars."

T.B.'s little eyes opened wide. That was a lot of money, but these were devices that should be in the possession of every reputable, private detective, and T.B. considered himself reputable.

"Twelve hundred," T.B. repeated as he eyed the counter filled with the selected bugging devices and gadgets. There were more gadgets than he really ever needed

"Twelve hundred," repeated the clerk.

"Do you give discounts to detectives?"

"If you have a license," said the clerk

T.B. tore the license from his billfold as if the sooner he showed it the lower the price would go. At the same time his mind rolled back into a novel he had read some time ago, forcing his memory into a nebulous chapter. Shell Scott had managed to acquire a handful of such devices with very little money down, if he recollected correctly, but how had he done it?

"That will give you a fifteen percent discount," said the clerk as he examined T.B.'s license.

T.B.'s brain was working full time. "Of course I'd like to

try out the devices. I'm not one to just purchase such electronics outright."

"I can guarantee everything works," the man answered.

"But if something doesn't, of course the culprit will get away."

The clerk scowled, not happy with the remark.

"I'd be happy to make a substantial down payment, however," said T.B., "as long as I can try out the package. If everything works, then we might consider the entire purchase."

T.B. waited for a moment as the salesman looked over the equipment. "How much down payment?" he asked.

T.B.'s memory was serving him well. "The Detective Association recommends ten percent. T.B. had no idea if such an association even existed, but Shell Scott might have said that.

The salesman raised an eyebrow as if he were considering the offer.

Leroy R stepped in with a comment. "I don't really think you need all this stuff, T.B."

T.B. gave Leroy a mean look, but the salesman's look was meaner. "Hold on," he said suddenly, becoming excited over the possibility of losing the deal. "Maybe we should examine this from a different perspective."

T.B. smiled. "Well, now, why don't we just do that?"

Carrigan Mulhouse slammed the phone down again and came back to the card table.

"Not in yet?" asked Sko.

"No, the little shit. I wonder where he is."

Reggie rubbed his stomach. "I'm getting hungry. What do you say we break for lunch?"

"Not until I take this final pot. Raise you a hundred fifty."

"Pass," said Pavlov.

"Pass," said Reggie.

"I'll call," said Carrigan, "just to keep you honest."

"So you see," Snuffy was explaining to the Princess and Johann, "it's quite simple. You two will be parked behind the hotel. When Coddington arrives in his Lincoln, you'll recognize it. It's a half mile long and so highly polished, you can see your face in it from a hundred yards."

Johann smiled as he lit up another cigarette.

Snuffy went on. "As soon as Coddington arrives, give us about five minutes. Then we go into our routine. Is that clear?"

"Yuh, yuh."

The Princess frowned. "I want to run through this just one more time, just to make sure I've got everything straight."

Snuffy was happy to accommodate beautiful Pam Allison, charming Pam with the strawberry blond hair, with the model body, with the pretty redlined lips and pretty Mona Lisa smile.

"Okay, one last time," he explained. "The eaglet coin box will be over on the shelf. You two will be outside. Johann, you'll be the first to enter..."

"I can't believe it even ran at all," the mechanic said as he wiped his greasy hands on a rag and slammed the hood down on the Chevy. "You only had a nubbin left for points, and the timing was so bad, it even made my Mickey Mouse watch look good.

T.B. said nothing, but looked to see if the mechanic was actually wearing a Mickey Mouse wristwatch. He was.

The mechanic went on. "There was no spark coming through the number six and eight cylinders so I replaced both wires and put in new plugs. I must have poured a gallon of cleaner down the carburetor."

"How's it run?" T.B. inquired.

The mechanic grinned as he opened the door and turned the key. It started immediately, and he raced the motor a couple times.

236

"Jesus!" T.B. had never heard it run so good. He cringed, expecting a hundred-dollar bill. "How much do I owe you?"

The mechanic wiped at his hands and tugged at his cap. "Got quite few parts there, thirty bucks worth at least."

"How much for everything?" T.B. asked again.

"Oh, sixty dollars ought to about cover it."

"Sixty dollars!?" T.B. exclaimed totally pleased with the amount.

The mechanic stared at T.B. like he had been slapped with a lawsuit. "I thought that was a fair price."

"It is! It is!" T.B. whipped the money out of his wallet like it had grease on it.

Even Leroy thought the amount was more than fair. "Are you a Marxist by any chance?" he asked the mechanic.

The man thought a moment, and when he removed his cap and scratched his head, Leroy was sure he was.

"No," the mechanic finally said. "But I've got a union card."

Leroy frowned, but T.B. was smiling from ear to ear. "That's just as good. Let's go, Leroy."

"By the way," the mechanic asked. "What happened to the roof of your car?"

"I used to be with the circus," T.B. answered. "An elephant fell on it."

As they backed out of the garage, they heard the mechanic holler after them, "Must have been a big one!"

They swung on to Wayzata Boulevard and drove back to the Interstate, and once on the freeway, T.B. pressed the accelerator to the floor. "Unbelievable," he said as he leaned forward to listen to the hum of the fine tuned engine.

"He had to be a Marxist," Leroy commented. "Listen to that engine, and all for sixty bucks!"

"You know, Leroy, he might have been at that." The speedometer showed seventy miles an hour. "Boy! This old tub has never been over sixty. Let's see what she'll really do!"

The two leaned back in their seats and watched the speedometer climb.

It had taken the better part of an hour to drive back to Fargo from Detroit Lakes. The Princess pulled the Volkswagen to a stop at the light opposite Bud's Roller Rink.

"So," she said, as she turned to Johann. "Do you think it will work?"

"I don't know why not. Snuffy seems to have everything under control."

"How much do you think a genuine eaglet coin box is worth?"

"Quite a few thousand according to Snuffy."

"Are you worried about tomorrow night?" she asked.

"I'm concerned." said Johann. "I've never done anything like this before."

"I hope everything turns out all right."

"Well, we'll know tomorrow, won't we?"

Pam didn't answer. She shoved the gear in low and drove on when the light turned green.

Pavlov, Reggie and Carrigan sat in Sko's car across from the Dutch Maid restaurant. Sko pointed to the letters on the front of the brick building that spelled *Dakota Business College.* "It's a tenant building now. Buckmeier owns it." An alley ran between the Dutch Maid Grill and the old college building, and along the outside of the old structure, an enclosed staircase acted as the fire escape for all three floors.

Sko pointed upwards "At the top of the staircase, a door leads to two small rooms. We'll be playing cards in the first one. There's a window on the other side facing the Mexican Village. Timing is critical."

He turned to the back seat. "Carrigan, you'll be in the Mexican Village parking lot. Reggie, you'll come up the staircase as soon as Carrigan signals you. Is that clear?"

"Yes." Reggie was as somber as he had ever been, his eyes fixed on the staircase in the alleyway.

Sko drove down the alley to the Mexican Village parking lot located behind the Dutch Maid. He parked in a strategic spot and turned to Carrigan. "This is where I want you parked." From where they sat, the window on the third floor of the Dakota Business College building was clearly visible. "Pavlov will signal you from there. Then you signal Reggie with that thing-a-ma-jig you're supposed to get. Everything clear?"

All three acknowledged.

Sko went on. "The building also has an inside staircase with an exit on Main. That's the fast way out. Once the ruckus starts, you can bet the other three will use the back way, and I'll go with them. Pavlov, you and Reggie take the outside staircase."

Pavlov was hesitant. "I wish we could rehearse everything."

"We just did," said Sko.

"It's risky," said Pavlov.

"I know."

"It could go haywire."

"The Princess could be beat to death by her husband, too." He checked their glum faces. "Look, if it does go haywire, you guys got nothing to worry about. I'm the guy who's gotta face Frank again."

Carrigan understood completely. "He's right, guys."

A long silence hung inside the car as they looked over the layout of the building and the alley.

"Everything straight?" Sko asked.

The others all nodded.

Sko started up the car and drove back to Carrigan's office.

"Dammit, dammit!" T.B. slammed a fist against the wheel. Only five miles from Fargo and he had to get stopped.

The redheaded highway patrolman slowly approached the Chevy, his eyes curiously examining the flattened rooftop. He stooped to peer inside the Chevy window. "Can I see your license, please?" he inquired. He was big.

T.B. played dumb. "What seems to be the trouble, officer?"

"Your license, please."

T.B. was trying to be cool. "I think an explanation is in order. You see, my partner and I are on a case, and we…"

"Step out of the car," the patrolman commanded.

"I think we can…"

The highway patrolman pulled on the door handle, and when he did so, T.B. rolled out onto the pavement. His magnum flopped from its place and clattered against the cement.

"Freeze!" The patrolman was faster than Wyatt Earp as he stuck the muzzle of his pistol in T.B.'s face.

"Oh, Lord!"

Leroy sat still as a statue, his hands raised in the air.

"Oh, Lord!"

It was almost nine pm when the phone rang in Carrigan's office. He stared at the three around the table, surprised the phone was ringing at this time of night. Verna, he thought as he got up and went to the other room.

Reggie dealt out the cards while Carrigan answered the phone. In seconds, he was back.

"Who was it?" asked Sko.

Carrigan didn't respond.

"Well?" Pavlov asked when he saw Carrigan's twisted face. "Did the little shit finally call?"

"Yeah, he's at 211 9th Street South," he said, as he arranged his cards.

Pavlov paused. "211? That's the county courthouse."

"It's also the county jail."

The others looked up from their cards.

"He got a citation."

"For what?"

"The usual stuff. Speeding, resisting arrest, insulting an officer and carrying a pistol without a permit." Carrigan looked at his cards again. "Did anyone open?"

The card game broke up at 11:45. Right afterward, Carrigan drove to the jail where a night guard buzzed him in. A second guard ushered him to an office where an officer was on duty.

"I understand you have a couple of my friends in custody," Carrigan said.

The officer, with drooping eyelids just nodded. "Yep." He nodded to his coworker who walked off to the jail cells and returned with T.B. and Leroy R a few minutes later.

"Hi, Carrigan," T.B. offered. "I think I can explain."

"Don't even try," Carrigan responded.

Twenty-Two
On Your Mark, Get Set...

Early the next morning, T.B. drove to the FM Community Theatre. He was ecstatic about his car; it was running great now. The day before he had been clocked at 82 miles an hour by the highway patrolman, and the radar was accurate. That was exactly the speed he had been traveling.

After he and Leroy were hauled off to jail, he handled the situation smoothly, like his hero, Shell Scott, would have done. He was granted one phone call, and so, naturally, he called Carrigan Mulhouse.

T.B. was afraid Carrigan was going to leave him there, but when Carrigan finally arrived, he had done some fast talking. The fact that he had acquired the electronic equipment Carrigan needed was his only saving grace. T.B. had never seen Carrigan so angry.

But that was last night; today was another day. T.B. made his way up the walk to the theatre, entered and found Marty, the director, on stage with his technical advisor, working out scenes for the next performance.

Marty saw T.B. and motioned for him to come back stage where he had assembled the necessary items T.B. requested.

"Police uniform, chauffeur outfit and two guns," Marty happily pointed out. It was difficult to look Marty directly in the eye, since one of them sort of looked at you and one sort of didn't. The one that didn't was his good eye. "I hope the guns work for you."

The uniforms were good, but T.B. raised an eyebrow at the weapons. "This is a real .38 police special?" he asked.

"No. It's fake. Plastic, best I could do."

"This other gun," T.B. said. "It looks like a cap pistol."

242

"But it fires blanks. You wanted a gun that fires blanks."

"But, it still looks like a cap pistol."

"T.B.," Marty said as his eyes wandered a bit. "You called me 36 hours ago. I did the best I could. Do you want them or not?"

"I do. Thanks Marty, you've been wonderful."

He picked up the items and hauled them out to his car wondering what Carrigan would say about the guns. Why did he need a policeman's uniform complete with a .38 pistol? And why a gun that fired blanks?

T.B. had the box of clothes and other items on his desk when Carrigan arrived at his office. Carrigan pulled up the piano stool and quickly examined the pants, the shirt, the coat, the hat. The police uniform was a fair match of the Fargo Police's uniforms, and everything seemed to be the correct size for Reggie.

"This is a .38 police special?" Carrigan asked when he lifted it from the holster. "It's plastic."

"I didn't want anyone to hurt themselves."

Carrigan examined the other pistol that was to fire blanks. "What the hell's this, a toy?"

"It's the best I could do with the time restraints you gave me. Granted it doesn't look very threatening, but it fires blanks. I tried it. It isn't as loud as my magnum, but it makes enough noise. Here, I'll show you."

"No! No! I believe you. What about the electronic stuff?"

T.B. held up two small devices, a control and a receiver. When he flicked the switch on the control unit, a red bulb blinked on and off on the second piece of equipment. "Works up to within 350 feet," T.B. explained.

"Good," was all Carrigan said. He looked at T.B. with a killing look. "How come you drove to Minneapolis?"

T.B. slouched in his chair.

"And why did you take Leroy along?'

T.B. maintained the slouched position

"I can forgive the speeding, but a detective without a gun permit?"

T.B. didn't dare look up.

Carrigan slapped the Minnesota Tribune down on his desk, opened to a particular page. "Did you by any chance have anything to do with this?"

T.B. glanced at the news report. He had already read the article. It was sketchy, and the police were not certain a robbery had been in progress or not. The article labeled the fracas as a *domestic argument*. Police were searching for two suspects who escaped on foot from the Gay Nineties Bar. One was armed and dangerous and the description of the two fit T.B. and Leroy R perfectly.

"Well," T.B. began, "I think I can expl—" He stopped when he saw the killing look still hanging on Carrigan's face. He dropped his head, so embarrassed. "I appreciate you bailing us out of the slammer."

"I hope to hell you do, Harvey. It cost me four hundred dollars."

"I'll pay you back." He was unable to look Carrigan in the eye. "Perhaps I could pay you back in services?"

"I won't be requiring your services anymore."

"But you said you needed a bagman to deliver the ransom money."

"I didn't say I needed one. You did. We'll take care of this ourselves." Carrigan stuffed all the clothing and items in the box, shoved it under his arm and stood up. "I don't want you or Leroy involved in anything anymore. I don't know what the hell you two were doing in the Gay Nineties Bar, but you're off the case. Understand?"

T.B. raised his head, looking like a plucked chicken. "Okay."

"You owe me," Carrigan said. He got up and left.

"You owe me," T.B. repeated quietly to himself once

Carrigan was gone. That was the same phrase he had used on Orville at the bank. Of course, he would pay Carrigan back somehow.

T.B. sat for a few minutes thinking and then called Leroy. "How you coming with the pictures you took in Minneapolis?" T.B. listened for a few moments. "Right. Get back to me as soon as you can. We owe it to Carrigan to figure this thing out."

He hung up and crossed the room to where the city map of Fargo-Moorhead hung on the wall. He had marked an X on Jerry Allison's office building, put one on the Allison home and one on Pam Allison's office building, which was the same as Carrigan's. He had also placed another X on Leroy's place in Moorhead, but as he studied the X's, there seemed to be really nothing strategic about them.

When he glanced at his watch, he said, "Aha!" In seconds, he was out the door and walked to Jerry Allison's office where he waited across the street, checking his watch occasionally. His timing was good. Jerry drove up in his car, entered his office, and ten minutes later, he came out and walked pass the post office headed toward Roberts Street. T.B. had a good idea where he was going, and he wasn't wrong.

Jerry Allison went directly to Epko Photography, where he and the fellow inside met briefly. T.B. had learned the fellow's name was Gordon Gelsper. Within a few minutes, Jerry and Gordon left the store and headed for P.D.'s Restaurant.

"Aha!" T.B. said as he trailed after them.

Things at the Powers Coffee House seemed normal this morning. Ruckles had already arrived and left, Wandering Eddie and Mumbling Mike were in a corner booth, both with huge breakfasts before them, and Hardnuts Brodigan was leaning against the counter talking to the Fargo-Burnout. Harriet, dressed in a bright green dress this morning, was having breakfast with another client, a bald, older man.

Carrigan had not seen the Iranian lately, which was understandable. He probably wouldn't be showing up where Brodigan hung out. Carrigan had put two and two together and figured out it was Hardnuts who had given the Iranian the beating, not Harvey.

All the members of the coffee group were at the table now. Reggie was the last to arrive, and Millie had just plunked his wheat toast in front of him. She shook the coffee container and hurried off to another table.

The guys had been somber all morning.

Carrigan eyed Reggie. "Your stuff is at my office. Pick it up after coffee." Carrigan lowered his voice. "Pavlov, you pick up the gun and blanks." He eyed Snuffy. "How are you coming along?"

Snuffy finished rolling a cigarette. "We've rehearsed everything. We're ready."

"Got the limousine?"

"Got it."

Carrigan wanted to remain calm, but he was nervous. He singled out the Princess and Johann, "When do you two leave?"

"We'll be in DL at two o'clock this afternoon," Pam answered.

"When does Coddington arrive?"

Snuffy answered. "Usually between four and six, but we want to be ready for him in case he shows up early."

Everything seemed in order, but no one was joking at the table this morning. Reggie ate away at his wheat toast, Pavlov finished up the eggs on his plate and Johann lit up another cigarette, although he already had one burning in the ashtray.

"Tonight's the night," Radio Sko said in passing. He hadn't tried to sell a radio buy to Carrigan in days, and today was no exception.

Princess Pam Allison was as beautiful as ever, but she was lacking the spirit she normally possessed. The entire coffee group looked glum.

The Princess spoke suddenly. "Let's call it off." All eyes at the table shifted to her. "This is...this is nuts. It isn't... fair to any of you."

"Fair? Shee-it," Pavlov retorted. "And deprive me of the opportunity to play a henchman? Shee-it."

When the Princess let out a slight snicker, the table finally loosened up.

"I'm going to nail those sons-a-bitches!"

"Ah'm gonna carry a big gun in mah belt."

"Careful you don't shoot off your penis."

"Haw, haw, haw."

"We can't let our Christian Mr. Coddington get away, can we?"

"I get to play cop. I've always wanted to play cop."

"You'll look good dressed up like Lavonya LaRue,"

"Yuh, yuh. I'm the peon. All I get to do is drive a car."

"Every job is important, Johann."

"Boy, are we going to stick it to Wimpy Wimpleton."

"Yuh, yuh, you betchum, Red Ryder."

T.B. was on to something. He could taste it, feel it in his bones. After Jerry and Gordon left Elm Tree Square, both returned to their offices. T.B. sat in his car now across from Jerry Allison's business. He was determined to keep Jerry under surveillance all day long.

It had occurred to him that he might case Jerry Allison's home in secret, but he also remembered how much trouble he had gotten into at Ruckles' home and at Harriet's apartment.

T.B. pieced it together nicely. Jerry Allison wasn't as dumb as he was made out to be. Either Jerry had the negatives of the Princess, or his friend, Gordon from Epko Photography, had them.

T.B. looked up the street, bored with the monotony of watching the front of Jerry's office. At that very moment, he saw Carrigan Mulhouse drive by in his car, and somebody else was with him.

T.B. started his car and drove after him. At the Mark Building, Carrigan and Pam got out of his car and entered Carrigan's office. A few seconds later two cars pulled up in front, and several of Carrigan's coffee table buddies got out and went inside. T.B. kept his eyes focused on the front of the building, wondering what was going on. After a few minutes, he drove back to Jerry's office, but Jerry's car was gone.

"Shit." T.B. drove directly to Epko Photography, and as he passed by, he looked through the window of the camera shop where Gordon normally sat behind a counter. He was gone, too.

"Shit," he said again and drove on.

The Princess and Johann von Meer crossed the viaduct that led to the north end and main shopping district of Detroit Lakes. Per Snuffy's instructions, they turned north at the Tourist Bureau and drove across the tracks. Snuffy had rented a garage behind the Lakes Publishing Company where they found Snuffy's pickup.

"I'm scared," the Princess said. "I don't know if I can go through with it."

"You've got to," said Johann. "Everybody's counting on us."

As they pulled up alongside his pickup and before Pam had a chance to shut off the engine, one of the garage doors to the building swung upwards, and Snuffy motioned for them to drive in.

Once inside, Snuffy pulled down the garage door, and there, in the next stall sat a black limousine—shiny, long and massive.

"Ooooh," Snuffy remarked when the Princess stepped from the car. "You look, just like her."

She did resemble the real Miss Lavonya LaRue in every

respect. The coal black dress with the pleats down the front and the red sash about her waist were a steadfast trademark of the celebrity. Her tiny, high heeled, black patent leather shoes with a strap running across her ankles added more class, and the set of diamond earrings and the matching brooch around her neck, though not genuine, certainly appeared so.

Her hair was dyed jet black and flowed downwards over her shoulders. The see-through shawl and the black patent leather purse with the strap over her shoulder set her off perfectly.

The Princess slipped a pair of dark glasses in place.

"Beautiful," said Snuffy. "Just beautiful."

Snuffy produced a set of clothes encased in a suit bag for Johann. The black coat and pants and white, frocked shirt were what he expected. A black tie and a chauffeur cap trimmed him out nicely. Snuffy even had a black pair of high knee boots.

"You look absolutely beautiful," Snuffy told the Princess again.

She smiled as she brushed her hair back over her shoulder. She took a long slender cigarette holder from her purse and showed it to Snuffy, then handed over a business card with her new name on it.

"Perfect," he said as he examined the items. "I'll be seeing you two a little later. Good luck," he said, as he exited the building. Seconds later, Johann and the Princess. heard Snuffy start up his truck and drive away.

Johann examined the clothes before him—the coat and pants, the knee boots, the chauffeur cap, the shirt and tie. "I hope this works."

T.B. stood patiently under the red glow of lights in the darkroom and watched Leroy as he immersed the photo paper into the chemicals. He gently maneuvered the paper around with tongs waiting for the image to appear. Several photos from the Gay Nineties Bar already hung from a wire strung from wall to wall above the chemicals.

Leroy R smiled widely. "Wait until you see this one."

T.B. watched as the image slowly began to appear.

"She sure had a good hold on you, didn't she?" Leroy R quipped. "Or was she a he?"

The, image had fully appeared now depicting T.B. and so-called girl whose name was Bert. It was obvious that she had a firm grip on the bulge in T.B.'s crotch.

"I don't think that's funny, Leroy."

Leroy overlooked the comment. "I'm only developing this photo for effect. Note the clarity of it." He pulled it from the first set of chemicals and dipped it into the equalizer. "I shot this from forty feet away and blew it up. It has nice tones in spite of the shadow."

"You should have let me shoot the son-of-a-bitch."

"Just because he was a little funny?"

"He was a damn flamer. I could have put out his flame permanently."

Leroy chuckled as he held up the photo. "Look how clear it is. Not much grain. I used fast film, yet I still got good clarity."

T.B. looked over all the photos hanging on the wire. They were all quite clear, clean shots, cropped nicely. Leroy had done a nice job of filming the interior of the bar. "So what does all this tell us?"

"Well," said Leroy R "once we dry all these and get a closer look, I think you'll find a couple of these shots have some interesting aspects." He removed one from the wire. "For example, this photo was shot from the stage area at about twenty feet. Notice anything unusual about it?"

T.B. adjusted his glasses and studied the photo. "Nope."

Leroy R smiled inwardly. "You will when we compare it to some photos I took at the Powers Coffee House."

Leroy R gathered up the photos, switched on the light to the darkroom and opened the door to the corridor within the house. He kept his drying machine in a small room next to his den. "How about a brandy while we wait for these?"

"Why not?"

Leroy R started the machine, and as belts and wheels started turning to a fine hum, T.B. procured two shots of the excellent brandy from the den and returned to where the photographs were rolling out from below a huge drum, dried, clean and ready to be handled.

Leroy R collected the photos one by one, and then the two returned to the den where they spread the photographs across his desk. T.B. sipped at the excellent vintage brandy, his eyes studying the photos, yet, he failed to see anything significant about them. Evidently, Leroy R thought there was something peculiar about them.

"Now, take this one, for example," Leroy R said as he held one up for T.B. "Take a close look at this. What do you see?"

It was already late in the afternoon. The Princess and Johann sat inside the black limo parked at the far end of the Holiday Inn a block away from away from Snuffy's cottage. From their vantage point, it would be impossible not to see Mr. Coddington's fancy Lincoln pass by.

They were facing the pool in which guests of the hotel were busy frolicking, diving, and bathing in the warm sun. A back entrance door to the hotel was constantly opening and shutting as people came and went, mostly younger boys and girls dressed in a wide and colorful array of bathing suits, carrying rubber floating devices or towels or flippers and goggles. Some either headed for the pool or swung past the limo in the direction of the beach at the front of the hotel.

Though the windows of the limousine were down, it was still extremely warm. Johann had shed his coat and the Princess her shawl.

She looked elegant in her black attire, enticing, like a black widow spider.

Miss Lavonya LaRue—famed antique collector from Chicago.

Articles about the woman and her flamboyant lifestyle had appeared in dozens of magazines. Anyone who was remotely interested in antiques would know who she was.

In reality, the real Miss LaRue was a relatively private person who owned a half million-dollar acreage in the vicinity of Arlington Heights, a northern suburb of the windy city. She was a young, vibrant person, and possessed a reputation for showing up in the most obscure places, and more often than not returning with some expensive antique she had acquired. Of course, such stories were what appeared in the collectors' magazines.

It was mostly circumspect, from Snuffy's point of view, that Mr. Coddington would not only know the name of Miss LaRue, but would also recognize her should he ever see her in person. He was counting heavily on his assumption, and if he was wrong, then everything that was transpiring this afternoon was for naught.

Johann and the Princess understood all of that as they continued staring down the narrow stretch before them. From where they sat, they could also view the old pavilion, a ramshackle hall, where Bobby Vee had begun his singing career some years ago. He and his band had stood in for Buddy Holly and the Big Bopper, both, who tragically died in a plane crash en route to Detroit Lakes for a night of rock and roll entertainment.

They waited some more.

At exactly five o'clock, Radio Sko and Pavlov parked around the corner from the Dutch Maid Grill. Sko was wearing his tan suit, tie snugged up to his neck, calm and completely in control of himself.

Pavlov was dressed differently today. He had donned a dark blue pinstriped suit with a gray pullover sweater underneath. To disguise his face somewhat, he had slicked down his curly hair with oil, parted it in the middle and flared it backwards over his ears on both sides. His jowls were puffed up from the cotton balls he had stuffed inside his cheeks, and he was wearing a pair of dark glasses, which he did not intend to remove for the rest of the night. Underneath his coat and tucked into his belt, yet visible if he ever thrust the coat aside, rested the automatic hand gun that fired blanks.

Pavlov Glitzberg may have appeared big and mean, but underneath all the show, he was scared. For all practical purposes, he needed to appear tough since he was supposed to be a henchman, a bodyguard. Sko had told him just to act like one, but Pavlov had hated drama in high school and college. As verbal as he was with his clients, Pavlov could not begin to deliver a five-minute lecture to a small group of people without choking up.

He was jittery and he knew it, but he did not want to tell Sko. At the bottom of the iron staircase, Pavlov admired how calm Sko appeared, how well he was doing, however, he had a real vendetta to fulfill.

They both glanced toward the dumpster at the end of the alley. Within an hour, Carrigan would be sitting behind it in his Oldsmobile with the piece of electronic equipment that would eventually send a signal to Reggie Richthoffen. It was a simple device. All he needed to do was flick a switch, and Reggie, holding a small receiver at his end would see a red bulb blinking.

It was clear to Pavlov what he was to do. It was clear to all of the men what they were supposed to do.

But as the two ascended the staircase to the third floor, Pavlov felt his knees weaken, and his throat was dry. He hoped to hell he could go through with it.

Just moments after Sko and Pavlov had started up the staircase, T.B. Harvey drove past the Dutch Maid Grill in his beat-up Chevy completely unaware of their presence. He continued north across the NP railroad tracks to the dead end, made a sharp right and left past the fire station and continued up Roberts Street.

T.B. had just come from Jerry Allison's house. Jerry Allison's car wasn't there, and neither was his wife's.

On a hunch, and even though it was near closing time, T.B. decided to check out Jerry's office. As he slowed the car, he searched the immediate area, but Jerry's car was nowhere around. He drove to Epko Photography and stopped directly in front, where he squinted his eyes, searching inside for Gordon, but he wasn't visible either. T B. waited patiently for five minutes. People came and went, but Gordon never showed up.

Jerry Allison was not in his office and Gordon was nowhere around.

"Shit," he said as he slumped back in the seat. All day long, neither of them had been in their offices. *So, where the hell are they?*

Plotting, T.B. was sure. Plotting how to have the money delivered.

Plotting how they would spend the money

But where are they plotting?

Obviously the two would not plot at Jerry's home.

Traffic was picking up now since it was after five o'clock, and the sidewalks were filled with people walking up and down the street.

"Shit," T.B. swore again, as he pulled away from the curb. He swung onto Roberts and headed back north to Fourth Street where he stopped for a red light.

His mind was in a half-daze, but as he glanced across at the Mark Building where Carrigan had his office, he saw the flash of a long, black coat disappear around the corner.

The office building was devoid of lights at the moment. T.B. heard a horn honk from behind him, shoved up a fist and then drove through the intersection and parked across from the Mark Building.

He got out of his car and crossed to the side door of the building where he thought he had seen the person in the long, black coat. The door was open, so he let himself in. A short staircase led upwards to a metal fire door. He eased himself up the stairs and cautiously opened the door. Carrigan Mulhouse's office was at the end of the hallway to his left, and at this end, a door led to Pam Allison's decorating business. Both offices were closed, both without lights.

T.B. listened for a few seconds, but he could hear nothing, no movement anywhere. Across and down the hallway about twenty feet, another staircase led to the second floor. Perhaps the man had gone upstairs.

T.B. silently made his way up a half dozen steps when he clearly heard the sound of a door closing downstairs. There, in the corridor with his back to T.B. was the tall man in the black coat.

"Hey!" T.B. shouted as he reached for the magnum inside his coat. The man quickly shoved his way through the metal door.

By the time T.B. came back down to the hallway, he could hear the man clatter his way down the steps to the outside.

In hot pursuit, T.B. pushed his way through the metal door and down the stairs to the parking lot just in time to see the rear door of the Flame Bar across from him swing shut.

T.B.'s nerves were crawling as he darted across the lot and disappeared inside to a haven of dim light. T.B. quickly glanced at the front entrance. The man didn't have time to reach it. He was still inside.

Smoke was heavy, and the foul smell of stale liquor ran through his nostrils. Pool balls smacked loudly, and from one corner, a jukebox pounded out an obscure song. To his left, an old duffer was fishing pull tabs out of a jar for a couple gamblers, and at the bar, several men were pressed in for their after-work fix.

The two men nearest him at this end were staring directly at him. It was then that T.B. realized he still was holding the big magnum in his hand. He jammed the handgun out of sight, and as he casually strode past the two, he whispered, "Narcotics."

He could feel their eyes penetrating the back of his head as he waded into the thicket of the crowd. Smoke was heavier now, the liquor smell thicker yet. Nowhere could he spot the man in the long black coat, and a man wearing a long black coat on a warm day like today would stand out in a crowd.

Something in the back of his mind was falling into place. *Where had he seen that coat before?* And then it came to him!

There were only two doors inside the bar at this end, and both led to the bathrooms. *The men's can!* That was the only place the man could have disappeared so quickly.

T.B. gulped and felt his nerves twinge. He stood erect, smoothed down his coat, patted the magnum underneath and felt his courage grow as he quietly let himself into the restroom.

There were two urinals against the wall, and two stalls to the right. The distinct aroma of week-old piss smacked at his nostrils. He stepped lightly into the center of the room, bent down and saw a pair of beat-up shoes poking out from a light colored pair of pant legs. *Facing him.* The man was sitting on the stool, or at least that was T.B.'s initial assumption. He was still bent over examining the shoes when the door burst open and slammed into his face. Stars shot through his eyeballs as his glasses crunched. When he hit the floor, he jolted his spine and more stars shot through his brain as the back of his head thumped against the cement. A few minutes later he felt the hands of two guys picking him up by the arm pits.

"Are you okay?" one of them asked.

"Shall we call an ambulance?"

T. B. was seeing out of only one eye, and although his glasses were still in place, his face was numb. Blood dripped down from the bridge of his nose where the pads in his glasses had dug in. He felt his nose, wiggled it around.

"Are you hurt?" one of the men asked again.

The numbness in his face was slowly subsiding, and now the pain was slowly taking its place, and his little bulbous nose was rapidly becoming a big bulbous nose. His back hurt, his head hurt, his face hurt, everything hurt.

"I'm okay, I'm okay," he managed to say. He felt inside his coat, surprised that the magnum had managed to remain in place. He straightened up and strutted toward the door and then turned to eye the two men staring back. "Get a mop and wipe up that piss on the floor. A guy could fall down and get killed in here."

Just as he turned to exit, someone else pushed the door in and slammed it against his face. He groaned and held his nose all the way back to his car.

Delray K. Dvoracek

Twenty-Three
Scam Night

Carrigan, sitting in his Oldsmobile behind the dumpster had no reason to feel nervous, but he was. He was no more than a stone's throw from the entrance to the Mexican Village Restaurant. He also had a clear view of the third floor warehouse window behind which he knew the card game was presently going on, and he could not help but wonder how Pavlov and Sko were holding up, and whether Sko was winning or losing.

Carrigan's part of the scam was simple. All he had to do was keep his eyes glued to the window. He had been looking upward for so long that he had a kink in his neck. On three occasions, Pavlov had appeared at the window and pulled at the shade simply to glance out, but each time, he had not given the signal, which, as stupid as it seemed, was nothing more than to give Carrigan the finger.

It was still early, yet, Carrigan was jumpy. It could well be another three or four hours before he would get the finger, that is, if everything was going well.

Carrigan glanced across the open parking lot to the street where a policeman was walking between two buildings. The policeman was, of course, Reggie Richthoffen strolling the sidewalk, dressed in the police clothes. From this distance, he looked very authentic. He stopped and twirled the Billy club he was carrying. He swung it upwards in a fancy spin, dropped it to his side and then repeated the maneuver.

It was the waiting that was killing Carrigan.

"Cop," said Pavlov as he looked down from the third floor window.

The Guys from Fargo

Frank Newsom looked up from his cards, then lifted his heavy frame out of the chair and came to the window. As he glanced out to the sidewalk, he chomped on his cigar and blew out a blue smoke stream. He knew the familiar twirl of the night stick, the fancy spin upwards. From where he stood, there was no doubt in his mind who he was.

Frank Newsom trudged back to his chair. "Brodigan," he said to the three at the table. "Don't know what he's doing this far down. His beat is usually on North Broadway."

Little Bucky sucked on a cigarette and grinned. "I wouldn't worry about him."

"I'm not," said Frank Newsom. He picked up his cards and examined them. "Fifty," he said, as he flipped a fin into the pot.

"Call," said Sko.

Frank had two pairs, but Sko's two pairs were higher.

"Goddamn you're lucky tonight," Frank grunted.

"Skill," said Sko with a smile as he raked in the pot. "Who's deal?"

"Mine," Wimpleton, the bald-headed Dean of the college, answered.

Sko stacked up the bills in front of him. He was ahead by almost four thousand dollars, he calculated. Yet, not once during the night had he consciously stopped to count the money. It would not be gambler-like.

Sko was especially alert to everything. He had been steadily winning since he arrived. As long as the other three were using a clean deck of cards, he knew he could beat them anytime.

This was exactly how the game some weeks back had begun. Sko had won heavily the first half of the night, and then someone had slipped in the marked deck of cards. Sko was four thousand ahead now, exactly where the other three wanted him, believing his luck was so good that he couldn't lose. Sometime during the night, one of the men would suggest a new deck, and it was then Sko had to be ready.

Strangely enough, at that very moment, Wimpleton suggested, "How about a new deck? These cards are getting cold."

"Suit yourself," Sko said.

The university man with the stoic, pug nose face unwrapped a new deck, shuffled them, had them cut and dealt them around. Sko made a quick inspection of the backs of the cards. This deck was not marked either. The three were going to let him get way ahead and then drop it all on him later on. *Good!*

Sko examined his five cards as Bucky opened with a ten spot. Everybody stayed and cards were dealt around. Radio Sko kept two kings and a jack. He drew a king and a four.

Twenty," said Bucky. Frank shoved in a twenty-dollar bill, Sko shoved in a twenty and raised the pot thirty. Wimpleton passed.

Bucky made a face and threw in an additional thirty.

Frank passed.

Sko laid down three kings.

"Damn," said Bucky. "You're lucky tonight."

"Skill," Sko repeated again. "Deal."

Sko won five of the next eight hands. Losing was not bad, since he played his cards only for what they were worth. In less than twenty minutes, he picked up another six hundred dollars.

As the foursome played on, Pavlov stood to the side, hands crossed in front of him, watching, waiting, knowing that if Sko's luck held, he would have a pile of money in front of him in another hour or so.

Pavlov crossed to the window again and moved the shade to the side. Reggie was gone, but across the alley, he could see the top of the Oldsmobile and a portion of the windshield. It was dark, but he knew Carrigan was sitting behind the wheel.

"You're making me nervous," Frank suddenly told Pavlov. "Why the hell don't you sit down?"

The Guys from Fargo

Pavlov had been cautioned about Frank Newsom's behavior. It would all be for show, Sko had informed him earlier. It was in Frank's nature to be tough, pissy and sarcastic, especially when he was losing.

So far Pavlov felt he was doing well. He had hardly spoken a word all night, had done everything Sko had instructed him to do. Just stand by, say nothing, act tough.

"I said why the hell don't you sit down!?" Frank snarled again. "And take off those goddamn dark glasses!"

Sko cast a curious glance at Pavlov wondering how he was going to respond.

Pavlov remained against the wall, dark glasses in place, the cotton balls inside his cheek jutting out his jowls. He looked mean, tough, just like he was supposed to be. He was about the same height as Frank, although Frank outweighed him by fifty pounds or more.

Pavlov left his glasses in place, but he unbuttoned his coat and made sure they all saw the handle of the pistol sticking out of his belt. It did resemble a cap pistol, but the handle was enough to get their attention, and by the look on Frank Newsom's face, he for sure saw the butt of the gun.

In a slow southern drawl, Pavlov spoke. "Ah ain't gettin' paid ta sit. Ah git paid to keep mah fukkin' eyes open."

Defiantly, Pavlov crossed to the window, pulled the shade aside and glanced out. When he turned back to the room, the four men at the table were still looking at him. Pavlov leaned against the wall, crossed his hands over his chest and stared directly at Frank Newsom.

Slowly, Frank let his eyes drop to the table. "Whose deal?" he said without looking up.

"My God! What happened?" Leroy R draped a wet towel over T.B.'s left eye. It was almost swollen shut. A heavy gash on the bridge of his nose looked nasty, but it wasn't bleeding any more.

"The Fargo-Burnout," said T.B. The towel covered both his eyes now as he leaned back in the leather chair letting the cool wetness of the cloth sooth his face. "I caught the bastard near Pam Allison's office and trailed him over to the Flame Bar. He got me from behind when I wasn't looking."

Skepticism was riding Leroy R's face. If the Fargo-Burnout had nailed him from behind, he should have a welt on the back of his dead. Actually, he did, but his eye was swelled up like a ping-pong ball full of yeast, and his glasses were flattened like they had been run through the rollers of an old washing machine.

When Leroy R shoved a shot of brandy into T.B.'s hand, he whiffed it, and without removing the towel, he gulped the shot down in one swallow. Leroy R filled the shot glass again.

"You're sure it was the Fargo-Burnout?" Leroy R glanced at the photographs laid out on his desk and selected one that depicted the Fargo-Burnout. "Was he wearing the long coat?"

"Yeah. And white dirty pants. He needed a shave, his hair was greasy and his fist was big."

"What was he doing at Pam Allison's office?"

"I don't know. Might have slipped a blackmail note under the door. I think he's our man."

Leroy R made a face. "I'm not so sure."

T.B. pulled the wet towel away and squinted through his good eye at Leroy R, questioning his response.

"I've been doing some more thinking about the photographs," Leroy R said. He turned them to face T.B. The top row depicted a few stripping shots of the Princess. The bottom row showed several of the photos taken from within the Gay Nineties Bar.

Leroy R pointed to the shots in which Pam Allison was stripping. "I think these are all professional photos."

"But you said they had a lot of grain in them, not as much clarity as yours."

Leroy R sipped at his brandy and scratched at the scraggly

hairs on his chin. "These photos could have been taken with a faster speed film thus giving more grain when blown up. Whoever blew them up cropped the sides and the top like a professional. The girl is in the center of each photo, and what's more, the lighting is perfect. Look at the shadow on the sides of the girl's body. Look at the depth of field. Look at the dimension overall. These are excellent shots even though they have more grain than mine."

T.B. slipped his spare set of glasses in place. Though they were an older pair, and though he couldn't see very well at a distance, the bifocals were still useful. And now, he was seeing fairly well out of his left eye. He lifted his head and examined the photos trying to understand what Leroy R was talking about. At a glance, he could see Pam's nude body was centered perfectly on each picture, and a shadow on the sides of her body gave her the dimension that he assumed Leroy R was talking about.

"So what are you telling me?" T.B. finally asked.

"I'm simply saying these photos of the nude girl were taken by a professional. I'd stake my life on it." Leroy R didn't look as if he were about to die soon, so T.B. figured he knew what he was talking about.

T.B. came back to the Fargo-Burnout. "What do you know about this guy in the long black coat?"

"Just what I told you the other day. He works periodically on the railroad docks, picks up odd jobs here and there."

"Maybe he was a photographer at one time," T.B. suggested

"He was in the service before he showed up here."

"Then where does that leave us?" asked T. B.

"You tell me."

"That brings us back to Jerry Allison and his camera buddy, Gordon Gelsper."

"You just told me the Fargo-Burnout was the blackmailer."

T.B. thought a moment, opened his mouth and paused. "Shit. I don't know. I had some suspects, but they aren't suspect any more. Now I've got some new suspects, but I don't know how suspect they are. Jerry and Gordon seemed like the best suspects, but then, what was the Fargo-Burnout doing in Pam's office building?"

Leroy R shrugged. "I don t know. Maybe you should ask him next time you see him."

"And get my face punched in again? T.B. draped the towel over his forehead and leaned back in his chair thinking out loud. "What the hell was he doing in Pam Allison's office building? Pam wasn't there. Nobody was there."

T.B. took the towel away, leaned forward again and scrutinized the photos Leroy R had taken in Minnesota. "Let's talk about these Gay Nineties photos again. You said this afternoon there was something peculiar about the angle of the photos. What did you mean by that?"

Leroy R hunched over the photos and scratched at his beard again. He adjusted the peasant cap perched on his head and held up a photo. "Well, take this one for example…"

"He's not coming," said Johann, as he ground out his sixth cigarette in the ashtray. Pam Allison was still in the back seat and had draped the shawl over her shoulder. It was dusk, but lights from the Holiday Inn were already on lighting up the parking lot and the pool across the complex as if it were day. There was very little activity in the pool at the moment, except for a few stragglers still jumping from the board, splashing, hollering.

From across the park, they could hear the thumping of old time music pouring out of the pavilion. Dozens of people had left the hotel and crossed through the park to the dance hall. The boards that covered the windows were swung upwards and hooked to the ceiling of the overhanging porch that surrounded the hall.

Occasionally, huge bursts of laughter rang from the building.

"He's not coming," Johann repeated as he lit up another cigarette. He was uncomfortable and irritated from sitting so many hours.

"Snuffy said he would arrive," she commented from the back seat, but now, she, too, was skeptical.

"But in the late afternoon," Johann retorted. "It's almost 8:30. He's not coming."

There it was suddenly. They both saw the flash of the white car for just a second. The fancy Lincoln without a doubt just passed by the hotel headed toward Snuffy's cottage.

"That's him!" Pam exclaimed.

"By God he did come." Johann felt his body come alive as he checked his watch. "We wait five minutes and make our move."

Pam Allison tensed in the back seat, tugged at her shawl, pulled the patent leather purse closer to her side. The Coddington scam was about to begin.

"I think you're bluffing, Sko," said big, ugly Frank Newsom as he rolled the cigar from one side of his mouth to the other.

Sko held the five cards tight in his hand and glared back at Frank without any hint of excitement in his face. "Might be," he said as he shoved a hundred-dollar bill into the pot.

"Fold," said Wimpleton.

"Me too," said Bucky.

Frank Newsom bit down on his cigar and spread his cards out for one last look, then threw them in. "Take it."

Sko placed his cards face down on the table and slid them into the deck. If no one called him, he didn't have to show his cards.

"What'd you have?" asked big Frank.

Sko reached for his winnings. "A straight."

Frank snarled and bit on his cigar, unaware that Sko had nothing more in his hand than a pair of fours. Frank Newsom had thrown away three sevens, a winning hand.

Pavlov was still standing against the wall, hands folded across his chest. Frank Newsom had not spoken to him since the earlier encounter, and now when he glanced up at Pavlov, he just as quickly glanced away and stood up for a stretch.

Sko stacked up the bills in neat piles. He had not been counting his winnings, but he estimated that he was nine or ten thousand dollars ahead.

"Beer," Frank Newsom growled.

Sko pulled four cans from a cooler in the corner. "Don't mind if I do." It was his second can all night long. He popped the beer top and took only a small mouthful. The other two men at the table stood up, they, too, ready for a stretch.

Wimpleton was wearing a smirk on his face. "By God, you're hot tonight."

Sko chuckled. "Doing all right." He took another drink but kept his eye on the three. Sometime soon, one of them was going to slip in the marked deck of cards. He was surprised they hadn't done so already, and he was pleased at the way he was playing cards. Even if they switched decks, now he, too, would know it, and he could read the spots just as well as they.

Pavlov eased himself away from the wall, walked to the window and pulled the shade aside. Reggie was visible on the street again, twirling his night stick. The Olds was still in the lot. *So far so good.*

"No, no, it's not too late at all," Snuffy was saying to Mr. Coddington. "I was just sort of cleaning up around the place anyway. Got another customer coming in soon, so I'm going to stay open for a bit."

Mr. Coddington cocked his head to the side and bowed slightly. "Most appreciative, most appreciative." He was throwing out the charm and elegance of a prince. "If you don't mind, I'll just browse around."

"Sure, go ahead," Snuffy told the Christian gentleman. While Mr. Coddington moved off into the center of the junk filled room, Snuffy slipped off into a different corner and began rearranging items, shifting chairs and tables. He was sweeping the floor when he heard the bell jingle at his back door.

Johann von Meer was standing in the doorway dressed in his chauffeur uniform. He looked suave from head to foot in the black suit and shiny black knee-high boots, and his beard was very natural for his role.

Mr. Coddington, too, turned when he heard the bell at the unusually late hour. He was amused to see a chauffeur in the doorway and more curious as he watched the chauffeur walk very stiffly to Snuffy Jamison's desk. Under the watchful eyes of Mr. Coddington, Snuffy and Johann began conversing in extremely low voices.

Coddington strained to hear the conversation, all the while pretending to be examining some glassware on a case in front of him. He saw the chauffeur remove his black leather gloves, watched as he tucked them neatly inside the front of his coat. It was then that Mr. Coddington turned his gaze to the outside. In the dim light, he could see the front end of the shiny limousine, its black color laden in reflection from the interior lights of the antique shop. Mr. Coddington shifted his gaze back to the two men near the desk.

"I can assure you, Mr. Coddington is also a reputable collector," Snuffy said in a little bit louder voice.

Coddington heard the phrase. When the chauffeur walked back outside, Coddington's curiosity drove him to the inevitable. He approached Snuffy, and as he did so, he caught another glance outside. The chauffeur had reached the car and was opening the rear door of the limo.

"I believe I heard my name mentioned," the Christian gentleman politely addressed Snuffy.

"That fellow just wondered whether they had arrived at an inconvenient time."

"They?" Coddington inquired, his little eyebrows jumping upward.

"He and the lady with him. The fellow in the black outfit dropped in yesterday and had a look around and said he would be back with someone interested in a purchase."

Coddington eyes quickly scanned the room. "Who might I inquire is this... lady?"

Snuffy was playing his role to the hilt as he rummaged through the scattered items on his desk. He pulled out a drawer, turned over some papers. I wrote the name down somewhere, but I can't seem to find it at the moment."

Mr. Coddington squinted and turned up his mouth. Snuffy knew the Christian bastard was extremely irritated because he did not produce a name.

The man offered a cordial smile. "Might I inquire what item was of interest?"

Snuffy looked about the room. "You know," he finally said as he scratched the back of his head. "I was outside most of the time. I don't really know what the chauffeur was interested in."

When the back door jingled, Mr. Coddington quickly turned away from the desk and crossed to where he had been before, but his eyes bulged out when he saw the lady who had just entered the shop. He was stunned with her appearance and knew without a doubt who she was. His nerves jumped as he strained his ears to hear the conversation going on, and he cursed under his breath when he could not make out what they were discussing.

Mr. Coddington observed the lady as she reached into her purse and produced a card. Snuffy quite casually glanced at the card and dropped it on his desk, and then the three moved off into a far corner of the room.

Mr. Coddington could hardly contain himself as he

inconspicuously as possible made his way to the desk. Could he be mistaken? She had the same black flowing hair draped over her shoulders, the black dress, the red sash. And the long strap running over her shoulder and attached to the petite black, leather purse.

Half way to the desk, he saw the lady open her purse and take out a long slender cigarette holder. She placed a cigarette in it, and immediately the chauffeur snapped a light for her.

Unable to resist, Coddington walked directly to the desk and glanced at the card. *My God, it is her!* His throat went dry. *Miss Lavonya LaRue here in Detroit Lakes!* Nervous energy raced throughout his body. The hair on the back of his head tingled. He stiffened and tugged at the bottom of his pin-striped suit coat, his interest suddenly shifting to the item the three were now examining. The conversation seemed to be only between Miss LaRue and Mr. Jamison.

A tense shock overtook him as he silently crossed the room. Now, close enough, he fixed his eyes on the eaglet coin box. From where he stood, the antique appeared to be in excellent condition. It would be valued at no more than three, perhaps four hundred dollars. But this was Miss Lavonya LaRue, the famous lady from Arlington Heights. If she was making an appearance here, it wouldn't be to purchase a three-hundred-dollar item. This lady collector dealt in thousands of dollars!

Mr. Coddington's mind was way ahead of his body. If the eaglet coin box were genuine… if it really were genuine… *Mr. Jamison said the chauffeur had made an appearance the day before...* He was no ordinary chauffeur. This must be Daniel Stone, her special driver and also a *very astute collector.* His specialty was gems, but no doubt he knew a great deal about other collectibles and art objects. He was every bit as good of a collector as Miss LaRue.

"Good heavens," Coddington whispered to himself. He suddenly realized that Mr. Jamison had no idea to whom he was speaking, nor did he have the faintest idea of the sort of price a genuine eaglet coin box could bring.

"I could offer sixteen for it," Mr. Coddington heard Miss LaRue say to Snuffy.

"Sixteen?" inquired Snuffy in words deliberately delivered with a sense of incomprehension about the amount.

The Christian gentleman cringed when he heard the offer, and his hands trembled. Obviously, the chauffeur had had time to examine the coin box the day before. Mr. Jamison even said he was outside when the chauffeur was looking around. The man had plenty of time to unscrew the back of the box and check for a serial number. The item was worth perhaps thirty or thirty-five thousand dollars!

Miss LaRue drew on the end of her cigarette holder and released a fine stream of smoke. "Eighteen thousand, then," she said to Snuffy.

Snuffy's eyes bugged out like his head was pumped full of air. "Eighteen thousand dollars?"

Coddington's heart banged away. *The dumb shit doesn't even know who he's dealing with, and he doesn't even know she's talking in thousands!*

Coddington stared at the coin box, the shiny brass eagles perched on the wires, the black trim along the sides. *It's in very good condition. No one in their right mind would offer thousands for a copy!*

Eighteen thousand, Coddington was thinking. That was an extremely low bid for this item. Far too low for such a precious collectible.

He moved in a little closer. "Excuse me," he said to the three. "I couldn't help but overhear your conversation."

Carrigan could understand why some people smoked. Sitting in a car for three hours even made him think about it. It made sense why undercover agents or FBI agents could easily get the habit. Sitting around doing nothing was no fun.

He had listened to the radio for a while, found a toothpick and ran that through every groove in his teeth until it was mush. He had tapped his ring on the steering wheel so many times that he was sure he had made a dent in it.

The first hour passed by with an average amount of monotony, the second hour with extreme monotony, the third unbearable. He had to take a leak now, but he did not dare leave his spot, and his neck was cramped from looking upwards at the third floor window. He wished now he had parked further back, but the parking lot was filled to capacity with cars. The Mexican Village was doing a good business tonight. And besides, he needed to be close enough to the window so he could see Pavlov give him the finger.

From here, he could easily see up and down the alley, and from this vantage point he would often see Reggie walk by. More minutes slowly ticked by. He was bored and tense, and his feet were stiff from sitting in one position.

"Come on, come on!" he said out loud. Not once in the last twenty minutes had he seen Pavlov appear at the window.

He began tapping his ring finger against the steering wheel again, wondering how Snuffy, Johann and the Princess were doing. By now, they should have concluded the Coddington scam, if indeed they had been successful. Perhaps Coddington didn't even show up. If he did, then the scam should be over.

He tapped the ring incessantly again. "Come on, Pavlov, let's get this over with!"

"It is Miss LaRue, isn't it?" Mr. Coddington inquired. "Miss Lavonya LaRue, I believe?"

Pam Allison's eyes focused on the neatly dressed man in the pinstriped suit, but she said nothing.

"I'm sorry to interrupt," he went on, "but I have read considerably about you. If I might be so bold as to introduce myself." He stuck out a warm hand. "Conrad Coddington."

Pam was playing her role nicely. She examined him from

head to toe with a flare of indignance, then drew in a breath of smoke through the thin cigarette holder and let it out slowly through her ruby rounded lips. Only then did she offer her hand.

"It is indeed a great pleasure to make your acquaintance, Miss LaRue," said Christian Mr. Coddington. "I couldn't help but overhear your offer of eighteen thousand for this coin box."

Pam did not respond, and Snuffy gave the appearance as if he were still in shock over the eighteen thousand dollar offer.

Coddington's voice trailed away from his normal syrupy tone into a cutting remark. "Of course, Mr. Jamison, you realize eighteen thousand is rather a pittance for this item."

Snuffy let his mouth gape in awe. "It seems fair to me."

"Mr. Coddington," the Princess interrupted sharply. "I believe the unwritten code of ethics allows me to conclude my dealings without interruption, does it not?" Her tone was snobbish enough, and a delight for Snuffy to hear. Coddington felt her cold approach. She was shrewd, like the articles stated she was, and she was now showing her arrogance and aloofness, two other traits that overshadowed an inscrutable collector.

Coddington's greed was pressing on him like a thousand-pound vice. "Of course. Miss LaRue, it is an unwritten code, as you so amply stated, however, I happened to notice this coin box earlier this evening when I first arrived. I just hadn't got around to dealing with Mr. Jamison."

All three knew that was a lie. Pam put on a snobbish smile, one that also smelled the greed pouring off of this insolent cheat. "Daniel," she said as she held up her cigarette holder.

Johann took the cigarette holder from her and looked about for an ashtray. Snuffy instantly produced one. Johann chucked the cigarette from the holder and handed it back. She promptly reached inside her purse and produced another cigarette, which she slipped into the holder. Johann flipped a lighter, and all three watched her draw in a long breath. She blew out the smoke in a fine stream. "Mr. Coddington," she said after a long and dramatic pause. "Daniel discovered this item yesterday."

Coddington gave a wide snide smile like a used car salesman. "Ahh, but you did not purchase it yesterday. He abruptly turned to Snuffy. "Twenty thousand."

"Twenty-two," Pam said without hesitating.

"Twenty-four," snapped Coddington.

Snuffy's eyes flicked back and forth with the bidding, feigning his surprise and shock.

Pam blew out another fine stream of smoke. "Twenty-five."

Mr. Coddington was silent, as if he were rethinking the situation. She looked at the coin box hoping she had not hurried her bid. Holding her composure, she waited patiently for his bid, and when it did not come, she turned to Snuffy. "I believe we can settle on twenty-five. Cash of course." She began to open her purse.

"Twenty-six!"

Pam turned to Snuffy with cold, staring eyes. "Mr. Jamison, I believe yesterday you said I could entertain the privacy of dealing with you alone. There was no mention of any other person being present for settlement on this item." She stuck her nose up in the air like an aristocratic snob. "How do you know for sure this Mr. Coddington is reputable?"

Coddington was insulted with the remark and frisky. "I can assure you I am!"

"W-well, ah," Snuffy stammered, "He has purchased other, ah…"

"Come Daniel," she interrupted. She spun on her heels and made for the doorway, but turned before she exited. She removed the cigarette from her holder, dropped it to the cement floor, ground it out and then left.

As soon as she and Johann were out the door, Coddington turned to Snuffy. "Rather poor sport, wouldn't you say?" His eyes gleamed with envy when he turned to the coin box. It was a grand find, and he had purchased it out from under the nose of the infamous Miss Lavonya LaRue. That in itself was enough notoriety to deserve an article on himself in one of the art magazines. He would, of course, turn over the coin box within a few months' time and make as much as eight or ten thousand dollars' profit, maybe more.

"Well, Mr. Jamison," Coddington said as he watched the limousine pull away, "I believe we can conclude this deal in short time."

"Y-yes, Mr. Coddington. If you'll make out a check, I'll give you a receipt.

"Oh, that won't be necessary," he answered, still wearing the greedy smile as he crossed to the desk. "I'll make a quick phone call and we can conclude this with cash. You don't have any objection to cash, do you? I prefer cash. That way I can, ah, well…"

He didn't have to finish the sentence. Snuffy knew it was in his nature to deal with cash, yet he was still surprised, since this was a huge sum of money. Coddington never did take a receipt since no documentation was as good as no transaction. That way he could resell the coin box for a nice profit without the IRS knowing about it.

Of course, this time, Coddington would be in for a real shock, but that did not bother Snuffy, since, after all, he was dealing with a Christian crook.

Coddington was at the phone whispering in a voice low enough so that Snuffy could not hear, and when he concluded, he came back to the coin box and ran his hands over it, rubbing the shiny finish. "It's a good price, you know," he said, "that is, a good price for you, a fair price, I'd say."

Snuffy smiled as he walked to his desk and sat down. He watched Coddington gloat over his grand purchase, nervous a bit, yet wanting to laugh out loud. He would laugh, eventually, but not until the cash was in his hand and the good Christian gentleman was on his way.

The money was piling up. Sko could only guess that he had about twelve thousand dollars in front of him. It was in stacks of tens, twenties, fifties and hundreds. It was still early for an all night card game, and he was rather surprised that the boys had not yet brought out a marked deck.

"It's that cop again," Pavlov muttered from the window.

"Forget the goddamn cop!" Frank Newsom barked. "It's just Brodigan."

"Ah doan' like it," Pavlov shot back at the cigar-chomping man. "Ah doan' like cops."

Frank leaned over and spoke to Sko "Where'd you find this goddamn rummy? Why don't you send him home so we can play some real cards? I don't like him standing around."

Sko gave Frank a quick glance but said nothing. When Frank returned his eyes to his cards, Sko said, "Fifty more."

Frank scowled and passed, and Sko raked in the pot.

Frank grunted as be watched Sko stack up the bills. He snuffed out his short cigar and lit up another. "What d'ya say we up the ante a bit?" He blew out a blast of blue smoke that hovered above the card table. "And maybe get rid of this fuckin' deck. It's gettin' cold."

Sko knew it was coming. "Suit yourself." As soon as they broke the seal on the cards, it would be three against one, and whichever of the three had the best hand would stick and rake in the pot. It made no difference that Sko could read the same cards. The odds were too heavily against him.

He was ready to signal Pavlov.

Pavlov would signal Carrigan.

Carrigan would signal Reggie, and within two minutes, Reggie would come running up the fire escape.

Frank broke out the marked deck and handed it to Wimpleton, who shuffled them and then plopped the deck next to Sko. "Cut?"

"Sure."

Reggie was still twirling the night stick in a fancy manner, nervous to a degree, but strolling down Main Street toward Roberts. He held the receiver in his hand, the small black box with the red bulb. When it blinked on and off, it was his turn to act, but so far, nothing.

Twice during the night, he had been stopped and asked for directions. Fifteen minutes ago, Ernie from the bookstore closed up his shop and mentioned to Reggie how nice it was to have the law patrolling the streets.

The night had been for the most part uneventful, except when a patrol car had passed by. The officer waved at him, and Reggie had waved back. After the car was gone, it occurred to him that the policeman might have stopped to talk to him. They surely would have recognized him as not being a member of the force, so from that moment on, he had spent a great deal of his time in dark doorways hidden from any passers-by.

He wished he could have spent all of the time in dark doorways, but Sko maintained it was important for him to be seen periodically by Pavlov and, hopefully, by one of the other card players. That would make his sudden appearance at the top of the stairs much more credible. So every time he approached the Mexican Village, he stuck around for a few minutes before he moved on.

It did make sense, but Reggie was now feeling uneasy. He had been patrolling the same two blocks for over four hours. Wouldn't someone on the street become suspicious of him?

Still, the night had been uneventful. Not too many people were walking the streets at this time. People were going in and out of the Mexican Village, and a handful of customers were doing the same at the Dutch Maid Grill. Those traveling by in cars were no threat at all.

He reached the corner of Main and Roberts now, and as he rounded the corner, he gazed across at the floating neon message on the bank building. He was reading the message for the umpteenth time. *A new car loan can...*

The loud *ker-thump* of metal against metal battered its way into Reggie's ears, so loud that he jumped. Two cars had just collided at the intersection. A horn blared in the calm of the night like a fire siren, while steam shot out from underneath a buckled hood.

When a door flopped open from one of the cars, the driver fell out onto the street, still holding fast to a bottle. A man from across the street came running, and now two teenagers zipped past Reggie to the scene. In less than a half minute a crowd of people had gathered.

"Someone call the police!" Reggie shouted as he neared the wreckage.

Half of the faces of those that had gathered were looking back at him as he approached. Reggie suddenly realized *he was* the police!

"Oh, Jesus!" he exclaimed. *What the hell do I do?* At that very moment, the red bulb on the device he was holding in his hand began blinking on and off. "Jesus!" he said for a second time.

Shivers ran up and down his spine as he stared at the blinking light. Amid shouts from the crowd, he hollered out the only thing he could think of at the moment. "Someone call the police! I've got a robbery in progress!"

He spun around and ran as fast as he could for the staircase at the bottom of the Dakota Business building. If anyone yelled after him, he wouldn't have heard it, since his mind was set, his direction clear, his heart pounding fiercely. This was it!

By the time he reached the staircase, he saw a set of flashing red lights and heard a siren. A police car was already underway.

Reggie threw the door open and headed up the fire escape. The interior was pitch black, and he stumbled after a few steps.

He groped for a side railing and found it, and now, he ran up two steps at a time, his eyes slightly adjusting to the dark. Half way up, he stumbled again but regained his balance and kept moving. The iron stairs beneath his feet rattled with each step. His heart pounded. His throat was dry.

"Oh, shit, oh, shit!" he groaned as he neared the top of the fire escape.

The four men around the card table looked up at the same time when they heard the siren. Most amazed were Pavlov and Sko as they eyed each other. The siren was nearer, louder.

Pavlov was shaking as he pulled back the shade and peered out. He had absolutely no idea what was happening, but now he could see the reflection of a flashing red beacon.

Frank Newsom looked up. "What is it?"

Pavlov was dumbfounded. "I don't know! It's a police car!"

Sko was the first to jump up from the table. "What?"

Now, all the card players were on their feet, and Frank was at the window looking out at the flashing lights. "What the hell's all that about?"

The thumping of Reggie's footsteps coming up the outside iron stairs caught everybody's attention. Everyone in the room froze, especially Frank Newsom as he heard a foot bang against the door.

"Police!" he heard. "Open up!"

Reggie was kicking at the door, and when it tore loose, he jumped into the opening, a pair of dark glasses on his face, the plastic pistol in his hand and leveled at the men. "This is a raid! Don't anyone move!"

Shocked with the sudden appearance of a police officer, Frank, Bucky and Wimpleton threw their hands up and Sko followed suit. Pavlov was right on cue. He whipped out the pistol with the blanks and fired it three times. The shots echoed loudly in the small room as Reggie gave a blood curdling yell and fell to the floor like a big sack of potatoes.

"Jesus fucking Christ!" Frank Newsom hollered. "He shot him!" He, Bucky and Wimpleton scrambled into the next room heading for the back staircase, howling like a pack of wolves. Sko motioned to the money on the table and ran after the three.

Reggie jumped to his feet, and after he and Pavlov gathered up all the money on the table, they hustled out the door down the fire escape.

Tromping down the inside staircase, Sko caught up with the other three, but big Frank in the lead was slow and cumbersome as he made his way down. Bucky and Wimpleton were practically screaming their lungs at him, rushing him at every turn.

At the bottom of the stairs, big Frank was panting as he fumbled with the two by four that blocked the exit door from the inside, his face as white as a ghost. "Jesus Christ, Sko!" he puffed. "He shot him! That fucking rummy shot a cop!"

When Frank finally got the door open, Bucky, Wimpleton and Sko ran right over him. His three-hundred-pound frame plummeted and rolled to the sidewalk. "You fuckin' idiots!" he swore at the three as he labored to his feet. "We're dead meat!" But the three were already out of ear shot, scrambling between the building and the Mexican Village.

Carrigan, sitting in his car, saw the first three men run past and recognized the third one as Sko. A few seconds later, big Frank Newsom lumbered by.

Red lights flashed from the corner as a siren sounded on Main from another direction. Carrigan was as confused as anybody over what had transpired, and just as he was about to pull away from the dumpster, Pavlov and Reggie shot past him. Before he could roll down his window and shout at them, they were at the end of the alley. Carrigan had never seen such speed.

At least the guys were safely out of the building. His

curiosity at a peak, he pulled out onto Main where he saw the two crunched cars at the intersection. Two police cars had stopped, their beacons flashing.

Carrigan laughed all the way through the intersection as a policeman directed him around, and he was still laughing when he pulled up at his office.

Twenty-Four
Adding Things Up

T.B. knew Carrigan wouldn't leave for coffee until about nine in the morning, which meant he was still in his office. He tried to vault the front steps to the Mark Building two at a time, but his legs were too short. When he fell, he cracked both shin bones against the steps and spilled the contents of the envelope he was carrying. He swore as he rubbed his shins, gathered up the photos and papers and jammed them back into the envelope.

Carrigan was behind his desk when T.B. walked in. "Got your phone call," he said as he pulled up a chair.

Carrigan could not help but notice his swollen eye, and his nose was as red as a crab apple. Carrigan was surprised and at the same time not surprised to see his battered face, but he did not at all want to know what happened.

Carrigan pointed to the box in the corner. "You can have your stuff back."

T.B. glanced at the box. In it were the police uniform, the guns and electronic device. He thought maybe Carrigan would explain why he wanted the props, but Carrigan said nothing. "Everything went all right, I presume?"

"Yes." Carrigan showed no emotion.

"You aren't still mad about me and Leroy ending up in jail, are you?"

"Yes."

"I'll pay you back, you know that."

Carrigan pointed to the box. "Your stuff."

T.B.'s face saddened, hurt from the short answers. "Is that all you wanted me for? To pick up the box?"

"Yes."

"You said you needed a bagman a couple days ago."

Carrigan glowered.

"You don't need one?"

"No."

"Someone has to deliver the money."

Carrigan clasped his hands together and leaned on his desk. "What makes you think I have the money?"

T.B. pointed to the box. "You're finished with the props."

Carrigan saw the little man's mind clicking. "We have most of it."

T.B. fidgeted. "Is the blackmailer supposed to contact you today?"

"Possibly."

"By phone, I imagine."

"I imagine."

Carrigan was still mad, and T.B. had no trouble discerning that by the curt answers he was getting. He slowly pulled the envelope from under his arm and laid it on the desk.

Carrigan eyed the envelope for a few seconds. "All right. What have you got?"

T.B. felt a sense of relief as he dumped the contents out and lined them up. "Leroy took these in the Gay Nineties Bar in Minneapolis. Look at the angle of the shots."

Carrigan studied the photos.

"Notice these were taken from a low angle, since the stage in the bar was raised three feet off the ground."

"So?"

T.B. pointed out two photos the blackmailer had sent. "These were taken from floor level."

"So?"

"So, whoever took the original photos had to be higher up, like in a balcony, and there is no balcony in the Gay Nineties Bar."

"But there was probably a spot light on her, wouldn't you think?" Carrigan challenged.

"Probably."

"So someone could have taken the photos from the position of the spotlight. Whoever that was was probably on a ladder or a platform. That would explain the shots."

T.B. frowned. He didn't like the answer, but what Carrigan had said was certainly plausible. He tried a different approach. "Look at the grain in the photos. It's not fast speed film."

"So it's not fast speed film. So what?"

T.B. had no answer. Leroy R seemed to have explained it all so simply the night before. Somehow the speed of the film was important, but now T.B. could not remotely figure out why. Maybe Leroy said the speed was fast, not slow.

"What about the shadow along the sides of the girl's body?" T.B. finally asked, as if he were now casting some new evidence on the photos.

"What about the shadow?"

"Shit." T.B. couldn't remember what was so important about the shadows either. Something about the lighting and professionalism, but nothing was registering clear in his brain. "Maybe Leroy should come in and talk to you. He understands..."

"Look, T.B.," Carrigan interrupted. "I sent you to Minneapolis to pick up some simple electronic equipment, which you did, and for which I'm very grateful. But what the hell did you do with the rest of the money? It was I who paid four hundred bucks to get you and Leroy out of jail."

T.B. hung his head down like a puppet without a string. "We got the photos."

Carrigan slowly raised out of his chair, his face turning red, as if he were growing a boil. "I didn't ask you to take any photos, and I didn't ask you to take Leroy along. And I didn't expect you to drive that piece of junk you call an automobile down there.

"I also did not expect to have to bail you out of jail, but I do expect you to get off the case! Is that clear?"

T. B. stared into the furious eyes across from him. "Does that mean you don't want to hear about my private investigation on Jerry Allison?"

Carrigan stood up and grabbed the sides of his head, unable to restrain his temper. "What the hell are you doing following Jerry Allison around!?"

The deep red color in Carrigan's face was finally making an impact on T.B. He felt his nerves crawl around inside him. "Ah, really it's Jerry's buddy, Gordon, the guy who works at Epko. You see, I followed…"

T.B. abruptly stopped talking when Carrigan began stuffing the photographs back into the envelope. He stomped around the desk, picked up the box of clothing and shoved it under one of T.B.'s arms, the envelope under the other. He spun T.B. around and pushed him toward the door. "You are off the case!"

"Does that mean you don't need a bagman?"

The deep red in Carrigan's face was now turning purple.

"Right. Off the case." T.B. walked out the door, marched down the steps and strutted confidently across the street to his car. Once inside, he slammed the door and set the box and envelope on the seat. He had presented his recent research badly. It was clear that Carrigan was not at all receptive to the photographs or the trip to Minneapolis with Leroy or his private investigation on Jerry Allison.

But after spending a short ten minutes with Carrigan, he now knew three important things; Carrigan and the group had somehow raised most of the ransom money, the blackmailer would probably call today, which meant that the ransom delivery was going to be made fairly soon.

Either today or tomorrow.

It all made perfect sense. Last night Carrigan had somehow raised the money, and although it plagued T.B. that he didn't know how, he still respected Carrigan. However he had raised the money, he must have done it in an honorable fashion, because Carrigan was an honorable man.

He did not have to wait long. Within minutes, and like he expected, Carrigan and Pam Allison came down the front steps of the Mark Building. T.B. knew the two would be at the Powers Coffee House for at least the next hour.

T.B. reached for the clothes next to him and pulled on the paint-stained coveralls. He plopped a paint hat in place and slipped on a pair of white gloves. From the trunk, he a retrieved a brush and paint can, a short ladder and a black case that contained the *necessary electronics.*

Loaded down with equipment, he crossed the street to Carrigan's Oldsmobile. He glanced about him, then pulled the small bug from the case and placed it against the metal on the inside of the front fender. He heard the faint click of the magnet hold the device firmly in place.

Pam Allison's Volkswagen was parked next to the olds. He placed another bug under the front fender of her car, then confidently marched to the back door of the Mark Building and banged his way up the steps to the inside corridor. It made no difference how noisy he was, for now he was nothing more than a simple painter in the building. Who would question the appearance of a painter?

He whistled as he set up his ladder near a closet door, and after removing the set of picks from his pocket, he kept whistling while he worked the lock. Four minutes later, the door opened. He hummed as he placed the black case on a shelf and set the dials. He had just closed the door when a lady came out of an office from the far end of the corridor.

"Good morning," T.B. greeted with a friendly smile. "Beautiful day for painting, isn't it?"

He had the brush out, slapping it against the wall, but after she disappeared into the women's restroom, he realized he was painting with a dry brush, but it made no difference.

"Oh, so-lo-mio," he sang as he moved his ladder nearer to Pam Allison's door. He had his picks out again, selected the prongs he needed and jammed them into the lock. He kept singing, and when he heard the toilet flush from the restroom, he once again grabbed his brush and began slapping it against the wall.

The lady passed by him on the way back to her office. "Beautiful day for painting," T.B. repeated. "I'll have her done in no time."

The lady responded with a slight smile this time, but when she reached her door, she stopped for a moment and examined the walls. With a strange look on her face, she entered her office and closed the door.

Three minutes later, he had Pam's door unlocked. He was about to push it open when the lady from down the corridor stuck her head out again and stared in his direction.

Nothing phased T.B. this morning. He picked up his brush, began whistling and added a creative tap dance to his routine.

Without losing a beat, he turned to face the lady fully and gave her a pleasant nod. She abruptly returned inside her office.

T.B. pushed the door open and slipped inside Pam's office. He put the bug in her phone and fifteen seconds later was back in the corridor. He gathered up his ladder and paint supplies and whistled his way toward the back door.

The lady from the office opened her office door as he passed by and stared at him.

"Ran out of paint," he told her. In no time he made his way outside to his car, shucked the uniform and stashed everything in the trunk.

Back inside his car, he retrieved disguise number two; a leather vest, cowboy boots, a huge Stetson and dark glasses. He made a quick inspection in his rear view mirror, although basically all he could see was the glasses.

"Next stop," he said as he started up the car. He drove around the block and parked in front of the Powers.

Pavlov was more excited than he had ever been. His voice

was hushed, and with each sentence his eyebrows jumped up and down. "I'm not shittin'! There were so damn many red lights flashing, I thought it was a real raid!"

"Haw, haw, haw!" A napkin swirled around as Reggie leaned across the table. "Two cars collided at the intersection, and before I knew it, a patrol car comes around the corner, red lights blinking, and I'm running like hell for the fire escape."

"Course I was calm all along," Sko said.

"Shee-it You were the first one out of the room."

"No, Frank was."

They all laughed.

"You guys were wonderful," said the Princess.

"How much did you guys get?" Johann asked.

Carrigan was talking under his breath. "Fourteen thousand four hundred. It's in my office right now."

"Whew!"

The Princess had a handkerchief to her eyes wiping away the tears. "You guys were wonderful."

"What's everybody crying about?" Snuffy, wearing his normal, grubby green sweater, sat down. He was also carrying a small leather briefcase.

"It's all here," Snuffy said in a low voice. "All twenty-six thousand. I ain't never seen so many hundred dollar bills in my life!" He practically shook with excitement as he looked over the gaping faces.

"J-Jesus Christ!" Pavlov stuttered. "Twenty-six grand?"

Snuffy was all smiles as he eyed Johann and the Princess. "Pam was great. Our Christian son-of-a-bitch thought she was the real Lavonya LaRue." He hooked a thumb in his sweater. "Johann was all right, but I was pretty good, too."

They all laughed.

"What would you like this morning, honey?" It was Millie, and she was talking to Snuffy.

"Oooh, honey!" said Pavlov. More ooohs and aaahs from the crowd.

287

Snuffy smiled back. "Junkman special this morning." Millie scooted away after she left a fresh pot of coffee.

Carrigan looked over the crowd. "That brings us around to one slight problem. We've got forty thousand four hundred dollars. We still need nine thousand six hundred. Divided seven ways that's about fourteen hundred apiece,"

Silence.

"Come on, guys," Snuffy said. Cough it up. I'll throw in my share."

The Princess' eyes lit up.

"Why don't we just give the blackmailer what we've got?" Pavlov suggested.

"I agree," said the Princess. "I can't ask you guys to give up your own money. You've done more than enough already."

"We can't take a chance," Carrigan countered. "We don't know who we're dealing with."

"How do we know we get the negatives?"

"We don't."

Carrigan looked around the table. "I'll give my fourteen. How much can the rest of you give?"

"Eight hundred is tops," said Reggie.

Pavlov nodded. "Me too."

Sko shrugged. "Five for me, and that's pushing it."

Johann offered twelve.

"Anybody keep count?" Carrigan asked.

"Forty-six thousand five hundred."

"I can give a thousand," Pam offered. "I'll have to take it out of my business account. That way I can hide it from Jerry."

Reggie looked up from his figuring. "Still need twenty-five hundred."

The table was silent again.

"I'll cover it," Carrigan finally said.

Pavlov wiped a hand across his face. "Jesus. I'll throw in a few more."

"Me too," said Reggie.

Sko just shrugged.

"Okay, we're covered."

Pam touched Carrigan on the arm. "I can't let you do that."

"It's a done deal. It's covered."

Millie shuffled in with Snuffy's breakfast and jiggled the coffee pot. "You guys aren't drinking much this morning." She hurried off to another table.

"You're throwing in the most, Carrigan," said Pavlov.

Sko shook his head. "I wish I could give more, but I can't."

"We do what we can, guys. It's settled."

The table finally got down to some serious conversation, even though it was hushed this time.

"We sure took care of that Christian son-of-a-bitch, didn't we?"

"I arranged the car accident to make it more realistic."

"Shee-it! You didn't arrange nothin'."

"You should have seen her. She was the spittin' image of Lavonya LaRue."

"Frank went through that metal door like it was paper."

"I can't believe how fast you guys were running!"

"Then, finally, this white Lincoln goes by."

"I really did think it was a raid."

"He shot me three times. I've wounds to prove it."

"I can imagine Frank is scared shitless."

"You guys are all so wonderful."

"You betchum, Red Ryder. You betchum."

"What's the matter with you guys? Your pot's still full."

While the guys were bantering, T.B. entered the Powers through the back door and found a seat near the wall farthest away from Carrigan's table.

"Ingenious," he said as he sat by himself, dressed in his cowboy disguise. A receiver was hooked to his shirt, and from it, a thin wire ran upwards into an ear piece. Earlier in the morning, he had placed a bug underneath the table where

Carrigan's group normally sat. He chanced the possibility that perhaps someone else might have occupied their spot, but he was in luck.

They were still bantering away, and he could hear everything quite clearly. They had collected over forty thousand dollars, some of it from a card game and most from a son-of-a-bitch named *Christianson*. He had no idea who this Lavonya LaRue lady was or what role she played in gathering the money.

However they had come by the money, T.B. considered it a magnificent feat, and it all had to be legitimate, because Carrigan would never be involved in something dishonest

Two of the members now excused themselves, and moments later, the rest of the group was gone except for Carrigan and Pam Allison.

"Stay in your office all day," T.B. heard Carrigan tell her. "And listen for the phone. He's bound to call. I'll be right down the hall. Leave your door open, and whenever your phone rings, I'll hear it."

"I'm scared," T.B. heard her say.

"Nothing to be scared of," Carrigan answered.

"Who'll deliver the money?" she asked.

"Whoever the blackmailer asks for."

There was a long silence at the table, and for a moment, T.B. thought his ear piece had gone bad. When he looked at them, he saw the girl give Carrigan a light kiss on the cheek. "Thank you," T.B. heard her whisper to him.

When they left, Carrigan took the leather briefcase with him. Amazing, T.B. thought to himself. Everyone from the coffee group had chipped in to make up the rest of the ransom. He could not help but admire their integrity. *Yes, sir. The guys from Fargo were quite special.*

T.B. glanced around the lounge thinking he might see the Fargo-Burnout, but he was not in. Wandering Eddie was in a corner by himself, but none of the other prior suspects were in today.

The Guys from Fargo

T.B. finished up his coffee and was about to leave when he heard a male voice through his ear piece say, "You were really super, Harriet, and so early in the morning."

T.B. heard a giggle in the background. "Not bad for twenty bucks, huh, honey? How about we have breakfast," Harriet was saying, "and then go back to my apartment and I'll give you the best saddle-job you've ever had."

Saddle-job? T.B. wondered what that was all about as he as he beckoned for Millie to bring him more coffee.

Millie poured a cup and left.

"... hook my spurs into you, baby," the man was saying. T.B. sneaked a look around the booth. At Carrigan's table, Harriet was sitting with a big husky cowboy, and like himself, the man was wearing a huge Stetson and big cowboy boots, size 13 or better, he guessed.

"Do all you cowboys have big cocks?" T.B. heard her ask him. He felt his own groin beginning to swell.

"Jes' the studs," the cowboy said

T.B. grinned when he heard the word *stud*. He leaned back in the booth and tipped his Stetson forward as he pressed the hearing device deeper into his ear. *You're going to have to wait, Leroy,* he muttered to himself.

It was almost ten-thirty when T.B. Harvey finally left the Powers Coffee House, just a few minutes after Harriet the whore and her cowboy stud boyfriend had left. Back in his car, he removed the cowboy gear and drove around the block. Carrigan's and Pam's cars were still in the parking lot in front of the Mark Building.

"Good," he said as he raced the car through an orange light. He swung past Jerry Allison's office, but his car was gone.

At Epko Photography, Gordon Gelsper was not behind the counter.

He drove to Jerry Allison's home. No car.

He drove across the bridge to Leroy R's mansion. He was in.

"How'd it go," Leroy R asked as T.B. sat across from him.

"He wasn't very receptive to the photographs," T.B. confessed.

Leroy R frowned, lifted the stopper from his cantor and poured two shots of brandy. "Can't understand why. Seemed clear to me those were professional photos. Did you point out the shadows?"

T.B. nodded.

"And the angle the shots were taken from? Without a doubt there was something peculiar about that."

T.B. had tried, but if he had had undisputable evidence and had been able to explain it properly, he still doubted Carrigan would have believed anything this morning.

"Did you mention the possibility of Jerry Allison and his camera friend being the blackmailers?"

"That's when he threw me out. We're off the case, Leroy."

"Of course we're off the case. We both knew that all along. We're doing this as a favor to Mr. M, aren't we?"

"Right," said T.B. That seemed to comfort him as he threw down the shot. Leroy R filled it immediately

T.B. ran his tongue across the lip of the glass on this second brandy. He loved the smoothness of it. The old lady had good taste in brandy. He wondered if she drank

T.B.'s mind was working. "Do you have access to a car, Leroy?"

"Why?"

"We'll need a chase vehicle when the ransom money is delivered."

"Chase vehicle?'

"When the blackmailer calls, we have to be ready."

"For what?"

"The chase. We've gotta catch the blackmailer red-handed. Carrigan will appreciate that."

The Guys from Fargo

"They've got the money?"

"All fifty thousand."

"Holy moly!" Leroy R rolled his eyes and took a sip of his brandy.

"Well, do you have a car? Mine is too recognizable."

Leroy R rolled his eyes again. My landlady has one."

"Does it run?'

"Of course. It only has fifteen thousand miles on it."

"Must be a new one."

"No. It's a Studebaker, 1947 I think. Green."

This time T.B. rolled his eyes as rose to his feet. "Well, let's have a look at it."

"Take a look at these photographs first." Leroy R handed him two photos. "I blew these up this morning. Notice anything particular?"

T.B. held a photo in each hand and looked back and forth.

"Do you see it?" Leroy R asked.

T.B. gasped. "You're damn right I see it!" He nervously gulped down his remaining brandy and held up the photos again.

Leroy R had already poured a third shot for him. "Yes, sir!" T.B. said excitedly. "You're damn right I see it!"

The phone call came at exactly five o'clock, Carrigan heard the ring, one of many during the day, and quickly hurried down the corridor to her office. As soon as he entered, the Princess picked up the receiver.

She didn't even have time to mention her office name. She looked at Carrigan, nodded her head vigorously and then hung up, her face full of fright.

"What'd he say?"

"Be at the phone at 12th and University at ten o'clock tonight."

"What else?"

"No police, and he said bring the money and the man with the gimpy leg."

"Meaning Johann?" Carrigan asked.

She shrugged. "Who else?"

"Johann," Carrigan repeated as he pondered the request. The blackmailer could have asked the Princess to come alone, but he must have suspected she would be fearful of the delivery. Johann would be a likely person to take along since he had a bad leg. He couldn't run very fast, and he was small and lightweight, not much of a threat to anyone.

"Did he say anything else?" asked Carrigan.

"No."

"Did he mention the negatives?"

"No." Carrigan eased himself into a chair and saw a deeper fright creep into her face. "I'm scared," she said. She nervously sat and folded her arms across her chest as if a sudden chill had pounced upon her.

"You know he's going to run you all over town to make sure you aren't being followed."

"I know."

"Just don't disappoint him. It'll be just you and Johann. I don't think we can chance following you."

"I didn't expect you to." The cold stare remained on her face, and then tears abruptly poured from her eyes. He was out of his seat and wrapped an arm around her. Then the sobs came as she hugged him, pulled him closer, as if closeness were her only means of protection.

"You'll be all right," he calmed her, as he stroked her strawberry hair. "You'll be all right."

She pulled away from him, her tears still flowing. "Maybe Johann won't go along with it."

"He will," said Carrigan. "Any of us in the coffee group would have. You know that."

She gained a little composure and pulled a handkerchief from her purse

"Come on," he said. "Johann's probably in his studio."

The Guys from Fargo

Leroy R sat behind the wheel of the green Studebaker. He and T.B. had been waiting and observing the front door to Carrigan's office for some time. They both saw Carrigan and the Princess leave the building, get into Carrigan's Oldsmobile and pull out of the parking lot.

T.B. and Leroy R studied the electronic graph between them. By the green blip, T.B. could tell Carrigan had turned the corner at the next block and was headed north.

"Well, it works," T.B. commented.

One more green blip remained on the scope, but it was stationary, the bug that remained under Pam Allison's car.

T.B. watched Carrigan's blip, saw the green spot stop. He looked up and gazed across the way. "That's where the artist's studio is located. Johann's his name."

"Why'd they go there?"

"Drive up and park across from the office and we'll know in a minute or two." Leroy started the car, ground the gear into first and jerked the vehicle as he let out the clutch. He drove all the way in low. When he hit the brakes, he almost sent T.B. through the windshield.

T.B. eyed Leroy, left the car and crossed the street. A few minutes later he came out the side door carrying a black case. Inside the car, he opened the lid and rolled the tape on the recorder. He punched a button and ran through several phone conversations before he finally found what he wanted.

A man in a whispered voice spoke; *Twelfth and University the phone booth tonight, ten o'clock. Drive your car, bring the money and the guy with the gimpy leg. No police.*

"The guy with the gimpy leg," T.B. repeated. "Johann's got a limp. That's why they went to see him. Let's go."

"Where to?"

"My office."

Leroy R started up the Studebaker and ground the gear again. He raced the engine and slowly pressed on the accelerator as he gently let out the clutch, trying to make a smooth start. The car jerked forward and nearly killed. Leroy gave it more gas, and the car jumped like a scared jackrabbit.

"Goddamn, Leroy. You drive this thing like you've never driven a stick shift before."

"I haven't," he answered.

Leroy ground the gear into second. Again the car lurched.

"How in the hell did you ever get a driver's license?"

Leroy R grinned. "Who said I had one?" He stared ahead and aimed the car down the street. "Kind of fun, though."

Twenty-Five
The Delivery

All of the guys in Carrigan's office looked on as he shoved the last eight hundred dollars into the briefcase. The case now contained the fifty thousand dollars in ransom.

Carrigan snapped the briefcase shut, checked his watch and looked up just as Johann lit up another cigarette. He was wearing his regular clothes; brown corduroys, jacket, Levis and boots. Pam Allison wore a simple tweed skirt and white blouse and had a black jacket snugged around her.

Snuffy rolled a cigarette and licked the edges shut. "I don't like it. We go to the trouble of digging up fifty grand and now we're letting the blackmailer go free."

"'What do you suggest?" asked Pavlov.

"A couple of us follow them."

"We can't," Carrigan protested. "It's too risky. Besides, most of the money isn't ours. I don't want anyone getting hurt."

Sko raised a good question. "Course, we have no guarantee we'll get the negatives."

"Look," said Carrigan. "The blackmailer will probably demand the money be dropped off someplace so he can pick it up later on. He's not going to play ball if he sees someone following Pam and Johann."

"What about the negatives?" Sko asked again.

"We may never get them." Carrigan looked at the concerned faces staring back and threw his hands up. "What would you do if you were a blackmailer and had the money?" He waited for a response but none came. "If it was me, I'd take the money and run. Maybe the negatives will be left in the same place he picks up the money, and if not, we may never hear from him after tonight."

Reggie agreed. "I think Carrigan's right. Just give the guy the money and let it go at that."

Pavlov nodded.

Snuffy dragged on his cigarette but said nothing.

"I agree," said Sko.

Carrigan checked his watch again. "Twenty minutes and you two have to be at the phone booth. You'd better get going."

Johann ground out his cigarette and took a firm grip on the briefcase.

"Don't play hero," Carrigan cautioned him.

Johann nodded. "I'm an artist, not a hero."

A block away, T.B. and Leroy R sat in the green Studebaker. Through the zoom lens of a sophisticated camera, Leroy R had been observing the goings on inside Carrigan's office. "The painter just picked up the briefcase," he said.

Moments later, Johann and Pam Allison walked down the front steps of the Mark Building and disappeared around the corner. T.B. checked the green glow on his graph. They had entered her car and the bug was working.

"They're headed north," T.B. confirmed. "At least we know their first stop is twelfth and University. That's across from NDSU. Let's go."

A fine mist was slowly dropping over the city. When Leroy R started up the Studebaker, he turned on the windshield wipers to brush away the droplets. With gears grinding, he pulled away from the curb in jerking motions, though somewhat smoother than he had done earlier in the day.

When he turned onto Broadway, Pam's yellow Volkswagen was just ahead, and she was driving.

"Don't get too close," T.B. cautioned.

"Right."

T.B. kept his eyes on the graph. Each quadrant was a block in distance, which would always give him the exact location of the Volkswagen, even if he couldn't see it. The graph was working very well and supposedly could track a vehicle for up to three miles.

As they trailed a few blocks behind the Volks, T.B. was jubilant. He had gotten smart and called Jerry Allison's office and asked for Jerry. He was told Mr. Allison would be out of town in California until next Tuesday. He also found out Jerry was registered at the LaCroy Hotel in Los Angeles in case of an emergency.

To T.B., it seemed all too convenient for Jerry Allison to be out of town during the delivery of the ransom money, so to check out the story, he had called the LaCroy Hotel and asked for Jerry Allison. A reservation had been made, but as of yet, Jerry had not yet registered. So T.B. drove to Hector Airport in Fargo and discovered that Jerry Allison had indeed booked a flight to Los Angeles. The flight left that morning at 7:35. Jerry should have long been in Los Angeles by late afternoon.

But he had not yet registered. That was suspicious.

During the day, T.B. had not been unable to trace Gordon Gelsper from the camera store, and that was suspicious.

The Fargo-Burnout had disappeared completely in the past few days, and that was even more suspicious, especially now. Millie, from the Powers, knew his real name was Tony Giocanni. T.B. surmised that the name itself could easily be Mafia related, so he looked up his name in the phone book and to his surprise discovered that he was listed. His mother, a talkative old woman, had answered. What T.B. learned was that Tony Giocanni had worked in a print shop for two years after he got out of the service.

Printers worked with cameras all the time! Maybe the Fargo-Burnout really wasn't burned out like everyone thought. His mother hadn't seen him or his car for a few days. Like Leroy R had said, the Fargo-Burnout actually owned a car, but he was gone, vanished into thin air.

That was suspicious.

There were at least three good suspects now, and T.B. was sure that one of them would surface tonight.

He shoved a hand up against his chest with the assurance that the big gun was inside the leather holster. With his eyes constantly trained on the graph in front of him, he noticed the Volkswagen had turned on Twelfth Avenue North and was headed toward the university.

"Go straight here," T.B. commanded when they reached the intersection.

"Right," said Leroy R.

"No, straight.".

"Right, straight." Leroy R crossed the intersection, jerking the car only slightly when he downshifted. They turned at the next corner, circled around and came down the one-way on University Avenue and parked in a lot across from the filling station.

From where they sat they had a clear view of the phone and the VW parked next to it. At a few minutes to ten, the phone must have rung, since Johann got out of the car and picked up the receiver. He glanced around for a few seconds and hung up.

Back in the Volkswagen, the two drove across University Avenue and headed west on Twelfth.

"Let's go," T.B. commanded.

The VW maintained a straight course across the viaduct and was now moving at a rapid clip. By the time the Studebaker reached the top of the bridge, a Jet whooshed above them with its engines whining, just short of landing at the airport.

Four blocks ahead, the yellow Volkswagen was vividly clear under the amber lights lining the thoroughfare. The mist had turned into a steady drizzle, and now drops splashed heavily against the windshield. With a distinct even hum, the wipers whipped away the rain cleanly. Visibility was still good, but puddles were beginning to form on the road.

"She just turned north on the Interstate," T.B. said, his eyes glued to the graph. "She's pushing it."

"Probably because the blackmailer gave them a time limit for the next point."

By the time Leroy R reached the Interstate, the green blip was already headed back east.

"They're on Nineteenth Avenue heading past the airport road."

"What's at the end of it?"

"University Avenue again. There's a liquor store and a pizza place on the corner. And a phone, too, if I recollect."

When they turned off the Interstate, Leroy pressed the accelerator to catch up. Within a half-minute, they were whipping along the thoroughfare at the south end of the airport and could see the VW way ahead.

As they neared the University intersection, the VW was already sitting near the outside phone.

"What do we do?" Leroy R asked.

T.B. felt a sense of panic since there was no place to pull over and park. "Just drive past. They won't know us."

As they drove through the green light, the two figures in the front seat were clearly visible. At the next corner, Leroy R turned left and parked.

"They're moving already," T.B. said as he checked the blip on the graph. "Jesus, whoever is calling knows their movements by the second. They hardly had time to talk."

The VW came their way, passed behind them and continued east. On Broadway, the VW headed north.

"Forward," said T.B. They continued to parallel the VW, which was now three blocks east of them. Both cars were headed in the same direction, and after a half dozen blocks the VW blip on the graph was again stationary.

The Studebaker swung off and slowed at Northport

Shopping Center. Across the Hornbacher's Foods parking lot near the bank, Johann was already on the phone. Leroy R. shut off the lights and coasted to a stop a block away.

Once again, the VW was underway headed north. The rain was coming down heavier now as Leroy R adjusted the wipers to a faster speed and trailed after the two.

Strange, T.B. was thinking. The blackmailer would have to be making phone calls from somewhere. How was the caller able to make these calls with such precision? Surely, he, too, would have to be in a car nearby to know when the VW would arrive at each point. Or perhaps the blackmailer had timed the route and knew exactly when to call.

Maybe the blackmailer had a phone in his car. Yes, a mobile phone was certainly possible, which still meant another car would have to be in the vicinity.

T.B. looked around, checking whether he remembered seeing a similar vehicle at the first few stops. It was impossible to know. There were simply too many cars in Hornbacher's lot.

Who did he know that had a phone in his car?

Nobody. Both he and Carrigan thought initially that the blackmailer was a weirdo, but someone was keeping very close track of Pam and Johann now. Whoever this person was had to be a professional. Yes, in every respect a professional at blackmailing and at photography.

"Where are they headed?" Leroy R asked interrupting T.B.'s thoughts.

"They'll come out on the Walltown Road if they maintain their course. That's a dead end." At the end of this stretch the VW would have to turn either right or left. Right would take them across the Red River to highway 75 and back to Moorhead. Left would take them back to the Interstate. There were no public phones in either direction that T.B. knew of.

The Studebaker wound through a wooded area that paralleled the river, a stretch, which even in good weather was quite treacherous. "Slow down and turn off your lights," T.B. cautioned.

The road was wet and slippery, and when the lights went off, Leroy R could barely see ahead, could not even see the yellow line. He downshifted and crept along at a slow speed. When they came out of the winding road, they would once again be in the open and they did not want their headlights visible to the VW ahead.

As they cleared the woods, the blip on the graph clearly indicated that the VW had turned left and was headed back toward the Interstate. T.B. pressed his mind. This lonely stretch circled the north end of the airport, and he could not recollect any businesses along the way.

When they reached the stop sign on the highway, the taillights of the VW were barely visible now, and the car was rapidly outdistancing them.

"After them, and faster!" commanded T.B.

"I can't see anything now." Leroy R sped up, hit the gravel on the right side of the road, corrected and spun onto the gravel of the left. He shifted into high and sped on.

"Faster Leroy!"

"What do you think I am, a goddamn bat?" He swerved again when the wheels touch the gravel. The back end slid around as he pulled up on the highway. "You, know, T.B.," he said. "If I can drive without lights in a pouring rain and stay on the road, I sure as hell should be able to pass a driver's test."

"You're doing fine," T.B. commended him. Under the circumstances, he was doing very well.

T.B. trained his eyes on the graph again. The VW had left the highway. Peering ahead through the pouring rain, they could barely make out the headlights headed north on a country road.

Leroy R followed when he reached the gravel, but the VW was way ahead, and even though they were on a flat open stretch, they could no longer see the taillights. Suddenly the blip on the screen was stationary.

"They stopped," T.B. said.

Leroy R crept along aided by an occasional lightning flash that lit up the road. They approached a turnoff, nothing more than a matted down path where T.B. calculated that the VW had turned off and was stopped no more than a few hundred yards away. When another bolt of lightning struck, they could see the path that led into a copse of trees. Somewhere in those trees Johann and Pam were probably meeting the blackmailer.

"What now?" Leroy R asked.

"We walk, unless you can think of a better idea."

"We walk."

They zipped their jackets up around their necks and crawled out of the car into the drenching rain.

As they hurried along the path, Leroy R questioned T.B. "Are you sure you know what we're doing?"

"No."

They reached the trees with the help of more lightning lighting the way, and after another hurried few minutes, they could see the VW headlights, the beams shining on the front of a small shack. A dilapidated fence ran around one side of the building. A garage stood off to the side, one of its doors missing. Above and swaying with the wind, a row of poplars emitted an eerie whine as the whipping rain blew through.

It gave T.B. the shivers as he looked over this perfect setting for a Halloween night.

Another flash of lighting struck in the distance, giving enough light to show that no other vehicles were nearby, and when the light faded, T.B. saw a dull light burning from within the shack.

The two made their way closer, and just as they came up from behind the Volks, the door swung open to the building and Johann and Pam stood in the doorway. When a third figure moved into the light behind them, T.B. gasped.

"My God!" he said. He could clearly see the long black coat on the tall man, the white pants, the black mop of hair. It was the Fargo-Burnout, and he was holding the briefcase of money in his hand!

T.B. fervently tugged at the .357 magnum and loosed it from his holster.

All three figures were clearly visible in the headlights, but T.B. could not tell whether the Fargo-Burnout had a weapon. As loud as he could, T.B. hollered out, "Down! Down! Get down!"

He was shouting at Pam and Johann, and he was sure they had heard him, but all three in the doorway seemed stunned to hear the voice coming from out of the pouring rain.

"Down! Get down!" T.B. shouted again, He aimed the magnum above the heads of the three figures and pulled the trigger. The gunshot boomed like a cannon, and immediately, Pam and Johann ducked down, and although the Fargo-Burnout squatted, he had not yet drawn a weapon that T.B. could see.

T.B. lowered the magnum and fired. A flame charged out of the barrel as the bullet ripped a chunk of wood from doorframe. Just as the Fargo-Burnout slipped from view, T.B. loosed another shot that sent a bullet spattering glass from a window.

"Go back and call the police!" T.B. shouted at Johann and Pam as he rushed for the door and flattened himself against the outside wall. The two still seemed stunned with his appearance.

"For crissake, call the police! I'll keep the bastard pinned down!" The two jumped into the VW and in seconds turned the vehicle around. As they headed back to the main gravel, T.B. caught sight of Leroy in the beam of their headlights. He was running faster than a greyhound chasing the bunny at a racetrack.

T.B.'s mind was back on the man inside the shack. He

gripped the magnum tightly and flung himself on the floor in the open doorway fully expecting a volley of shots to come at him, but nothing!

The drone of the VW engine was slowly fading in the distance, and now T.B. was again hearing the pelting rain all around him. His face was wet from rain and sweat, and heat was building up underneath his jacket. *Goddamn!* he was thinking. *This is the moment of truth! Move over Shell Scott!*

He jumped to his feet and ran inside the room keeping the gun leveled. With nervous energy beating at him, he accidentally fired the weapon, and for a split second he thought that the man inside had shot at him. He collected his thoughts and realized he was in a one-room shack with hardly any furniture. A couple candles were burning on a table, the only source of light. At the end of the room, rain whipped through the opening of another doorway.

T.B. delivered a whoop as he charged through to the outside. When his feet hit the ground, his shoes slid out from underneath him and he went down hard, and again his weapon fired. He quickly scrambled to his feet and stood staring into the night through his rain-spattered lenses.

He knew he had fired four times and had only two shots left. A thunderous roar charged from overhead as a heavy wind blew fiercely at him almost knocking him over. A flash of lightning struck so close that the ground shook beneath him, and during the short but bright flash, he saw the white pant legs of the Fargo-Burnout fifty yards away. He was scrambling up a slight incline and still carrying the briefcase.

With another cavalry whoop, T.B. took off on a dead run, water splashing under his feet, heavy brush whipping at his shins, feet slipping and sliding until he reached the spot where he had last caught a glimpse of the man.

Light tore across the sky again, and when he saw the white pants, he fired again. The recoil from the weapon nearly ripped the gun from his slippery hand. Instinctively, he was running again, fighting the weeds and mud. He puffed and wheezed until his lungs were about to burst. Another piercing light in the night gave him a glimpse of the man. He was tearing across a meadow, his strides outpacing T.B.'s by threefold. Charged with adrenaline, T.B. kept up pursuit in spite of the fact that he knew the long-legged man would outdistance him. It was only a matter of time, yet he pressed on. When the man changed direction, T.B. whooped again as rain smacked him in the face, his glasses now nothing more than a dribbling haze of water. He lowered his head and charged on, his legs relentlessly untiring. He could see nothing over the lenses without his glasses and absolutely nothing through them.

He kept running and then suddenly felt himself jumping off into space. He heard himself cry out as he fell downward off of a cut bank. When his feet finally hit the ground, he rolled head over heels down a steep embankment. As he tumbled, he had no fear of hurting himself, but God forbid if the pistol loosed from his grip. He held on to the weapon doing somersault after somersault until finally he splattered against a hard surface.

In a half daze he lifted his head and stared up into the falling rain. Surprisingly, his glasses were still in place. He was lying on a hard, gravel surface now, and as he stirred feeling every bone in his body out of whack, he heard a faint rumbling noise. At first he thought it was thunder, but then a set of headlights were coming at him at a rapid pace, and it was all he could do to muster enough strength to roll himself to the side as the car sped by. Instinct brought him to a sitting position. He aimed the magnum at the taillights of the car and squeezed off the last shot. The sound practically deafened him, but the car kept going.

He watched through his rain-drenched glasses, everything fuzzy now, the taillights of the fleeing vehicle nothing more than a red blur as they slowly faded into the night.

"Shit," he said, as he struggled to his feet.

"Shit," he said again as he began the long struggle back up the bank. He was mud from head to foot as if he had spent a week wading through a slough.

A half hour passed before he managed to find his way back to the Studebaker. The rain had lessened, and the lights from the airport runway to the south were producing enough reflection off of the rumbling clouds above to light his way.

When he crawled into the car, Leroy R was sitting calmly behind the wheel listening to the radio.

"How'd it go?" Leroy R asked as if T.B. had just returned from a boy scout outing.

T.B. slumped into the seat exhausted and wheezing, trying to catch his breath. "The bastard had his car waiting on the road. He got away."

"Tough," Leroy R consoled.

"Damn," T.B. said after a few more breaths. "You got back here in a hell of a hurry. No guts?"

"Oh, I got guts. I just like to keep them inside here," he said as he patted his stomach. "Especially when people start shooting. I call it survival."

T.B. wanted to laugh, but his whole body ached, and now the pain in his rib cage was tearing at him. He had never run so hard or fallen so hard in his life.

"At least we know who the son-of-a-bitch is," he said triumphantly. "I'll get him. I won't let Carrigan down. Let's go."

"Where to?"

"Back to my..." He stopped in mid-sentence. He was looking at the graph on the seat. The green blip depicted Pam's Volkswagen less than two miles away on the highway. It was in a stationary position, but by now the car should have long been off the graph and the police should have arrived.

T.B.'s mind whirled. "Back to the highway!"

Leroy R started up the car and switched on the lights. Once they reached the highway, they headed back east, retracing the path they had taken only an hour earlier. The green blip was still on the screen, directly ahead no more than a mile.

They passed the turnoff that lead to Fargo and kept going until they reached the river.

"Slow down," T.B. cautioned as he studied the graph.

"Stop," he commanded. When Leroy R jerked the car to a halt, they were in the very center of the bridge.

The fear struck them both. They clambered from the car and peered over the side of the bridge to the river below. There, submerged in the water, was the faint glow of a pair of headlights.

"Oh, my God," said T.B.

Twenty-Six
Into the gloom

It was early Saturday morning when Carrigan parked near the bridge. T.B. Harvey was with him. The two got out of the car and walked hurriedly past several other cars that had lined the road.

A police car with its lights flashing warned oncoming vehicles of the huge crane in the center of the bridge. Carrigan and Harvey stood in the crowd of onlookers, all staring down into the water where the long steel arm of the crane reached toward the sunken Volkswagen. Two divers in wet suits with tanks on their backs had just come to the surface, and when one of them signaled, the man in the crane set the machine in motion. The motor ground, wheels turned and gears clacked as the slack came out of the cable.

Less than a minute later, the yellow roof of the Volkswagen broke the surface, water spewing from the open window of the driver's side. The churning wheels of the crane clacked some more as the car emerged. Water from the doorframes and undercarriage dripped and spilled back into the river. Carrigan shook, expecting the worst.

When the crane gently dropped the vehicle to the surface of the bridge, two policemen were at the vehicle and simultaneously opened both doors allowing water to gush out to either side of the pavement.

Carrigan lowered his head, felt the knot in his stomach, felt the nausea creep into the back of his throat.

T.B. nudged Carrigan as he pointed in the direction of the VW. The water had drained away now with the doors open, and clearly, no one was inside the vehicle. Carrigan felt the blood drain back into his face.

The two approached the vehicle but were stopped before they were within twenty feet. "Do you know whose car this is?" one of the policemen inquired. Carrigan realized how conspicuous he must have been

"Ah, no," he answered as he slowly moved back from the officer. "I was just curious."

The policeman kept his gaze on Carrigan, long enough for him to feel a threat coming from behind the officer's dark glasses. Carrigan walked back to his car thinking it was quite possible the two had escaped from the vehicle. The window on the driver's side had been wide open.

At his car, Carrigan again turned to view the vehicle and saw one of the policemen walk to the far side of the bridge. When the officer leaned over the side, it was then that Carrigan and T.B. saw two men slip an aluminum boat into the water. The boat floated lazily downstream for a few seconds until one of the men got the motor started. As the. boat passed under the bridge, Carrigan could see the ropes and grappling hooks used for dragging. Carrigan studied the riverbank down river. Here, near the bridge, the current was swiftest, but in the distance near the first bend, the current was less strong. If Pam and Johann had escaped from the vehicle, they might well have drifted downstream to that bend. It was possible the two could have escaped from the river, but if they had, Carrigan was sure he would have heard from one of them by now.

But this was Saturday morning, eight hours after the accident had occurred. *Eight long hours.*

"It was the Fargo-Burnout," T.B. told Carrigan.

"Impossible," said Carrigan.

"I saw him. I know it was him."

Fire burned in Carrigan's eyes. "Just how the hell close did you get to him?"

T.B. lowered his head. The closest he had been was perhaps fifteen or twenty yards. "I saw his long coat and white pants. He's got that mop of hair. It was the Fargo-Burnout, I'm telling you, Carrigan. It was him."

Carrigan scowled, shook his head as he started the car. "Impossible. The guy hasn't got enough brains to blackmail anybody."

Carrigan's hands shook. He scolded Harvey. "Goddammit, T.B., I told you, you were off the case. Goddammit, I told you!"

The anger in his words shook T.B. to the bone, and no matter what he told him now, Carrigan was in no mood to listen. He felt terrible remorse over the two who plunged into the river, and Carrigan must be feeling worse yet, since they were his friends. It did not look good.

Carrigan turned the car around and was heading back to Fargo when T.B. finally spoke again. "Are you blaming me for their deaths?" T.B. felt the gloom and pang Carrigan was going through, and the despair on his face was more than he could stand.

"No," said Carrigan. "They must have..."

"It was raining," T.B. interrupted. "They must have slid off the road."

"Yes, I know."

Carrigan turned onto Broadway and wound his way along the curvy road through the trees past Trollwood Park.

T.B. broke the silence again. "It was the Fargo-Burnout, Carrigan."

Carrigan didn't respond.

T.B. was pleading now. "I even saw him once at the Mark Building near Pam's office. He was..."

"Harvey," Carrigan stopped him short. "I don't want you to say anything about this to anybody. Understand? Not to the police, not to anybody."

"I understand. You see, one day I was at the Mark Building and this..."

"Harvey," Carrigan interrupted again. He looked directly at the little man noticing for the first time how scratched up

312

his face was, how the frames on his glasses were bent out of shape, and one lens had a crack through it. He looked like a little puppy that had been spanked for crapping on a carpet. Carrigan softened the blow. "Harvey, I appreciate your wanting to help me, but please, you are off the case. Do you understand, off the case?"

Yes, sir." T.B. had a lump in his throat.

"If anybody asks you, you never had a case with me. Understand?"

"Yes, sir."

"You don't know anything about this matter, you don't even know me, do you understand? You never were on this case, and you are not on this case now. Do you understand?"

"I understand."

"You are completely off this case one hundred percent."

"One hundred percent."

"I don't want to hear another word about it."

"Not another word."

"I don't even want to see you around town."

"But I live here."

"Go away, take a vacation, take a month off."

"If I do, will you see me after that?"

Carrigan drove on silently past Northport Shopping Center, past North High into the heart of town on Broadway. He pulled up in front of Harvey's office and never did answer Harvey's question.

Carrigan was staring straight ahead as T.B. opened the door, and when he stepped out, Carrigan still hadn't moved his head.

"Ah, Carrigan. About the Fargo-Burnout. Maybe 1 could investigate…"

T.B. shrank back when he saw Carrigan's head slowly fall forward and bang against the steering wheel.

T.B. closed the door and crossed to the storefront of his office. Before he went inside, he cast another glance at

Carrigan. He still had his face slumped against the wheel.

By the time T.B. reached his office, he was feeling badly about everything. He thought he and Leroy R had done a remarkable job of detective work, but in the final analysis everything went wrong. Of all the suspects, who would have guessed the Fargo-Burnout was the blackmailer.

Jerry and Gordon Gelsper were the more likely suspects. They had a friendship in common, and Gordon was a professional photographer. The Fargo-Burnout was a nobody.

They were all wrong. He, Carrigan and Leroy R would have never picked the Fargo-Burnout. Where had T.B. missed something on the man? What had he overlooked about the man's past?

He could be anywhere by now. Probably in California hiding in Muir Woods near Sausalito. He could live on nothing and live anywhere and be happy.

The man was gone, and T.B. would never find him. Gone with fifty thousand dollars. *What would Shell Scott do?* T.B. let his mind grind away and finally pulled several folders from a drawer.

Photographs of all the people in the Powers Coffee House.

Photographs of the nude girl, Pam Allison.

More photographs from the Gay Nineties Bar.

Notes, papers, reports, information supplied by Carrigan.

Checking and savings account from the Allisons.

Character analysis of all the suspects—Hahmeed, Ruckles, Hard-nuts, Wandering Eddie, Mumbling Mike.

Weeks of research all stuffed into a few manila envelopes. Somewhere in all of this research and paperwork was a clue he had missed. If Shell Scott had this case and was starting over, he would begin with a hunch.

That's what T.B. needed—a hunch. He began wading through the material from anew, not sure what he should be looking for. After a few minutes, his fingers came upon two photos held together with a paperclip. These were the two photos of Pam Allison, one taken at the Powers Coffee House, the other, one of her nude photos. These were the two photos he and Leroy R had found so interesting a few days ago. Both were blown up, extreme close-ups of the girl's face.

He put the pictures side by side and examined them carefully. The glaring significance was there, just as it had been a few days ago. At the time, the photos meant something, but now that the Fargo-Burnout turned out to be the blackmailer, the photos seemed to have much less meaning.

But T.B. needed a hunch to work on, an alternative to everything that had gone wrong.

Maybe these were the photos to begin with. Maybe he should back up a few days and look at these two photos differently. How would he view these photos if he were just starting the case from scratch and had absolutely no suspects?

He churned the photos over in his mind for a half-minute. "Aha," he said excitedly. "Aha!"

Twenty-Seven
Black Monday

Carrigan Mulhouse read over the headline and the short article for the third time.

CAR PULLED FROM RED RIVER IN
WALLTOWN BRIDGE MISHAP

An apparent one-car mishap occurred sometime late Friday evening or early Saturday morning on the Walltown Bridge between Fargo and Moorhead.

Early Saturday morning police officials received an anonymous phone call reporting an automobile had left the bridge and plummeted into the Red River. Investigators later verified the silhouette of a car submerged in the water. The vehicle was retrieved about ten a.m. the same day, but no persons were reported within. The owner of the automobile has been identified, but information is being withheld pending notification of next of kin.

Dragging operations have continued since the mishap. It is not known how many persons may have occupied the vehicle. According to the police report, no evidence has been found to indicate how the accident occurred. Dragging operations will continue through this week.

Carrigan put the paper down and reached for his coffee cup. Snuffy picked up the paper and began reading the article.

Radio Sko lit up a cigarette.

Reggie stirred his coffee, put in a second sugar packet and stirred it some more.

"They're dead," said Carrigan. "No one's to blame."

"No one's to blame," repeated Sko.

"And the fifty thousand is gone," said Pavlov. He sat

forward, hands clasped together, his eyes glued to a nervous set of twiddling thumbs.

"We can't tell the police?" said Snuffy.

"No, we can't," Carrigan agreed.

"What about this Fargo-Burnout character?" asked Snuffy. "What did Harvey have to say about him?"

"It couldn't have been him. He's just a vagabond. He can hardly talk."

"But Harvey said he saw him," Pavlov shot back.

"I know, I know, but it just isn't right."

Millie came around with a new coffee pot, shook the one on the table and moved on.

"They're dead."

"Aha!" T.B. Harvey exclaimed as he came out of the storefront a block away from his office on Broadway. He jubilantly skipped along the sidewalk until he came to the parked Studebaker, jumped in and grinned at Leroy R.

"Aha!" he said as he checked his watch. It was a few minutes after nine. They had to hurry if they wanted to be on time.

"Next stop," T.B. commanded. "And step on it."

Leroy R didn't bother to check traffic. He raced the engine and dropped the clutch leaving a black streak ten feet long as he squealed around the corner and turned up Roberts. They passed the Mark Building and circled around the block and stopped in at the rear of the Burlington Northern warehouse where the artist had his office.

"Come on, Leroy. This shouldn't take long."

"Could we have our bill, Millie?" Carrigan asked. The entire group was still around the table and had finished what coffee they were going to drink. No one had ordered breakfast this morning.

One by one, each of the coffee members produced some

317

loose change and tossed it on the table. Carrigan was gathering up the coins when he heard the front door slam open and bang against the wall.

T.B. Harvey and Leroy R strutted through and walked directly to Carrigan's table. They did not invite themselves, rather, drew up two chairs, slid them into place and sat down.

Harvey was carrying a manila envelope under an arm and Leroy R was holding a long, folded sheet of brown paper with pieces of masking tape holding the flaps shut.

Carrigan was at a loss for their sudden appearance. The other members' curiosity peaked as they examined the odd couple. Reggie was the only one who had met T.B., yet all of the guys knew who these two were. Snuffy shuffled his chair back as if he were going to leave,

"No, please," T.B. beckoned. "I believe it would behoove everyone to remain a few minutes more." He examined the faces around the table, his own face ecstatic, his whole being in full control. He adjusted his glasses, in which one of the lenses was cracked. "You're all here, I see, everyone except the girl and Mr. von Meer. I trust you all read this morning's paper?"

Obviously they had, since the paper was on the table.

Carrigan pulled a face. "Harvey, if this is another one of your hair-brained presentations, then I..."

"Oh, it is indeed a presentation," he interrupted, a cocky tone prevalent in his voice. "It is indeed a presentation, and a final one concerning this case. I presume you are all terribly shocked with the apparent drowning of Pam Allison and her artist friend."

No one said a thing.

"They're dead," Carrigan said quietly as he looked around the room.

"Ah, yes, they are indeed dead." T.B. hesitated for effect, then, "That is, for this group they are, for all practical purposes, dead."

Heads turned at the table as the guys conversed among themselves.

"Leroy, if you will, please," T.B. indicated with a swoop of the hand.

All eyes were on Leroy R as he pulled a series of photographs from the manila envelope. He placed one on the table so all of the members could see it. "A photograph. of the nude girl," he pointed out and placed another photo on the table. "The same girl taken here in the coffee house, and at this very same table, I might add."

"So?" said Carrigan.

Leroy R produced two more photographs, both enlargements of the same two photos, both headshots of Pam Allison.

"Note the earring the girl is wearing," said Leroy R. "It's a pearl."

Everyone leaned in on the enlarged photos. Leroy R produced a third set of photos, extreme close-ups of Pam's earlobe. "The earring is a little grainy and fuzzy," Leroy R pointed out, "but those are identical earrings. One photograph was taken supposedly several years ago in Minneapolis, the other was taken only a few weeks ago here in the Powers Coffee House."

"So what," said Carrigan. "Pam Allison liked jewelry. So they're the same earrings. My wife has a pair I gave her over fifteen years ago."

T.B. took over the lead now and placed a copy of a check on the table. "Mrs. Allison had a habit of noting on every check what she purchased. Note in the lower left corner she has written, *pearl earrings*. This check is dated less than six months ago."

The check was passed around the table and finally ended up in Carrigan's hand. He scrutinized the notation and looked up unimpressed. "Pam Allison probably has several pairs of pearl earrings."

"That is indeed possible," he agreed, "and we thought of that." From the manila envelope, he pulled out another smaller envelope and passed it around. "Note from the return address, this is from the Williston Post Office. What can one acquire from the Williston post office that one can easily acquire from a local post office?"

"Stamps," said Pavlov.

"What else?" The grin on T.B.'s face was wide enough to shove a ruler in sideways.

The envelope ended up with Carrigan again. He held the envelope firmly as a calmness came over his face. "A passport."

"Exactly," T.B. agreed. "Or passports." He emphasized the *"s"* on the end of the word.

Then like some magician completing his act, T.B. laid the long brown folded paper on the table and loosed the masking tape from the ends. He quickly jerked out a long, pink, plume feather.

"Jesus Christ!" Pavlov said.

"Yes," T.B. said triumphantly. "The same plume on the photographs."

"I'll be damned," Reggie said, his face flushed.

Carrigan's jaw dropped. "Where did you find it?"

"Where we found the empty envelope from the post office. In your artist friend's studio."

The guys at the table gaped at the plume lying in the center of the table

"We also happened to find these." T.B. poured the rest of the contents from the manila envelope. Two rolls of negative film dropped on the table. Carrigan anxiously grabbed one of the rolls, held it up and scanned the poses.

"Forty-two different shots in all," said T.B. "And the black curtain used as a backdrop is in the studio wadded up in a corner. And we found this." From his pocket, he dropped a thin strand of black cloth. "I believe it's called a G-string."

The Guys from Fargo

Carrigan looked at the faces around the table, his face carrying a dumb but happy smile. "They're alive!" he said in an excited whisper.

He challenged T.B. again. "But you said they met the Fargo-Burnout and he took the money."

"I know," T.B. agreed. "I confess I don't understand what his function was. I chased him and he had the briefcase. I know he did. I saw it."

The Powers Coffee House members were so engrossed in their discovery that none of them had even noticed the tall, greasy haired man standing next to the table. In his hand, he was holding onto the briefcase.

"C-Car-i-gan M-Mul-house?" the tall man in the black coat asked in a stammering voice

All of the members focused on the Fargo-Burnout.

"It's him," T.B. said excitedly.

"M-Mr. M-Mulhouse?" he repeated.

Carrigan was on his guard. "Yes?"

Everyone stared at the briefcase when he placed it on the table. Carrigan quickly unsnapped the briefcase expecting to see the fifty thousand dollars. However, the only content was an envelope with Carrigan's name written on the front.

The Fargo-Burnout was stammering again. "Sh-she said to b-bring it b-back. Sh-she gave me m-money." He pulled five one hundred dollar bills from his pocket as if to prove she had done so. Then, as if he had no other care in the world, he walked off to the counter and sat down.

Carrigan's eyes focused on the envelope. He tore it open and retrieved the letter from within. It was in Pam's handwriting.

He read it out loud, very slowly and in a very low voice.

My Dearest Carrigan,
Johann and I had been planning this for months. Over the past several years, I learned so

much about you. You have always been so kind and so thoughtful, and so vulnerable, too. I'm almost sorry I had to take advantage of you, but it was such a beautiful opportunity. You have consistently supported me, especially concerning the terrible marriage to my big, dumb husband, so I knew I could count on you to help me. And you really did come through this time, you and all the guys.

I must confess I was somewhat worried in the beginning when you hired a private detective. T.B. is so sweet, isn't he? As it turned out, he even seemed to help things along. You must thank him and Leroy for their marvelous performance.

That night when we took the briefcase full of money, we made a few stops at phone booths just to see if anyone was watching. I really didn't think you would have a car following us that night, but I guess I misjudged you. I know you won't go to the police, because you will have a hard time explaining to them how you acquired the ransom money, so Johann and I aren't worried about that. Actually, we didn't have any idea how you would raise the money, but we just knew you would.

Johann and I have been madly in love for so long. Of course, we could never show it. We rarely saw each other over the past year because we were afraid big, dumb Jerry might somehow find out. You know how he is, and I know you won't say anything to him, since it would break his poor, dumb heart.

Thank you, sweet Carrigan, for your everlasting friendship, and tell the guys goodbye for me.
Love, The Princess

P.S. I wonder if they will ever find our bodies.

Carrigan folded up the letter and placed it back in the envelope. When he looked up, all of the members were smiling, even T.B. and Leroy.

"Ain't that something?" Reggie said.

Snuffy began to roll a cigarette. "She was a princess, wasn't she?"

"Way-al ah'l be gah-dammned," Pavlov said with his southern accent. "Ah think we all been fukked."

He said the remark so loud that those customers nearest to the table turned their heads.

Carrigan looked over the guys and their grinning faces, and when Millie swung by, he stopped her. "Millie, breakfast for everybody, and I'm buying."

"My," she said. "What are you guys celebrating?"

Carrigan looked around the table. The guys all broke out laughing. And they laughed and they laughed and they laughed.

THE AFTERMATH

Jerry Allison returned to Fargo from California after having been notified of the possible drowning of his wife. On the same black Monday following the mishap, Pam Allison's purse was found in the Red River a mile downstream from the bridge. A few weeks passed before the Fargo Forum published the contents, which were a billfold with her driver's identification and a half dozen credit cards, a cosmetic bag, a pair of pearl earrings and forty-two dollars in cash. To this day, Jerry Allison firmly believes his wife drowned, although the body was never recovered.

Two months passed before the landlord of the Burlington Northern warehouse building reported that he had not received his monthly rent check from Johann von Meer. An investigation of Johann's studio found it completely intact, and as a result, he was placed on the missing person's list. Johann von Meer had no living relatives, thus his case lies buried in the files of the Fargo Police Department, his disappearance a life-long mystery, at least to the police.

Sko Skofield still lives in Fargo and is retired from the radio business.

After the supposed raid of the card game and shooting of the *police officer*, Frank Newsom and Bucky Buckmeier left town, and a few months later, Dean Wimpleton died of a heart attack. Not surprisingly, Conrad Coddington, the Christian gentleman, never returned to Snuffy's Antique shop to contest the purchase of the eaglet coin box.

Paul Glitzberg left the insurance business after many years and now deals in securities. He and his wife are still good friends of the Mulhouses.

Reggie Richthoffen retired from Moorhead State and spends a great deal of time enjoying his grand children and fishing at his cabin on Shell Lake.

Damon Jamison, known as Snuffy, eventually turned to making small wooden toys for a living but returned to the antique business after accidentally sawing off half of his right forefinger. He travels from flea market to flea market and resides in the same house in Detroit Lakes near the Holiday Inn.

Leroy Ridgebutte's landlady died shortly after the blackmail incident and left her entire estate to him, which included the 1947 Studebaker, the dilapidated mansion and one hundred thirty thousand dollars in stocks and bonds. Leroy and T.B. Harvey moved to Minneapolis and formed a business called *Gladkijzad and Associates Detective and Photography Agency*. Six months later, when the business folded, T.B. remained in Minneapolis, working for a big brother organization that caters to homeless and abused children. Leroy R, still a Marxist, returned to Fargo where he occasionally unloads freight at the Northern Pacific Railroad docks. He eventually became an avid duck and goose hunter.

Carrigan Mulhouse still runs a small advertising agency, although he has moved his business from place to place. After twenty some years, the Hornbacher Food Stores are still his major client. Carrigan turned to writing after having suffered a mild stroke and is still in the process of making a name for himself as a prominent author.

None of the guys from the Powers Coffee House group ever learned for certain what happened to Johann von Meer and Pam Allison, but a few years after their disappearance, Carrigan discovered an art magazine in which a few paintings very closely resembled the style of Johann. Coincidently, the artist's name was listed as *Jeremy von Meer*, a resident of the Dutch city of Leide, the birthplace of Rembrandt. Though the magazine did not depict von Meer's photo, the author of the article did make reference to the artist's limp. He also stated that von Meer's wife, Patricia, owned a small, elite dress shop on Vermeer Allee. The author described her as beautiful as a fairytale princess with hair that was golden like the sun.

Many of the original buildings in *The Guys from Fargo* have changed names by now. Ruckles Chemical Company never did exist. It was once a printing business, and is now the City of Fargo's Assessment office. Strauss Clothing moved to the West Acres Shopping Center, and the three-story affair in the rear, which contained T.B. Harvey's office, now bears the name of *The Stearns Building.*

Elm Tree Square still contains a prominent collection of small shops, however, P.D.'s Restaurant has changed names and owners several times.

Moorhead State became Minnesota State University Moorhead.

The bus depot, the main stop for transients at the Powers, moved to NP Avenue. After the Powers Hotel was sold, the Coffee House became several different restaurants. For many years, it was named *The 400,* because it was located on 4th and Broadway. That name remains on the marquee outside the hotel, but the present restaurant is called *Juano's* and caters to Mexican cuisine.

The Mexican Village Restaurant on Main has consistently been a mainstay of the city because of its reputation for good food, and it remains so. Oddly enough, it was owned and operated for many years by an Iranian family.

The Dutch Maid Grill on 8th Street has been gone for over a decade, and several of the stores on that first block south of Main have disappeared or become different businesses, including Ernie's bookstore. The Dakota Business College building bears the same name, but it never was in operation, even when this story took place. The enclosed fire escape on the south wall is still intact.

Perkins is gone and so is Pratt's Coats on Broadway as well as the porn shop that once occupied the Roxy Theatre. Epko Photography, which was next to Phil Wong's restaurant on NP Avenue, and, where Gordon Gelsper supposedly worked, disappeared long ago. The building in which Jerry Allison supposedly had his office is called the Lincoln Mutual Insurance Company.

The third floor southeast corner of the Burlington Northern Railroad warehouse building north of the BN tracks is where Johann had his studio. This is the exact location where Pam Allison was filmed in the nude. The building acted as refrigeration storage in earlier years for the railroad and was home to a variety of businesses including a café, bakery and restaurant, and has become, for the most part, an office building. Next to the BN building is the old, white structure, also a storage building for the BN railroad, where Wandering Eddie and Mumbling Mike hung out. Windows were manufactured there for a period of time, and then it became the Mental Health Center. The sign for the center is still up, but that business has disappeared, and the building is no longer occupied.

The Mark Building at 400 Roberts Street, where Carrigan had his office, is the same today as it was in 1983 and still hosts a few small businesses. It was originally a church and at one time functioned as a funeral home. Ivers Funeral Home, across the street, hasn't changed in years, except someone recently put up a new neon sign.

The Flame Bar to the north of the Mark Building was for many years a thriving hangout for locals. It contained several pool tables, and during the last few years of operation offered strippers as entertainment. In the early nineties, it was remodeled into The Market Place, a business that housed several advertising and marketing firms, including Carrigan's Advertising Firm for a few years. Today it goes by the name of Byte Speed Computers, a company that manufactures computers for schools.

The one main architectural structure on Broadway that has maintained its function and name since 1923 serves as the cover photo for this novel. It is the Fargo Theater and lies a half block south of the Powers Hotel. Although it played no role in this story, the theatre is a landmark building, beautifully restored inside and out to its original decor. It is the only remaining theatre in downtown Fargo that shows films daily and is home of the famed annual Fargo Film Festival.

The Gay Nineties Bar in Minneapolis still caters to its own special clientele.

Seven years after the blackmailing incident and after the statute of limitations had expired, Carrigan Mulhouse received a registered letter from a law firm in Paris. In it was certification that he was the recipient of a fifty-thousand-dollar insurance policy, payable as a result of the presumed death of Pam Allison. *Presumed* to Carrigan Mulhouse was a misnomer, since he well knew what had transpired. He gathered the guys from Fargo together and returned the money that they had contributed out of their own pockets toward the ransom note. Of the remainder, Carrigan gave a thousand each to T.B. Harvey and Leroy Ridgebutte and divided the rest equally among the coffee group.

The Fargo Police Department closed their files on Pam Allison once she was declared dead, however, the mysterious disappearance of Johann von Meer still remains an open case. To this day, Carrigan still suspects that sometime in the future, the Princess or Johann, or both, will show up on his doorstep.

* * *